COMING HOME TO TUPPENNY BRIDGE

SHARON BOOTH

Storm
PUBLISHING

To request permissions, contact the publisher at rights@stormpublishing.co

Ebook ISBN: 978-1-80508-637-6
Paperback ISBN: 978-1-80508-638-3

Cover design: Debbie Clement
Cover images: Shutterstock

Published by Storm Publishing.
For further information, visit:
www.stormpublishing.co

Summer at the Country Practice

Christmas at Cuckoo Nest Cottage

The Moorland Heroes Series

Resisting Mr Rochester

Saving Mr Scrooge

The Witches of Castle Clair Series

Belle, Book and Candle

My Favourite Witch

To Catch a Witch

Will of the Witch

His Lawful Wedded Witch

Destiny of the Witch

The Other Half Series

How the Other Half Lives

How the Other Half Lies

How the Other Half Loses

How the Other Half Loves

To all the Josephs and Summers in the world. Thank you for caring.

ONE

'So, what are your thoughts, Mrs Marshall? Do you have any questions?'

The estate agent's voice was calm, but her eyes were eager, hopeful. Bethany almost felt obliged to gush about the house she'd just been shown around. The poor woman had, after all, been very thorough with the viewing, pointing out all the features she considered plus points and skipping very deftly over any potential downsides to the property.

Not, Bethany had to admit, that there were many downsides. On paper it had seemed perfect, and even now, having been shown around with such care and diligence, she couldn't honestly pick faults. It was just...

She sighed inwardly. This woman was so young and had probably convinced herself that Bethany would snap the house up. Maybe she should. After all, she had to live somewhere. She couldn't keep drifting forever.

Even as the thought crossed her mind, though, she knew she wouldn't. This house, as beautiful as it was, was going to end up just like all the others she'd viewed over the last couple of years. Dismissed and forgotten about. She wished she knew why.

'It's certainly a lovely house,' she said, not wanting to crush the estate agent just yet. 'I'd really like to give it some thought before I go any further, though.'

'Oh, of course.' The woman—had she said her name was Nancy?—gave her a wide smile which didn't stop Bethany from noting the disappointment in her eyes. 'It's a big decision. Naturally you'll have to take your time. You have my card?'

'I do,' Bethany assured her. 'Thanks so much for showing me around.'

'Oh, it was my pleasure.'

Locking the front door behind them, the two women headed down the drive to their respective cars.

'I'm so sorry I was late for the viewing,' Bethany said, feeling the need to apologise once more even though she'd already done so once. It was guilt pricking at her. If she'd decided to take the house she wouldn't have given her lack of punctuality a second thought.

'Don't worry about it. Did you say you'd come straight from the airport?'

'Yes. I just flew in from Fuerteventura,' she said.

'Ooh, how lovely. It's quite warm there in March, isn't it? Were you just there for a week or—'

'A bit longer than that,' Bethany said hastily. She felt embarrassed to say she'd been there for two whole months. It felt indulgent and selfish somehow. 'I was initially house hunting over there, but I changed my mind and decided to resume looking back home.'

She'd only actually looked at two properties while she'd been away, quickly realising that she had no more inclination to settle in the Canary Islands than she had in England.

'I have to say, I'd pick Fuerteventura over here any day,' Nancy said with a guilty laugh. 'I shouldn't say that, should I? Don't want to talk you out of putting in an offer.'

'I won't be going back abroad,' Bethany reassured her, deftly avoiding any promise of an offer. 'At least, not house hunting.'

She unlocked the door of her bright blue hatchback and smiled awkwardly. 'Well, thanks again.'

'I look forward to hearing from you,' Nancy said hopefully.

Bethany waved the business card that had been handed to her earlier but didn't reply with anything other than a brief nod. Thankfully, she slid into the front seat and started the engine.

Driving back to Somerset she thought she really needed to get her act together. Here she was, fifty-four years of age and, to all intents and purposes, homeless. Obviously, it wasn't as bleak as it sounded. She was hardly short of money and had just come back from a long and luxurious holiday in sunnier climes. Now she was heading to the home of her long-time friend, where she'd been invited to stay until she found somewhere suitable to live.

But therein lay the problem. She really couldn't keep relying on Helena's hospitality—although she rather suspected Helena would be glad of her company. She had, after all, lost her husband just over a year ago and was still grieving. Bethany would never have left her at all had Helena's two grown-up children not decided they should be with her for the difficult first anniversary of their stepfather Ted's death, and Helena had suggested they, and her grandchildren, might prefer to be alone with her so they could grieve together as a family.

It had seemed easier all round to take the opportunity to get away for a while. She knew she had no right to grieve for Ted, even though she'd once been married to him herself. They'd been divorced for years after all. But even though their marriage had ended she still missed him. There was never any chance they'd lose touch with each other because he'd married Helena, and over time he'd become a good friend in his own right.

Their friendship had, she recalled, been the result of a lot of hard work after the traumatic discovery of Ted and Helena's affair. She'd thought, for a while, that she'd lost them both, which had made everything so much worse. Eventually she'd realised she needed them in her life and to make that happen she was going to have to get over what they'd done. Helena had been her best friend since they were twelve years old and she couldn't imagine life without her. After some time, the anger and hurt had subsided and life had settled. She and Ted built a new kind of relationship, and her friendship with Helena survived. She'd always be grateful for that. Without Ted and Helena she'd have had no one.

But with Helena grieving for her husband Bethany felt awkward about expressing her own sense of loss, so had spent the year pretending it hadn't mattered as she focused on getting Helena through such an awful time. Although she'd felt a pang of sadness that Helena's children didn't want her around, she realised it had left her free to go away, switch off her phone, and just be. Somewhere new and different. Somewhere she could work through her sadness alone.

She hoped Helena wouldn't be cross that she'd made herself unavailable. Maybe she should have stayed in touch these last couple of months. But she had to be honest; it had felt good to be cut off from everything back in England. The only people she'd spoken to were tourists and locals who knew nothing about her or her life at home. She'd quite liked it that way, which was why she'd considered moving to Fuerteventura permanently. Until she'd realised that anywhere she lived she would be expected to reveal little parts of her life, bit by bit. Strangers wouldn't stay strangers. The past wouldn't stay buried. Wherever she lived she couldn't escape her own story. House hunting had quickly lost its appeal.

It was a bit cold, she thought, as she headed towards the village of Churleigh Magna, where Helena had bought a large cottage for herself after finally selling the house she'd shared with Ted. It had also been the house Bethany had shared with him, as it had been in his family for several generations. She had no real attachment to it and didn't feel any sadness that she'd never see it again. She was glad Helena seemed to be settling in her new home, but then, Helena wasn't particularly sentimental and never had been.

She put the heating on and turned up the radio, joining in with The B52s as they sang about a Love Shack. She didn't have the best voice in the world, but she loved that song and since she was alone, she felt no embarrassment about singing at the top of her voice, drumming her fingers on the steering wheel. It took her mind off Helena and Ted and house hunting and all the other things that kept nagging away at her. She'd spent two months having as much fun as possible, and she didn't want to let that feeling slip away.

Churleigh Magna was a pretty Somerset village with stone houses, criss-crossed by a gentle stream. Helena's new home, Chimneys, was on the edge of the village, set in an acre of land. It had five bedrooms and had been built in the mid nineteenth century, so wasn't as old as some of the other properties in the neighbourhood.

Bethany had sent her a text message early that morning telling her she'd be home late afternoon, and Helena had replied with a brief, *Looking forward to seeing you*, which wasn't quite as enthusiastic as she'd expected, but she supposed there wasn't really an awful lot more her friend could say in a text. She was sure they'd have a lot to catch up on over dinner.

She'd only just switched off the engine and stepped out of the car when Helena came rushing out of the front door and hurried down the drive to meet her. Bethany slammed her car door shut and locked it, then turned to her friend with a warm smile.

'I'm back! How have you been?'

She was relieved to see Helena was smiling. They embraced briefly then pulled apart as her friend surveyed her critically.

'How was it? Did you have a good time? You've got a bit of a tan! How was the hotel? What was the food like?'

'Crikey, Hels, let me get a word in edgeways.' Bethany laughed and slipped her arm through her friend's as they headed towards the house.

'Your luggage—'

'Oh, leave it. I'll collect it later,' Bethany said. 'How are you? Did you have a good time with the kids?'

'I did, thank you. It was lovely to see them.' Helena closed the front door after them, and they went down the hallway into a welcoming, cosy living room. Bethany sighed with relief and sank into the leather armchair.

'Glad you've got the heating on. It's so much colder here than it was in Fuerteventura.'

'What time did you land?' Helena asked. 'I'll put the kettle on. A cup of tea will warm you up nicely.'

'Actually,' Bethany admitted, 'I've been back hours. I've been viewing a house.'

'A house?'

Helena had been on her way to the kitchen but paused, eyeing Bethany in surprise. 'When did you arrange that?'

'While I was away. I saw it online and thought, why not? It's on the Somerset/Dorset border so not too far away from you, but far enough so I don't get on your nerves.'

Helena laughed. 'You'll never get on my nerves, Bethany. You know that.' Her eyes narrowed. 'So, are you interested?'

'I'm afraid not. Same old story.'

'Cold feet?'

'I guess you could call it that.' Bethany hated the term, but she couldn't deny it summed up what happened every time she came close to settling down somewhere. 'Anyway, don't worry, I'll find somewhere eventually and then I'll get out of your hair, I promise.'

'You know you're welcome to stay here as long as you want

to,' Helena said gently. She bit her lip and Bethany noticed a look of anxiety in her eyes.

'Is something wrong, Hels? You look worried.'

'I'll make that tea,' her friend said, turning to go, but Bethany had other ideas.

'Never mind the tea. What's wrong? Has something happened?'

Helena sighed and sat down in the other armchair. 'I'm sorry. I really didn't want to tell you this the minute you got home, but it's not something I feel I can keep from you either. I wanted to tell you this morning when you finally switched your phone back on, but it's not really the sort of thing one can say in a text or over the phone.'

'Okay, now I'm really scared,' Bethany said. 'Just tell me. It can't be as bad as all that, can it?'

Helena leaned forward, her hands clasped in her lap and her eyes troubled. 'I'm so sorry, Bethany, but I've had a message about your brother.'

Bethany's heart thudded. Of all the things she'd expected to hear, this hadn't even crossed her mind. 'Joseph?'

Helena nodded. 'His friend—a man called Clive—got in touch with me. He was desperately trying to find you. You see, Joseph was ill. Very ill. Clive thought you should know, and that maybe you'd like to see him.'

Bethany swallowed. So many thoughts were rushing through her mind she didn't know how to begin to process them. Joseph was ill? She couldn't even imagine it. He was so fit and healthy and strong. Then again, she was remembering a man in his early thirties. He'd be, what, sixty-five, sixty-six now. She could hardly believe it.

But to see him again?

She didn't know what to feel about that. After all these years, could she really face him? How did she even know he'd want to see her? He'd shown no desire to meet all this time, so would illness change that? Or was this Clive person making assumptions? Did Joseph even know Clive had been in touch?

'I—I'm really not sure...' Her voice trailed off as she saw the look in Helena's eyes. Her pulse quickened and her throat felt dry.

'I'm afraid it's too late, Bethany,' Helena said gently. 'Clive messaged me a couple of days ago. I'm sorry, but Joseph has passed away.'

TWO

It was raining, which seemed appropriate, given Bethany's mood. Her thoughts were as gloomy as the grey skies which hung heavy overhead, as she drove carefully over the stone bridge across the River Skimmer and into the market town of Tuppenny Bridge.

Home.

Well, hardly. Officially, perhaps, she should call it her hometown, but it had been a long, long time since she'd thought of it that way. Honestly, she'd tried not to think of the place at all.

Sometimes it caught her unawares. A brief, golden memory of a happy moment during her childhood. Mostly when she'd been with her mother before she withdrew from the world entirely, which meant she must have been seven or younger at the time. Christmas was likely to remind her of those golden days if she allowed it. And sometimes her birthday.

Always though, the momentary pleasure was dimmed by the misery of later memories of those same events. Christmases and birthdays had never been perfect, but they'd become much worse after her mother died. She tried not to think about the better times at all really, because it only made all those bad times that much harder to bear.

Ahead of her she could see Green Lane, which would take her past the village green. She remembered many gatherings there: the carol concert each Christmas Eve; the bonfire night displays; the summer fair; even a May Day event complete with maypole when she was very little, although she recalled that had stopped when she was a teenager.

But she wasn't going down Green Lane. It would take her to the market square, and to All Hallows Church, and that was the last place she wanted to see. Well, almost. No, she would drive past The Black Swan and turn down River Road. It was the most direct route and she'd be less likely to spot someone she knew.

Although, after over thirty years away from Tuppenny Bridge, she wondered how many people she *would* know. Places like this were struggling. Despite her personal feelings, she couldn't deny that this was a beautiful little market town, and set as it was in the glorious Yorkshire Dales, she had no doubt that many of its properties had been turned into holiday homes. Maybe she wouldn't know anyone. Could she possibly be that lucky?

She flicked on her left indicator.

Don't do it. Don't do it.

Even as she turned the steering wheel Bethany's internal voice was screaming in protest. *Why? Why put yourself through it?* Yet, somehow, she couldn't stop herself. Five minutes back in this town and already she was becoming weaker.

Market Street took her directly to All Hallows, which stood at the corner of Forge Lane, on the edge of the market square. She pulled over and stared at the beautiful Norman church, remembering the many times she'd come here with her mother.

She'd never understood why. Not then. Her mother would tell her they were going to the shops, but inevitably when they reached All Hallows, she'd squeeze Bethany's hand and say, 'Let's just pop in here for a few minutes, shall we? Gather our thoughts.'

But she never went inside the church. Instead, she'd lead Bethany along the path around the side of the building to a bench by a tree, where she'd sit quietly, saying nothing.

Bethany would get bored. Back then she had little appreciation for the peace and tranquillity of a churchyard, nor the stunning views of the rolling hills in the distance, nor the glorious trees that provided shelter in the rain and shade in the sunshine, nor the bleating of the sheep she could hear in the distant paddock.

What Bethany saw then were all those creepy gravestones.

And her mother's tears.

She'd grown to hate that churchyard. Her mother never told her why she sat there and cried. She never acknowledged her tears at all. And the funny thing was, she never made a sound. It wasn't as if Bethany had been forced to endure her mother's noisy sobbing. If Bethany hadn't turned to say something to her she would never have known, but after that, she realised it was every single time, and gradually it dawned on her that her mother's entire reason for visiting the churchyard was to cry. To release the pain and the sadness.

Bethany understood that now, but it didn't make it any easier to deal with.

She sat quite still, her hands gripping the steering wheel even though the car was safely parked.

Just go. Leave. It's too late now. It's all too late.

Even as the words entered her head, she knew she was going to ignore them. It was as if some force was compelling her to move, although she knew it was going to make things harder for her. As if today wasn't hard enough.

She shut the car door, pulled up the hood of her coat, and took a steadying breath.

A furtive glance around showed her there was no one in sight who she recognised. In fact, there were few people around at all. Even the market square looked empty. Was it the rain or was it because they were all at the church? How many of the townspeople had been invited, she wondered?

She forced herself to move, even though she hated herself for doing so. Across the road, through the gate, up the path...

She could see the church door ahead of her, but it was closed. Maybe everyone was inside. She rounded the building, following the familiar path, past the Garden of Ashes. She glanced at the bench where she used to sit with her mother, but it was too painful to linger there. She hurried on, her heart pounding in her chest as she turned the corner.

A gasp escaped her, and she pressed herself against the wall of the church, peering cautiously out across the grounds to where a group of people, dressed in black, were gathered around an open grave.

She didn't recognise the vicar. This one seemed quite young, not like the one who'd been here when she was a resident of Tuppenny Bridge. She narrowed her eyes, not entirely certain but thinking perhaps she recognised Miss Lavender, and that the Pennyfeather sisters were likely standing close to her. Possibly. It was hard to be sure since everyone was wearing black, and most had their backs to her. There were, however, two shocking pink umbrellas visible above the crowd and if anyone would carry pink umbrellas to a funeral it would be those two.

No one was looking her way. They were all focused on what was happening in front of their eyes. Her hand flew to her mouth as she tried to stay calm.

So Joseph was being buried in the family plot. Why? She could hardly believe he would have chosen that, and yet, why not? Maybe he was more his father's son than even she'd realised. Maybe, after she'd left, the two of them had reached an understanding. Maybe, with her out of the way, they'd settled into a more comfortable and happier life.

Well, if that was what Joseph wanted, so be it. Why should she care? All she knew for sure was, nothing and no one would bury her in that hole in the ground when her time came. She was going to be cremated, her ashes scattered to the wind. She would be free, not shackled to that family for eternity.

Had she ever really known Joseph at all?

Tears caught her unaware, and she tried to blink them away, but failed dismally. As they streamed down her cheeks she frantically swiped at them, furious with herself at her weakness. After all these years?

But that was her brother they were laying to rest. That was Joseph. The boy she'd loved and adored. The man she'd hated and had never forgiven.

The coffin was gently lowered into the ground, and even though she'd known what to expect by coming here today it didn't stop her heart from shattering into a million pieces for the third time in her life.

Turning away, she stumbled blindly out of the churchyard and back to her car, where she sat for a few minutes, her head on the steering wheel, trying to calm her thoughts and control her emotions.

She should never have gone to All Hallows. She should never have come back to this town.

She lifted her head and dried her eyes, filled suddenly with a determination to regain the control she'd fought so hard for during the previous decades. She had a job to do, and she was going to do it. And as soon as she was done, she would leave here and never come back.

She and Tuppenny Bridge were finished.

* * *

Clive was quite glad it was raining, even though it was, as Joseph would have said, bucketing it down now. The rain, he hoped, camouflaged the tears that he simply couldn't stop, no matter how hard he tried to be stoic and brave.

A part of him couldn't help thinking that Joseph would have been shaking his head right now, his eyes wide with astonishment.

'What the heck do you think you're larking at, soft lad? Crying like a baby over me? Give over!'

Joseph, he knew, had never realised quite how much he meant to Clive. He wished he'd told him.

As the vicar, Zach Barrington, gave the blessing over the grave, Clive scanned the crowd gathered around. His heart went out to Summer Fletcher who was sobbing openly, as her boyfriend, Ben, tried to comfort her. Summer had worked for Joseph at the Whispering Willows Horse Sanctuary, and she'd adored him.

Not only was she going to miss Joseph from a personal point of view, but she now had the worry of what was going to happen to the residents of Whispering Willows. She wasn't the only one. He'd been worrying about that himself.

He could only hope the new owner was a horse lover.

Ben met his gaze and a look of understanding passed between the two of them. Ben was also a vet, and worked for Clive at Stepping Stones Veterinary Surgery, which backed onto the village green.

The two of them had recently had several conversations about the future of the sanctuary. Ben was worried about Summer, and how she'd react if it didn't continue. He confessed he was quite glad she was going to Australia with her father after all. The trip had been booked for months, but Summer had asked her dad to cancel her ticket because of Joseph's illness. Unknown to her, her mum had secretly told her dad not to do that because there was a chance she'd still be able to make it.

With Joseph gone, Summer was definitely in need of a break, and when Clive had solemnly sworn to work at the sanctuary in her place, and their teenage volunteers, Maya and Lennox, had promised to help before and after school each day, she'd finally agreed to accompany her dad to visit her older sister, Billie, and brother-in-law, Arlo, in Melbourne.

Ben would miss her, but it would be better for Summer to be away while things were sorted out at Whispering Willows. He and Clive were concerned about the welfare of the horses, ponies and donkeys who lived there, and were hoping they could find alternative homes for them, should that become necessary, before Summer returned.

Clive's gaze shifted to the Lavender Ladies, and he thought that Joseph would have been beside himself with glee to see Rita and Birdie Pennyfeather dressed all in black. Well, almost.

He smothered a grin as he noted the bright red wellingtons they were wearing, as well as the orange scarves around their necks, and the purple hairbands in their dyed red hair. Even their umbrellas were bright pink.

Miss Lavender might have nagged them into wearing black coats as a mark of respect, but you couldn't keep the Pennyfeather sisters down for long.

His humour dimmed a little as he eyed Eugenie Lavender. She was standing stiffly, as elegant as always in a smart black coat and gloves, black boots, with a black trilby hat over her silver hair. Her great-nephew, Noah, was by her side, holding a black umbrella over the pair of them.

Clive wondered why Eugenie had turned up at all, given that she hadn't spoken to Joseph in decades. It had always puzzled him, but if Joseph had known the reason why, he hadn't shared it with him. He supposed she considered it her civic duty to be there, given that she had somehow decided that

Tuppenny Bridge was *her* town, and her responsibility, even if that had never been officially acknowledged, other than the fact that she was a member of the parish council.

No sign of Noah's wife, Isobel Lavender, which didn't really surprise him. She'd told him she hated funerals, and although she'd happily taken the money to provide all the flowers for this one, she'd dropped plenty of hints that she wouldn't be there in person. Not that it mattered. To his knowledge she'd had little to no contact with Joseph anyway.

All the people who mattered were here. Like Jonah. As a farrier, he'd visited Whispering Willows regularly, and had been fond of Joseph. He was clearly upset today, standing arm-in-arm with his partner, Kat Pennyfeather, great-niece of Rita and Birdie.

In fact, looking round, Clive could see that most of the people gathered here were visibly upset. Joseph's work had touched many hearts, and they were keen to pay their respects to someone who'd dedicated his own life to doing good, even if he hadn't mixed with them much.

His eyes narrowed. Where was Joseph's sister, Bethany? What a shame his own flesh and blood couldn't make the effort. Helena Marshall, who was the second wife of Bethany's ex-husband, had confirmed that Bethany would soon be back in the country, and that she would pass on Clive's contact details and his urgent message to her.

He'd heard nothing from her, though. Even when he'd contacted Helena again to tell her the sad news of Joseph's death and given her the details of the funeral, there'd been no word.

Bethany had made no effort to be here at her own brother's funeral. Whatever had happened to drive her out of Tuppenny Bridge, Clive thought long enough had passed now for her to put it all behind her. Joseph didn't deserve such callous treatment.

It didn't bode well for the future of the horse sanctuary. If Bethany Marshall, née Wilkinson, was so heartless, would she keep the place going? Personally, he couldn't see it. All Joseph's efforts would be for nothing. His legacy wiped out. It made his blood boil at the thought of it.

And yet, Joseph hadn't had the foresight to leave a will. As his only living relative, his entire estate, including Whispering Willows, would pass to his sister. Why? If he'd known what she was like, why had he done nothing to prevent that?

He supposed, when it came down to it, blood must be thicker than water.

He could only hope Joseph's faith in Bethany would be repaid.

THREE

As the windscreen wipers worked hard to clear the rain from her vision, Bethany leaned forward slightly and peered at the sign by the gate.

'Whispering Willows Horse Sanctuary,' she murmured, then frowned. 'Since when?'

It was the first she'd heard of it and her heart sank at the thought of it. Surely there wouldn't be any animals remaining? When Joseph got ill he must have made other provision for them. He wouldn't have just left them here for her to sort out. Would he?

She drove slowly and reluctantly down the drive, her stomach doing an involuntary flip when she saw the old house in the distance. Her mouth felt dry, and she swallowed hard, trying to calm herself. What was she even doing here anyway?

She pulled into the stableyard and turned off the engine. The solicitor had given her the keys and she knew she should really make a dash for it. The rain was still pouring, and she'd get soaked if she dawdled. Even so, every part of her rebelled at the thought of rushing inside that house.

Anyway, she was already wet from visiting the churchyard.

Her own fault. All of this was her own fault really. All she'd had to do was instruct an estate agent to put the house up for sale. She could have got rid of the whole shebang and never gone near the place. So why hadn't she?

She'd told herself that it was because she wanted to see the state of the place for herself so she could make sure the estate agent wasn't ripping her off. Besides, she ought to oversee the disposal of the furniture and personal belongings. No point in paying for house clearance when there might be things that could go to charity, for example.

Deep down, though, she knew she was lying to herself. What she really wanted from visiting Whispering Willows was closure, and the pathetic thing was that she knew she'd never get it. Not now. It was way too late.

Bracing herself, she climbed out of the car and slammed the door behind her, then gazed around in dismay, her breath catching as the wind gusted around her. Even though the heavy rain made it harder to get a clear view of everything, it didn't prevent her from realising that the house and stables were in a dire state.

She rattled the keys in her hand, trying to pluck up the courage to head indoors, but instead found herself walking towards the stables. Best to check them out, she told herself. After all, they could be a selling point. Outbuildings were always in demand, even if they were more often converted into holiday accommodation or office buildings rather than used for horses.

The nearer she got to the stables the slower her steps became, and she stared at them in despair.

What on earth had happened? One block, which she remembered had contained two looseboxes and a feed store, as well as the tack room, was bulging at the sides. It looked as if a giant had sat on it and squashed it, forcing the walls to spread, like buttercream filling oozing from a sandwich cake. The rest of the buildings weren't as bad but even so, they looked in dire need of some care and attention.

For a moment she almost imagined she could hear Pepper stamping around inside one of the looseboxes. Tears pricked her eyes at the thought of him and she mentally shook her head. Pepper would be long gone. She was being ridiculous.

Unbolting the top half of the door to one of the looseboxes she peered inside, shocked to see water dripping through a small hole in the roof, landing with a plop in a tin bucket beneath.

'How on earth could you let this happen?' she murmured, as if Joseph could hear her and would provide her with an explanation.

She closed the door and tried the next one, jumping back in surprise to find a horse staring back at her. Her heart leapt for a moment before she pulled herself together. This wasn't Pepper. How could it possibly be after all this time? Besides, this was a black gelding of around fifteen hands. Pepper had been fourteen hands and a beautiful, bright bay with a white blaze and black points.

'What are you doing in here?' she asked, as if the horse would answer her. She glanced around the loosebox. At least there was no bucket catching leaks in here. The bedding looked fresh, and the horse had water and a full hay net. She wasn't sure why it was inside, as most horses were quite happy to be out, rain or no rain, and this didn't look like a blood horse, but she was more concerned with why the top door had been shut. Surely it made more sense to leave it open? Horses rarely liked to be shut in like that. It must be like being in prison.

She swung the top door open wide and latched it to the wall to keep it in place.

'There. A bit of fresh air for you,' she told the horse, who blinked and turned away from her, as if he couldn't care less whether the door was open or not. She eyed him thoughtfully. He was obviously getting on in years. His eyes were sunken, and he had grey hairs around them and on his muzzle. His back was hollow, and his coat dull. He looked as weary as she felt.

So just how many horses was she now responsible for? She'd hoped someone had rehomed them all, but it seemed she'd been left with at least one, and possibly more.

A quick check of the other looseboxes yielded no more surprises, and she mentally crossed her fingers that there was currently only one resident for her to find a new home for. She tried not to think about who on earth would want such an old horse.

Water was dripping off her hair and running down her face, the wind was whipping her skin, making her eyes water, and she knew she was being ridiculous. She needed to go indoors and see for herself what condition the house was in. Having seen the stables she wasn't particularly optimistic, but surely Joseph had done at least basic maintenance? He couldn't possibly have allowed it to deteriorate as much as the stables, could he?

She glanced quickly into the open loosebox as she passed, noting the gelding was standing listlessly in a corner. Was he ill or just old? She needed to find the person who'd been in charge of this place while Joseph was ill. Maybe there'd be an explanation and a contact number somewhere in the house?

Her fingers shook as she tried to unlock the door. It had been so long since she'd last stood on this doorstep, fumbling with her keys. She remembered, as if it were yesterday, how she'd walked out for the last time, and the relief she'd felt when she'd dropped these very keys at her solicitor's for safekeeping, hoping never to return.

The key turned and she took a deep breath then pushed the door open. Her nose wrinkled as she stepped inside, aware of a stale, musty smell in the hallway. It was dark and gloomy, and she fumbled for the light switch, her mouth falling open in dismay as she saw the shabby wallpaper and the worn stair carpet. She almost wished she'd remained in the dark.

She walked to the end of the hall and pushed open the door she knew led to the kitchen, automatically switching on the light.

Before she could even begin to register the condition of that room she reeled back in alarm as a white missile launched itself at her and she was subjected to a series of short but increasingly frantic yaps.

'A dog!' She groaned in frustration. As if horses weren't enough to deal with, now it seemed Joseph had also owned a dog. A bichon frise if she wasn't mistaken.

She crouched down and made soothing noises in an attempt to calm it. The dog was practically dancing on its hind legs, and she eventually scooped it up and stood, rocking it gently as she stroked its head.

Despite herself she couldn't help but acknowledge that it was a cute little thing, and once it stopped yapping and surveyed her with interest through dark eyes, her heart might just have melted a little.

'So what's your name?' She turned the disc over on its collar and found the required information. 'Viva, eh? Pleased to meet you, Viva. And, more importantly, who's been looking after you?'

Viva rewarded her with several licks to the chin, which made Bethany laugh, despite herself. She kissed the little dog's nose then gently returned her to her bed.

'Right, let's see what state the rest of this place is in, shall we?'

As she got to her feet, her gaze turned to the ceiling and she mentally shook her head. No need to go up there. She wouldn't be checking out the bedrooms today.

It took her less than ten minutes to explore the rest of the downstairs, and her worry grew with each room. They all needed redecorating and re-carpeting, and that was just for starters. She wondered what the state of the boiler was, and the roof, and the wiring. At this rate she'd be paying someone to take Whispering Willows off her hands, never mind selling it for a profit.

She couldn't help but feel cross with Joseph. There was no excuse for letting it go to rack and ruin like this. She wondered what her mother would say if she knew. After all, it had been in her family for generations.

Viva trotted into the living room as Bethany sank onto a sagging sofa. Literally. The middle seemed to have no support and she felt as if she were practically sitting on the floor. Nervously she shuffled her way to the end cushion and placed Viva on her lap.

Some of this furniture had been here when she'd lived at Whispering Willows. Evidently Joseph hadn't cared that it was ugly, old, and in some cases barely fit for purpose.

'This is a real mess, isn't it, girl?' she whispered. 'Where do I even begin?'

Viva's dark eyes surveyed her sorrowfully and Bethany realised that this little dog must be grieving for Joseph.

'I guess you're my problem now,' she told her ruefully. 'I have no idea what to do first. I don't suppose you've got any information for me?'

Viva lay down and put her head on her paws and Bethany sighed as she stroked the dog's ears.

'A horse, a dog, and a house that basically needs gutting from top to bottom,' she murmured. 'Welcome home, Bethany.'

FOUR

The White Hart Inn was packed to the rafters with Tuppenny Bridge residents keen to pay their respects to Joseph. Sally and Rafferty Kingston, who owned the pub, had laid on a tasty buffet free of charge. Since Summer was Sally's daughter they felt it was the least they could do for a man who'd been so kind to Summer, and who she'd thought the world of.

As everyone mingled over sausage rolls and sandwiches, nursing glasses of alcohol and wondering aloud what would happen to Whispering Willows now, Clive took the opportunity to slip out of the pub and leave them all to it.

He didn't feel guilty about walking away from Joseph's wake. He knew his old friend would understand all too well. Besides, he needed to check on Chester, the latest arrival at Whispering Willows. Really, he should have said no when Mrs Evans begged him to take the horse, but how could he? Besides, Summer would never have forgiven him.

He could almost hear Joseph's laughter at that.

Got you wrapped round her little finger already, hasn't she? Told you she would.

He had indeed told him. Summer was desperate to save

every horse, pony, and donkey no matter what the cost or the circumstances. Clive had been warned by Joseph that it was up to him to be the head of the operation, while Summer would always be its heart.

'You'll need to toughen up with her,' he'd said, and Clive had assured him that was no problem. He was, after all, a vet, and used to making difficult decisions.

Well, that had lasted a long time, hadn't it? Joseph hadn't even passed away when Chester arrived at the sanctuary, and somehow Summer had persuaded him to take the poor old horse in. He hadn't mentioned it to Joseph.

Driving along Market Street he forced himself not to turn his head towards the churchyard. It had hurt him to leave his friend there, but it was what Joseph had wanted. Insisted upon, in fact.

Turning left onto Lavender Lane, he drove a short distance before indicating right and driving through the open gates of Whispering Willows.

This was the moment he'd been dreading. Since Joseph's passing he'd kept himself busy, dealing with official paperwork and organising the funeral, as well as overseeing the work at the sanctuary and continuing part time in his own job at Stepping Stones.

Now, though, it was time for real life to encroach. A new normality. He needed to pack up his belongings and take them back to his own flat above the veterinary surgery. He couldn't honestly say he'd be sorry to leave this old wreck of a house behind and return to his comfortable, immaculate flat, but it would be a wrench to say goodbye to Joseph yet again. He was everywhere in Whispering Willows.

At least the rain was easing off, which was something, although the wind was still gusting. So much for April showers. More like April monsoons.

His heart thudded as he noticed a bright blue hatchback

parked up in the stableyard. There was no sign of its driver, and he glanced around, his eyes narrowing as he noticed the top half of Chester's loosebox door was wide open.

Hurrying over he unlocked the bottom door and went inside, checking Chester was dry and comfortable and had enough to eat and drink. Carefully he closed both halves of the door behind him and bolted them shut, then strode to the house, his eyes darting left and right for any sign of someone loitering nearby.

If there was no one in the stableyard and no one in the paddocks and fields nearby, that meant only one thing. Whoever had visited had keys to the house. And the only other person who would have keys to the house was Bethany Marshall.

Clive's mouth tightened in anger. So she could come to the house but hadn't even bothered to attend her own brother's funeral? Well, he had a few words to say to Ms Marshall.

The door was unlocked, and he pushed it open, his pulse racing as he checked the kitchen and living room for signs of life. Where the hell was she?

'Can I help you?'

He spun round, instantly deflating as he saw a puzzled looking woman with a tousled honey blonde bob standing in the kitchen doorway, Viva in her arms. Evidently she must have been in Joseph's office.

She was, he knew, a couple of years younger than him, making her about fifty-four. She was wearing dark trousers and a thick, cream jumper, looking smart but casual. He was surprised by how short she was. She couldn't have been more than five foot two if that. Not really what he'd expected at all, and hard to stay angry at someone who looked so tiny and—yes, he had to admit it—vulnerable.

'Bethany?'

She nodded and put Viva on the floor. 'That's right. I'm afraid you have me at a disadvantage. Who are you?'

He stepped forward, almost reluctantly, and held out a hand to shake. She grasped it with surprising firmness and shook it.

'Clive,' he said. 'Clive Browning. I'm—I was—Joseph's friend.'

'Oh, I see.' She sounded weary. 'I suppose those are your wellies and coat in the hall then? I knew they were far too big to have been Joseph's. Have you been living here long?'

She didn't wait for a reply and pushed past him, heading into the living room. 'Perhaps you could tell me why this house has been allowed to get into such a state. And when did my brother start his horse sanctuary? Assuming it *was* his. It's not your sanctuary, is it?'

'Mine?' Clive's eyes widened in astonishment. 'Of course not. And the house is in something of a state,' he added indignantly, 'because all Joseph's money went on the horses. Which reminds me, was it you who opened that loosebox door and fastened it to the wall?'

She shrugged. 'Yes. In my opinion it's cruel to keep a horse locked indoors like that. I don't see why it's not outside anyway. A bit of rain never hurt any horse.'

'You're an expert, are you?' he asked, struggling to keep his tone civil.

'I rode a lot when I was younger,' she said. 'We had horses here. My father...' Her voice trailed off and she scooped up Viva and sat in an armchair, hugging the little dog to her as if afraid Clive was going to take her away. 'Well anyway, I just thought it would be better for the horse to get some fresh air.'

'Chester is an old horse,' Clive explained. 'He was brought here after his owner died. She'd treated him like a pet, keeping him inside whenever she thought he might get a bit cold. He's used to being stabled and gets anxious if he's outdoors in bad weather.'

'Well, that may be the case,' she said uncertainly, 'but there was no need to shut the top door on him was there? That seems unnecessarily cruel.'

'It would have been crueller if some of the roof slates had fallen on his head while he was looking outside,' Clive responded. 'It's been blowing a gale out there and if some of them came loose and slipped... I decided it was safer to keep the door shut for the time being. He wouldn't mind that.'

'Oh, wouldn't he? And *you're* an expert, are you?'

'I'm a vet,' he said. 'Joseph left the place in my care until you arrived. I was just doing my job, as I promised him.'

'Well,' she said, clearly a little uncomfortable, 'I'm here now. I can take it from here.'

He shook his head, hardly able to believe she could be so stubborn.

'You know nothing about the sanctuary or its residents,' he pointed out. 'You're going to need some help whether you like it or not.'

'Are you telling me there's more than one horse here?' she asked, clearly dismayed.

'There are thirteen residents altogether.' Realising she wasn't about to ask him to take a seat, he sat anyway, taking care to avoid the middle bit of the sofa. 'Three horses, four donkeys, and six ponies. And you've met Viva, of course,' he added, nodding at the bichon frise who was lying comfortably on her lap, and thinking what a traitor she'd turned out to be.

'So Viva *was* Joseph's dog, not yours?'

'I don't have a dog,' he told her. 'Although, if you don't want her I'd be happy to take her off your hands.'

The last thing he wanted was to dump poor Viva on someone who clearly didn't care much for animals, although he had to admit Bethany seemed quite taken with the bichon frise, and Viva seemed equally smitten with her. Dogs were supposed to be a good judge of character, weren't they? Well, he wasn't sure about Viva's judgement in this case.

Bethany hesitated. 'I—I'm not sure yet. I'll have to think about it.'

'Really? Well, let me know when you've made up your mind,' he said, unable to keep the sarcasm from his voice.

'You sound as if you're judging me, but I didn't know about any of this,' she reminded him. 'The message you left for me about Joseph's death didn't mention it. How was I supposed to know that my family home had become a horse sanctuary, or that I'd be expected to find homes for thirteen equines and a dog? How do you expect me to react?'

'Find homes for them?' Clive's heart sank. 'So, you're not planning on keeping the sanctuary going?'

She gave him an incredulous look. 'Are you joking? Why would I do that?'

'Because it mattered to Joseph!' he burst out. 'It was his life's work. Surely you must realise that? All right, he didn't make a will, which was foolish of him, but he would have known you'd inherit everything by default. He must have trusted you, believed you'd take over from him.'

'I highly doubt that,' she said. 'Why would he? He didn't even know me.'

'He was your brother!'

'A brother I haven't seen or spoken to in over thirty years,' she pointed out. 'He couldn't possibly have assumed I'd want to take on all this responsibility, and if he did—well, that was his error, not mine.'

'Wow!' Clive shook his head, unable to think of any other response.

'What's that supposed to mean?'

'Well, I guessed you'd be a pretty heartless sort of person, but this...'

'You think I'm heartless?' She shook her head. 'I can see you've made assumptions about me.'

'It's hard not to,' he said coldly, 'given that you couldn't even be bothered to turn up for your own brother's funeral, despite me giving you plenty of notice.'

'Who says I didn't turn up for it?' she said, her chin tilting in defiance. 'For your information I was by the church, watching.'

'You were there, and you didn't say anything?'

She shifted uncomfortably. 'I didn't feel right there. I hate funerals. And anyway, I'm sure Joseph wouldn't have wanted me there.'

Clive hardly knew what to say. His mouth dropped open and he stared at her in amazement. 'How can you say that? Why do you think I was so desperate to find you? He wanted to see you!'

'Did Joseph tell you that?'

'He didn't need to! I knew him, and I knew how much he missed you.'

'Perhaps,' she said carefully, 'you didn't know Joseph as well as you think you did. And you certainly don't know me, so maybe you ought to refrain from making snap judgements about me, and putting words into Joseph's mouth that I'm certain he would never have uttered.'

Clive steadied himself, determined not to have a full-blown argument with this woman. Not today, of all days. But she had a bloody cheek, telling him he didn't know Joseph when she hadn't so much as picked up a phone to call him in over thirty years.

'How long do you intend to stay?' he enquired at last.

She gave him a faint smile. 'Can't wait to see the back of me? Will my presence here cramp your style?'

'As a matter of fact,' Clive said, thanking his lucky stars that he wasn't a permanent resident, 'I'll be going home today. I just came back to pack my things actually.'

He realised he'd caught her off guard with that response. Her eyes widened and she tilted her head slightly, watching him.

'So you don't live here?'

'I was just staying here while Joseph was too ill to be left alone. Someone had to take care of him.'

Her head lowered and she focused on Viva as she gently stroked the dog's ears.

'Was it—I mean, did he suffer?'

Clive was tempted to yell the truth at her. What did she think? Of course Joseph had suffered! If she'd bothered to turn up she'd have seen that for herself, and just maybe she could have alleviated some of her brother's pain by being there for him.

'It wasn't pleasant,' he said at last. 'He spent the last few days in a hospice, and they made him as comfortable as they could. He wasn't really aware of anything in the end.'

His voice caught and he blinked away tears.

She said gently, 'I'm sorry for your loss.'

'He was your brother,' he replied. 'It was your loss too.'

'I lost Joseph a long, long time ago.' She gave him a brittle smile and, just for a moment, he thought he saw a gleam of tears in her own dark blue eyes. 'Anyway, before you go upstairs and pack, perhaps you could fill me in on this place. When did it become a sanctuary? And who's in charge of all these animals now? Someone must have been caring for them since Joseph got ill. You say you're a vet, so I presume you were too busy to work here full time.'

Clive leaned back in the sofa and nodded. 'Joseph employed a young woman called Summer Fletcher. She's been an absolute godsend, because even though Joseph couldn't afford to pay her much she worked hours every week for nothing. Then, when Joseph got really ill, we managed to get an army of volunteers in to help, although they could only do bits and bobs, fitting it around school and—'

'School?' she asked, clearly surprised. 'You're telling me this place was run by schoolchildren?'

'No. I told you; Summer runs the place. The two schoolkids help out at weekends, and they were here every day during the Easter holidays. And Summer's stepsister came up from Norfolk to help out, too, as well as Jamie and Eloise. Jamie's the younger brother of my colleague, Ben, and Eloise is his girlfriend.'

'And these are all teenagers?'

'They are, but they're hardworking and reliable.' He shifted a little. 'However, I've extended my leave from the practice to help here for a few more weeks, because Summer's going away in a few days. To Australia.'

'Going away?' Bethany gasped. 'Really? Couldn't she have picked a better time to jet off to the other side of the world?'

Clive's irritation grew as he thought about all the unpaid hours Summer had put in at Whispering Willows ever since she'd arrived in Tuppenny Bridge.

'That's not fair! Her dad's taking her to visit her sister who lives there, and it's been arranged for months. Summer nearly cancelled it, but we all talked her out of it. She needs a break. She's been working herself into the ground, and besides, she's grieving for Joseph. A few weeks away from this place will do her the world of good, and we weren't about to let her make yet another sacrifice.'

'Well...' Bethany sighed. 'Okay, I get that. It's just, she'll know all about the residents' needs and I know nothing.'

'You don't have to know anything. Like I said, I've taken leave, so I'll be here to do the work,' he said reluctantly. 'Maya and Lennox will be here during the weekends and before and after school. They know a lot, and Summer will leave a detailed set of instructions no doubt.'

'I suppose it's only temporary. Maybe by the time Summer gets back the problem will be resolved.'

He eyed her with suspicion. 'Meaning what?'

'Well, maybe by then we'll have found homes for the animals,' she said hopefully.

'So soon? Surely there's no rush? You could take your time, think about it. You might change your mind when you get to know them all.'

'That won't happen I'm afraid,' she said. 'I can't sell this place with a load of old horses, ponies, and donkeys as part of the deal.'

'Sell? You're planning to sell Whispering Willows?' Clive could almost hear the groan of despair from Joseph.

'Well, yes. You can't really have expected anything else?'

Had he? He supposed, when he thought about it, it was obvious that she'd want rid of a place she clearly had no love for, or why else would she have stayed away for so long? But a part of him had hoped that Joseph had known what he was doing, seeing no need to make a will ensuring his sister didn't get her hands on Whispering Willows. Had he really believed she would take over running the sanctuary from him? Clearly, Bethany was right. Joseph hadn't known her at all.

'I'll go and pack my things,' he said, getting to his feet with some difficulty, given the terrible condition of the sofa.

'Okay. Er, I don't suppose you'd be able to take Viva home with you tonight, would you?' As he gave her a puzzled look she added, 'I've booked a room at The Lady Dorothy and pets aren't allowed.'

'You're not staying here?'

She pulled a face and cast a despairing glance around the room. 'Not for a million pounds.'

'I'll take Viva,' Clive agreed briefly, before heading upstairs to collect his belongings.

He couldn't believe this woman. She had no heart whatsoever. She couldn't even bring herself to stay in this house for a night, let alone move in here. And all she wanted was to sell the place, which meant the end of the horse sanctuary.

Summer would be devastated. And where were they going to find suitable homes for all these animals? Did Bethany even care about them? Did she care about anything?

What on earth had Joseph been thinking?

FIVE

'And then she just coolly announces that she's putting Whispering Willows up for sale. I mean, can you believe that?'

Clive finally stopped to draw breath and Ben seized the opportunity to interrupt.

'Here, have a Penguin,' he said, holding out Clive's favourite chocolate biscuit. 'Get your breath back for a minute. Besides,' he added, nodding at the mug on the counter next to where Clive was leaning, 'your tea's getting cold.'

Clive managed a smile. 'Have I been going on a bit?'

Ben grinned back. 'A bit. But, quite honestly, I can't say I blame you. She sounds pretty awful. Are you sure she's Joseph's sister?'

'It is hard to believe, isn't it?' Clive unwrapped the Penguin and took a bite, hoping the chocolatey crunch would soothe his troubled nerves.

'Why on earth didn't Joseph make a will?' Ben mused. 'Maybe his sister didn't used to be so cold. Maybe she's changed in the last thirty odd years since he last saw her. I mean, people do, don't they? And didn't you say she's in her fifties now? Well, a young woman in her twenties would be very different to a woman of that age. Who knows what happened to make her so cynical?'

'More than cynical,' Clive said, hastily swallowing the biscuit. 'Downright heartless, that's what she is. This is Joseph's legacy and she's just planning to dismantle the whole thing as if none of it ever mattered. When I think how hard he worked over the years to keep that sanctuary going. Not to mention all the money he spent on it.' He shook his head, thinking about it. 'She just doesn't get it.'

'Well, maybe you should make her get it,' Ben suggested. 'We can't just give up and let her sell the place. Summer will be devastated. Oh hell, she's never going to agree to Australia now, is she? Once she knows Whispering Willows is going up for sale and all those animals are being packed off elsewhere, she'll refuse to set foot on that plane, and who can blame her?'

'Don't tell her,' Clive said immediately. 'You're right. She'll refuse to go, and she needs this holiday. She's worked far too hard recently. Besides, what good will her staying here do? I doubt very much that she'll be able to change Bethany's mind.'

Especially given how outspoken Summer could be when it came to the welfare of her beloved equines. She could really put Bethany's back up and drive her into doing something even worse than she'd already promised. Maybe she'd send the animals for slaughter instead of trying to find them decent homes. He couldn't risk that happening, and he wouldn't put anything past Joseph's spiky sister.

'It doesn't seem right keeping it from her, though,' Ben said doubtfully. 'If she comes back from Melbourne and discovers the house and residents gone, she'll never forgive me.'

'Oh, come on!' Clive took a sip of his lukewarm tea and pulled a face. He liked his tea hot. 'That won't happen. All the legal wrangling after a death can take ages to sort out. Won't she need to apply for probate or something before she can sell it? To be honest,' he added, 'I can't see her getting rid of it for ages. Far too much to deal with, and even if it was quite straightforward, look at the state of it! She's not likely to make much money from it. Might be wiser for her to do it up a bit before she even thinks about putting it on the market.' He stroked his chin thoughtfully. 'Mind you, there'll be inheritance tax to pay. She'll only have around six months before she has to stump up the cash, so that might put a fire under her.'

'Unless she's not bothered about that,' Ben pointed out. 'Didn't Miss Lavender say she'd married a wealthy man? Okay, they were divorced, but she probably got a huge settlement from that. Maybe she couldn't care less about making a profit as long as she gets rid of Whispering Willows. And where will that leave the horses?'

'Like I said, the legal aspect will slow everything up,' Clive reassured him. 'It takes time for inheritances to be sorted, and meantime, I'll do everything I can to try to persuade her to change her mind. Maybe, if she doesn't need the money, she'd consider putting Summer in as an official manager and paying her a salary? She wouldn't even have to live at the house. She could rent it out or something and go back to wherever it is she blew in from.'

'You really don't like her, do you?' Ben said. 'Not like you, Clive, to make such hasty judgements about people.'

'I don't know her,' Clive admitted. 'But I don't like what she did. Or rather, what she didn't do. She could have seen Joseph before he died, I'm sure of it. She could have attended his funeral properly, instead of lurking in the churchyard somewhere. And she could respect his wishes now and keep the sanctuary going. It seems to me she's done nothing but let him down. She obviously doesn't care about him at all.'

'I suppose the fact that she stayed away for over three decades pretty much warned us that would be the case,' Ben said.

'Aye, well...' Clive looked out of the window at the overcast skies. He supposed, deep down, he hadn't been able to believe that any sister of Joseph's could behave in such a fashion. He realised he'd been making excuses for her for months, but now he'd run out of them. Bethany Marshall was nothing like her brother, and it was a huge disappointment to him. 'Funny how different two siblings can be,' he mused. 'Joseph would do anything for anyone, whereas she...'

Ben drained his mug of tea and straightened. 'Hey, changing the subject a little, but would you be free to come over for supper on Saturday night?'

'Me? To yours, you mean? Daisyfield Cottage?' Clive frowned. 'Are you sure?'

Ben laughed. 'Of course I'm sure! Summer's leaving for Australia early on Monday, so we're having a farewell meal at ours for her. Sally and Rafferty will be there, too, and Mum's cooking.'

'She doesn't mind you inviting me?'

'Why would she?'

Clive shrugged. 'Well, when all's said and done it's a family thing, and I'm not family. I'm just your boss.'

'Don't be daft,' Ben said, clapping him lightly on the arm. 'You're family, too. Mum will be pleased to see you anyway. She's been worried about you.'

Clive put his mug carefully on the counter. 'Has she?'

'Of course!' Ben's tone softened. 'She knows what it's like to grieve, remember? She knows how much you cared for Joseph, and she understands how that feels. She doesn't want you to cut yourself off from people the way she did all those years.'

'Aye,' Clive said quietly. 'I suppose that makes sense. It's very kind of you all.'

'So you'll come?'

'Why not? Should I bring anything with me? Wine, perhaps, or a bottle of whisky?'

Ben grinned. 'Just bring yourself, Clive. We'll take care of everything else.' His smile faltered and he said, 'So you really think we should keep all this from Summer? About Bethany selling the sanctuary, I mean?'

'If you want Summer to get on that plane then I think it's our only option, lad,' Clive advised. 'Like I say, there's nothing she can do to change things, so why put her through all that anguish? Let her have a few weeks with her dad and her sister. She needs a break after all the work she's put in. And when she gets home... Well, there'll be plenty of time for her to deal with all that then.'

Providing there wasn't somehow a miraculously quick sale naturally. Who knew how low Bethany would drop the price if she wanted rid of Whispering Willows that fast? Thank goodness the legal wheels turned notoriously slowly. Bethany wouldn't be able to sell her inheritance anywhere near as quickly as she obviously wanted to.

And when probate was finally granted? He could only mentally cross his fingers that, somehow, he would be able to talk her into carrying on Joseph's legacy.

He didn't, in all honesty, hold out much hope.

* * *

Breakfast at The Lady Dorothy was basic but at least Bethany had the option of eating in her room rather than going downstairs—an option she took with relief. She refused the full English breakfast, settling instead for toast and a soft-boiled egg, plus the obligatory pot of tea.

She accepted the tray from the landlady and closed the door behind her, then carefully climbed into bed and settled back against the headboard, her eyes closed for a moment as she contemplated the day ahead.

Having opened the curtains slightly she was grateful to see that the bad weather of yesterday had rolled away, leaving a brighter, dryer day in its wake. That should make everything a little more bearable. Not much, but anything was an improvement on yesterday.

As she sipped tea she considered the events of the previous day, her heart sinking as she remembered the state of the house, and the fact that she was now responsible for finding homes for thirteen horses, ponies, and donkeys. Then there was Viva to consider. She had to admit she was rather taken with the little dog, but with her own plans so up in the air she wasn't certain she could keep her.

At least, she thought wryly, slicing the top off her egg, that awful Scotsman seemed willing to take Viva if necessary. That was something.

He'd really annoyed her yesterday, being so judgemental and rude. He knew nothing about her, but he'd clearly formed an opinion—based, no doubt, on Joseph's view of her. She wondered what her brother had told his 'friend' about her. Somehow, she doubted it was the whole truth.

Well, today she'd brave that place again and take a proper look around. She'd make an inventory of what was inside—most of it would be destined for the local tip from what she'd seen—and then get onto an estate agent as fast as possible. The sooner the place was up for sale the better.

As for the horses...

Bethany had no answer to that one. If they were all in a state like Chester, she knew they would be hard to rehome. Maybe another sanctuary would take them? Although, the way things were these days with the economy and the cost-of-living crisis, she suspected more people were trying to get rid of horses than taking them in, and knew that many animal sanctuaries were being overwhelmed with new arrivals. It probably wouldn't be easy to find them alternative homes.

And until she'd done that, she could hardly sell the house, could she? Unless, by some miracle, the estate agent found a buyer who had lots of money to spend doing up the stables as well as the house, and a passion for broken down equines. Not likely.

An hour later, showered and dressed, Bethany headed out to Whispering Willows. She decided to leave the car in the pub car park and walk. Fresh air would do her good.

She noticed there'd been some changes in Market Place since she left.

Pennyfeather's was still there, of course. Although, looking more closely at it as she passed she realised it was no longer Pennyfeather's Wool Shop, but Pennyfeather's Craft Shop, and above it was a new sign for The Crafty Cook Café. Seemed Rita and Birdie had made some changes to the old place. Good for them.

The doctor's surgery and the chemist's shop were still there, although they'd definitely been smartened up. She doubted very much that old Dr Gedney was still around, and she thought the chemist's name had changed, too, but at least they were still being used for the same purpose.

Taylor-Made, the children's clothes shop run by old Mrs Taylor that had stood on the corner of Little Market Street, was now The Corner Cottage Bookshop. It gave her a pang of sadness as she remembered her mother taking her into that shop to buy her new clothes. She'd got a lovely navy-blue winter coat one year. It had been so warm and smart, and she'd adored the little red and black buttons in the shape of ladybirds. She'd never forgotten it.

The White Hart Inn looked much smarter, too, she thought. It had been brightened up, and she loved the hanging baskets and window boxes of spring flowers that adorned the front of the building.

Hurrying past the church without glancing in its direction, she headed briskly down Market Street and onto Lavender

Lane, then crossed the road and turned towards Whispering Willows.

She slowed as she noticed a car turn into the drive.

Visitors! She couldn't imagine any of the teenage workforce had cars, and besides, they'd be at school today. Her heart sank as she realised it must be that awful vet again. What did he want now? Come to talk her out of selling up? He'd be wasting his time if that was his plan.

As she neared the stableyard, though, she realised it wasn't the vet at all. She wasn't sure whether to be relieved or dismayed to see Miss Lavender standing at the front door. Well, that hadn't taken her long, had it? Although, remembering what Miss Lavender had been like she shouldn't have been surprised.

She wasn't alone, either. She was chatting to a young woman with shoulder-length brown hair, wearing jeans and wellies and a grey jumper.

As Bethany approached, they both looked up and Miss Lavender's face broke into a wide smile. It occurred to Bethany that she'd aged massively. Then again, it had been, what, thirty-five years since she'd last seen her, and the middle-aged woman was now an old lady. She must be around eighty now, surely? She supposed Miss Lavender was thinking how much she'd aged, too, which was a depressing thought.

'Bethany! Oh, my dear, how wonderful it is to see you again.'

There was genuine warmth in her voice and her eyes, and Bethany experienced a pang of guilt that Miss Lavender was obviously so pleased to see her, while she'd been full of dismay when she'd realised who was waiting for her. She should be more open and welcoming. After all, Miss Lavender had done nothing wrong. On the contrary, after Bethany's mother had died, Miss Lavender had been a listening ear and a shoulder to cry on. Considering Bethany hadn't even kept in touch with her she was being remarkably forgiving.

'Miss Lavender.'

She hurried forward and found herself in a touchingly affectionate hug. Miss Lavender held her at arm's length and surveyed her closely.

'You're looking very well, my dear.'

'Very old you mean,' Bethany said, managing a laugh. 'I expect I've changed a lot since we last met.'

'Well, haven't we all?' Miss Lavender sighed. 'You're as pretty as a picture, just as you always were.'

She straightened and laid a hand on the young woman's arm. 'Bethany, let me introduce you to Summer Fletcher. She runs Whispering Willows. That is, she ran it, when Joseph was alive. Oh, dear. Well, she's the one to ask if you have any questions about the sanctuary.'

Bethany saw Summer's anxious expression and felt sympathy for her. This was, after all, her livelihood. She should put her out of her misery right now, tell her the truth about the future. Even so, she didn't have the heart to break that to her so soon after the loss she'd experienced and she found herself saying, 'I have lots of questions, naturally. Perhaps we should go inside, and I'll make us some tea.'

Summer looked slightly less pensive and, trying to ignore the guilt, Bethany unlocked the door and led them inside. She was tempted to apologise for the state of the place, but realised they'd probably seen it many times and wouldn't be surprised.

It seemed she was wrong, though, because as they all headed into the kitchen Miss Lavender looked appalled.

'What on earth has happened to this place? It was such a beautiful house! Look at the state of it!'

Bethany filled the kettle and switched it on. 'You haven't seen it recently, Miss Lavender?'

Miss Lavender looked rather shamefaced. 'I haven't been here since—well, since your father passed, dear. And, quite honestly, I rarely visited after you left. I only called now and then just to check everything was as it should be.' She shifted in her seat, clearly feeling awkward about something.

'Not once?' Bethany couldn't imagine it. Miss Lavender had made it her business to keep an eye on things after Bethany's mother had died. It seemed, once Bethany had left Tuppenny Bridge, Miss Lavender had washed her hands of Whispering Willows and the people left behind. Of Joseph. Was that because of what had happened? Had she discovered the reason Bethany had walked out?

But that wasn't my fault, was it? I didn't ask her to take sides!

'I see,' she said. 'Take a seat. Tea won't be long.'

She knew where everything was after checking all the cupboards yesterday and was glad that someone—probably Clive—had put fresh milk in the fridge.

'Oh,' Miss Lavender said, sitting at the table and looking round sadly, 'I can't believe how much this house has deteriorated. But it's so good to see you again, dear, and to see you back in this kitchen... I know it can't be easy for you, and in such trying circumstances.'

Summer cleared her throat. 'Look, I can see you two have a lot to talk about and I've got work to be getting on with. Come and find me when you need me, Bethany.'

'Oh, but I was making tea—'

'It's fine. I've not long had a drink. I'll leave you both to it.'

'Well,' Bethany said, feeling uncertain, 'if you're sure...'

Summer headed back outside, and Bethany made the tea for herself and Miss Lavender. She sat at the table and put her head in her hands.

'I didn't expect any of this,' Bethany admitted.

Miss Lavender sighed. 'It must have been a dreadful shock, finding out about Joseph's death. I'm very sorry for your loss, Bethany.'

Bethany gave a bitter laugh. 'You and I both know I don't

deserve any sympathy. I hadn't seen or heard from him in decades. Joseph and I were hardly family any longer. That's why I don't understand this. Any of it. Why didn't he make a will? He must have known that as his only living relative I'd be expected to take care of these horses.'

'But you're his sister!' Miss Lavender said, surprised. 'Who else would he trust them with?'

'Anyone!' Bethany shrugged. 'What about that Clive person? He was obviously very close to him.'

'Clive was an extremely good friend to Joseph,' Miss Lavender admitted. 'Even so, he's not family, is he? Clearly, Joseph trusted you and expected you to do the right thing for those poor animals. As he should.'

Bethany disagreed. Joseph had no right to expect anything from her. Hadn't she done enough for him already?

'This horse sanctuary,' she began hesitantly. 'I can't believe he didn't let me know.' The more she thought about it the angrier she felt. 'He had no right! What's it all about anyway? And how long had he been running it?'

Miss Lavender blew on her tea. 'It must be twenty-five years now. Just three years after your father died, in fact. Joseph seemed to withdraw from the outside world, rarely leaving this place. Then the next thing we knew he'd started taking in stray animals. It was completely out of the blue.'

'He left the brewery?' Bethany couldn't imagine it. Joseph had loved the Lusty Tup Brewery, and on the rare occasions when she'd allowed herself to think about him at all, she'd pictured him in his office there.

'Oh no, that came much later. He took early retirement but that was only around ten years ago. I suppose he was waiting for a pension or something. After he left there, he became even more reclusive. We rarely saw him around the town. He spent all his time cooped up here with the horses.' She gazed around the kitchen with some distaste. 'He became a sort of hermit, really. If he hadn't had Clive, I really don't know what would have happened. Clive was his link with the outside world and coaxed him into attending occasional events. Without him, I doubt Joseph would have bothered.'

'Clive's a vet, I understand?'

'That's right. He came to Tuppenny Bridge about twenty-eight years ago from Edinburgh, around the time your father passed. When our previous vet retired, Clive took over the practice and bought Stepping Stones from him. Naturally, he was called out to Whispering Willows many times, and the two of them struck up a friendship.'

Bethany sipped her tea, saying nothing.

'Clive's been wonderful these last few months,' Miss Lavender admitted. 'He moved into this house to take care of Joseph, employed a locum to help Ben as he couldn't be at the vet practice so much, and employed help for Summer.'

'Employed?' Bethany frowned. 'I thought the teenagers were volunteers.'

Miss Lavender shook her head. 'No, Summer confided that Clive paid them out of his own pocket. He just told Joseph they'd volunteered so Joseph wouldn't worry or feel bad. Clive's a good man. A kind man.'

He hadn't seemed particularly kind yesterday, Bethany mused. Then again, grief could affect people in different ways, and it was without question that Clive was grieving. She supposed she hadn't helped matters by telling him she planned to offload Whispering Willows either. She could have broken that to him more gently she thought ruefully.

'How are you feeling, anyway?' Miss Lavender asked her, her faded blue eyes warm with sympathy. 'You've lost your Yorkshire accent, my dear.'

Had she? Bethany hadn't been aware of that, but she supposed being around Ted and Helena with their polished tones for so many years she might well have done.

'It must be hard for you, coming back here after all this time.'

Bethany glanced around her and pulled a face. 'You could say that. I really don't know what I'm doing here, Miss Lavender. I can't believe Joseph didn't make provision for all these horses and ponies. I mean, what am I supposed to do about them? He must have known I wouldn't stay here, so what did he think I was going to do with all these animals?'

'You're not going to stay?' Miss Lavender's face crumpled. 'Oh, Bethany, dear. Are you sure?'

'Surely you of all people know I can't possibly come back here after everything that happened?'

'It was such a long time ago, dear. Another lifetime. You've done so much since then.'

'Yes, I have! And that's why I can't risk letting all that hard work go to waste. If I came back here, I'd be dragged back into that awful feeling. That helpless, hopeless feeling, like all the air's being sucked out of my lungs. I already feel a bit like that and I'm not even staying in this house. I've booked a room at The Lady Dorothy because I can't bear to be under this roof.'

'But it could be your home again if you just give it time.'

'It could never be my home!' Bethany said fiercely. 'It's *his* home! It will always be his home, and I can't live with all these memories of him and the living hell he turned this place into.'

Miss Lavender sighed. 'I suppose I can't blame you for that. How long do you intend to stay?'

Bethany deflated. 'That's just it. My intention was to spend only a few days here, sorting through belongings and getting an estate agent to view it. I had no idea there was a horse sanctuary here, or that I'd be expected to find homes for thirteen animals. Fourteen if you count Viva. Although Clive's taken her for now until I decide what to do with myself.'

'So you're definitely selling?'

'Definitely. Unfortunately, it's not going to be as straightforward as I'd supposed. I can't sell the house until I've found homes for the animals and look at this place! I'll be lucky to give it away the state it's in. I don't know.' She shook her head, feeling helpless. 'All I know is my flying visit to Tuppenny Bridge is going to last a lot longer than I'd anticipated.'

'Well, in that case you must stay with me at Lavender House,' Miss Lavender said at once. 'You can't stay in The Lady Dorothy indefinitely, and you'd be more than welcome in my apartment.'

Bethany wasn't so sure about that. The last thing she needed was Miss Lavender sticking her oar in every five minutes, however well-intentioned she knew the old lady was.

'Honestly, I'm fine at the pub,' she began, but Miss Lavender had made up her mind.

'I'm there on my own now the boys have gone,' she said, 'and I'd be glad of the company.'

Bethany frowned. 'What boys?'

'My great-nephews. Oh, of course, you won't remember Noah, and you weren't here when Ross was born. They are the lights of my life, Bethany, and I've had the pleasure of raising them almost as my own. I must leave in a moment but as soon as we get the chance we'll have a proper catch-up. Oh, I have such a lot to tell you. So much has happened since you left Tuppenny Bridge!'

SIX

When Miss Lavender finally left, having managed to extract a promise from Bethany that she would, indeed, move into Lavender House, Bethany decided it was time to bite the bullet and face Summer.

With growing trepidation she pulled on her coat and zipped it up, bracing herself for her employee's anger and disappointment when she broke the news of her plans. She didn't relish the prospect but knew it was only fair to give the girl warning that things were not going to stay the same at Whispering Willows. If nothing else, it would give her more time to find alternative employment.

Heading out into the stableyard she was taken aback to spot Clive, rather than Summer. Of course, she should have expected he'd be here, given that he'd already told her he'd arranged to cover for Summer while she was away, and was probably helping now to get used to the routine.

'Good morning.' She hoped her voice sounded certain and strong. She didn't want him to know how uncertain and weak she was actually feeling. He was clearly determined that Whispering Willows was going to stay open and would seize upon any sign of doubt, using it to manipulate her. That was not going to happen.

Clive glanced up and nodded briefly at her. 'Morning.'

He was picking out Chester's hooves. The gelding looked, if anything, even older as he stood patiently in the yard than he had in the dim light of the loosebox yesterday.

'Oh my,' she said, her voice softening with sympathy despite herself as she surveyed the elderly horse, 'he's really looking sorry for himself, isn't he?'

Clive nodded. 'Aye. Not a happy fella, are you, eh?' He rubbed Chester's nose affectionately.

'How old is he?' She shouldn't really be making conversation with Clive, but she couldn't help herself. Her sympathies were aroused, despite the pep talk she'd given herself last night. Looking at the poor old animal now she couldn't for the life of her imagine anyone else wanting to take him on. If Whispering Willows closed where would that leave him? Maybe Clive would take him? He obviously cared for the old boy.

'Around thirty,' Clive said briefly.

'Oh gosh, quite an age. So does he have any other health problems?'

'Nothing that doesn't come with being old. The main problem with Chester is he's grieving.'

'Grieving?'

'Like I said, his owner treated him more like a pet. The two of them were each other's world. Now she's gone he's missing her badly.'

'Maybe it would be better for him if he had some company. Being shut up in the stables alone can't be good for him.'

Clive sighed. 'As I explained, he's used to being stabled in bad weather and gets quite distressed if he's out in it. Yesterday was definitely bad weather.'

'And today?'

Clive shrugged as he looked up at the sky. 'Today, as you

can see, the weather is fine, so I'll be turning him out in one of the paddocks with a couple of Welsh cobs. They've become friends so he'll be quite happy there.'

'I hope so.'

He looked surprised that she was concerned, which she supposed she couldn't blame him for. She hadn't, after all, given him much of an impression that she cared one way or the other.

'How's Viva?' she asked quickly before he could comment further on her sudden interest in Chester's welfare. 'Did she settle at your place all right?'

'Eventually,' he said briefly. 'She's another one grieving. Now she's not only lost her owner but she's probably losing her home, too, just like Chester. It's hard on animals. I don't think people give enough thought to how grief and change affects them.'

Bethany bristled. 'I'm sorry, but you must understand I couldn't possibly take her with me to The Lady Dorothy. Pets aren't allowed in there at all.'

'But you could move in here,' he pointed out. 'Why not? It's a big old house that's just standing empty. All it needs is some love and attention.'

'Yes, well, I'm sure the new owner will provide that,' she said, anxious to head him off before he could start to harangue her again about keeping Whispering Willows. 'Do you know where Summer is?'

'She's just taken Barney up to Harston's Hill. He's one of our native ponies. I'll explain about him later. What do you need Summer for?'

He sounded suspicious and she couldn't help wondering what it had to do with him why she needed Summer. For some reason, though, she found herself saying, 'I want to speak to her about the future of this place.'

Clive's sandy-coloured eyebrows knitted together in a frown as he slipped the hoof pick in his pocket. 'What about it?'

Honestly, did he want to know everything? She couldn't see why she had to run any of this past him. It was her business, not his.

'She needs to know where she stands,' she replied curtly. 'It wouldn't be fair to keep her wondering. The sooner she knows the sooner she can start job hunting, and—'

'Job hunting!' Clive sounded horrified. 'You're not going to tell her you're selling up? She's about to go to Australia!'

'I think it's always best to be honest with people,' she said firmly. 'It's hardly my fault she's swanning off on holiday, is it?'

'I explained that to you,' he said, his tone disapproving. 'Summer's been an absolute godsend here. Joseph simply couldn't have managed without her. She deserves better than this.'

'So what do you want me to do?' she demanded. 'If she's been such a godsend, she deserves plenty of warning that she's going to have to find herself another position. And the good thing is, if she's the asset you say she is then she'll have no trouble finding work elsewhere, will she?'

He glared at her. 'Round here? With horses?' He shook his head. 'You're living in cloud cuckoo land. She's going to be devastated. And it's not just her she'll be worrying about. Summer lives and breathes these horses. She'll worry herself sick about their future, and how is she going to relax in Australia if she's got all that going through her head?'

Bethany was almost sure she was blushing under the pressure of his accusing stare. 'Look, I'm sorry about that, but I don't see what else I can do.'

'Don't tell her!' The sharpness in his tone took her aback, and she noted that he bit his lip, as if he'd recognised how brusque he'd sounded. The expression in his eyes softened and he said quietly, 'Please, just don't tell her. Not now. Let her go away and rest for a few weeks before you spring this on her.'

His concern for Summer's welfare was quite touching she thought. Even so, it didn't feel right to her to lie.

'She's bound to ask me what my plans are for this place and what am I supposed to tell her? Should I make out that everything's going to carry on as normal?'

'Can't you fudge it?' he asked hopefully. 'Sort of get round it by not answering her directly. Just tell her your plans are still up in the air at least.'

'But they're not,' she said, gazing steadily at him and noticing that his eyes were more grey than blue, like the sky on a rainy day. 'I've already made it clear to you that my plans are to find new homes for these animals and sell Whispering Willows so I can get out of here as soon as possible.'

Clive sighed and turned back to Chester. He patted his neck and said, 'Hear that, old lad? You're going to be turfed out of here, too, just as you were starting to settle.'

'Don't do that!' she snapped.

He glanced round at her. 'Do what?'

'Emotional blackmail. Manipulation. It's not right and it's not fair. I didn't ask for any of this. I don't know what you want from me.'

'All I'm asking,' he said heavily, 'is that you put off telling Summer the truth until she gets back from Australia. I'm not joking, she won't go if she knows what's going to happen. She needs this break. If you'd seen her these past few months—if you'd just been here...'

She stiffened, not sure if that was yet another dig at her. 'Well I wasn't,' she said defensively. 'However, I take your point that it's probably true Summer won't leave here if she thinks I'm going to sell up. I'll do as you ask, but the moment she gets back I'm going to be honest with her. It's not fair to do otherwise.'

Clive nodded. 'Thank you. And now I'm going to turn Chester out. Would you like to come with me? Meet the horses he'll be sharing the paddock with?'

Bethany hesitated. Was this another trap? Was Clive hoping that she'd fall in love with the residents of the sanctuary and change her mind about selling? He would be disappointed if he was. She had, she decided, nothing to fear. She wasn't going to back down now.

'Okay,' she said with a shrug. 'Might as well start somewhere. With Summer gone I suppose you'll be needing my help here.'

'Aye, that would be grand,' he agreed. 'And after all, they *are* your responsibility.'

'Don't push it,' she warned him as he took Chester's halter rope and turned the horse towards the paddock. 'They might be, but not for long.'

Though if she couldn't find homes for them all, what then? It really didn't bear thinking about.

It's not my problem she told herself fiercely as they walked slowly out of the stableyard.

Sadly, the gnawing feeling in the pit of her stomach reminded her all too clearly that, actually, it was.

Lavender House had once been a grand, stately home belonging to Josiah Lavender, the famous Georgian artist, and his independently wealthy wife, but was now a museum and art gallery dedicated to the memory of Miss Lavender's illustrious ancestor.

Bethany had only visited the place on two previous occasions, both times when she was a little girl. Her mother had taken her to tea with Miss Lavender, and they'd been shown into their host's private apartment at the back of the building.

She vaguely remembered her mother warning her to sit still and be quiet, as she fidgeted on the old-fashioned sofa and tugged at the hem of her best dress, and her relief when Miss

Lavender had eventually suggested she might like to play in the garden and burn off some of her energy.

There were formal gardens at the house, which visitors could pay to walk around, but Miss Lavender had her own private garden at the side of the building, which was walled, ensuring privacy from prying eyes and a safe space for her yellow Labrador, Binks, named after one of Yorkshire's finest cricketers, according to his proud owner.

Now, as Bethany headed into the house all these years later, her small suitcase in hand, she wasn't sure what to expect, and couldn't help wondering how she'd allowed herself to be talked into moving in with Miss Lavender.

The woman seated at the reception desk in the hall nodded and smiled a greeting at her, so she supposed she was expected by the museum staff as well as its owner. She glanced around, trying to get her bearings. It had been a long time since she'd last visited the house. It was hard to remember the route to the private quarters.

'Bethany Marshall?'

She turned at the sound of a male voice calling her name. A tall, dark, handsome man with black hair and a neatly trimmed beard was heading towards her, his dark eyes smiling a welcome.

She nodded, wondering who this vision was. 'That's me.'

He held out his hand and she shook it weakly. 'I'm Ross. Ross Lavender. Aunt Eugenie's expecting you. Would you like to follow me?'

This was Miss Lavender's great-nephew? Wow, he was gorgeous. Then she remembered that she was fifty-four and probably old enough to be this man's mother, and telling herself she ought to know better, she followed him meekly to the back of the house through a door marked 'Private' then through another door which led to the apartment.

Ross ushered her inside, calling out as he did so. 'Aunt Eugenie, your guest's arrived!'

Two Yorkshire terriers dashed to investigate her, yapping loudly.

Ross rolled his eyes. 'Don't mind them. Their bark's definitely worse than their bite.'

Bethany crouched down and patted the two little dogs, laughing as they tumbled over each other in an effort to be the closest to her.

'They're so cute! Bit different to Binks.'

Ross smiled. 'Oh, you remember Binks? I never met him but Aunt Eugenie's always talking about him. These are Boycott and Trueman.'

Bethany couldn't help but laugh. 'Still a cricket fan then, your aunt?'

'You could say that.' Ross gestured to the big, squashy, rather chintzy sofa, and said, 'Make yourself at home. She won't be long.'

With that, his great aunt hurried into the living room looking rather bashful.

'Sorry about that, Bethany. Call of nature. I'm afraid as you get older trips to the bathroom grow ever more frequent.'

Bethany had been about to say she knew exactly what Miss Lavender meant, but then remembered Ross was standing right there, and decided not to comment.

'You've met Ross then? Ross, this is Bethany, the lovely lady I was telling you about. She's Joseph's sister, remember?'

'We met in the reception,' Bethany said hastily. 'He kindly showed me the way as I seem to have forgotten it.'

'Ah well, I'll get you some keys cut, and you can come through the side gate and the back door,' Miss Lavender told her. 'Saves you having to come through the house.'

'Oh really, there's no need,' Bethany assured her. 'I won't be staying here that long.'

'It's no trouble, dear,' Miss Lavender said, waving a hand and dismissing her protests instantly. 'Now, would you like tea or coffee?'

Ross excused himself and left the apartment, closing the door gently behind him. Bethany realised she was staring wistfully after him and mentally shook her head. What on earth was wrong with her? Though, it had to be said, he really was good looking.

'What did you think of Ross then, dear?' Miss Lavender asked, smiling at her with a knowing look in her eyes. 'Rather a charmer, isn't he?'

Bethany was sure she was blushing. 'He seems, er, very nice,' she said feebly.

'Oh he is. A darling. Both my boys are. He's an artist, you know. He's settled up at Monk's Folly now. Do you remember Monk's Folly?'

Bethany lifted an eyebrow in surprise. 'The Callaghans' place?'

'Yes, that's right. Except it belongs to us now. We've completely refurbished it and turned it into the Arabella Lavender Art Academy. Ross oversees it and lives in the house. At the moment only day classes are running, but the residential courses open for business at last in a couple of weeks. We're having an open day and Ethan Rochester, no less, is going to perform the ceremony. You know, the owner of Rochester's Department Stores? He's a distant cousin of Rafferty Kingston, who owns The White Hart Inn. You must come to that.'

'Thank you. And what about Jennifer and Julian?' Bethany asked. 'Do they still live in Tuppenny Bridge?'

A shadow flitted across Miss Lavender's face. 'Jennifer does,' she said quietly. 'Unfortunately, Julian passed away some fourteen years ago.'

'Oh no, how awful!' Bethany's hand flew to her mouth as she remembered the friendly man who'd sometimes visited

Whispering Willows. He'd worked with Joseph at the brewery, she recalled. Joseph had spoken very highly of him. 'Didn't they have a son, too? A little boy?'

'Leon.' Miss Lavender sighed. 'I'll put the kettle on. There are some things you ought to know about the Callaghans.'

Bethany glanced at the suitcase, noting that Trueman and Boycott were investigating it thoroughly, but seeing that they were hardly likely to damage anything she followed Miss Lavender into the kitchen.

'Leon,' Miss Lavender explained, taking china cups and saucers from a cabinet, 'was killed in a car accident fourteen and a half years ago. Jennifer went to pieces. Well, she had two other children to care for.' She flicked the switch on the kettle. 'Ben, who was fifteen at the time, and poor little Jamie, who was just a baby when his father and brother died. Unfortunately, the responsibility for the house and his family fell on Ben's young shoulders, as Jennifer withdrew into herself and became a recluse. I'm afraid he had a very difficult time of it.'

'Ben...' Bethany frowned. 'I think Clive mentioned that the vet he works with at Stepping Stones is called Ben. Not the same one, I suppose?'

'As a matter of fact, yes, he is. After Julian died Clive took him under his wing. He and Julian were great friends, you see. In fact, I believe it was Joseph who introduced them. Of course, Julian was far more sociable than Joseph, so although Clive spent a lot of time with your brother, when he wanted to go out and see something of other people, he was with Julian.' She put spoonfuls of loose tea into a teapot, her eyes thoughtful. 'He took it badly when Julian died. I suppose he thought helping Ben would be the least he could do for his friend's son.'

'Helping Ben? You mean by giving him a job after he qualified as a vet?'

'Oh, more than that, dear,' Miss Lavender assured her. 'Milk? Sugar?'

'Yes please, and no thanks,' Bethany said.

'I really should cut down on sugar,' Miss Lavender admitted, adding two well-rounded spoonfuls to her cup. 'Where was I? Oh yes. Well, Clive basically did all he could to get Ben into veterinary school. The Callaghans didn't have much money, and I know for a fact that he paid for his textbooks and contributed towards the cost of Ben's studies. I don't know if Ben could have done it without Clive's help. And of course, he gave Ben work experience and holiday work and then promised him there'd be a job waiting for him as soon as he graduated. Clive was as good as his word. There was. And Ben's been at Stepping Stones ever since.'

'He's been very fortunate then,' Bethany said, thinking with some reluctance that Clive clearly had a good heart, given what he'd done for Ben and also for Joseph.

'He has,' Miss Lavender agreed, as she poured hot water into the teapot. 'In that sense, anyway. But don't think he's had an easy life, because I can assure you, Ben has suffered since the death of his father and brother. In fact, it's only since he fell in love with young Summer Fletcher that things started to change for him.'

'Summer Fletcher? You mean the girl who works at Whispering Willows?'

'That's right. She moved to Tuppenny Bridge a year last Christmas to be with her mother, who married Rafferty Kingston. They run the pub together. Anyway, she and Ben started courting, and she helped him come to terms with his grief. That's when he was finally able to let go of the past and sell Monk's Folly to me.'

'So where do the Callaghans live now?' Bethany asked.

'Do you remember Daisyfield Cottage?'

Bethany frowned, trying to picture it. A pretty little building on River Road, she seemed to recall.

'The Eckingtons' place?'

'That's right. Mrs Eckington passed away, and Mr Eckington lives with their daughter now, so he sold the cottage to Ben. They're much happier there than they ever were at Monk's Folly, and we've spent a fortune restoring Monk's Folly to its former glory, so everyone's happy.'

'And Ross runs it?'

'He's a brilliant artist,' Miss Lavender said proudly. 'It will be safe in his hands.' She poured tea through a strainer into the cups and confided, 'It's just what he needs. He was a bit—*restless* for a time. His mother's Italian, you know.'

Bethany smothered a smile. Clearly, Ross's mother being Italian explained everything as far as Miss Lavender was concerned.

'And now,' Miss Lavender continued, adding a drop of milk to each cup, 'he's courting at last. A lovely young girl who works in the bookshop in Market Place. They're absolutely smitten with one another. It's rather sweet.'

Bethany took the cup and saucer from Miss Lavender's hand and thanked her. They headed back to the living room, where they found Trueman lying contentedly on top of the suitcase while Boycott snored beside it, his little nose pressed into the thick, pile carpet.

'Aren't they beautiful?' Miss Lavender gave them an adoring smile as she settled herself on the sofa beside Bethany.

'You said you had another great-nephew, didn't you?' Bethany asked. 'Noah, wasn't it?'

'That's right.' Miss Lavender sighed. 'He's the headmaster of our local primary school now. Done very well for himself. Such a hardworking and decent young man.'

'And is he, er, *courting*?'

'Oh, he's been married for years,' Miss Lavender explained. 'To Isobel. She owns Petalicious, the florist's shop on the green.'

Something in Miss Lavender's tone told Bethany that she was worried about something, but she didn't ask what it was. If

Miss Lavender wanted to tell her she surely would. She was rarely backwards in coming forwards as far as Bethany recalled.

'Anyway, tell me about yourself,' the old lady said, giving her a warm smile. 'I was so sorry to read about your husband's death, my dear. Well,' she added hastily, 'your *ex*-husband's death. I was sorry to hear *that*, too.'

Bethany took a sip of her tea, her hand shaking slightly causing the cup to rattle in its saucer.

'Oh, it was an amicable divorce,' she assured her. 'Ted and I remained friends to the end. He was—' She swallowed. 'He was a good man. A kind man. I was very lucky.'

'Clive tells me that he made contact with you via Ted's second wife,' Miss Lavender said carefully. 'You got on with her, too?'

Bethany gave her a wry smile. She knew all too well that Miss Lavender was fishing for information, but she couldn't see the harm in her knowing the truth. Well, some of it at any rate.

'Very much so. Of course, it wasn't easy at first. We were, after all, still married when Ted fell in love with Helena.'

'Oh, Bethany!' Miss Lavender stared at her in dismay. 'I'm so dreadfully sorry. How awful for you. I can't believe you even speak to that woman after she did such a terrible thing to you.'

'Helena was my friend,' Bethany explained. 'A good friend. Frankly, I didn't want to lose her. It would have hurt me more than losing Ted.'

'But she betrayed you!'

'It wasn't that simple,' Bethany admitted. 'Ted and I had been drifting for a long time, and Helena was always far better suited to him. They behaved quite honourably for years, and I think they did all they could to make things easy for me. In fact...' She hesitated, wondering if she should admit this to anyone, let alone Miss Lavender. She'd struggled to admit it to herself for a long time, after all.

'In fact?' Miss Lavender coaxed gently.

'In fact, looking back on it, it was the best thing that could have happened,' Bethany told her. 'Does that sound awful?'

Miss Lavender considered the matter. 'Not awful, no. Surprising, yes. And rather sad if you don't mind me saying so. I'm so sorry things didn't work out for you, dear. When I saw the announcement in the newspaper about your marriage, I'd really hoped that you'd found happiness at last.'

'I wasn't unhappy,' Bethany said hurriedly. 'Like I said, Ted was a good man. He took great care of me. I wanted for nothing.'

'I'm glad to hear it. I wonder, do you ever hear from Glenn?'

Bethany's cup clattered again, and she hastily placed it on the occasional table close to the sofa.

'Not since before I left Tuppenny Bridge.'

'Me neither. He never came back here as far as I'm aware. Such a shame that didn't work out for you. He seemed such a charming man.'

She peered closely at Bethany, but if she was hoping for more information on that particular subject she was to be disappointed. Bethany had already spilled her thoughts more than she had in years. She wasn't prepared to discuss Glenn, of all people.

'So, Miss Lavender,' she said brightly, 'do tell me what else I've missed in Tuppenny Bridge. How are Birdie and Rita?'

That did the trick. Miss Lavender rolled her eyes and began to tell her all about how much she despaired of her old friends, even though it was quite clear that she thought the world of the pair of them.

Thank goodness, Bethany thought with relief, for the crazy, eccentric Pennyfeather sisters.

SEVEN

Miss Lavender showed Bethany to her room and left her to unpack, assuring her that there was no rush and lunch wouldn't be ready for at least an hour.

The room was a decent size, with fitted wardrobes and another plush carpet. There were French doors opening out onto the garden, but white drapes afforded privacy, and there were thick teal curtains for night-time.

Bethany sank onto the double bed and gazed around her, not really taking in her surroundings. She'd slept in so many strange bedrooms in recent years that it was just one more to add to the list.

She smirked, aware suddenly of how that would sound to a stranger. But the fact was, she'd been alone the entire time. There was no one special in her life. Those strange bedrooms were in temporary accommodation—hotel rooms, holiday cottages, friends' homes. Well, not even friends if she was being really honest with herself. Acquaintances. People she'd got to know over the years through Ted, but with whom she had more of a polite relationship than a true one.

Since her divorce she hadn't had a place to call home. Her

solicitor had said Ted should be the one to leave the marital home, but Ted didn't want to move out. And, as he said, the house was far too large for one person and, after all, it had been Ted's home before Bethany had even met him.

He was right of course, and as much as it hurt her to admit it, the place had never really felt like home to her anyway. The truth was she didn't feel she'd ever really had a home at all. Not her marital home, and certainly not Whispering Willows. Well, maybe when she was very young, before her mother changed and she'd been left in the care of her father and Joseph. Maybe then it had been a home. Her mother had attempted to make it into some sort of home at least. When she'd died it was just a house. Nothing more.

Sighing, she made a half-hearted attempt to unpack her suitcase. How many times had she done this over the last few years, she wondered, as she hung various items of clothing on coat hangers. Too many times. Sometimes she longed for somewhere she could finally put down roots and stay. Somewhere she could spend the rest of her life.

After her divorce she'd travelled quite a bit, looking for somewhere special. After Ted died, she'd moved in temporarily with Helena, but always hoped to find a place that called to her. A place that would fill her heart with such joy, and such a sense of belonging, that she'd have no alternative but to seek out a house there and begin her new life somewhere that finally felt like home.

When she sold Whispering Willows, what then? When she was finally free to put Tuppenny Bridge behind her for good... what? Where would she go?

'I'll stick a pin in a map,' she murmured to herself, as she draped a blouse over a coat hanger and hung it on the rail. 'That's probably the only way I'll decide. Or I'll put a few places into a hat and draw one out.'

It was, she admitted, possibly her only option if she was to move forward. And maybe if she bought somewhere she'd grow to love it eventually. She would make it a home by decorating it to her taste and filling it with furniture and belongings she loved, and then, gradually, it would feel like her own little sanctuary. It would win her heart. Bit by bit she'd settle at last.

After emptying her suitcase, she pushed it under the bed, out of the way, and sank back onto the bed. Now what?

Then she remembered she'd promised to call Helena and let her know how things were going, and that she hadn't done so.

She fished her mobile phone out of her handbag and rang the number. It rang four times before a breathless Helena said, 'Bethany? Well, it's about time!'

Bethany smiled. 'Sorry. I've been a bit preoccupied. Are you okay? You sound out of breath.'

'I heard the phone ringing, and I'd left it in the other room. I ran! You wretch, you didn't answer my texts! I was worried.' Helena paused. 'Are you okay? How's everything going?'

'I'm sorry. I was a bit busy. I'm fine. Everything's going fine.' It was her standard answer, given automatically. Usually, that was enough to placate most people, but not Helena.

'Okay, and how's it going *really*?'

Bethany rolled her eyes and shuffled back to rest against the headboard. 'Pretty much as I expected. Well, worse actually.'

'Worse? Oh no. I'm sorry to hear that. Worse in what way?'

'I'm not even sure where to begin.' Bethany glanced around the room. 'I'm calling you from the spare bedroom in Miss Lavender's apartment. I've moved in with her. She insisted.'

'Miss Lavender?' There was a question in Helena's tone but then she said, 'Oh! The artist's descendant who thinks she rules the town?'

'That's the one.' Bethany laughed, but then felt a bit guilty. After all, Miss Lavender had been kindness itself to her. 'She's actually been lovely to me and didn't like to think of me staying at The Lady Dorothy. It's just a bit...'

'Too much?' Helena said sympathetically. 'Feeling crowded already?'

'Yeah,' Bethany admitted, grateful that she didn't have to explain. 'At least at the pub I didn't have to make any effort.'

'Maybe it will do you good,' Helena said gently. 'You've been on your own for too long. Time to connect with other people again, don't you think?'

'I've been living with you for over a year!' Bethany said indignantly.

'That's not what I meant, and you know it.' Helena sighed. 'Anyway, how was it? Going back to Whispering Willows, I mean.'

'Awful.' Bethany shuddered at the memory. 'Bad enough just being there again. All those memories! But honestly, you should see the state of the place.'

'Grim?'

'Grim doesn't begin to describe it. It's a dump. It needs gutting if you ask me.'

'Well, that's not your problem, is it? You're getting rid of it, aren't you? Just sort out the contents and hand the lot over to an estate agent. Let them worry about it.'

'It's not that simple,' Bethany said grimly. 'There's something of a fly in the ointment there.'

'Oh?'

'It turns out that the place is now a horse sanctuary, and I'm suddenly responsible for thirteen horses, ponies and donkeys.'

'You're what?'

'I know! Nobody warned me about that, did they? I was horrified when I found out. I mean, what am I supposed to do with them all?'

'Sell them?' Helena suggested doubtfully.

'I don't think that's an option. I've only briefly met them, but I think they're all too old or damaged to just blithely sell on.'

She thought about poor old, hollow-backed Chester, and little Barney the Exmoor pony who was plagued by sweet itch and spent half the year swathed in barrier cream and a protective coat and hood.

Then there were Diamond and Sapphire, two elderly donkeys whose owner had died and who had been left alone in a paddock, forgotten about until the owner's nephew thankfully remembered them. And four Shetland ponies whose previous owners had apparently neglected them dreadfully and had been planning to abandon them until an acquaintance had tipped off the owners of the sanctuary in East Yorkshire, where Summer had previously worked.

The sanctuary owners hadn't had room for the Shetlands, apparently, but Joseph had taken them in. Summer had told her this, her eyes shining as she recalled how generous and kind Joseph was.

Whatever their problems, Bethany couldn't deny that her brother had been good to the horses in his life.

'Wouldn't another sanctuary take them?' Helena asked hopefully.

'In today's economic climate?' Bethany shook her head, even though her friend couldn't see her. 'I highly doubt it, although I'll have to try. You never know, I might get lucky. I don't know what else I can do to be honest.'

'So make the calls and get them sorted, then you can stick the house up for sale and get out of there,' Helena said, sounding more cheerful. 'Time to start hunting for your new home. You need to put down some roots, don't you think?'

'I think there'll be a delay on that, too,' Bethany admitted, uncomfortably aware that it might sound as if she was deliberately putting obstacles in her own path. 'It's the house. Like I said, it's a mess. Really needs gutting. I don't think it would be a good idea to put the house on the market the state it's in. I was thinking, maybe I'd do it up a bit. Well, it would definitely increase the asking price if I did, so...'

'But you hardly need the money!' Helena's voice was puzzled. 'You got a very generous divorce settlement from Ted, and you still have most of your own inheritance, and I'm sure that's more than enough to buy your own place and then some. What does it matter if you don't make much from Whispering Willows, as long as it's off your hands. That's what you wanted, isn't it?' She hesitated. 'It is *still* what you want, isn't it, Bethany?'

'Of course it is! It's not the money really. It's...' Bethany shook her head helplessly. What was it? Why didn't she just walk away and leave everything to Clive and Summer and the estate agent? Surely, between them all, they could sort the whole mess out. Why should she be bothered? '...The horses,' she finished weakly. 'I must think of their welfare. I can't leave until they're safely rehomed, so I might as well spend my time productively, improving the house.'

She was sure she heard Helena sigh.

'I suppose so,' her friend said at last. 'These horses—I hope you've got help with them? Thirteen is an awful lot to care for by yourself.'

'Oh yes, there's Summer and—and Clive.'

'Who are they?'

'Summer's worked for Joseph for ages apparently, and she's devoted to the animals. Only a young girl, early twenties. She seems nice enough. Very earnest and a bit idealistic, but her heart's in the right place.'

Would people once have described her in that way? She realised with a sinking feeling that they very well might have. She hoped Summer would always be a bit idealistic and that life wouldn't show her too much of its dark side, the way it had her.

'And Clive?'

'Clive...' She thought about the big, sandy-haired, grey-eyed Scot. 'Clive was Joseph's friend. He's a vet but he's helping at the stables because Summer's going to Australia to visit family and Clive's volunteering in her place. He's—capable.'

And kind-hearted, and pig-headed, and caring, and bossy. He clearly didn't think much of her and had idolised Joseph. She wondered how well he'd really known her brother.

But more than anything, Clive was grieving. She could see the pain in his eyes every time she looked at him. Miss Lavender had said that he'd also been great friends with Julian Callaghan, who'd died over fourteen years ago. So Clive had lost two good friends. He'd grieved twice over. It was a lot. She supposed volunteering at the sanctuary was his way of doing something constructive with all that grief. She couldn't blame him for that.

'What about his job? Seems a lot to fit in, being a vet and volunteering at the horse sanctuary.'

'He's got a locum covering his shifts at the surgery. He's been in place for a while, actually. Clive took leave to move in and care for Joseph in his last few months.'

'Wow.' Helena was clearly impressed. 'Sounds like a very special man.'

'Joseph seems to have inspired great loyalty,' Bethany said. 'Summer can't speak highly enough of him. She's in tears every time she mentions him, but that doesn't stop her telling me how Joseph would react to any given situation, and making sure I know just how wonderful he was.'

'Have you...' Helena paused, clearly considering her next words. 'Have you changed your mind about Joseph at all?'

Bethany frowned, almost sure she caught an uneasy tone in Helena's voice.

'Has time and distance made you think differently about him?'

Had it? Bethany thought about the dedication her brother had shown to the animals in his care. He'd obviously neglected himself and the house dreadfully to make sure those horses, ponies, and donkeys were looked after and cherished. He'd also clearly made a great impression on Summer and Clive.

She couldn't deny he'd always been wonderful with animals, showing a real affinity with them. But it had taken him a long time to find the courage to protect them all. She still remembered that day when he'd first done so. The first horse he'd ever rescued. How scared he must have been. She'd been so impressed. Awestruck even. She'd thought he was absolutely wonderful.

But that hadn't lasted, had it? The sudden warmth she'd felt towards her brother evaporated, replaced by the coldness she was more familiar with. He might have been eager to protect horses, but he'd not been so great at protecting her. In fact, he'd hurt her more than anyone ever had before.

And the worst part of it was that he wasn't even sorry. Not really. He'd let her go and hadn't bothered to contact her since. There wasn't any room for Bethany in Joseph's heart, clearly. It was too full of wretched horses.

She gripped her phone as her eyes narrowed. 'No, nothing's changed. I know what Joseph was and he may have fooled Clive and Summer, but I know the real him.' She blinked away tears. 'You're right, of course. I'll make some calls. See if I can find new homes for the horses, then I'll contact the estate agent. The sooner I'm out of Tuppenny Bridge the better.'

EIGHT

Clive paused at the gate of Daisyfield Cottage and took a deep breath. Nerves had taken hold of him, despite the stern lecture he'd given himself before setting off. He straightened his tie and smoothed his hair.

A mirthless 'Huh!' escaped his lips as he realised what he was doing.

Honestly! What was wrong with him? It was just a friendly dinner with his work colleague and his girlfriend, and their families. No one would give him a second glance. The focus would be on Summer, and quite rightly so. She was, after all, the one jetting off to Australia on Monday. This evening was all about her, and he needed to remember that.

Even so...

He closed his eyes briefly, then walked slowly up the garden path. Vaguely he registered that the front garden was looking very pretty, its borders bright with spring flowers, but he didn't have time to think more deeply about that as the door opened before he'd even reached the step.

'You made it!'

Ben grinned at him, his blue eyes twinkling, and Clive swallowed.

'How did you know I—'

'I was looking out of the window. We wondered if you'd turn up, but I'm really glad you did. Come in!'

Clive tried to arrange his facial features into a smile and allowed Ben to usher him into the hallway before being led into the living room.

He'd never been in here before and was pleasantly surprised. It was a light, bright room with a contemporary feel. He knew it had been recently decorated, and the Callaghans had thrown out all the old, dark furniture from Monk's Folly and replaced it with modern light oak units and a grey three-piece suite that looked extremely inviting and put the one at Whispering Willows to shame.

Summer, her chestnut hair loose around her shoulders for once, was sitting in an armchair, smiling a welcome. She was, he noted with surprise, wearing a dress. He wasn't sure he'd ever seen her out of jeans before, apart from at her mum's wedding when she'd been a bridesmaid. Oh, and Joseph's funeral, though even then she'd worn black trousers.

Her mum, Sally, and stepfather, Rafferty, were on the sofa.

'Isn't this lovely, Clive?' Sally asked him eagerly. 'I don't know about you but it's not often we get invited out to dinner. This is a proper treat.'

'Great to see you out and about, Clive,' Rafferty said. 'How are you?'

There was sympathy in his tone and Clive knew he was referring to his recent loss, but he didn't want to get into all that. Not tonight. It would be too much to deal with.

'Ah, you know,' he said with a shrug. 'Getting on with it.'

Rafferty nodded. 'No other option really I guess.'

Clive didn't reply, but sat, rather awkwardly, on the free

armchair. Ben's younger brother, Jamie, was perched on a beanbag and Clive frowned.

'Did you want this chair, Jamie?'

Jamie grinned. 'You're all right. I often sit on here. I like it. Besides, not being funny but if you sat on this beanbag you'd probably never get up again.'

'Don't be so cheeky,' Ben reproved him, but Clive gave him a rueful smile.

'You're probably right,' he acknowledged. 'I'm safer here in this chair, that's for sure. Where's your mum, by the way?'

'In the kitchen, naturally,' Ben said. 'Before you say anything, she wouldn't let us help her. We all volunteered but she insisted she wanted to do everything herself.'

'She did,' Sally assured him. 'Mind you, that's probably for the best. If I'd helped her cook anything none of you would want to eat it.'

'You're very good at prepping though,' Rafferty reminded her, and she beamed at him.

'I am, aren't I? We all have our strengths and weaknesses.'

The door to the kitchen opened and Jennifer hurried in. Clive glanced up at her, and his heart gave its customary flutter which, as always, he refused to acknowledge.

'Oh, you're here,' she said, smiling at him. 'I didn't hear the door. Sorry. Well, you're just in time because dinner's about to be served. Would you all like to come through to the dining room?'

Everyone immediately got to their feet—Clive couldn't help noticing with some envy that Jamie fairly sprang up from the beanbag with no difficulty at all—and followed Jennifer into the dining room, where a large table had been laid.

'Now, just sit down and make yourselves comfortable,' Jennifer said. 'I'll be back in a minute with the starters.'

'What are we having, Mum?' Jamie asked, taking a seat

before anyone else had even thought about it. He nodded at the bowls that had been placed on the table. 'I'm guessing soup?'

Jennifer looked a bit bashful. 'It's nothing much, I'm afraid. Yes, you're right, Jamie. Just a simple carrot and coriander soup with home baked bread rolls. I hope that's okay.'

Everyone agreed that was more than okay, and Jennifer hurried back into the kitchen after refusing everyone's offer of help.

'Well, this is nice,' Clive said, hoping he didn't sound too tense as he sat down.

Ben and Summer sat opposite him, and Ben gave him a reassuring smile. Clearly, he understood how nervous and ill-at-ease Clive was feeling and was doing his best to make him feel comfortable.

Maybe, Clive thought with a sudden pang of guilt, he wouldn't make such an effort if he knew the main reason for Clive's unease.

As if on cue, Jennifer returned carrying a large tray with a huge bowl of soup and a plate of bread rolls. She placed it in the centre of the table and picked up a ladle.

'If you'd like to pass me your bowls I'll fill them for you,' she offered.

Clive noticed her hands shook as she performed this simple task, and he couldn't help but lift his gaze to study her face. She wasn't looking at him, which didn't surprise him, but was biting her lip, her focus obviously all on serving the soup without spilling any.

He realised it had been a long time since he'd been this close to her, and that she'd aged more than he'd noticed on the brief occasions they'd been in the same room together. He thought the last time had probably been at the open event at Monk's Folly—he really must stop calling it that as it had been renamed *The Arabella Lavender Art Academy*—but she'd been in the kitchen then, a proud, if clearly nervous, member of staff, and hadn't so much as glanced in his direction.

Although she had more lines on her face than he remembered, there was a serenity about her that was reassuring. She'd always been shy and a bit awkward, even before Julian passed, but after he died she'd become a hermit. Ben had worried himself sick about her, and Clive had wished with all his heart there was something he could do to take that worried, haunted look from her face.

Now, though, with a new home and a job at the art academy, and the burden of Monk's Folly finally lifted, she seemed like a new woman. Her skin was clear, and she'd filled out a little. Despite her obvious nerves about tonight, there was an underlying calm to her, and he thought with some surprise that she radiated contentment.

It had been many years since he'd seen her this way, and the thought came to him that—if he was being brutally honest with himself—he wasn't sure how he felt about it.

Ashamed, he almost dropped the bowl of soup when she handed it to him, and her eyebrows shot up in alarm.

'Sorry!'

'Whoops, nearly.' She smiled at him, her blue eyes bright with amusement, and his heart flip flopped.

Look away, you moron. Do you want people to notice the way you're gawping at her?

He put the bowl on the table and reached for a napkin, his eyes never leaving the soup. 'This looks grand, Jennifer. Thank you.'

'You're very welcome. After all, it's a special occasion.' Jennifer served the last portion of soup and took her seat at the head of the table. 'How are you feeling, Summer? Excited?'

Summer hastily gulped down her spoonful of soup and nodded. 'I am, but I'm a bit nervous, too. It's a long flight, and I've never been on an aeroplane before.'

'You'll be fine, love,' Sally promised her. 'I'd never been on an aeroplane either until we went to Paris for our honeymoon, but I loved it. Besides,' she added, giving Summer a knowing look, 'I reckon you'll be that busy making sure your dad keeps calm you won't have time to worry.'

Summer grinned. 'You're probably right. Dad would never go on a plane,' she told Ben. 'Mum wanted us all to go on one of those cheap package holidays to Spain when we were kids, but he refused point blank to fly, and it would have taken that long to go by coach Mum decided it was easier to just book a caravan in Skeggy again.'

'Well, all that time on a coach with two kids in tow!' Sally sounded horrified. 'No thanks. Not to mention how travel sick I get, remember. Bugger that for a game of soldiers.'

Clive smiled, grateful that Sally and Summer's easy banter had broken some of the tension in the room. Not that anyone else seemed to have noticed it anyway. Just him then?

He risked a sideways glance at Jennifer, but she was concentrating on the food, so he looked away again before anyone noticed where his attention had strayed to.

'How's the job at Monk's Folly going, love?' Sally asked Jennifer.

Clive watched Jennifer's face, noting the way her eyes lit up and her face creased with pleasure at the mention of her new career as cook at the art academy.

'Oh, it's going really well,' she said enthusiastically. 'Obviously, we haven't really got started yet. It's just day students right now, and it's simple enough to prepare either a cooked meal or a picnic lunch for them. But the first residential students arrive in a week and then I'll really be able to get to work.'

'How are you finding working for Ross Lavender?' Rafferty enquired.

'He's a lovely boy,' Jennifer enthused. 'And he doesn't interfere at all. Lets me make all the decisions about what to cook, which is a relief.'

Summer grinned. 'I expect he's too loved up with Clemmie to care what you cook,' she said. 'Probably doesn't even notice the food at all.'

Jennifer's eyes twinkled. 'They are quite sweet together,' she admitted. 'He's courting her properly—you know, the old-fashioned way. Proper dates and no staying the night. It's so charming to see.'

'Clemmie's potty about him,' Summer told her. She gave a sigh of pleasure as she swirled her spoon round in the last of her soup. 'I'm so glad for them. They waited a long time to be together and they really deserve to be happy.'

'What about the new art teacher?' Rafferty enquired, pushing his empty bowl away. 'How's he shaping up?'

'Callum? Seems pleasant enough,' Jennifer said, thinking about it. 'I can't say we've spoken much but he's polite when we do. Rather quiet but Ross says he's a very good teacher and is passionate about art, which is all he cares about I suppose.'

She glanced round at them all. 'Is everyone ready for the second course?'

'Give me a moment!' Jamie scraped his third bread roll around the edges of his all-but-empty bowl and stuffed it in his mouth. 'Okay, go for it!'

'Oh, Jamie,' Jennifer said mournfully, 'you have no manners whatsoever.'

'Bet he wouldn't have done that if Eloise had been sitting here,' Ben said with a sly grin.

'Never mind all that,' his mother said hastily, as Jamie gave his brother an indignant dig in the ribs. 'Who's going to help me collect the dishes?'

Clive's immediate instinct was to volunteer, but he was too afraid of the rebuttal that he was sure was inevitable, so he said nothing.

Sally and Summer both offered, but Jennifer refused their help. 'It was a rhetorical question,' she explained. 'Jamie, give me a hand please.' She smiled round at them all. 'It's a paella. I hope you all enjoy it. It's the first time I've made it.'

Everyone hurriedly assured her that it sounded marvellous, and she collected some of the dishes then took them into the kitchen, a reluctant Jamie trailing behind with the rest of the soup bowls.

'Are you all packed then?' Ben said, turning his attention back to Summer.

She nodded and swallowed. 'I'm really going to miss you.'

Clive noticed the emotion in Ben's face and his heart went out to the lad. Young love!

'It's not for long,' he reminded them gently.

'Three weeks.' Summer sounded wistful. 'I'm really looking forward to seeing Billie and Arlo again, and to spending time with Dad, but it does seem a long time to be away. I'll miss you so much, Ben. I'll miss all of you. And I can't help worrying about what might happen at Whispering Willows while I'm gone.'

'I've told you,' Ben said, squeezing her hand, 'everything will be fine there. Clive's on the case, aren't you, Clive?' He gave Clive a meaningful look, and Clive straightened his face immediately, nodding briskly at Summer.

'Absolutely. You don't have to worry about a thing. Maya and Lennox are going to be popping by every morning and some evenings after school, and they'll be there at weekends. They're good kids.' He didn't mention that he'd offered them a bumper bonus if they'd put in the extra hours. As far as Summer knew they would be on the standard rate he'd been paying them ever since Joseph got ill.

As far as Bethany knew they didn't get paid at all and were doing it out of the kindness of their hearts. To be fair he thought

Maya probably would have done. Lennox needed a bit more incentive.

'But what about Bethany?' Summer persisted, as Jamie and Jennifer returned to the table.

Jamie was carrying plates and Jennifer held a huge dish of paella which, as distracted as Clive was, he couldn't help noticing smelt delicious.

Summer didn't even acknowledge their arrival. She'd clearly worked herself up into a bit of a state as she thought about the sanctuary, and Clive noticed the anxiety in her green eyes as she turned to him, a plea in her voice.

'Has she said anything to you about what she plans to do with the place, because she's said nothing to me. I tried to get her to tell me *something* at least, but she was so vague. Said she was still thinking it all over.'

'Well,' Sally said heartily, 'I expect it's a lot for her to take in. Fancy her not knowing her old home was a horse sanctuary! I'd need a bit of time to think it all over if I was her.'

'But according to the town grapevine,' Rafferty added, 'Bethany was always horse mad when she lived here before. She had her own pony and adored him. The Wilkinsons were a very horsy family, weren't they?'

Jennifer nodded as she began piling up the plates with paella. 'They were. Well, not so much the Wilkinsons as the Parkinsons. They were Coral's family.'

'Coral?'

'Joseph and Bethany's mother,' she explained, passing the first plate along. 'The Parkinsons were an old, well-established family in Skimmerdale. They were the ones who originally built Whispering Willows, and it belonged to Coral, not Terence Wilkinson. Even though,' she added darkly, 'the way he strutted around you'd have thought it was his by birthright. Odious man.'

Clive's curiosity was piqued, so even though he was hesitant about direct contact with Jennifer he couldn't resist asking a question.

'What was she like? Coral, I mean. Joseph rarely mentioned her, and I wasn't sure how he really felt about her.'

Jennifer held his gaze for a moment then tilted her head to one side thinking. 'I barely saw her,' she admitted. 'Apparently, she and my mother had been good friends when they were in the same class at the primary school. They only drifted apart after Coral was sent to St Egbert's when she turned eleven. And then, of course, she met Terence when she was still a teenager. My mother said she became terribly reserved and kept herself to herself.' She passed another plate along. 'Sadly she died when I was just a little girl. My mother was very upset as I recall.'

The spoon paused over the paella dish as she considered.

'Although, I do remember her telling my father that poor Coral would finally get some peace from her husband, which was a blessing. I also remember her saying it's a pity that Joseph and Bethany wouldn't get the same reprieve, and that there was no justice in the world, because if there had been it would have been Terence who died, not Coral.' She shook her head slightly then dished out the last of the paella. 'I remember that time clearly,' she confessed. 'It was all so sad. Everyone was very shocked.'

'Shocked?' Sally asked. 'Was her death unexpected then?'

Jennifer exchanged a fleeting glance with Clive. 'I suppose it was,' she said hesitantly. 'Although she'd been ill for some time.'

Clive felt a pang of sympathy for Bethany. Her childhood, he realised, had hardly been the sort of happy time he'd experienced in his own. She must be carrying a lot of pain inside her.

'Parkinson?' Rafferty sounded thoughtful. 'I know that name. Where do I know that name from?'

'The Lusty Tup Brewery,' Jennifer said immediately. 'It was Albert Parkinson—Coral's great-grandfather—who founded the brewery way back in the nineteenth century. That's where most of their money came from. Not all of it, but most.'

'That's right,' Rafferty said. 'I remember reading about them. So Joseph was related to the brewery owners?'

Clive shook his head. 'No. The Parkinsons had sold Lusty Tup to another company for a fortune long before Joseph was born. However, he did work there and was passionate about the place, right up until he took early retirement to focus on the sanctuary.'

'At one time,' Jennifer said sadly, 'the Parkinsons were considered to be more important than the Lavenders round here.'

'Crikey, don't let Miss Lavender hear you say that,' Ben spluttered. 'You know she thinks she's royalty in this town.'

'Yes, well, what she forgets is that the Parkinsons gave employment to a great many people in Tuppenny Bridge. Lots of townspeople worked at the Lusty Tup Brewery.' Jennifer sighed. 'Julian was one of them, and Leon, too, although of course, it didn't belong to the Parkinsons by then.'

There was a moment of silence and Clive wondered if everyone else was thinking how amazing it was that Jennifer could talk about her lost husband and son so easily after being a prisoner to her grief for so long.

Summer said, 'So the Parkinsons were a big deal round here then? Why did someone like Coral Parkinson marry someone like Terence Wilkinson? What did he do? Was he important, too?'

Jennifer laughed. 'Hardly. I remember my parents thought he was a failure in every way. His various so-called business ventures collapsed every time. Coral's family despised him, and they were in despair when she seemed to fall for him. But then he was very good looking back in the late fifties, according to my mother, and the more her parents tried to break them up the more charming he seemed to Coral. In the end, it was quite easy for him to seduce her. She found out she was expecting Joseph, and the wedding was a done deal. But I know my mother was adamant that he'd got her pregnant on purpose and wangled his way into the family. It was all about the money with him, not poor Coral herself.'

'He sounds awful,' Sally said with a shudder. 'Poor Coral. And poor Joseph and Bethany having a father like that. I presume he wasn't much of one to his kids?' she asked, looking at Clive.

He hesitated then shrugged. 'I can't say Joseph ever spoke much about him either. When I arrived in Tuppenny Bridge he'd only just passed away and Joseph only ever mentioned him briefly. Mind, it was without any sign of affection, so possibly not.'

It wasn't for him to reveal some of the more private things Joseph had confided in him. There was a lot he could say about Terence Wilkinson, but what good would it do now?

'Sounds like quite a tragic family,' Sally said with a sigh. 'Coral and Terence were obviously not happy together, and Joseph and this Bethany had some sort of falling out and didn't speak all them years, until it was too late to make it up.' She shook her head. 'Such a shame.'

'And now Bethany's back in her old home,' Rafferty added. 'Must be a strange feeling for her after all this time. Clearly Joseph wanted her to have the place, though, so he must have had some affection for her, even if they hadn't spoken for all those years.'

'What do you mean?' Jennifer asked, sounding puzzled.

'Well, he didn't leave a will, did he? He must have known that Whispering Willows would go to her by default, as his only living relative, so he must have cared enough about her to let that happen or he'd have made damn sure his will stated otherwise.' Rafferty shook his head. 'I can't quite believe Joseph was so careless in that regard, you know. Everyone should make a will. The trouble it can cause when people don't bother...'

'I'm sorry,' Jennifer said, her eyes wide with amazement. 'You've got that all wrong.'

Clive's heart thudded as everyone paused in their eating and stared at Jennifer in surprise. 'You mean, Joseph *did* make a will?' he asked, hardly daring to believe it.

'I mean,' Jennifer said, glancing round at them all, 'Whispering Willows wasn't Joseph's to leave to anyone. The house belonged to Bethany. It always did.'

NINE

Bethany spent that Saturday evening in her bedroom at Lavender House, poring over the account books and receipts that she'd purloined from Whispering Willows. Summer had shown her where Joseph kept them, and she'd apologised profusely for the mess they were in.

'I did try to tidy them up,' she promised Bethany, 'but I didn't have access to them all. Just last year's accounts really. It was all such a jumble, but Joseph seemed to like it that way. Said he knew where everything was, and he didn't need to do anything else with it.'

Bethany had assured Summer that it wasn't her fault, nor her responsibility, and had sent the young woman off to her farewell dinner at Daisyfield Cottage with a smile, before turning back to the dresser in the kitchen and staring in horror at the contents of the drawer.

Hours later she was still lost among the scraps of paper and pencil jottings that passed for Joseph's accounts and was developing a headache.

She was almost relieved when there was a tap on her door and Miss Lavender popped her head around.

'Goodness, you do realise how dark it is in here? How on earth can you see?'

Bethany hadn't really noticed the dusk creeping up on her, although she'd been squinting through her reading glasses with increasing frustration.

Miss Lavender switched the light on. 'Are you all right, dear? I wondered if you'd care for some supper? You've been hidden away in here for hours.'

Bethany immediately apologised. 'I'm so sorry. You must think I'm incredibly rude. I'm afraid I got sidetracked by this...' She waved a hand over the stack of papers on her bed and sighed. 'I didn't realise the time.'

'Oh, I don't mind if you want to spend the evening in here,' Miss Lavender assured her, entering the room fully at last. 'I was just worried you'd be hungry. And now I see you've been working away in here in the dark like a little mole I'm very glad I decided to see if you were okay. It's terribly bad for your eyes, you know. You shouldn't really work in such poor light.'

'I know.' Bethany took off her glasses and rubbed her eyes wearily. 'Actually, I think I've seen more than enough for today. I'll get back to it tomorrow.'

'That sounds like a good idea,' Miss Lavender agreed. She peered down at the bed. 'Accounts?' She sounded rather uncertain, and Bethany wasn't surprised.

'What passes for them,' she said grimly. 'I have to say, from what I've seen so far it's a miracle Whispering Willows has kept going as long as it has. Do you know, it's not a registered charity? How does that even make sense? If you're going to run a horse sanctuary surely that's the first thing you'd think of?'

'Perhaps Joseph was worried he'd have to get your permission,' Miss Lavender said thoughtfully.

'My permission? Why would he...' Bethany's confusion cleared. 'Oh, you mean because it's being run from my property? Maybe. Or maybe it's because he knew he'd never be granted it with the state the stables are in right now. I don't know what the rules around these things are. It seems to me he's been very foolish and irresponsible. When I think of all the money he must have spent on these horses over the years! He must have been nearly bankrupt.' She sighed. 'I have a feeling I won't need to apply for a letter of administration.'

'I'm sorry, dear?'

'Apparently, if there's no will, the next-of-kin is supposed to apply for a letter of administration so they can access the deceased's bank account for example. But if the estate is quite small most banks will release the money without that.'

'I believe,' Miss Lavender said cautiously, 'that Joseph received quite a sizeable inheritance after his father died? At least, that's what I was given to understand. After all, he managed to keep this house and the sanctuary going even after he'd retired without, as you say, gaining charitable status for it. Although,' she added, 'he did receive the occasional gift from the Tuppenny Bridge Fund. We were happy to help where we could.'

Bethany gave a brittle laugh. 'Believe me, Miss Lavender, Joseph would have received nothing when our father died. My father had no money of his own. Everything we owned came from my mother's side of the family.'

'I knew it was the Parkinsons who were the wealthy ones, of course,' Miss Lavender said. 'But surely your father's business interests—'

'Failed miserably every single time. All my father did was spend my mother's money until she worked out a safety net with her solicitor.' Bethany's face twisted into the semblance of a smile. 'She wasn't as stupid as he thought she was. She managed to tie up her inheritance in trusts for Joseph and me, so my father couldn't get his paws on the money. He was completely reliant on Joseph's generosity after Mother died.

And Joseph was way too kind to him. I never understood it. It was almost as if Joseph felt sorry for him.'

Miss Lavender shuffled uncomfortably. 'I—I would hardly say that, Bethany. And I'm sure, when you think about it, you'll agree with me.' She cleared her throat and tentatively sat on the edge of the bed. 'I've often thought,' she admitted, 'that all this charitable work Joseph did was more a way of easing his own conscience. Don't you think?'

Her hooded eyes held a trace of anxiety and Bethany frowned. How much did Miss Lavender know? But how could she possibly know anything? Joseph was the only other person involved who knew her, and he would never have told her what had happened. Would he?

'Guilt, Miss Lavender?' she asked, not wanting to give anything away if she was wrong.

Miss Lavender took her hand, and Bethany noted with some alarm that there were tears in the old lady's eyes.

'I know this is a long time coming,' she said, shaking her head sadly, 'and really, my dear, I can't tell you how sorry I am. I must apologise. I must apologise now for the way I let you down so badly back then. I have never been able to forgive myself. When I think of how you must have suffered! And of course you ran away. Why wouldn't you? I never blamed you for that, dear. Only myself for not being brave enough to interfere. For not offering you a home there and then. A refuge under my roof.'

Bethany stared at her, at a loss to understand what she was talking about.

'Your mother would have been ashamed of me,' Miss Lavender continued. 'I don't know why I didn't say anything. Why I didn't step in. When I think of the suffering that must have gone on under that roof it makes my blood curdle. I was full of shame when I heard you'd gone, you know. That's why I made it my business to search the papers for any mention of you. I was so delighted when you married Ted Marshall. I knew you'd found happiness at last. Well, I thought you had...' She sighed and dabbed at her eyes with a handkerchief.

'Miss Lavender,' Bethany began, but the old lady shook her head.

'I never spoke to him again from that day until this,' she swore. 'Of course, I felt terribly sorry for him when he was ill. One wouldn't wish that on one's worst enemy. And we always tried to help with sanctuary funds, as I explained, because really, one cannot take it out on the animals because of the actions of their owner. But personally, I could never get past what he'd done, my dear. I couldn't bring myself to go to Whispering Willows again after your father passed. I'm sorry, but there it is.'

Bethany was trying to make sense of Miss Lavender's jumbled outpouring but had to admit defeat.

'I'm sorry, Miss Lavender. Could you please tell me what you're talking about?'

Her hand was gripped even tighter.

'I'm talking about Joseph's disgusting behaviour, my dear. What else?'

Bethany was conflicted. She wasn't entirely sure what it was about Joseph's behaviour that Miss Lavender found disgusting, and despite her own feelings towards her brother, she was wary of agreeing wholeheartedly with the old lady in case she'd be agreeing with something she actually *didn't* agree with. Not at all.

'Er...'

'I saw them!' Miss Lavender said, her eyes wide. 'In the stables!'

Bethany closed her eyes briefly. It didn't bear thinking about. Poor Miss Lavender. She'd be traumatised for life. No wonder she hadn't gone back to Whispering Willows since.

'I'd knocked at the door of the house but there was no

answer, and I'd brought a basket of homemade pies for you all,' Miss Lavender continued. 'I was about to leave when I heard voices coming from the stables. Raised voices. Naturally, I had to see what the noise was about.'

Naturally, Bethany thought wryly.

'What I saw will live with me forever,' Miss Lavender said dramatically. 'Joseph and your father! Your poor father.'

'My poor...' Whatever she'd been expecting to hear it certainly wasn't this. And she'd never heard anyone refer to her father as *poor* before. Not in that context anyway.

'What exactly did you see?'

'Your father was cowering in a corner,' Miss Lavender said, her voice shaky, 'and there he was—Joseph—standing over him, threatening him. Threatening him, Bethany!' She shook her head. 'With a horse whip!'

Bethany's hand flew to her mouth. 'When—when was this?'

'Just a few months before you left. I'm so sorry. If I'd just said something to someone. The authorities...'

Bethany's mind was whirling. Her brother had threatened their father with a horse whip? Had he been up to his old tricks then?

A memory resurfaced of her brother's face, dark and menacing, his knuckles clenched and bleeding. Her father lying on his back in the stableyard, his lip cut and swollen, his eyes wide with shock.

She'd been crouched down beside the loosebox door, trembling with fear. She'd never seen Joseph behave that way before. Joseph had hurried over to her, his expression softening when he saw how scared she was.

'It's going to be right, Beth,' he promised her. 'Haven't I always told you that? It's all going to be right.'

But she was still terrified.

Terrified of what their father would do to him.

Except, he hadn't done anything, had he? Bullies seldom

retaliated when their victims finally fought back, and Terence Wilkinson was a bully all right. Joseph—her wonderful hero of a big brother—had stood up to him at last, and she'd thought that had been the end of it.

Yet now, Miss Lavender was telling her that Joseph had been threatening their father with a horse whip? Just months before she'd left, too. Which meant only one thing. Their father had reverted to his old behaviour and Joseph had been forced to stop him once more. And Miss Lavender had seen and had assumed...

All those years, and poor Joseph had been blamed for his actions that day. That was why Miss Lavender had ignored him afterwards. Why there'd been few visits to Whispering Willows. Why she'd blamed him for Bethany's leaving.

'You thought Joseph hit me,' she murmured.

Miss Lavender reared back a little. 'Why—yes. Are you saying he didn't?'

'Oh, Miss Lavender, you couldn't be more wrong, you really couldn't. Joseph never raised a finger to me. Never. My father—he was the bully. He was vile. Cruel. Oh, he never harmed us physically, don't get me wrong. No,' she said coldly, 'he had far more effective ways of punishing us. What you saw that day was Joseph trying to stop him from doing something unforgivable. Believe me when I tell you, whatever you think you saw, you were wrong. Joseph was not to blame that day. The fault lay entirely with my father.'

Miss Lavender looked dumbfounded. 'But—but a *horse whip*, Bethany?'

'I know how it must have looked to you,' she said, realising as she looked down that tears were rolling down her cheeks and landing in her lap. How odd because she hadn't even been aware she was crying. 'You must trust me on this. Joseph acted out of kindness. My father would have done something despicable if my brother hadn't been there to stop him.'

'I—I really don't know what to say,' Miss Lavender said. 'So you're saying I was wrong? All these years when I blamed Joseph for you leaving home, that wasn't the case?'

Bethany took a deep breath. 'I'd really rather not discuss why I left home,' she said at last. 'Not now. It's still too much and besides, it would only require more explanations than I'm willing to give you. I'm sorry.'

'No, no, it's quite all right.' Miss Lavender squeezed her hand. 'I was so angry with myself, Bethany. I thought—that day —I thought I should have notified the police. I remember it so well. Joseph just walked past me, his head held high, as if he'd done nothing wrong. He snapped the whip in two and threw it on the muck heap. I hurried over to help your father to his feet. He was shaking, but so angry. I offered to call them, you know. The police. But he refused. Said it wouldn't be fair and it was a family matter.'

'I'll bet he did,' Bethany said grimly.

'I was worried. I wasn't sure what to do. And when you left Tuppenny Bridge I was tormented. I thought, what if Joseph had been treating you that way? What if he hit you with a horse whip? Was that why you'd left? I felt so bad about it, my dear. I kept checking on your father to make sure Joseph hadn't harmed him. He was so grateful to me. Told me he appreciated my concern and that I shouldn't worry, Joseph had seen the error of his ways...'

Her voice shook and Bethany was appalled to see tears spilling from her eyes. She put her arms around the old lady and hugged her tightly.

'My father was a manipulative liar,' she said heavily. 'Don't feel bad that he fooled you. He fooled a lot of people.'

'So when you said... When you said *he* made Whispering Willows a living hell, you didn't mean Joseph? You meant—'

'My father. I'm so sorry, Miss Lavender. I wish I'd known. I promise you; I was never in any danger from Joseph. None. But if it's any consolation, my father never raised a hand to me either. I swear it.'

'Well,' Miss Lavender said, her voice muffled against Bethany's shoulder, 'I suppose that's something I must be grateful for. Although,' she added bleakly, 'it now seems I did Joseph a terrible injustice. And, sadly for both of us, it's far too late for me to ever make amends.'

TEN

Clive had brought bacon sandwiches for Maya and Lennox, which pleased them. It was a cold Monday morning, so he thought it the least he could do, given that they were teenagers who'd miraculously managed to drag themselves out of bed at this ungodly hour to be at the stables before school.

'Tuck in, kids,' he said, handing the foil-wrapped packages over. 'Let's fill up before we start work.'

Viva danced around him, her nose twitching as she caught the scent of the bacon she'd watched him grilling just twenty minutes earlier.

'We've had this conversation,' Clive told her. 'You can't have bacon. It's bad for you. Anyway, you've had your breakfast so you can stop looking at me with those pleading eyes, you wee monkey.'

'She does look sad,' Maya said, sounding guilty.

'She'll look even sadder when she's got pancreatitis,' Clive said darkly. 'No bacon for her please.'

They leaned against the stable walls in companionable silence, enjoying the thick sliced white bread and not too crispy bacon that Clive had cooked with his own fair hands. He pretended not to notice when Maya gave Viva a bit of her bread crust.

'Just think, Summer will be on a plane now,' Lennox said dreamily. 'Lucky cow.'

'Bet she'll hate Australia,' Maya said. 'All them spiders. Ugh! The ones in the stables are bad enough, but they're the size of dinner plates over there. They crawl up the toilet and bite your bum when you're having a pee. You don't see that on *Home and Away*, do you?'

'I think there's a bit more to Australia than spiders,' Clive said. 'Anyway, it will be good for her to spend time with her dad. I know she's missed him. And of course, they'll be staying with her sister and brother-in-law so I'm sure she'll have a brilliant time.'

'I think just getting away from here for a bit will do her the world of good,' Lennox said, with surprising wisdom. 'She looked knackered lately.'

'Bet Ben will miss her,' Maya added.

Clive had no doubt about it. He thought it was probably a good thing that Ben had a busy day ahead of him at the surgery. It would stop him brooding. It was going to be a long three weeks for the loved-up couple.

At least he'd managed to reassure Summer on Saturday night, after Jennifer's little bombshell had dropped, causing Summer to panic.

'But if Bethany already owns Whispering Willows, she won't have to wait for any of the legal stuff, will she? If she wants to sell the house she can go right ahead,' she'd gasped, as realisation had set in.

It had already occurred to him, and his heart had sunk at the prospect, even as he wondered how he'd never known that the house and sanctuary didn't belong to Joseph at all. He supposed the subject had never come up. Why would it? He'd naturally assumed that Joseph owned it because, after all, he was the only son of Terence and Coral Wilkinson, and a lot older than Bethany. It seemed odd that Coral had bypassed Joseph and made Bethany the main beneficiary of her will. Why?

Evidently, Sally had been wondering the same thing because she'd asked Jennifer what on earth Coral had been playing at.

'Joseph was too soft with his father,' Jennifer said. 'Maybe she thought if she left it to him Terence would have forced him to sign documents handing it over or something. I wouldn't put anything past that man. Coral probably wouldn't have dreamed, when she made that will, that Bethany would still be a child when she inherited. My mother said that the main thing, though, was that Coral didn't want Bethany to end up in the same situation as herself. She wanted Bethany to have independence and to be able to live her life without needing a man to keep her, and probably hoped Bethany would have more sense when it came to men and finances than she'd had. My understanding is that Whispering Willows and the bulk of her fortune was held in trust until Bethany turned thirty, although some of her money was to be released to her on her twenty-first birthday.'

'Sounds like Coral had good advice,' Rafferty had mused. 'Given everything we've heard about Terence, she clearly thought he'd find a way to sell the house at the first opportunity.'

'What about Joseph's inheritance?' Summer asked, sounding hurt on his behalf. 'He must have got something from someone! How else could he have kept the sanctuary going all these years?'

'Oh, Joseph got a very generous financial settlement,' Jennifer assured her. 'He just didn't get the house and land.'

'Yet Bethany allowed him to continue living there, even after she left?' Clive said, frowning. He'd have thought that, after whatever had happened to cause her to leave, she'd have turfed him out after their father died. She probably could have done. Certainly after she turned thirty she could have sold the house outright and Joseph wouldn't have been able to stop her.

For some reason, she'd not done that. She'd allowed her brother to stay, and only now, when he'd passed away, was she determined to offload Whispering Willows. What had taken her so long? It wasn't what he'd expected to hear, and he thought maybe there was more to Bethany than he'd given her credit for.

'She could have sold it ages ago if that was her plan,' he'd said to Summer, hoping it would reassure her, even though he felt bad at his deception. 'I wouldn't worry. I'm sure Whispering Willows is safe.'

Ben had looked uncomfortable but didn't contradict him.

'Clive's right, love,' Sally said. 'I reckon now she's back she might well stay. Hey, you never know,' she added eagerly, 'she might put you in charge of the place and pay you a proper wage for it. That would be grand, wouldn't it?'

Summer grinned. 'You think that's a possibility?'

'Stranger things have happened,' Clive had said, avoiding Ben's gaze. 'Jennifer, this paella is absolutely fantastic.'

He hadn't felt good about deceiving Summer, and he knew Ben hated it, but they'd both agreed she would never get on that plane if she was worried about the future of Whispering Willows, and she needed that holiday. Mind, she wasn't the only one. He was ready for a break himself.

Thank the lord for Maya and Lennox because he wouldn't have been able to manage at the stables without them while Summer was away. Making them breakfast was the least he could do. He'd make them a daily three course lunch if they asked him.

'Would have been even better with ketchup,' Lennox told him, nodding at his half-eaten sandwich. 'Just for future reference, like.'

'For future reference,' Maya said firmly, 'ketchup is vile on bacon butties. It's brown sauce all the way.'

'Aye, well, I wasn't sure which you'd prefer, if any, so I didn't put any on to be on the safe side. And *for future reference*, maybe tomorrow it's your turn to make me a bacon butty. What do you reckon?'

Maya's eyes widened. 'I haven't got time for that!'

'Me mam wouldn't like me messing about in her kitchen,' Lennox said quickly. 'Especially not at that time in the morning. Anyway, I don't think we've got any bacon.'

Clive laughed. 'Seems like I'm on butty duty every day then.'

They looked relieved. 'You can deduct it from our wages if you like,' Maya said hesitantly, earning a disapproving look from Lennox.

'Ach, you're all right,' Clive assured her. 'I reckon I can stretch to a butty every morning. Mind, it won't always be bacon. I'm not made of money.'

He didn't want them taking him for granted, after all, he thought with wry amusement. He glanced over his shoulder, surprised to hear a car approaching. They all straightened and exchanged bemused looks as a bright blue hatchback pulled up in the stableyard. Viva let out a yap, warning whoever it was that Whispering Willows was protected by a bichon frise who would take no prisoners if they meant any harm.

'What's *she* doing here at this time of the morning?' Lennox muttered. 'Must be crackers.'

'*You're* here,' Maya pointed out.

'Exactly.'

Clive scrunched up the foil that had held his bacon sandwich and stuffed it in his pocket, then gathered Viva into his arms as Bethany stepped out of her car looking surprisingly elegant for so early in the morning, dressed in smart navy-blue trousers and a grey sweater.

'Morning!' she called, smiling at them before reaching into the back seat, and retrieving a huge pile of papers.

That was possibly the most cheerful she'd sounded since she'd got here, he thought with surprise. She had a lovely smile and he wished she'd smile more. It really brightened her face.

'Er, morning.' He glanced at the teenagers who gave him a knowing look.

'Come to check up on us,' Lennox whispered.

'We'd best get to work,' Maya added.

'Finish your sandwiches,' Clive instructed them. 'You're entitled to some breakfast. Besides, you're volunteers as far as she's concerned. What's she going to do, sack you?'

'Fair point,' Lennox said with a shrug, taking a huge bite of his bacon butty and fixing Bethany with a defiant stare, as if she was planning to snatch his breakfast from his hot little hand.

Bethany gave them a cheerful wave and headed towards the house. 'Lennox and Maya, right? Thanks so much for turning out this early. I'll put the kettle on, shall I?' she called as she neared the door. 'Shall we say five minutes?'

With that, she entered the house and closed the door behind her, leaving all three of them standing there in stunned silence.

'What's got into her?' Maya asked Clive, as if he'd know. 'Summer said she was a cold fish, but she seems all right to me.'

He thought a cold fish was a bit harsh. She'd had a rough time at Whispering Willows so she was bound to feel a bit out-of-sorts here. And she had, after all, allowed Joseph to stay here when she could have sold the place from under him years ago.

Maybe he should be a bit friendlier towards her. Maybe she'd cared more about her brother than she'd let on.

Although, if that was the case, why hadn't she come to see him when he needed her most?

Don't get carried away, Clive, he told himself as he headed slowly towards the house. She probably charged Joseph an extortionate rent or something.

Now that was a point. He wouldn't be at all surprised.

ELEVEN

The kettle had just boiled when the kitchen door opened and Clive, Maya and Lennox walked in. They all looked a little awkward, and Bethany hurried to make them feel at home.

'You're just in time. Would you like tea or coffee? Clive, there's a bowl of water down there for Viva.'

She and Clive ended up with mugs of coffee while the two teenagers plumped for tea. She was a little taken aback when Lennox asked for four sugars in his.

'Wow, that's—that's a lot of sugar,' she managed. 'Are you sure?'

'It's for energy,' he assured her. 'My mam swears by it.'

Bethany couldn't help wondering whether his mother had any of her own teeth left but said nothing as she dutifully heaped four spoonfuls of sugar into Lennox's cup of tea.

They certainly knew their own minds she thought with some amusement. Lennox had warned her that he could only drink tea so strong you could stand the spoon up in it, while Maya had announced she basically wanted tea flavoured water.

'Just dip the teabag in it,' she instructed. 'Can't stand tea to be honest.'

'I can make you coffee?'

'Oh no, that wouldn't be right. Got to have a cup of tea for breakfast, right?'

Defeated by that logic, Bethany did as she was asked and placed two mugs of tea in front of the teenagers, who'd settled themselves at the table. She exchanged a wry look with Clive, noting the twinkle in his grey eyes as he sipped his coffee.

'I just wanted to say hello to you both,' she told Maya and Lennox. 'And to thank you both for turning out so early this morning.' She glanced at her watch and her eyes widened. 'So *very* early,' she amended, noting it was only six thirty. 'I really do appreciate it, and I want you to know I'll be here every morning to make you a good breakfast before you start work. You too, Clive, naturally.'

'That lets me off butty duty then,' he said, winking at the teenagers.

'Great,' Maya said. 'Thanks very much, Mrs Marshall.'

'Bethany. Just call me Bethany.' Bethany crouched down and fondled Viva's ears, glad to see the little dog again and noting she looked healthy and happy, despite the upheaval she'd had recently. 'You're welcome. I really am very grateful for your help. With Summer away for the next three weeks I don't know how we'd manage without you.'

'It's Clive that will be doing most of it,' Lennox said grudgingly. 'We'll be at school all day, although we'll be dropping in after hours two or three times a week to finish up. But he'll be here all day, remember.'

'And he's had to pay a locum to do his proper job for him,' Maya said, giving Clive an uncharacteristically adoring look. 'Summer says he's a superstar, and I reckon she's right. Mind you, my dad says he must want his head read, and I think *he's* right, an' all.'

Maya laughed and, despite the guilt she was feeling about

how much these three were putting themselves out, Bethany laughed, too.

'I think both those things might be correct,' she agreed. 'Anyway, I shall cover the cost of the locum, naturally.'

Clive put down his mug. 'Oh, there's no need for that,' he assured her.

'I insist,' she said. 'It's only fair. Why should you be out of pocket?'

'Because I'm doing this for Joseph,' he said firmly. 'He loved these horses, and he loved Summer. I promised him I'd take care of the situation and that's what I plan to do, so thank you for your generous offer, but it's my responsibility and I intend to see it through.'

Bethany hesitated, aware that Maya and Lennox were watching them closely, clearly waiting to see what would happen next and who would give in.

She couldn't deny she felt a bit put out that Clive had rejected her gesture so soundly. She'd been trying to make amends for her earlier prickly attitude, but clearly he wasn't interested.

'Very well,' she said stiffly. 'If that's what you want.'

'It is, aye.' He picked up his mug again and took a long drink. 'Good coffee,' he told her approvingly.

She narrowed her eyes as he watched her, realising at last that it was his way of thanking her and letting her know his decision was nothing personal. She relaxed a little.

'I'm glad you like it.'

She was rewarded with a grin that had a surprising effect on her. As her heart skipped she wondered what on earth was wrong with her lately. Look how she'd been staring at Ross Lavender, and now bloody Clive—Clive...

She frowned. 'What's your surname?' she enquired, realising with embarrassment that she'd quite forgotten, even though she was certain he'd already told her once.

'Browning,' he reminded her. 'Clive Browning.'

'Like the poet,' Maya said.

'Or gravy browning,' Lennox added helpfully.

'Gravy browning!' Maya said, rolling her eyes. She gulped down her tea. 'Hurry up, Len, we need to get on with the work. Time's getting on.'

'What will you be doing this morning?' Bethany enquired.

'Changing their water first,' Maya explained. 'Then we'll turn out the horses who have been stabled overnight, muck out their looseboxes, and I'll see to Barney.'

'Barney? Oh, that's the little pony with sweet itch, right?' Bethany nodded. 'Does it take long to sort him out?'

'Not really, now I've got used to it. I'll get his barrier cream and his rugs done and take him out.'

'I'll be poo picking mostly,' Lennox said gloomily. 'Making sure the fields are clear of manure. Lovely job.'

'I'll check all thirteen of them over,' Clive said. 'Make sure there are no lumps or bumps or cuts. Actually, a couple of them are due to be wormed so I'll do that later, too.'

'Is there anything I can help with?' Bethany asked, more because she felt she should rather than because she wanted to. It had been a long time since she'd had anything to do with horses and she wasn't sure she'd even know where to begin these days.

'You could take Viva for a walk,' Clive suggested, sounding doubtful. 'It would save me a job. Mind, only if you want to.'

'I'm sure I could manage that,' she said at once, feeling she'd got off lightly.

'Well, I'm ready, Len. How about you?' Maya jumped up and scraped back her chair, the sound of its wooden legs on the stone floor making Bethany wince.

Lennox sighed. 'Yep. Let's get on with it.'

They thanked Bethany again for the tea, and also thanked

Clive for some bacon sandwiches he'd evidently made for them, then headed out into the yard.

'They're good kids,' he said fondly.

'They seem it. Not many teenagers who'd be willing to turn out at this hour of the morning,' she said. 'I'm impressed. They're very nice.'

'Well,' Clive said, sounding suddenly awkward, 'thanks for the coffee. I'd better get out there and start work.'

'Clive, I don't suppose...' Bethany hesitated, wishing that she'd never started this conversation now. She glanced down at Viva. 'Oh, it doesn't matter. Forget it.'

Clive frowned. 'What was it? Is something wrong?'

'No, no. Nothing like that. Well, apart from the state of these accounts,' she added, giving a rueful nod to the pile of papers she'd dumped on the table. 'I've certainly got my work cut out for me there. No, it's just...' She took a deep breath. She might as well just say it now. 'I don't suppose Joseph ever mentioned Poppins and Pepper, did he?'

Clive cleared his throat. 'Poppins and—Pepper? Not sure, to be honest. Should he have done?'

'I suppose not.' She shrugged wistfully. 'It's just, Poppins was our dog—mine and Joseph's. Gorgeous little cocker spaniel. And Pepper was my pony. I—I had to leave them behind when I left, and I always wondered...'

Always wondered? The guilt had eaten her alive. Of all the regrets Bethany had about the past, leaving Pepper and Poppins behind at Whispering Willows had been the biggest. She wasn't sure she'd ever forgiven herself.

Clive was staring at the floor.

'It's okay,' she said. 'If he didn't mention them...'

'Neither of them were here when I first came to Whispering Willows,' Clive said slowly.

Bethany swallowed. 'I see. Thank you.'

Clive watched her closely. Too closely. She didn't want him

to see the tears pricking her eyes. To her relief, Viva trotted up beside her and she scooped her up, grateful to be able to hide her face in the little dog's soft, white fur.

'Poppins...' Clive murmured. 'You know, I think I do remember Joseph telling me the wee thing had passed away in her sleep, aye. He was very fond of her. Black cocker spaniel, yes?'

'That's right. She was eleven when I left so I suppose she wouldn't have lived much longer.'

'Yes. I saw a photo of her. And Pepper... little bay pony, right?'

Bethany's eyebrows lifted in surprise. 'Yes! You met him?'

'No, no. I'm afraid not. But Joseph did talk about him. About all the horses you used to have. He, er, sold them. Found them good homes.'

Bethany stared at him, her heart thudding. 'Sold them? All of them?' Her mind raced. As well as Pepper, her own beloved pony, there'd been her father's horse, Jet, and Joseph's own horse, Magnus. Why would Joseph sell them? 'When?'

Clive cleared his throat. 'I believe he sold them just after you left home,' he admitted. 'But they went to very good homes. He was very thorough.'

'And Father let him?' Bethany said disbelievingly.

'I think your father was struggling to ride, with his arthritis,' Clive said hastily. 'And Joseph was so busy caring for him and working at the brewery that he didn't get much time to spend with them himself. He thought it would be kinder to let them go to good homes where they'd get more care and attention.'

'I see.' She didn't though. Not really. He'd sold their beloved horses, yet just a few years later he'd started taking in waifs and strays. Her eyes narrowed. This was punishment, no doubt about it. He knew how much she loved those horses—how much she loved Pepper. He'd sold them to spite her. Because he hated her.

'I'd better get to work,' Clive said awkwardly. 'You're sure you don't mind me leaving Viva here with you?'

'Not at all,' she told him. 'I've got to get on with these accounts, so I'll be here all day anyway, but I'll take her for a walk in a couple of hours, don't worry.'

He nodded and left the house, seeming quite relieved to get out of there. She could see in his face that he knew more than he was letting on and she'd bet anything that Joseph had admitted to him that he'd sold Pepper especially because he'd known how much she loved him. She really couldn't believe her father had agreed to part with them, though, especially Jet. How had Joseph managed that?

She kissed Viva's nose and sighed. It was just another question that she'd never know the answer to.

TWELVE

The grand official opening of The Arabella Lavender Art Academy took place on Sunday the twenty-eighth of April. Miss Lavender was beside herself with excitement and beaming with pride, not least because Ethan Rochester himself had agreed to cut the ribbon.

Jonah Brewster, the local farrier, had grinned from ear to ear when Bethany mentioned that she would be attending the event.

'Wouldn't dare miss it, would you? Not that she'd let you. And you *are* living under her roof so there's no escape. Mind you, there are plenty of us in this town wondering how many ceremonies this art academy needs.'

'What do you mean?' Bethany leaned against the stable wall, watching as Jonah trimmed one of the donkey's hooves. She found the farrier easy company. This was his second visit to Whispering Willows since she'd been here, and he had a kind nature and a friendly manner.

'Well, there was an open day for all us Bridgers to admire the work they'd done. Proper champagne laid on, an' all! Can't say she skimps on things like that, can we? Then there was another open day which was for prospective students. Then there was a mini opening ceremony when the first day students arrived to start lessons. Now this! I reckon this is the one that matters most to her, though. I mean, Miss Lavender's a canny old bird. Got Ethan Rochester to perform the ceremony, and of course, the local paper will be covering it all. Lots of publicity on local news and for their website, too.'

'She keeps banging on about Ethan Rochester,' Bethany admitted with a smile. 'Is it true he's related to Rafferty at The White Hart Inn?'

'That's right.' Jonah patted Moonflower's neck. 'There you go, girl. That's you done and dusted for a few weeks.' He straightened and rubbed his back. 'Think they're distant cousins or something. Ethan's mum was a Kingston, so Kat says. I can't keep up with it. Anyway, he's forking out for a scholarship and donating a cup and a cash prize for a competition in his wife's name, so he's obviously keen to help. Ethan, I mean, not Rafferty. Although Rafferty's an art nut, too. He's studying for a degree in art history, so Kat says. No idea how he finds the time to be honest. Any road, the Kingstons love art, so it's no wonder Ethan Rochester was persuaded to attend the opening event.'

'Will you be going?' Bethany asked hopefully. In a town full of people who were mostly strangers she thought it would be good to see a friendly face. Miss Lavender would likely be too busy playing hostess, and she'd rather avoid Rita and Birdie as much as possible. They'd only be digging for information.

'Oh, we wouldn't miss it for the world!' Jonah rolled his eyes. 'Probably won't stay long, though. Me, that is. I'll take the kids home after an hour or so, cos they'll only get bored, but Kat will no doubt stay longer.'

'I'll look forward to meeting her,' Bethany said.

'Actually, you've already met her, although you probably won't remember her.'

'I have?' Bethany frowned. 'When? Who is she?'

'Katherine Pennyfeather. Rita and Birdie are her great aunts.'

Bethany's eyes widened. 'Oh, the little girl at The Black Swan! Good heavens, I remember her. Fancy you being married to her!'

'Not married yet,' Jonah said sheepishly. 'Engaged, though. Wedding's on the eleventh of May. Summer was fuming when she found out because she's not back until the thirteenth, bless her.'

'That's amazing. I forget, you see,' she said wistfully. 'I forget how long I've been away, and that the adults I see walking around this town might well be the little children I left behind. I must admit, it was quite a shock when I saw Miss Lavender looking so old.' She grinned suddenly. 'The Pennyfeathers haven't changed much, though. They still look just as outlandish as they always did.'

'Aye, they'll never change,' Jonah agreed, his eyes twinkling in amusement. 'Hearts of gold, the pair of them. And before you ask, no Kat doesn't share their taste in clothes!'

'I don't think anyone does,' she said, laughing. 'Well, now that I know you two will be there I'll definitely go.'

So that Sunday she accepted Miss Lavender's gracious invitation of a lift up to Monk's Folly, as she still thought of the place, and braced herself for a lot of curious stares and awkward questions.

She'd almost backed out several times but had decided— after a stern talking to from Helena—that it was better to pull the sticking plaster off rapidly.

'Get it over with,' Helena had advised. 'If people want to ask you questions, let them. You don't have to tell them anything you don't want to. And once you're out there, the fuss will die down. Hiding away is what will make them curious.'

She was right and Bethany knew it, so she put on a pretty

summer dress and teamed it with a light jacket and court shoes, applied make-up, combed her hair, and headed out, determined to enjoy herself and help Miss Lavender do the same on what was, for her, a big day.

She had to admit she was taken aback by the appearance of Monk's Folly. She vaguely recalled it being a bit of a grim house, standing halfway up a hillside on the far bank of the River Skimmer. As the car made its way through smart new gates and up the short drive, she thought it looked far from grim now. Its paintwork was new and gleaming, its awful old windows had been replaced, and the overgrown garden had been landscaped. The tatty old garage that had always seemed on the verge of falling down had gone. In its place was a smart new building that was obviously a studio.

'Even the stonework has been power washed,' Miss Lavender said proudly. 'Doesn't it look beautiful?'

Bethany realised Miss Lavender wasn't expecting an answer. She was too busy gazing out of the window, her eyes shining with excitement. Naturally, as the car approached the crowd that had gathered outside the house, the old lady gave a regal wave before pulling into the small car park and parking faultlessly.

'Quite a few people here,' she said, turning off the engine. 'Now, are you ready for this, my dear?'

'Me?' Bethany raised an eyebrow. 'It's your big day, not mine.'

'I know. Well, strictly speaking, it's Ross's big day,' Miss Lavender said modestly. 'Nevertheless, I do understand how difficult this must be for you, facing the town after all these years. Don't think for one moment that I don't appreciate the effort you're making.'

Bethany felt quite touched that Miss Lavender had considered her feelings.

'It's not a problem,' Bethany reassured her, patting her arm. 'I'm sure people are far more interested in the new art academy than anything I've got to say. You look lovely by the way.'

Miss Lavender glanced down at her cornflower blue dress and jacket. 'Do you think so? My dear father always said this colour brought out the blue in my eyes.' She smiled. 'He'd be so delighted that Monk's Folly is back in our family, you know. And for the art academy to be named after our dear Arabella, whose art has always been so overlooked—well, he'd be over the moon.'

'Shall we go in then?' Bethany asked, smiling fondly.

'We shall, dear. We shall.' Miss Lavender opened her car door. 'Ooh, I do hope the Rochesters are here already, and that Ross has been making them feel at home.'

'Did you spot them in the crowd?' Bethany climbed out of the car and smoothed down her dress.

Miss Lavender gave her a surprised look. 'Of course not! Ross was under strict instructions to take them inside, give them refreshments, and introduce them to the press people. We don't want them hanging around outside with the townspeople, do we?'

'Of course not.' Bethany smothered a grin. 'Silly me.'

They avoided the crowd at the front of the house and Bethany followed Miss Lavender round the back, where the door was opened before Miss Lavender had the chance to knock on it. Someone had clearly been expecting her.

'Come in, Miss Lavender,' said a woman, probably a bit older than Bethany. She seemed familiar, but Bethany couldn't quite place her. She had grey-streaked brown hair and bright blue eyes and looked a bit nervous. 'The guests have arrived, and so has the reporter and the photographer from *The Skimmerdale Herald*. They're in the drawing room with Ross and Clemmie. I've served them canapés as you instructed.'

'Thank you so much,' Miss Lavender said graciously. 'Oh, Bethany, I don't know if you remember Jennifer? Jennifer Callaghan.' She gave Bethany a knowing look. 'And Jennifer, this is Bethany Marshall. Used to be Bethany Wilkinson. Remember?'

'Of course I remember.' Jennifer held out her hand and shook Bethany's warmly. 'We were at school together, but I was two years ahead of you, so we didn't have much to do with each other, I'm afraid. My mother was friends with yours, though. At least, when they were at primary school together.'

At the mention of her mother Bethany's stomach tightened. 'I—I hadn't realised,' she admitted. 'About our mothers, I mean. It's nice to see you, Jennifer. I was so sorry to hear about Julian and Leon.'

She saw the same look flicker across Jennifer's eyes as she imagined had been in her own just seconds earlier. Grief was easily recognised by fellow sufferers.

'Thank you,' Jennifer said. 'I appreciate that.'

'Shall we go through, Bethany?' Miss Lavender said heartily. 'Jennifer here is the new cook at the academy. She really is excellent at her job. I can't wait to sample some of her canapés.'

Jennifer and Bethany exchanged a look, each recognising that an order had been subtly given.

Grief was replaced by amusement and Bethany gave Jennifer a resigned nod as Miss Lavender ushered her out of the gleaming, newly fitted kitchen.

'Sorry about that, dear,' she whispered in Bethany's ear as they headed down the hallway, 'but Jennifer's been so fragile for so long and any mention of her loss... The last thing I need is for her to fall to pieces today of all days.'

She pushed open a door and ushered Bethany through. Bethany felt awkward and ill-at-ease as she found herself in a room full of strangers. What, she wondered, was she even doing here? She should be outside with the rest of the plebs!

At least she recognised Ross, who gave her a friendly smile as he held out his arms to welcome his great aunt.

'Aunt Eugenie! We were just talking about you,' he said, kissing her on each cheek. 'And, Bethany, nice to see you again. Thanks so much for coming.'

'My pleasure. Thanks for inviting me,' Bethany mumbled.

She barely lifted her gaze so didn't really take in the faces of the other guests, but luckily Miss Lavender was quickly in full flow, introducing herself to the press and making it quite clear that the art academy was going to be a huge success and a massive boost to the local economy.

She greeted Ethan Rochester like an old friend, and Bethany noted the air kisses she exchanged with a rather bemused strawberry blonde woman who also seemed a bit shy.

'It's so lovely to see you both again,' Miss Lavender assured them. 'And how well you're both looking. Bethany, this is Ethan Rochester, and this is his wife, Cara,' she added, indicating the strawberry blonde. 'Ethan, Cara, this is Bethany Marshall. She's staying with me at the moment. She's been away from Tuppenny Bridge for some time, but she's recently returned because her brother sadly passed away.'

Two pairs of sympathetic eyes immediately swivelled in her direction and Bethany tried hard not to feel like a total fraud, as both Ethan and Cara assured her how sorry they were for her loss. If they knew the truth about her relationship with Joseph, they wouldn't waste their sympathies.

'Bethany, this is Clementine Grant. She's, er, Ross's young lady,' Miss Lavender said, rescuing her from the Rochesters' compassion.

'Clemmie,' the young woman said immediately.

'Only *I* call her Clementine,' Ross added, giving his girl-friend an affectionate look.

'I wouldn't let anyone else get away with it,' Clemmie said, nudging him.

She was a pretty thing, probably in her late twenties. A round face, blonde hair, and big blue eyes that shone with love for her boyfriend. Bethany could hardly blame her. He was quite a catch.

'Clemmie works—' Miss Lavender suddenly frowned and looked round the room. 'Ross, where on earth is Callum?'

'Running late,' Ross admitted. 'He said to start without him.'

'Well, that's a good start to his new career as our art teacher,' Miss Lavender said indignantly.

'Not his fault, Auntie. He had a puncture.'

Miss Lavender pursed her lips. 'Hmm. I suppose... Anyway, as I was saying, Clemmie works at The Corner Cottage Bookshop in Market Place.'

'Ah. I saw that when I arrived,' Bethany said. 'It used to be something else in my day. A children's clothes shop called Taylor-Made. I must confess I was quite sad to see that had gone, but I'm sure a bookshop is very popular here.'

She noticed that Miss Lavender had drifted off to talk to Cara and Ethan and could hardly blame her. They were her honoured guests, after all. Not to mention the fact that the reporter seemed more interested in the Rochesters than the art school, something which Miss Lavender had no doubt picked up on and was determined to put right. She also realised there'd been no offer of any canapés, despite Miss Lavender's assertion that she couldn't wait to try them.

It didn't matter. Bethany had to admit that she was happier chatting to Clemmie, who seemed nice and normal and not intimidating.

Miss Lavender called Ross's name, and as he excused himself to join his aunt with the Rochesters, Clemmie turned eagerly to Bethany.

'Isn't this awful? I don't have a clue what I'm in here for. I mean, what do I know about art? And having to stand here and make small talk with the Rochesters... Oh, it's been horrendous. Thank goodness you arrived.'

Bethany grinned at her. 'I was just thinking thank goodness for you,' she admitted. 'I don't know anything about art either. I'd far rather have waited outside with the others, but I'm living with Miss Lavender at the moment so I could hardly refuse, could I?'

'Refuse Miss Lavender?' Clemmie's eyes rolled. 'No chance! To be fair, I could hardly say no to Ross. It means such a lot to him, and I wanted to support him. Dolly's furious because she's stuck outside.'

'Dolly?'

'My aunt. She owns the bookshop. Ross said I could invite her in, but I know Dolly. She'd have a few too many glasses of champagne and hog the Rochesters, just to annoy Miss Lavender.' She looked immediately contrite. 'That makes her sound awful and she's not, really she's not, but she does have a wicked sense of humour and although I usually love her for that, I couldn't take any risks. Not today. It's going to be bad enough controlling her when they let everyone in.'

She turned and her gaze settled on Ross. As if he'd been alerted by some mystical force, he turned and smiled at her.

Bethany couldn't help but feel a sudden joy at their obvious love for each other. It was lovely to see a couple who so clearly adored one another. It made her think of Ted and Helena. They'd been the same, and although it had hurt her terribly when she'd first seen that look between them, as time went on she'd realised she was glad of it. They were both such good people. They deserved to feel that way.

It had also made her realise, once and for all, that she'd never felt that way about Ted. About anyone.

Not even Glenn.

'I think it's time we went outside,' Miss Lavender announced, glancing at her watch. 'The invitations did say two o'clock and it's a minute past. Ethan, are you ready?'

Ethan assured her that he was, and Ross gave everyone a nervous look.

'Right then. I guess this is it. Time to cut the ribbon and officially open The Arabella Lavender Art Academy.'

THIRTEEN

Ethan did a splendid job of the official opening ceremony. He made a fine speech about the importance of art, and how marvellous it was to see an overlooked female artist in the limelight thanks to her distant relatives. He talked about Josiah Lavender's excellence, and how it was clear talent ran in his family, what with Arabella herself and then Ross (Ross shuffled awkwardly at this point and stared at the ground while Clemmie and Miss Lavender fairly beamed with pride), and how gratifying it was to see this wonderful new venture. He added that he hoped the academy would introduce art and the joy of creating it to many more people in the years to come, and how thrilled he was to be able to contribute in some small way to something he firmly believed could enrich and even change lives.

He then declared The Arabella Lavender Art Academy officially open and cut the ribbon to cheers from the waiting crowd, as the camera flashed and the reporter hurried forward to get some quotes.

The doors at the front of the house were pushed open and people invited to enter and partake in refreshments.

'Thank the lord that's done,' someone muttered as they brushed past Bethany on their way into the house. 'Been standing out there for bloody ages. There'd best be champagne on offer, or I'll be fuming.'

Bethany had lost Clemmie somewhere in the crowd and couldn't even see Miss Lavender, but she decided it was best to just go with the flow. They were bound to be somewhere inside.

As she made her way up the path a voice in her ear made her jump.

'I wasn't expecting to see you here.'

She turned, and for some reason her stomach flipped as she saw Clive beside her.

'I wasn't expecting to see you here either,' she said, wondering why she felt so nervous speaking to him. 'I thought you'd have work to do at the stables.'

She realised immediately, from his narrowed eyes, that he'd taken that as a criticism.

'I've caught up with everything I needed to do,' he assured her. 'And I'll be going back after I've finished here. It's just, I didn't come to the other events here, and I felt I owed the Lavenders at least one visit.'

'I'm sorry. I didn't mean...'

The tide of people jostled Bethany and carried her further away from Clive, rendering her unable to finish her sentence. She looked back and saw he was now engaged in conversation with Ben. Oh well, if he wanted to take everything she said personally that was his problem. Right?

The guests filed into the powder blue hallway of Monk's Folly and were gently ushered into the dining room where a long table, dressed in a snowy white tablecloth and groaning with delicious looking food, was standing beneath the window. There was a multitude of chairs placed around the edges of the room, ensuring guests who didn't wish to or were unable to stand could sit down and eat in comfort.

There was already a queue for the buffet, but Bethany's stomach was rumbling and she had no hesitation in joining it. She'd worry about finding a chair later.

'You got here then.' There was a smile in the statement and Bethany smiled back as Jonah joined the queue just behind her.

'I did. And looking at the food on offer I'm glad I made it.'

'Aye, looks good,' he agreed. 'Miss Lavender never skimps on these dos, I'll give her that. Kat said to ask you if you'd like to sit with us,' he added, nodding over at the far wall where a dark-haired woman was sitting chatting with two young children. 'She's saved you a chair just in case.'

'Oh, that's really kind of her,' Bethany said, touched. 'Thank you. I'd be glad to.'

It would, she thought, be much better than standing around like a spare part, wondering who everyone was and trying to dodge small talk, or even worse, questions. There would be inevitable interest as people realised she was Joseph's long-lost sister. She hadn't been back in this town long, but long enough to have already realised that people had thought a lot of him. She'd interpreted several looks that, although hurriedly masked with smiles, had revealed that some people in Tuppenny Bridge thought she should have done more to be with her brother before he died.

If sitting with Kat and Jonah would protect her from some of those people she thought it could only be a good thing. Ten minutes later, plate piled high with various yummy food items, lovingly prepared by Jennifer and another member of the kitchen staff, Bethany headed over to sit with the Brewster/Pennyfeather clan.

She carried with her a small plate of food for Tommy, who was Jonah's seven-year-old son. Jonah, who wasn't far behind her, had filled plates for him and Kat, and assured her that fifteen-month-old Hattie would happily share theirs and didn't need her own plate.

Tommy tucked in with relish as soon as he got his hands on the goodies, and Kat sat Hattie on her knee before introducing herself to Bethany.

'Jonah said you remembered me,' she said, smiling. 'I suppose I've changed quite a bit since you last saw me though.'

'You certainly have,' Bethany said. 'Last time I saw you I think you had long plaits, and you were covered in mud and carrying a jam jar and a fishing net.'

'Oh yes?' Jonah gave Kat an enquiring glance and she laughed.

'Never caught anything other than a couple of tiddlers,' she admitted. 'Still it never stopped me trying. Well, what did you expect when we lived right opposite the river?'

He nudged her fondly. 'Always were a bit of a tomboy.'

Bethany's stomach rolled as Rita and Birdie pulled up chairs to join them. Uh-oh. No escape now.

'I wasn't,' Kat said indignantly.

'Yes, you were,' her Great Aunt Birdie, resplendent in a shocking pink dress and orange cardigan, nodded. 'Nothing wrong with that anyway. Came in useful at times. You allus got us a great haul when you went brambling. Remember the pies we used to bake when you brought them to ours?'

'I do,' Kat admitted wistfully. 'I haven't been brambling in years.'

'I'd love to go brambling,' Tommy said eagerly. 'Can we go brambling tomorrow, Kat?'

'In April?' She laughed and shook her head. 'You'll have to wait a few months, I'm afraid, Tommy.'

'Well, when the brambles are out will you take me? And then Auntie Rita and Auntie Birdie can make me a pie, can't you?' He turned pleading eyes on the Pennyfeather sisters, who visibly crumbled in the face of such a heartfelt appeal.

'Of course we can,' Rita assured him, adjusting the collar on her turquoise blouse. 'And you can help us bake it, how's that?'

Tommy looked thrilled, and Bethany swallowed down a lump in her throat. What a happy family they all seemed. So far removed from her own experiences of family life—if she could even call the people in her life family.

Nibbling listlessly on a feta cheese pastry parcel she recalled what things had been like at home when she'd been Tommy's age. No loving parents, no baby sister, no caring great aunts to bake with.

Her mother, she knew, had loved her to the best of her ability. The trouble was, she was so closed off, so wrapped up in her own misery that she didn't seem to have the energy to spend time with her young daughter. Her father was often out—thank goodness—and when he was home he was usually in a bad mood, and certainly didn't waste time making small talk with his children.

There'd only been Joseph, and for a long time she'd been grateful for him. Even after he'd started work at the brewery once owned by their mother's family, he made sure to spend time with her and look out for her. He taught her how to ride, she recalled, and he'd been patience itself.

He'd also tried his best to be there for their mother and had done all he could to coax her outdoors and make sure she had some fresh air and a bit of fun in her life. Bethany couldn't remember how many times he'd succeeded, but she suspected it hadn't been often. Their mother had been determined to wallow in her own misery.

For many years, Bethany had felt sorry for her. Now, though, she wondered if Coral Wilkinson could have done more to help herself. If not for her, then for the two children who desperately needed her.

She'd been like a ghost long before she finally slipped away and left them for good, at the mercy of their father's rages and epic sulks, his manipulation and gaslighting. His disgusting cruelty.

No, life for Bethany and Joseph had been nothing like it would be for Tommy and Hattie. Looking at their smiling faces now she could only be grateful that these two beautiful children had a better chance of happiness than she'd had.

'Penny for them?'

Bethany blinked as she realised Rita had asked her a question, and that Birdie was watching her shrewdly.

'Oh!' She forced a smile. 'Just thinking about bramble pie and how long it is since I tasted some.'

'How are you finding it, being back here in Tuppenny Bridge?' Birdie asked.

Bethany only just understood the question, since the old lady's cheeks were bulging with sausage roll when she asked it.

'Er, it's a bit strange,' she admitted. 'I'm getting used to it, though.'

'Did you see the changes to our shop?' Rita asked eagerly. 'It's a craft shop now. And there's—'

'It's not *our* shop any more,' Birdie reminded her. 'It's Kat's shop now. A craft shop as well as a wool shop. The upstairs belongs to Daisy, though.'

'Daisy?' Bethany wasn't familiar with that name.

'Daisy Jackson,' Kat explained, wiping pastry crumbs from Hattie's chin with a tissue. 'She's originally from Upper Skimmerdale, but she's moved here and turned my old flat into a craft café.'

'Oh wow!' Bethany's smile was genuine. 'That's a great idea.'

'We've not been open long,' Kat said, sounding delighted at Bethany's reaction. 'Even so, it's doing really well so far, and we're hoping business will boom in the summer when the tourists come back in bigger numbers.'

'Is Daisy here?'

'She is actually. I saw her a few moments ago.' Kat looked

around, scanning the crowd for her business partner. 'Oh, there she is! She's talking to Noah and Isobel.'

Birdie screwed up her nose. 'Poor sod. How did she get stuck with them? Someone rescue her.'

'Noah's all right,' Jonah said indignantly.

Rita laughed. 'Notice you don't rush to defend his wife, though.'

Kat and Noah exchanged looks then Kat gave Bethany an apologetic smile. 'Sorry. We're not being horrible, honestly. It's just, Isobel can be a bit...'

'Of a cow,' Rita finished helpfully.

'She's a cow?' Tommy asked, his eyes wide.

'Certainly not!' Kat hastily offered him a sandwich and shook her head at her great aunts.

'Isobel's just a bit prickly,' Jonah said quietly. 'Not as sociable as Noah, shall we say?'

'Although Noah barely mixes with anyone these days,' Birdie pointed out.

Bethany wondered if people had talked about Joseph in the same way. He was apparently supposed to have become quite the hermit after all. If not for Clive, Miss Lavender had said. She looked around, wondering where Clive was.

'He's the headmaster of the primary school,' Kat said in a stage whisper. 'Noah, I mean. Isobel runs Petalicious, the florist's shop on Green Lane.'

'I know,' Bethany assured her. 'I've heard all about them from Miss Lavender.'

Rita and Birdie chortled. 'Of course you have! Fancy you living with Eugenie. Bless you. You deserve a medal.'

'She's been very kind to me,' Bethany said quickly.

'Oh I'm sure she has. Heart of gold has Eugenie,' Rita agreed. 'Just... Bloody hell, imagine living with her! I'll bet all you've heard is Josiah this and Arabella that, Noah this and Ross that... Go on, admit it!'

Bethany hid a smile. It wouldn't do to give the Pennyfeather sisters ammunition. She remembered that much from all those years ago.

'How long are you planning on staying here, Bethany?' Kat asked, as if deciding that Bethany needed rescuing from her great aunts.

'Honestly, I haven't decided yet,' Bethany admitted. 'There's a lot to sort out. I had no idea that Whispering Willows was a horse sanctuary. It's been a bit of a shock finding that out.'

Not to mention the state of the house and stables, she thought ruefully. She dreaded to think how much work needed doing on that bulging stable block. When she'd ignored Ted's advice to make sure Joseph signed a proper tenancy agreement, insisting she would rather let him live there for free so long as she didn't have to bother with the place again, she'd not considered for a moment that he would let it fall into such disrepair. Would she have put things on a more formal footing if she had?

Probably not, she admitted to herself. She'd just been happy to put the whole place out of her mind. Ted had suggested a couple of times that she put it up for sale.

'Maybe Joseph would like first refusal?' he'd asked hesitantly, aware that she hated hearing her brother's name. 'You could at least ask him, via a solicitor's letter, but if he doesn't want to buy it, or can't, well then put it on the market and you'll never have to think about it again.'

'I don't have to think about it now,' she'd pointed out frostily, 'except when you bring it up.'

They hadn't talked about it again.

Why hadn't she sold it? Sometimes she'd wondered that and had told herself that selling it would mean having contact with Joseph, even if only through a solicitor. Deep down, though, she acknowledged that there was a part of her that didn't want to evict him or put him through the stress. She didn't need the money. Let things continue as they were.

Perhaps she'd been unwise. She should at least have sent someone round now and then to check on the place. But it had honestly never occurred to her that Joseph would neglect the house. It had been their mother's home and he'd loved his mother. And she knew he had a good job at the brewery and a large inheritance from Mother, so hadn't seen any reason why he couldn't afford to maintain Whispering Willows, especially as she'd never charged him a penny in rent.

More fool her. He'd obviously cared as little for the family home as he cared for her.

'Anyone sitting here?'

A couple—probably in their mid-forties—hovered hopefully over them, champagne flutes in hand. Bethany's eyebrows rose when she saw the man was wearing a dog collar. Was this the vicar who'd given the service at Joseph's graveside that day she'd arrived in Tuppenny Bridge? She hadn't seen him close up, but he looked vaguely familiar. He was a kindly looking, rather handsome man, with broad shoulders, tawny-coloured hair, and blue eyes.

The woman was svelte and elegant, with hazel eyes and dark hair. There was something about her that oozed class. Even before she opened her mouth Bethany had guessed that her accent would be nothing like the vicar's. He spoke in a local dialect, but as the woman thanked Kat and took a seat next to Rita, her cut glass tones confirmed that she came from different stock entirely.

'Isn't it splendid?' she asked, nodding over at Ethan and Cara Rochester, who were still embroiled in a discussion with Miss Lavender and Ross, and Sally and Rafferty who had just joined them. Clemmie, Bethany noted, had escaped, and was now chatting animatedly with a plump dark-haired woman with a silver fringe—perhaps her infamous Aunt Dolly. 'I can't believe how different Monk's Folly looks, can you? And how wonderful to have an art academy on our own doorstep.'

'Will you be having lessons then, Ava?' Kat asked.

Ava gave a careless shrug. 'Hadn't really thought about it.'

'You should, love,' the vicar said. 'You used to like painting, and it would do you good to take up a hobby.'

'I'll consider it,' she said, before taking a sip of champagne. 'Goodness, how rude of us! We haven't even introduced ourselves.' She leaned forward and beamed at Bethany. 'Ava Barrington. Although,' she added ruefully, 'most people round here just call me the vicar's wife.'

'Nothing wrong with that,' Birdie said. 'That's what you are.'

'Apparently so,' Ava said with a sigh. 'It will be on my gravestone, you know. "Here lies The Vicar's Wife. She made a lot of tea." I often imagine that years from now people will read that inscription and have no clue who or what I really was.'

'Well,' the vicar said, shaking his head in apparent bewilderment, 'I know who you are, and now so does everyone else here, so perhaps I'd better introduce *my*self.'

'Oh, darling, everyone knows who you are,' she assured him, poking his dog collar. 'This gives you away every time.'

'Well, yeah, I'm the vicar,' he said, 'but she doesn't know my name.'

'Does it matter?' Ava asked pointedly. 'Isn't "the vicar" enough?'

Bethany saw Rita and Birdie exchange knowing looks and thought an intervention was called for.

'I'm certainly not going to call you the vicar's wife,' she assured Ava. 'You're a person not an appendage. Pleased to meet you, Ava. I'm Bethany. And you are...?' She smiled encouragingly at the vicar, who was looking a bit subdued, as if he'd realised he'd somehow offended his wife but wasn't in the least bit sure how.

'Zach,' he said, realising she was speaking to him. 'Zach Barrington.'

'The vicar's wife's husband,' Birdie said, and cackled with glee, which somehow broke the tension as Ava started to laugh.

'I've heard so much about you,' she confided in Bethany. 'I've been dying to meet you at last. How are you finding it, living with Eugenie? Isn't she a darling? Well, perhaps a bit scary at first, but a darling when you get to know her.'

'She's been lovely,' Bethany agreed. 'Although, she always was lovely to me, even when I was a little girl.' She thought about the misunderstanding Miss Lavender had been labouring under about Joseph's behaviour, and how she'd ignored him all those years, and felt sad for him. At least, she realised with relief, Ava hadn't commiserated with her over her brother's death. 'It's not too bad staying at Lavender House. Better than staying at Whispering Willows anyway.'

'I can imagine,' Ava said sympathetically. 'I visited Joseph several times over the last few weeks of his life, and I was shocked at the state of that house. I don't know how Clive stood it there, especially when you think how lovely his own flat is above Stepping Stones. Isn't Clive wonderful? I don't know what Joseph would have done without him really, and now here he is helping you out with the horses. What a gentleman.'

She turned and saw Zach sitting disconsolately, his half-empty champagne glass clutched in his hand.

'Oh, darling, look at your face! How can I possibly resist?' She planted a kiss on his lips and Bethany was amused to see his eyes immediately light up. Clearly, Ava could wrap Zach around her little finger.

'Ava's father was Giles Wilson-Davies,' Kat said, a hint of mischief in her voice. She fixed Bethany with a challenging look.

Bethany turned to Ava in surprise. 'Oh, the explorer! How fabulous.'

She was aware of some distinct mumblings of surprise to her other side, and Ava's face positively radiated joy.

'Oh, you've heard of him!'

'Of course. He was an amazing personality, wasn't he? Very lively and jolly. I saw him interviewed on television several times. My ex-husband had his autobiography actually and we both read and enjoyed it. What an incredible life, and how he embraced it!'

Ava seemed lost for words. Her mouth opened and closed several times, and it was Zach's turn to reach out to her. He took her hand and squeezed it gently, and Bethany noticed that Ava squeezed his fingers in return.

'He did embrace life,' she said quietly. 'He made the most of every second. I was very lucky to have him as a father.' She dabbed at her eyes then shook her head. 'Goodness me, how ridiculous to be so emotional after all this time. It's the champagne, of course. Bluebell *would* insist I have another glass.' Her face brightened. 'Have you met Bluebell Fairfield? She's my dear friend, and she owns the Cutting it Fine hair salon in Market Place.'

'No, I haven't.' Bethany sensed that Ava wanted to change the subject and was happy to go along with it. 'Is it a good salon? I'm going to need a trim soon.'

'Oh, it's awfully good,' Ava assured her. 'Of course, it's not a top salon, but then it doesn't charge top salon prices, so there's that. Ooh, talk of the devil!'

A heavily made-up brunette of around Ava's age waved a half-empty glass of champagne over her friend's shoulder as she gazed at them all in obvious excitement.

'Have you seen the new art teacher?'

Ava shook her head. 'Eugenie said he'd been delayed. Why, has he arrived?'

'Has he arrived? O.M.G.' Bluebell rolled her eyes. 'I'll say he has, and all I can add to that is phwoar!'

Birdie's and Rita's eyes lit up in anticipation.

'We haven't seen him yet either,' Birdie admitted. 'Where is he, Bluebell?'

'Over there, talking to Clive and Ben,' Bluebell said, waving a hand in their vague direction. 'You can't miss him. Think Richard Armitage. Seriously.'

'Ooh, really?' Even Kat's head swivelled at that description, making Jonah give an indignant, 'Oy!'

Bethany naturally had to look, too. After all, she didn't want to be impolite, did she? Following the direction of Bluebell's pointed finger she quickly found the new art teacher, along with Clive and Ben. They seemed to be getting on famously.

'He's absolutely scrummy,' Ava admitted. 'Sorry, darling.'

'That's all right,' Zach said with good humour. 'I say the same about Jennifer Aniston.'

'He does, too,' Ava confided. 'Isn't it awful? Such a cliché.'

'I have no idea who Richard Armitage is,' Rita confessed, 'but if he looks like that I wouldn't say no.'

'Honestly, Rita, you're eighty-two years old,' Kat remarked.

'What's that got to do with anything? Never too old for a bit of eye candy,' her great aunt told her. 'If I ever stop looking you might as well have me put down.'

'What do you think, Bethany?' Birdie said, giving her an eager look. 'Nice, eh? His name's Callum Knight according to Eugenie. Knight in shining armour, eh?' She winked at Bethany. 'I think he's about fifty, so more your age group than ours sadly. Divorced. I'd get in there if I were you.'

'Hey, I saw him first,' Bluebell reminded them all.

'It's okay, I'm really not on the market for any man,' Bethany assured her. She turned back to the children, who were completely oblivious to the adult women's shameless behaviour as they munched on what was left of their buffet food.

Her stomach was fluttering and doing the weirdest things, and she felt peculiarly trembly. If she didn't know better she'd say she actually fancied that man! But seriously, she hadn't felt like that since... Oh God, it had been years. Decades. Why now? Why him?

And the worst thing was it wasn't Callum Knight who'd had that effect on her. Watching that little group of men chatting to each other, she'd barely noticed the new art teacher. No, all her attention had been on Clive. Clive, of all people!

This was all she bloody needed.

'Hey up, here's Jennifer with fresh supplies,' Jonah announced, and Zach sat up straight, looking eager.

'I see cake,' he said happily. 'I hope she's done a Victoria sandwich. They're my favourite cakes ever.'

'I'll tell Mrs Kensington that,' Ava said, her eyes twinkling mischievously. 'She keeps baking you coffee and walnut cakes because you once told her *they* were your favourite. She'll be devastated.'

'Well...' Zach pulled a face. 'Okay, let's just say they're joint favourites. Anyway, whatever Jennifer's made, I'm ready for a slice.'

They all watched as Jennifer set a couple of plates on the now half-empty buffet table. She exchanged a few words with one of the guests and laughed.

Kat sighed. 'Isn't it wonderful to see her out and about like this? I can't believe she's actually got a job after all those years hiding away. I'm so happy for her.'

'Me too,' Zach said. 'So good of Ross to hire her when she's been unemployed for so long. Many employers wouldn't, you know.'

Bluebell was craning her neck. 'Ooh, I think she's done a chocolate cake too. I'm going to nab myself some of that. Laters, kids!'

She hurried across the room towards the buffet table and Ava shook her head, laughing.

'What do you think, Bethany?' she asked. 'Shall we go over

and grab some cake before Bluebell demolishes the whole thing?'

Bethany nodded, but really she wasn't thinking about cake. Her mind was full of something else entirely. Something that had quite thrown her. Clive had turned away from the conversation with Ben and Callum and, despite trying to look casual as he sipped at his champagne, Bethany could see that his attention was elsewhere. He kept glancing across at Jennifer, and the look in his eyes told her that it wasn't the cake he was interested in.

Did Clive *like* Jennifer?

No one had mentioned it, which was unusual in this town, and Clive certainly hadn't breathed a word. But then, why would he, and to her of all people? He barely knew her.

She swallowed down her disappointment then chastised herself. What did it matter who Clive liked? He was nothing to her.

Even so...

She glanced around but it was obvious no one else had noticed, and since neither Ava nor Kat—nor, most tellingly the Pennyfeather sisters—had mentioned it, she could only assume that no one else had picked up on his feelings. Had Jennifer?

She knew she wasn't being fair to Clive, but resentment bubbled up inside her as thoughts of Glenn and Ted resurfaced. She'd never been enough for either of them and her old feelings of rejection and being second best attacked her all over again.

This, she reminded herself grimly, was why she didn't get involved with people. She wasn't meant to meet anyone special. She wasn't meant to have a home, a family. She'd been stupid to allow herself to dream, however briefly.

'Cake?' Ava repeated, eyeing her curiously.

Bethany forced a smile. 'Cake,' she agreed.

FOURTEEN

Bethany was in the middle of cooking breakfast in the grim kitchen at Whispering Willows again, despite Miss Lavender's assertion that she was quite mad, getting up so early each morning and heading out to prepare a meal for Clive, Maya, and Lennox.

'I'm sure they're fed quite adequately at home, dear. You don't have to make them breakfast, you know.'

Bethany felt, though, that it was the least she could do, given their hard work. More than that, it made her feel as if she were part of something. She hadn't really got involved with the sanctuary or its residents and didn't feel she'd be much use if she tried. It had been far too many years since she'd had anything to do with horses and that time in her life was in the past. But by being here each morning and feeding the little workforce, she'd felt as if she was contributing in some small way, other than taking Viva for a daily walk.

Part of the team. Part of the Whispering Willows family.

She mentally shook her head. Maya and Lennox had their own families and really didn't need her.

And Clive?

Since seeing him at Monk's Folly yesterday she'd realised it was possible that if Clive wanted to be part of any family, it was the Callaghans. Or had she overreacted? Imagined things because fear had taken over when she'd realised she was developing an attraction to him?

She wondered again about his background. She knew, of course, that he'd grown up in Scotland, but that was about it. Were his parents still alive? Did he have any brothers and sisters? Maybe Julian and Joseph had been his brothers in a way, and now he'd lost them both. She couldn't help but feel sad for him.

He'd never married, though. She knew that much because she'd asked. Miss Lavender had said there'd never been anyone as far as she was aware.

'Married to his job,' she'd said, nodding briskly. 'Some men are, you know. And if you ask me it's a good thing when they recognise it and avoid making a promise to another person that they can't possibly keep. At least Clive acknowledged that no woman could compete with his work and didn't inflict a life of misery on some poor wretch.'

Had he never been in love as a young man? Never wanted to be with anyone? Never wanted children?

Maybe some people just didn't want family life. It wasn't for everyone, she supposed. Look at her. And yet, if she stopped to think for a moment, she knew the familiar ache would return. It was an ache she tried hard not to dwell on, but it nagged away in the background and sometimes popped up unexpectedly, attacking with a ferocity that startled her. The ache for a home and a family. The need to belong somewhere— to someone.

It was too late for children, of course. She'd become reconciled to that years ago. Ted had been unable to father them, and she'd told him it didn't matter. They had each other, after all. Except, she knew they didn't really have each other. Ted had his own interests and she... Sometimes it seemed that she'd had nothing.

She tutted impatiently. What was the point of dwelling on all this now? She had a breakfast to cook, and the hungry hordes would be here any minute.

As if she'd conjured them up the door flew open and Maya and Lennox tumbled in, pink-cheeked and laughing. Bethany thought they were hardly typical teenagers. Weren't most people of their age supposed to be lying in bed until lunchtime? Didn't they grunt answers and refuse to engage in conversation with anyone over twenty? She thought she'd been rather lucky to find these two. Not that she had, of course. That was down to Clive, too. Everything came back to him in the end.

'Sit down,' she said, smiling at the two new arrivals as they greeted her cheerfully. Their early wariness of her seemed to have dissipated now that she fed them regularly. How easily they'd been bought! 'Breakfast is nearly ready.'

'Isn't Clive here yet?' Lennox asked. 'He's usually here before us.' He grinned at Maya. 'Finally, we beat him to it! Result!'

'I'm sure he won't be long,' Bethany said, placing mugs of tea on the table. 'Extra strong for you, Lennox and extra weak for you, Maya.'

'Perfect. Ooh, can you just give me—'

'Two sausages but four rashers of bacon,' Bethany finished for Maya with a grin. 'Already on it. And three rashers for you, Lennox, but three sausages.'

'You ought to get a job in a café,' Lennox said, clearly impressed. 'You're good at this.'

The door opened again, and Clive headed in, Viva tucked under one arm. Bethany's heart made a dangerous leap into her throat—at least, that's how it felt to her. Unfortunately, or perhaps not, he wasn't even looking at her. He was on his mobile phone and seemed distracted.

'Whereabouts is this? Oh yeah, I know where you mean. Sounds serious. Of course, I'll be straight there.'

He ended the call and shoved his phone in his jacket pocket before giving Bethany a brief smile as he put Viva down.

'Sorry, I won't be able to eat that today. I've got to go on a call out.'

'Sick animal?' Maya asked worriedly.

'It's a bit more than that,' he admitted. 'That was Jessie who works for the Upper Dales Equine Welfare Association. She's asked me if I can meet her at Grenley Hall over in Larkspur Common. There's an issue with some horses there and she says it's quite serious. Sorry, but looks like I'm going to be late today.'

His apology was addressed to Bethany, as if she was his actual boss or something. She wondered if that was because of the stupid comment she'd made at the opening of the art academy. She really hadn't meant it to sound that way and was mortified that he might think of her as some draconian employer, cracking the whip.

'Don't be daft, we can manage,' Maya said.

'Absolutely. Main thing is you sort them poor horses out,' Lennox said.

'Thanks. I'd better get off.'

'Haven't you even got time to wait while I put something in a sandwich to take with you?' Bethany asked.

Clive shook his head. 'Best not. I need to get to the horses as soon as I can.'

He turned to leave and impulsively Bethany asked, 'Could I come with you?'

Clive slowly turned round, and the look of incredulity on his face matched the ones on Maya's and Lennox's faces.

'Come with me?'

Bethany wondered why on earth she'd blurted out such a stupid question.

'Sorry. I suppose that's a no. You wouldn't want me in your way.'

Maya and Lennox stared at her, then at Clive, who rubbed the back of his head looking awkward.

'I—er—'

'Forget it,' Bethany said hastily. 'It was silly of me to suggest it. Besides, I've got breakfast to dish out for these two.'

'I can dish breakfast out,' Maya said immediately. 'And I can put some aside for you two as well, so you can have it when you get back. She can go with you, can't she, Clive?'

He looked cornered and Bethany felt sorry she'd ever mentioned it.

'Honestly, it doesn't matter,' she assured him. 'You go.'

He was eyeing her steadily and she could see he was trying to figure out why on earth she would want to go with him when she'd never shown any interest in the horses at Whispering Willows.

'Okay,' he said at last. 'But can you hurry? There's no time to lose.'

'You'll turn the grill off and make sure—' Bethany began, but Maya waved her hand.

'I'm not daft. Go on, get off. We'll have something ready for you to eat when you get home. And don't worry about Viva either. We'll see to her and leave her in the kitchen when we head off to school.'

Bethany grabbed her coat and followed Clive who was already striding towards his SUV. She couldn't help wondering what on earth had come over her. It had been an impulse request. For that moment, she'd just thought it would be good to see him in action as a vet, and to maybe be part of something useful.

Maybe she'd made a huge mistake, though, as Clive barely spoke a word to her as they drove out of Tuppenny Bridge towards the Hall.

. . .

Larkspur Common was a former estate village, which lay just a few miles from Tuppenny Bridge, although it could have been another world.

It lacked the charm of its closest town, and although it couldn't be expected to have as many facilities, given that it was a village, it seemed to Bethany that it had no facilities at all.

It consisted, as far as she could see, of a collection of uniform cottages and an old Methodist chapel which was clearly no longer in use.

There was a solitary bus shelter, and she noticed four or five bored looking youngsters sitting on the bench inside it, while an older man stood outside, clearly not keen to risk sharing the bench with them.

'Don't they even have a shop here any longer?' she asked. She was almost sure there used to be a general store of some sort. Come to think of it, she thought there'd been a fish and chip shop, too. She was certain some of her primary school friends had raved about the "Larkspur Chippy".

'Nope, that closed about five years ago,' Clive told her. 'They haven't got anything here now—except a bus which calls here on its way between Tuppenny Bridge and Lingham-on-Skimmer. Shame, isn't it?'

'So where's the Hall?' she enquired, unable to picture it in her mind's eye.

'Just past the village centre. Don't get too excited though. It's practically derelict. Trouble is, people have been grazing their horses in its grounds in recent years and it's not exactly lush grazing land. I got called out last year to one who'd got caught in barbed wire.' He pulled a face. 'That wasn't a pleasant job.'

'Do they have permission to graze their horses there?' Bethany asked, surprised.

'Definitely not. I've had discussions with the UDEWA and the local council before. The horses get moved on, but they're always replaced by more. We're monitoring the situation but it's not ideal. With the cost-of-living crisis people are struggling, and they use what's left of the grounds as free grazing, rather than renting suitable land. But some of the land really isn't great for horses. Anyway, let's see what we've got today, shall we?'

The car pulled up in a lay-by and Clive unclipped his seat belt.

'Ready?'

Bethany nodded, still not sure why she'd asked to join him. She hated the thought of seeing any animal neglected or hurt. She wasn't entirely sure she wanted to follow him at all.

Even so, she found herself climbing out of the car and trailing after Clive, who was heading for the nearby gate, where an old Land Rover was parked.

The Hall was shielded from the road by trees, so it was difficult to see much until they entered through the gate.

Bethany could tell immediately that the house, which had probably once been stunning, was now in a state of ruin. She also realised that, even though it was almost May, the grazing wasn't in any way adequate. She gazed round in dismay.

'Oh my God. All this junk!'

'I know. More like a municipal tip, isn't it? You can see what's been happening here.'

A short, dark-haired woman approached them and held out her hand to Clive.

'Good of you to come, Clive. Appreciate it. Anonymous caller tipped us off. Tipped being an appropriate word. Quite obvious there's been a lot of fly-tipping here.'

She gave a bleak smile as she waved an arm around the wild and overgrown garden.

'Any spare land and what do they do? Dump all their rubbish on it. Humans, eh? Makes you proud. I reckon our friendly anonymous caller was only here to dump their own rubbish. Mind you, at least they had the decency to make the call.' She eyed Bethany with obvious curiosity.

'Sorry,' Clive said hastily. 'Jessie, this is Bethany Marshall. She's the owner of Whispering Willows—Joseph's sister.'

Jessie brightened immediately.

'Oh! Joseph was an absolute star. We were so sorry to hear of his passing. Whispering Willows was a godsend to us on a few occasions.' She shook Bethany's hand then turned back to Clive. 'You'd better come and see for yourself. Poor little fella's in a pretty pickle.'

Nervously, Bethany followed Jessie and Clive through a tangle of bushes and trees at the end of the so-called garden, into what had once probably been a decent paddock but was now a patch of land overgrown with weeds, its fencing broken and its gate missing. Bethany gasped as she noticed a small, dejected strawberry roan mare standing by a pile of rubbish.

'Oh, poor wee thing!' Clive said. He wasn't looking at the roan, and Bethany suddenly realised that a chestnut foal was lying on its back between two old mattresses. Beside it, an old fridge lay on its side on top of one of the mattresses, along with a couple of torn black bin liners which had rubbish spilling out of them. Old tyres were dumped on the ground around the area, and someone had left a load of old bricks and tiles.

The foal didn't even attempt to get up. Not that it could have. For one thing it had become well and truly wedged in the gap between the mattresses, but for another even Bethany could see it wasn't well enough to manage it alone.

'The state of him! Oh, the poor little mite,' she cried.

Clive was already kneeling on the mattress at the side of the foal. 'Very emaciated. Seems like he's just given up trying.' He shook his head. 'Poor mum, keeping an eye on him. She must be frantic.' He turned compassionate eyes on the pony who was standing close by. 'Don't worry, sweetheart. We'll sort him out. We'll sort you both out.'

'Will he be okay?' Bethany asked anxiously. She felt sick as Jessie crouched beside the foal on the dirty torn mattress and soothed it with kind, gentle words.

'Look at the state of his hooves,' Clive said. 'Shockingly overgrown. Mind, his mum's no better. She must be having awful trouble hobbling around.'

'Should we try to get him on his feet?' Jessie asked, and Clive nodded.

'Aye. Let's see if we can manage it. He's not exactly going to be a heavy load,' he said with a sigh.

Bethany turned and cast her eye over the mare who was standing nearby. She clearly wasn't well nourished, her eyes were dull, and her ribs protruded. As Clive had pointed out, her hooves badly needed trimming, and it was obvious she hadn't been groomed for a long time. Yet she was obviously a pretty pony, with large eyes and a dish shaped face.

'She's a Welsh pony, isn't she?' she said, frowning.

Clive glanced over. 'Aye. Section A, I'd guess. Welsh Mountain. Look how small she is, bless her.'

Bethany agreed. The mare couldn't be more than 11.2 hands high.

Her gaze ranged around the paddock, and she noted that, even though there hadn't been any spells of heavy rain for over a week, much of this area was boggy and unsuitable for horses.

Even the drier half of the land was in poor condition. There were lots of nettles and worn tracks from tyres. It was evident that someone had driven a vehicle down the gravel drive at the side of the house and directly into the paddock. Which probably explained the broken fence and missing gates, she thought grimly. They'd come here specifically to dump their rubbish, and had gone ahead, despite knowing the danger it could pose to the mare and foal.

The roan threw up her head and stamped anxiously, and without thinking Bethany moved to comfort her.

'It's okay. Everything's going to be all right. We'll rescue your baby, don't worry.'

She stroked the mare's nose, murmuring soothing words to her.

'That's done it,' Clive announced, and she turned to see the foal standing beside the mattresses, its head hanging low as Clive checked him over.

'Oh lord, look at the state of him,' Jessie said.

'He's got a nasty wound to his hip, and pressure sores,' Clive said. 'I'd guess he's probably got a severe case of worms, too.'

The foal sank to his knees and Clive shook his head. 'He's not in good shape. Not at all. He needs warming up and while I'm doing that I'd suggest you ring Walter Harding over at East Midham. This young lad's going to need hospitalising and I just don't have the facilities at Stepping Stones.'

'Will do,' Jessie said, taking out her mobile phone. 'I'll be honest, I did try calling him before I called you, but his wife said he was out dealing with a difficult calving. Fingers crossed he'll be back now.'

Bethany wondered if Clive was offended that he was Jessie's second choice, but if he was he certainly didn't show it. He was far too busy trying to warm up the foal, and she turned back to the mare who was clearly worried about what was happening to her offspring.

No wonder the foal was emaciated, she thought. This poor mare was clearly undernourished herself, and it was no doubt affecting her milk production. The foal was very young and would still be feeding from her. Or trying to. Her blood boiled at the thought of them being left here in this awful place to slowly starve to death. Lack of money was no excuse. If the owners couldn't afford to keep them they should have done everything they could to find them a suitable home, not just abandon them in this wasteland. She hoped Jessie would track them down and make sure they were punished.

Bethany's eyes filled with tears as she looked at Clive. 'Is he going to be okay?'

'Honestly? I'm not sure. But he'll have the best chance with Walter Harding. Any luck, Jessie?' he asked as Jessie tucked her mobile back in her jacket pocket.

Jessie looked relieved. 'He's only just got home, poor thing, but he's coming straight over with a trailer.'

'Have you any idea who owns them?' Bethany asked, her voice choked with anger.

Jessie shook her head. 'Afraid not, but I wish to God I did. There's not even a fresh water source here. Just an old trough that seems to hold a bit of leftover rainwater. I wouldn't trust whoever owns them to refill it now the rainy spell seems to be over. My feeling is that these horses have been abandoned. They certainly wouldn't be the first.'

'I'd agree,' Clive said. 'I've seen way too much of this sort of thing in recent years.'

'Good thing is that the sale of this place has finally gone through,' Jessie told them. 'It's all getting flattened and they're building a housing estate here, so that will at least put an end to the grazing. If you can call it grazing.' She sighed. 'I'll put an abandonment notice on the gate. I don't expect anyone will come forward to claim them.'

They sat together while they waited for the other vet to arrive, all keeping close to the foal to make sure he stayed warm, while the mare tried to find a little grass to eat, periodically returning to check everything was okay.

'Why can't you treat them at Stepping Stones?' Bethany queried.

'I don't have stables there. But don't worry, Walter Harding has state of the art equine facilities. He does a lot of work with the racing stables over in East Midham, so these two will have the very best care. If anyone can get this wee laddie back on his feet it will be him.'

'Couldn't you build stables at Stepping Stones?' she asked. 'Or did you just not want to work with horses?'

'If I could have I would have,' Clive assured her. 'It was my dream to do so, but there simply wasn't the room.'

Bethany frowned. 'I barely remember visiting Stepping Stones when I was a child,' she admitted, 'but my recollection of it is that it had a large piece of land at its side that could have been used to build stables. Am I wrong?'

'No, you're not,' Clive told her. 'Unfortunately, my predecessor sold off that land a year before I arrived in Tuppenny Bridge. Did you not see the cottages next door to the veterinary practice? They weren't there in your day. Built on land that he sold to developers sadly.'

'Oh, of course.' Bethany groaned. 'You know, I thought there was something different about that area when I drove past. The cottages weren't there when I left. What a shame.'

'Joseph and I did talk about putting hospital facilities at Whispering Willows,' he admitted hesitantly. 'Sort of an outreach from Stepping Stones. We both thought it made great sense at the time. I'd pay rent and the sanctuary is such a short distance from the surgery...'

'So why didn't you?' Bethany asked, surprised. 'I'd have thought that made perfect sense.'

'I don't know.' Clive shook his head. 'He just went cold on the idea, and I never knew why. Although now I think about it, maybe it was to do with the fact that Whispering Willows was your property, not his. He'd have had to ask your permission.'

'Which would mean getting in touch with me,' she said bitterly. 'God forbid.'

Clive stroked the foal's face. 'Maybe there was another reason. I don't know. We'll never know now, will we? Anyway, the main thing is this wee one will soon be safe and sound at Harding's.'

'And what about afterwards?' Bethany blurted. 'When they're well enough to leave hospital, I mean. Of course they must come to Whispering Willows, mustn't they? They'll need love and care, and we can provide that. And we've a vet on hand, so what could be better?' She saw the surprise on Clive's face and blushed. 'Well, it makes sense, doesn't it? At least for now.'

'Are you sure?' His grey eyes fixed on hers. 'It's a big commitment. We've already got thirteen of them to rehome and—'

'Rehome?' Jessie gave her a look of dismay. 'Seriously?'

Nothing prepared Bethany for the guilt that immediately attacked her.

'Well, yes,' she said falteringly. 'But that won't be for some time. These ponies will be welcome, and they'll be given the chance to recover properly. We can think about what happens next later.'

'Perhaps,' Clive said slowly. 'Although... like I said, he's in a bad way,' he reminded her, gazing sadly at the foal who was lying beside him, his head on Clive's lap. 'Don't—don't get your hopes up, okay?'

Bethany's heart sank. He had to make it. He was so young. He didn't deserve to die like this because of some cruel, heartless owner.

'He should have a name,' she said sadly. 'I'll bet he's never had one and that's the least he deserves.'

Clive gave her a gentle smile. 'Any suggestions?'

'Something Welsh,' she said. 'How about Dylan Thomas?'

Jessie nodded. 'Grand name for a fine little fellow,' she said.

'What about his mum?' Clive said. 'I doubt we'll ever know her name, if she even has one. What would you like to call her?'

Bethany blanked. 'I don't know any other Welsh poets,' she admitted sheepishly. 'Not female ones anyway.'

'How about a songstress then,' Jessie suggested. 'Shirley Bassey.'

Bethany and Clive exchanged glances.

'Sounds good to me,' Clive said.

Bethany managed a smile. 'Okay. Shirley Bassey it is. Oh, I hope they both make it. They deserve so much more than they've had so far.'

Clive lifted his head. 'Do I hear a vehicle coming down the drive?'

'Not more fly tippers, I hope,' Bethany said furiously. 'If I get my hands on them they'll be sorry!'

'Easy, tiger.' He grinned at her, and part of her wished he wouldn't. His smile did funny things to her.

'Trailer,' Jessie said, relieved. 'Walter's here. He didn't waste any time.'

Walter Harding was a stocky man in his early forties. He greeted Clive and Jessie like old friends, so he'd clearly had dealings with them both before. He looked the foal over and agreed with Clive that he desperately needed hospitalising.

Bethany got to her feet and went over to soothe Shirley Bassey, who was clearly worried that someone else was now hovering over her foal. Jessie joined her, and as she slipped a halter on the pony they could hear the two vets muttering about an infected wound and surgery.

The trailer was roomy and well bedded with straw. The mare was safely tied up and given hay to eat while the foal lay quietly among the bedding as Jessie shut the door. Clive and Walter had a brief conversation and shook hands.

'You'll let me know how they're getting on?' Clive asked. 'If you're stuck we'd be happy to take them at Whispering Willows once they're fit to leave your place.'

'Really? I'd heard Joseph had passed away,' Walter said. 'I wondered what was happening to the residents there.'

'This is Bethany,' Clive explained, waving a hand in her direction. 'She's Joseph's sister and she owns the sanctuary. She's happy to offer them a temporary home where they can recuperate.'

Walter smiled at Bethany. 'Thank you. And don't worry, I'll keep you both informed.'

'Let's just hope they both make it,' Clive said. He shook his head. 'Sometimes I despair, Walter, I really do. He can't be more than four months old, poor wee soul. Oh, and by the way, his name's Dylan Thomas, and his mum's Shirley Bassey. For your records.'

He was so kind, she thought wistfully, and so genuinely concerned about animal welfare. Look how he'd given up his time to help at the sanctuary. She realised suddenly that she'd been a bit thoughtless, considering foisting another two animals on him without even asking if it was okay. Maybe it was time she gave him a hand. After all, they *were* her responsibility.

She thought about the state of the stables and hoped they had enough decent looseboxes. Barney needed to stay in overnight until the end of summer, and Chester was stabled in bad weather, which they'd had a lot of recently, so they were in the best part of the stabling. The mare and foal could share a loosebox, of course. She hoped they had another good one that didn't leak.

Although, once the animals had been properly treated by Walter Harding they could probably be turned out in one of the paddocks.

She'd done a tour of the Whispering Willows land and had been relieved to find that, at least, was well cared for, with decent grazing, no weeds, secure fencing, a good water supply and safe shelters.

The mare and foal would probably be fine outside, rugged

up. Drier, warmer weather was coming at last. She'd seen the forecast for May. It would work out anyway, one way or the other.

She thought maybe she ought to invest in getting the roof and doors of those stables repaired though, and she definitely needed to get a builder in to look at the bulging block. She couldn't leave it like that after all.

Not that she planned to stay of course. She wasn't entirely sure what she intended to do. But if—no, *when*—she sold Whispering Willows, having decent stables could only improve her chances of a quick sale, surely?

'Thanks for offering to take them,' Clive said ten minutes later, as they drove back towards Tuppenny Bridge, the horse box following behind them. 'It's very good of you, and I must admit, I'd like to be sure they're being well cared for once they leave Walter's place.'

'Don't be daft,' Bethany said. 'What else could I do? Those poor animals—I'll never forget the sight of that little foal lying there on his back, and his poor mum looking so ill and scared.'

'Aye, you see all sorts in this job,' Clive admitted. 'I was surprised you wanted to come to be honest. I didn't think you wanted anything to do with horses.'

'It's not that,' Bethany said quickly. 'Honestly, I've always loved them. It's just—just I suppose I had to harden my heart. Walking away from Pepper was so unbelievably painful. It devastated me to leave him behind.'

'Joseph told me that pony meant the world to you,' Clive said quietly.

Bethany folded her arms. 'Yet he still went ahead and sold him the minute I left, instead of taking care of him for me.'

Clive's hands, she noticed, tightened on the steering wheel. He really couldn't bear to hear a word against his precious friend, could he?

Nevertheless, Bethany needed to explain. 'After I left

Pepper and Poppins behind I never owned another animal. I suppose I just thought, well, maybe I didn't deserve to own one. I suppose I was punishing myself really for leaving them.'

'I expect...' Clive hesitated then ploughed on. 'I expect you had good reasons to go away, and that you did what you had to do. You can't go on punishing yourself forever.'

Bethany gave him a sideways glance, wondering exactly how much Clive knew. Just what had Joseph told him? Surely not the truth?

'Anyway,' she said at last, turning to gaze out of the window as they drew near to Tuppenny Bridge, 'I think maybe it's time I stopped avoiding animals. While I'm here I'd be happy to help at the stables. Obviously, I'm a bit out of practice but I'm sure you could teach me, and I'd do my best to meet your high standards.'

Oh God! Did that sound as if she was flirting with him?

He smiled. 'That's great. I'm sure any help would be appreciated. Although, it's Summer's high standards you should worry about. I'll be back at my real job in two weeks, remember?'

She'd completely forgotten and was dismayed at how her spirits sank.

The truth was, despite everything, she *had* started to think of them as a little family—her, Clive, Maya, and Lennox.

She'd forgotten Summer would be back from Australia soon. Forgotten that Maya and Lennox would revert to working weekends only. Forgotten that Clive would go back to work at Stepping Stones.

Forgotten, most of all, that when it came to home and family, for her it was only ever a temporary arrangement. How could she have been so stupid?

FIFTEEN

Maya and Lennox had headed off to school by the time Bethany and Clive returned to Whispering Willows. In the kitchen Maya had left a brief note telling Clive what jobs they'd done before leaving, explaining that she'd plated him and Bethany cooked breakfasts which were keeping warm in the oven, and adding that she hoped whatever emergency Clive had been dealing with all had gone well.

'They're such good kids,' Clive said, fussing an eager Viva who was clearly delighted they'd returned. He washed his hands then sat down to breakfast. 'I was really lucky to find them. Although, strictly speaking, Maya practically begged me. She's horse mad.'

'Doesn't she have her own pony?' Bethany asked, placing a plate of bread and butter on the table before sitting down opposite him.

He shook his head. 'No way they could afford it. Her dad's a farm labourer and doesn't earn much, and her mum works part time at Millican's. You know, the chippy in Market Square? Ponies are expensive to keep. That's why so many of them end up like the poor mare and foal at Larkspur Common.'

'I hope they'll be all right,' Bethany said with a shiver. She chewed some bacon, thinking about it. 'We'll need to get another loosebox ready, just in case. Is there one that doesn't leak? I mean, apart from the ones you use for Chester and Barney?'

'There are a couple of others that aren't too bad,' Clive said, slicing into his fried egg. 'I'll see what I can do.'

'I was thinking...' Bethany hesitated. 'I was thinking perhaps I ought to invest some money in doing up the stables. Just a new roof, new doors, that sort of thing. I mean, when I sell this place the outbuildings would be an asset, and the better condition they're in the more it will rack up the price, right?'

He frowned, not looking entirely sure. 'These days,' he said, sounding almost reluctant to put into words his thoughts on the matter, 'it's more likely that the stables would either be pulled down, or they'd be converted into something else. Round here there's a big demand for holiday accommodation and the stable block would make good holiday cottages. I'm not sure I'd waste my money.'

She stared at him in surprise. 'I thought you'd have been biting my hand off! I'm offering to improve the accommodation for the horses and you're saying not to bother?'

'There just doesn't seem much point,' he said heavily. 'If you were staying and planning to keep Whispering Willows running then of course I'd be all for it. But as it is...'

She prodded listlessly at a mushroom. 'I suppose you're right.'

'If you want to spend some money on the place, I'd start with the house. Anything you do to improve that will increase your profits. Having said that, there are no guarantees. After all, the new buyer might have plans to demolish everything. If they can get planning permission who knows what they'll put up in its place.'

'Demolish Whispering Willows?' Bethany frowned. 'Why

would they do that? It's a perfectly good house.' She gazed around her and sighed. 'Well, it used to be.'

'Aye, I'm sure it did, but it needs an awful lot of work doing to it. And like I said, there's a demand for holiday accommodation round here, and with all this land, who knows? It could even be turned into a holiday park of some sort. You can't really rule anything out.'

Bethany hadn't even considered that. She'd just imagined someone would buy Whispering Willows, spend a lot of money restoring it, and live in it forever more. She realised now that she'd been extremely naive.

'So you're saying I shouldn't spend any money on it at all?'

Clive shrugged. 'It's not for me to say, is it? Maybe you should discuss it with the estate agent. Get his views on the best thing to do.'

He sounded a bit off, like he had other things on his mind.

'Are you worried about Dylan Thomas?' she asked anxiously. 'You do think he'll make it, don't you?'

'Honestly? I'm not sure. All I can say is he's in good hands and he'll get the best care. I think Shirley has a much better chance, once she's been wormed and fed properly and had those hooves trimmed, but the little one's had a really rough time of it. I wouldn't like to say what his chances are.'

Bethany pushed her plate away, suddenly not hungry.

Clive sighed. 'Bethany, I feel there's something I should tell you. I haven't been entirely honest with you.'

'About the foal?'

'No.' Clive put down his knife and fork. Evidently his appetite had deserted him too. 'About Joseph.'

Her eyes narrowed. 'What about him?' she asked suspiciously, while her mind raced with all the possibilities. He could be about to tell her anything. Nothing much would surprise her about her brother.

'What I said about Pepper...'

Bethany's heart thudded. 'What about him?'

'I told you Joseph sold all the horses.'

'And he didn't?'

He rubbed his forehead, obviously dreading what he was about to tell her.

'He sold his horse and your father's horse,' he said slowly. 'But Pepper—Pepper was already dead. I'm so sorry.'

'Dead?' she whispered. She shook her head. 'But he wasn't even old. When I left he was, what, eleven, twelve? What did he die of?'

To her surprise Clive reached for her hand. 'There's no easy way to say this, Bethany. Your father shot him.'

Bethany stared at him. Thoughts of her beautiful bay pony with the black points and white blaze fluttered through her mind. His gentle nicker in a morning when she went to greet him; the way he always nudged her pockets, searching for mints; his dozens of quirks and habits that made him so special to her.

'Shot him?' She imagined her father aiming a gun at him and felt sick. Had he known? Had he been afraid? Had he thought of her, wondering why she hadn't come to save him? Her stomach heaved and she covered her mouth as tears filled her eyes.

'I'm so sorry. I didn't want to tell you, but you were so angry at Joseph for selling him, and you thought it proved he didn't care about you. I had to explain. You deserve the truth.'

'Explain what exactly? All you've told me is that my father shot Pepper. Why did he do that?'

Clive bit his lip as he studied the table for a moment.

'Don't lie to me again,' she warned him. 'I need to know what really happened.'

He nodded. 'I suppose you do, aye. The fact is, he shot Pepper because of you. Because you left home. He was furious when he found you'd gone, and since he couldn't find you to punish you...'

'He punished Pepper instead.' Tears rolled unchecked down her face. She could well believe it. It was just the sort of thing her father would have done. Why hadn't she considered that? What had she been thinking, leaving her beloved pony in that monster's hands? 'Joseph. Did he try—?'

'Unfortunately, Joseph was at work, but it seems your father deliberately timed it so he heard the shot just as he was arriving home. There was, shall we say, an altercation. The next day, Joseph sent Magnus and Jet to a livery stable a few miles away and instructed the owner to find new homes for them.'

'And Father allowed that?'

'He had no choice. He'd pushed Joseph way too far. Joseph threatened to call the police if he tried to stop him. After that there were no animals at Whispering Willows until after your father died. You see, that's when it started—Joseph wanting to make amends to horses for the things your father had done. I—I know what he was like. What was going on here when you were kids. Joseph couldn't always stop him then, but he did everything he could to make up for that when he was able.'

'He used to whip them,' Bethany said slowly, the memories she'd tried hard to bury bubbling up inside her. 'He never hit us. Never raised a finger to us. He didn't need to, you see. He knew what would hurt more. If we did something he didn't like, it was our horses he punished. We quickly learned to behave ourselves.'

'I know,' Clive said quietly. He squeezed her hand tightly. 'I'm so sorry.'

'Miss Lavender saw Joseph threaten Father with a horse whip,' she told him, tears spilling down her cheeks. 'She had no idea what had been going on. She just saw Father cowering in the stables and Joseph looming over him with the whip in his hand. She assumed Joseph was the bully, the bad one. That's when she stopped coming to Whispering Willows. When she stopped liking Joseph. She thought I'd left home because Joseph had done the same to me.' She shook her head slowly. 'All those years. I only found out after I moved into Lavender House. I put her straight of course, but it was too late by then.'

'So that's why she had nothing to do with Joseph!' Clive gasped. 'I never understood it. That man!' he added furiously. 'Correction, that *so-called man*, has a lot to answer for.'

'We *all* have a lot to answer for!' Bethany cried, wrenching her hand from his grasp. 'All this wretched family. Don't you see that? Oh, it's easy to just blame Father. He was a tyrant and a sadist, no question about it. He made Mother's life a misery, bullying her and cheating on her repeatedly. Hard to believe any other woman would want him, but somehow they seemed to fall for him. He tormented me and Joseph. He whipped the horses to punish us and keep us in line. So yes, blame Father. But the rest of us aren't innocent.'

Clive frowned. 'Meaning what?'

Bethany ran a hand through her hair, hardly able to keep up with the jumble of thoughts that were swirling around in her head.

'My mother was weak and feeble. She did nothing to stand up to him. Nothing to stand up for her children! This house belonged to her. The money was hers. Why didn't she throw him out? Why didn't she take a stand? Why did she sit back and let him do what he liked, making us all so miserable?'

'I suppose she—' Clive began, but Bethany wasn't in the mood to listen.

'And Joseph! He was older than me. A young man by the time Mother died. Why didn't he stand up to Father? Why didn't he do something?'

'He did!' Clive said, clearly indignant. 'I've just told you—'

'When it was too late! Oh, I'm not saying he didn't do *any*thing. I remember when he was about nineteen he plucked up the courage from somewhere and punched Father to stop him whipping Magnus. It was such a big deal. I couldn't believe he'd actually done it, and Father was so shocked he didn't touch the horses after that—at least, I always believed he didn't but then Miss Lavender told me what she saw so who knows... Joseph must have been protecting the horses as much as he could.'

'So?'

'It wasn't enough! He should have called the police or something. He was weak, just like Father. Oh yes,' she added angrily, 'Father was weak. That was our mistake, you see. We thought he was strong, but he wasn't. He was pathetic. Using a whip on a defenceless horse to punish his own children. Bullying a woman who had no way of standing up to him. That's not strength. That's cowardice, plain and simple.'

Clive said nothing. He was simply staring at her as if he had no words.

'And me,' she finished bitterly. 'I'm the worst of the lot. I should never, never have left those horses behind for that man to punish. I should have known what he'd do, but I just wanted to get away. I wanted to escape. I told myself things would be fine and that I needed to put myself first, but I was selfish. You see?'

She gazed at Clive through tear-filled eyes. 'That's my family for you. Weak, selfish, and thoroughly pathetic.'

Clive squeezed her hand. 'Aw, Bethany, that's just not true,' he said gently. 'When the so-called head of the house is a sadistic bully it's hard for children to stand up to him. You'd have grown up living in a dark shadow caused by his behaviour. Grown up in fear. No one can blame you or Joseph for not having the courage to stand up to him. You both did the best you could. Joseph by stopping your father from attacking the horses, and you by escaping. Putting yourself first. It's self-preservation and you shouldn't beat yourself up about it.'

'And our mother,' she said bitterly. 'Letting it happen when we were too young to do anything for ourselves then...'

Then leaving us alone with him forever.

She could still recall that awful day when she'd heard the news. It had been Joseph who broke it to her, sitting beside her on her bed, stroking her hair as she cried her little heart out. She'd wept bitterly, though even now Bethany wasn't certain if she'd been crying with grief or because she'd been afraid, already realising that she and Joseph would be even more at their father's mercy.

'It's going to be right, Beth,' he'd said, as he so often had before. 'Haven't I always told you that? It's all going to be right.'

'It must have hurt,' Clive said gently. He took her hand again. 'You were so young when she died.'

'Seven.'

'Joseph said she'd been ill for a long time,' he said. 'It must have been hard for you all.'

She stared at him. 'Did Joseph tell you *how* she died?'

The look in his eyes told her that he knew all too well.

She spluttered with anger and grief. 'So you know she wasn't ill! She took her own life! She abandoned us—left us to *him*. That's how much she loved us.'

'But she *was* ill,' Clive said. 'There are many different types of illness and mental illness is just one of them. She was clearly depressed and suffering or she would never have done what she did. I'm sure she loved you dearly, just as Joseph did.'

Bethany wiped her eyes and stared at him. 'Joseph? He said that did he?'

'Not in so many words, no,' Clive said. 'He didn't have to. I saw it in his eyes. I heard it in his voice every time he mentioned you.'

'He mentioned me a lot then?' she challenged.

Clive lowered his gaze. 'Not often,' he admitted eventually. 'But when he did—'

'Oh please!' Bethany gave a harsh laugh, ignoring the pressure from Clive's hand as he squeezed her own. 'When I left home I didn't hear a single word from Joseph. Not a word.'

'Did you leave an address?'

'Even Miss Lavender knew where to find me!' she snapped. 'She read the announcement of our wedding in the newspaper. If she could find me so easily, why couldn't Joseph? I wasn't exactly difficult to find once I met Ted. He was a high-profile businessman. It wouldn't have taken him long to find me, but he didn't bother.'

'Did *you* bother to write to *him*?' Clive asked pointedly.

She was about to blurt out that she hadn't, and that there'd been a very good reason for that. Instead, she said, 'This is getting us nowhere. Thank you for telling me what happened to Pepper. Do you happen to know what happened to him afterwards? After he died, I mean? Where did he go?'

Clive hesitated. 'I do actually. He was taken to the equine crematorium in Ravensbridge.'

'And his ashes?' she asked anxiously.

'I'm sorry, I have no idea what Joseph did with those,' he said, his eyes full of regret.

'I just hope they're not buried here,' she said sadly. 'I'd hate to think of him stuck here in this prison where he'd been treated so badly. Trapped here, just like my mother was. Like Joseph was all those years.'

'I'm sorry I can't be of more help. If it's any consolation, though, I doubt Joseph would have seen it like that. If Pepper *is* buried here he'd probably see it as him coming home to the place where he'd once been loved dearly by a young girl who'd thought the world of him.' He hesitated, frowning. 'Is that how you really see it? About Joseph, I mean. You think he was trapped here?'

'Don't you? He should have moved on. Left all those

horrible memories behind. Why did he stay? Guilt? Grief? I don't understand him.'

She seemed to have left Clive lost for words.

Bethany scraped back her chair and got to her feet, her vision blurry with tears. 'I'd better get to Lavender House,' she said. 'Can you scrape the plates when you're done, and I'll wash up when I come back later this afternoon. I—I have things to do.'

He didn't speak but merely nodded, his eyes never leaving her face. She blinked away her tears and saw the compassion in his face. It was way too much for her to deal with. It had been an emotional morning, and it wasn't even half over yet.

Yet again, her overriding thought was to escape from this house.

Whispering Willows held nothing but sadness for her.

SIXTEEN

Clive had endured a largely sleepless night. Thoughts of Bethany kept replaying in his mind.

She'd really thrown him yesterday. He'd been amazed when she'd asked to accompany him on his mission because he'd convinced himself that she had no real interest in horses any longer. Then her reaction to the mare and foal had really surprised him. He'd seen a side to her that he'd never have expected. A loving, compassionate side that had made him look at her differently.

But then, back at Whispering Willows, when he'd told her about Pepper... He thought about what she had said and how she had looked. It made his heart swell with grief and sorrow for her. She had so much sadness locked away inside of her. So much unresolved pain. She might try to put on a brave face, but he'd seen the truth in her eyes and he'd wanted to hold her and take all that anguish away. His response to her emotional outburst had taken him aback as his own protective instincts kicked in. It was all very new and odd.

He found himself pondering, too, on what she'd said about Joseph being trapped in his life in Whispering Willows.

Was she right? Clive had never thought of it that way before. He'd always taken it for granted that Joseph owned the house for a start. But more than that, he'd assumed that his friend had wanted to stay there because he loved it so much. It held memories of his mother, after all, and Joseph had clearly thought the world of her. He seemed to hold no bitterness towards her, the way Bethany did.

Even so, now that he thought about it, the house must also have held bad memories for him. He remembered what Bethany had told him about Miss Lavender catching Joseph threatening his father with the horse whip. Knowing Joseph the way he did, he knew he must have been pushed to desperation levels to do such a thing. Joseph wasn't a violent man. Clearly his father's reputation was well-deserved. He'd been a bully and a tyrant and had obviously given the occupants of Whispering Willows—human and equine—a life of misery.

Given that, why *had* Joseph stayed?

He'd had money. He could have left the house and gone anywhere. Started again. Made fresh memories and lived a life free of worry and responsibility.

Was Bethany right? Had he stayed out of guilt and grief? Grief was understandable, but what did Joseph have to feel guilty about? Because he couldn't save Pepper? Is that really why he'd decided to dedicate the rest of his life to rescuing other horses—because he was trying to make amends for the one who'd died on his watch?

He shouldn't have done that. It was a waste of his life. Clive was suddenly overwhelmed with sadness for his friend. Joseph had done a noble thing, but at what cost? He'd lived in poverty, watching the house crumble around his ears, all to keep his horses fed and well and loved. But he'd had no life of his own. No friends, other than Clive. No partner. No family. Even his own sister had abandoned him.

If Joseph had really sacrificed all those things out of guilt and grief... It didn't bear thinking about. Bethany was right. It would mean Joseph was just as trapped as his mother ever was.

As light began to creep through the slight gap in the curtains he sat up in bed and stared miserably at the duvet, not seeing it as another thought occurred to him.

Was he trapped, too?

He'd been so concerned about Joseph all this time, but was his life much better? Oh, he was better off financially than Joseph had been, and Stepping Stones was in far better condition than Whispering Willows. He'd spent good money modernising and decorating the flat above the surgery, condemning the old kitchen and bathroom to the tip and replacing shabby carpets with good quality wooden flooring. But was it a home when the only person who ever saw it was himself?

He had friends. Well, more like acquaintances if he was honest. Joseph had, of course, been his best friend for years, and then there'd been Julian...

Clive swallowed. He couldn't believe it had been almost fourteen years since Julian had passed away. Where had all that time gone? Fourteen years of grieving and wishing and hoping and feeling guilty because he shouldn't be feeling what he was feeling. What sort of friend had he been to Julian really?

Guilt and grief. Just like Joseph. Maybe it was true. Maybe he really was as trapped as Joseph had been, and for the same reasons.

'I can't be like him,' he murmured to himself, feeling a sudden panic at the thought. Why had he not seen it before? He was stuck. Unable to move on. Unable to love again. All the things he'd missed out on because he'd been too ashamed and afraid to speak up. Well, he couldn't let that continue because if he didn't speak up now he really would end up like Joseph.

He didn't want to spend his dying moments regretting all the chances he'd never taken. All the opportunities he'd missed.

All the wonderful things that might have been if he'd only dared to put his thoughts into words. He'd been a coward for far too long.

It was time to be brave.

Clive couldn't help wondering what on earth he was doing as he trudged up the path of Daisyfield Cottage. It was Saturday and Ben was doing the morning surgery at Stepping Stones, but Jamie might be in, and if he was what excuse would Clive have for visiting?

Come to that, what excuse did he have if Jennifer answered the door? He couldn't just blurt out the reason for his visit. It needed careful handling—a slow building up to telling her how he felt about her.

At the thought of that, he swallowed hard and almost turned round again. Only the thought of Joseph dying with a head full of regrets prevented him from running away as fast as he could from this ordeal.

But what if she laughed at him? Or was outraged?

What if she's been waiting for me to say something?

He ran a hand through his sandy-coloured hair, his mind whirling with confusion.

Maybe he should just wait a bit longer...

The front door flew open, and Jamie hurried out. He looked surprised to see Clive but didn't ask questions.

'Morning. I'm just on my way out but Mum's in. Go straight in, she won't mind.'

Dazed, Clive watched as he hurried down the path without showing the slightest interest in why Clive was there. Clearly he'd been overthinking this.

Despite Jamie telling him to go straight in, Clive knocked hesitantly on the slightly open door and called Jennifer's name.

He heard a slightly surprised response and then Jennifer appeared in the hallway.

'Oh, Clive!' She looked anxiously around, and he realised she wasn't anywhere near as calm as she'd been when they'd been in company, having dinner at the cottage.

'Sorry. Jamie said it was okay to come in.' Even though he hadn't obeyed the instruction, as he was still hovering on the doorstep.

Jennifer seemed to realise that as she shook her head impatiently and said, 'I'm so sorry. Of course, come in.'

He took a steadying breath and told himself to remain calm, then followed her through to the kitchen where she immediately put the kettle on.

'Tea? Coffee?'

'Tea would be grand, thank you.'

He didn't really want a drink at all and couldn't imagine being able to swallow a single mouthful of the stuff, but it was what people did, wasn't it? Drank tea and made polite conversation. Oh hell, he really wished he hadn't started this.

'So, what was it you came for?' Jennifer asked. Her blue eyes, so like Ben's, were wide and anxious. 'There's nothing wrong, is there?'

'Oh no, no.' He hurried to reassure her. 'Everything's fine.'

'And how's it going at Whispering Willows?' She busied herself making tea, her back to him now. 'Are you getting on well with Bethany? It was lovely to see her again after all this time. She seems very nice.'

'Aye, she's all right,' he admitted, surprised to find himself agreeing with her statement. Not so long ago he would have said she was a nightmare, but he'd softened his opinion of her lately. Like Lennox and Maya he was grateful that she'd turned up every morning to cook them a breakfast. She really didn't have to do that, but she'd insisted, and he had to admit it was good when they sat together in the kitchen, chatting and laughing with the two teenagers.

And then there was her reaction to the rescued foal and mare which, he couldn't deny, had touched him deeply. He hadn't expected her to get so emotionally involved after how adamant she'd been that she wanted rid of Whispering Willows. She'd even helped a bit with the mucking out and poo picking, which had amused Maya and Lennox no end.

And what she'd said about her mother and the rest of her family... She was obviously grieving deeply and carried a lot of emotional baggage. It had given him a new insight and understanding of her character and made him think she wasn't anything like the woman he'd assumed her to be after their first meeting.

'I really liked her. She's been through a lot,' Jennifer said, handing him a mug of tea.

'Haven't we all?' The words were out before he could stop them, and he could have kicked himself as she paled slightly and hurriedly turned away.

'Shall we go through to the living room?'

She led the way and he followed meekly, cursing himself for reminding her of everything she'd been through. The last thing he wanted was for her to start dwelling on the past again. She needed to look to the future and all its possibilities. They both did.

They sat on opposite sides of the living room, as if they couldn't put enough space between them. Clive sipped tea and cringed inwardly at the awkward silence. He just couldn't think how to start the conversation.

In the end, it was Jennifer who broke the impasse.

'So, what's brought you here, Clive?'

His stomach flipped with nerves, and he carefully put the mug on the occasional table next to his armchair.

'It's—it's a bit difficult to explain.' His mouth felt dry, even though he'd just sipped tea. He was finding it hard to formulate a sentence, never mind pour his heart out to her.

'That sounds ominous,' she said. 'It's not about Ben, is it? Don't tell me you're cutting his hours or laying him off?'

'Oh no, nothing like that! I really couldn't manage without him. He's an absolute godsend.'

She smiled. 'I'm so glad. He thinks the world of you, you know, and he's so happy at Stepping Stones.'

'I think the world of him, too,' Clive admitted. He rubbed his forehead, trying to muster up the courage to add, *and you.*

'You can tell me anything,' Jennifer said gently. 'I think I know what this is about anyway.'

His head shot up. 'You do?'

'Oh, Clive, you and I have known each other a long time. Did you really think I wouldn't know?'

He gulped, wishing there was whisky in his mug instead of tea. Although, if there had been he'd have drunk the lot by now.

'It's Joseph, isn't it?' she said kindly. 'I understand, I really do. He was your best friend, and it must be so hard being without him. Especially since you're at Whispering Willows every day, where his presence must be everywhere.'

Clive's shoulders sagged with relief. 'Oh.'

'I know exactly how you feel. It was so hard being at Monk's Folly. I could feel Julian and Leon everywhere. I thought the pain was going to crush me, I really did. It felt, sometimes, as if I were being buried alive. But you know, Clive, it will get better. It really will.' She nodded reassuringly at him, her eyes warm with sympathy. 'Especially when Summer gets back from Australia, and you can return to your own job. A break from Whispering Willows will do you the world of good and you'll start to move on at last. I promise you.'

Clive nodded dumbly, misery settling on him like a heavy cloak. How could he tell her now, after that little speech? He should go. This was getting him nowhere.

He was about to get to his feet when something stopped him. The thought of Joseph, lying in that hospice bed during those last days of his illness. Had he been thinking of the years he'd wasted? What had been going through his mind in his last hours of lucidity? Regret?

Clive couldn't let that happen to him.

'Talking of moving on...' It wasn't how he'd meant to start the conversation, but she'd given him an opening and he seized on it. 'Jennifer, I'm here to talk about us.'

He could see from the look of shock on her face that it was the last thing she'd expected.

'Us?' she asked faintly.

He nodded. No going back now. As that television quiz show host often said, he'd started so he'd finish.

'You know how I feel about you.'

Jennifer gripped the mug of tea and stared at him. 'Clive...'

'I love you,' he told her desperately. He had to say it out loud right there and then or he probably never would. 'I've always loved you. Ever since the day I met you, even though I tried so hard not to. But you know that, don't you?'

'Clive, don't.' Jennifer put down her mug of tea and faced him calmly. 'This is ridiculous. All these years! Surely you've put this nonsense behind you by now?'

He felt icy cold suddenly. 'Nonsense?'

She shook her head. 'Oh, come on, Clive. We've known each other years. Whatever you might have once felt for me you should be past all that now. We've barely spoken since—since Julian passed.'

'I didn't know what to say to you,' he admitted. 'I was lost. Drowning in my own grief for him, and so ashamed. He was one of my best friends. I should never have let my feelings for you develop, I know that.'

'It was all a long time ago,' she said firmly. 'I can't think about all that now, I really can't.'

He gave her an anguished look. 'But as you said, it was a long time ago. Time to move on, surely? We can't be alone and unhappy forever. Julian would understand, you know he would, and—'

'Oh, I'm quite sure he would,' she said bitterly. 'But do I get any say in this?'

His heart sank. She didn't feel the same, did she? If she did, surely she'd be glad that he'd brought the subject up? She looked as if she wished he'd never come here today. He was wishing the same thing.

She seemed to recognise the look of desolation on his face because her expression softened.

'Clive, you're a good man, you really are. The fact is, though, I don't love you. And if you really think about it, you'll see that you don't love me either. This is just something you've told yourself all these years to justify your feelings for me back then. To make it matter. The truth is, as you say, we've barely spoken for over fourteen years. That's not love. You're clinging to the past, and I don't blame you for it. I did the same thing, after all. I wallowed in it, in fact. But that's over now. I don't want to go back; I want to go forward. I have a job now, and a lovely new home where I'm very happy. My children are doing well and they're happy, too. I don't need a relationship—particularly one as complicated as it would be with you.'

'It doesn't have to be complicated,' he mumbled.

'You're Ben's employer. You were Julian's dear friend.' She shook her head. 'You know as well as I do it would be exceptionally complicated, and all packaged up in bad memories, pain, and unhappiness. I don't want that, and neither should you.'

'So what do I do now?' he asked desperately. 'Have you any idea how hard it's been to wait for you?'

'Not that hard,' she said. 'Be reasonable, Clive. If it had been that bad you'd have spoken to me long before now. I think you've just convinced yourself that your future lies with me, and now that Joseph's gone you're panicking. You don't want to end up with regrets, so you've decided it's time to act.'

Her perception staggered him and left him unable to answer her. She smiled.

'I can see I'm right. You're a good man and you deserve so much more. Your future's not with me, Clive. You need to look elsewhere and let this dream go.'

'Elsewhere?' He gave a short laugh. 'I don't think that's going to happen, do you?'

'I wouldn't be so sure.' She narrowed her eyes. 'How are...'

She shook her head, evidently having decided not to finish what she'd been about to say.

Clive watched her, puzzled. 'How are what?'

'It doesn't matter. Forget I said anything.'

'But you didn't say anything,' he pointed out. 'Not really. Yet you clearly want to, so why don't you just say it?'

'Maybe,' she said thoughtfully, 'because I don't know if you're ready to hear it.'

He heaved a sigh. 'The kind of day I'm having I might as well hear whatever you've got to say to me.'

She hesitated then nodded. 'Okay, well if you must know, I was just going to ask how you and Bethany are getting along.'

He gave her a puzzled look. 'Me and Bethany? What does that have to do with...' Suddenly realising what she was implying he stared at her in amazement. 'You can't be serious? Me and Bethany?'

'Well,' she said, picking up her mug and taking a sip of tea before shrugging slightly, 'I wouldn't rule it out. Oh, don't look so dumbfounded! It must have crossed your mind?'

When he continued to stare at her she said, 'Really, men are so oblivious at times. I saw her at the open day at Monk's Folly. She couldn't take her eyes off you, Clive. Did you really not notice?'

He opened and closed his mouth, too staggered to reply.

'I'll take that as a no,' she said, her eyes twinkling with amusement. 'If the Pennyfeather sisters were taking bets on it, I'd definitely place my money on you and her getting together. She looked quite the smitten kitten. Trust me. I notice these things.'

'B—Bethany?' He couldn't quite believe it. Of course it hadn't crossed his mind. Why would it? Then he thought about his reaction to her grief yesterday and how thoughts of her had kept him awake for most of the night. Remembering how he'd wanted to take her pain away and protect her from all those bad memories, he wondered if he was being completely honest with himself.

But he'd noticed nothing in Bethany's behaviour to indicate she was interested in him. Jennifer said she'd been watching him at Monk's Folly? Seriously?

His heart thudded at the thought, and he reached for his tea, stunned by this unexpected turn of events.

'I'm not the woman for you, Clive,' Jennifer said gently. 'But maybe Bethany is. Why don't you give her a chance?'

'She's—she's leaving Tuppenny Bridge soon,' he said, feeling dazed. 'There'd be no point.'

'Maybe she wouldn't leave if she had something worth staying for,' she pointed out. 'Isn't it worth exploring anyway? Better than wasting your life away dreaming of something that's never going to happen.'

Wow, that was brutal! But she had a point. Even so, *Bethany?*

He wasn't sure how to feel about it all. She was Joseph's sister, and given how she felt about him, that could be even more complicated than a romance with Julian's widow.

He gulped down the rest of his tea, not sure what to think any more.

'I can see you're a bit confused,' Jennifer said kindly. She got to her feet. 'Wait there. I've baked the most delicious red velvet cake and I'd love you to try it. You can give me your verdict while you think about what I've just said.'

He nodded and as she passed he said, 'Thank you.'

'For the cake or the advice?' She smiled. 'Either way, you're welcome. It's what old friends do, isn't it? And that's what we are. Old friends.'

He nodded.

Message received and understood.

SEVENTEEN

Bethany settled in the sagging armchair in the living room of Whispering Willows and lifted Viva onto her lap. The little dog seemed content to be with her, and her presence was a comfort to Bethany. It had been so many years since she'd owned a dog—not since Poppins, in fact. She hadn't realised how much she'd missed the companionship. Ted hadn't been a dog lover, so she hadn't pushed it, and deep down she'd thought maybe she didn't deserve to own another dog anyway. It would have felt disloyal, given that she'd abandoned Poppins the way she had. Now, she thought she'd quite like to have her own dog again one day. Maybe she'd even give Viva a home. If she ever found a home to give her, of course.

That, she decided firmly, was a problem for another day. She couldn't give any headspace right now to house hunting. She had enough on her mind trying to decide what to do with Whispering Willows. It was keeping her awake at night, worrying about the estate and the animals that lived on it. Not to mention Summer and, to a lesser extent, Maya and Lennox. They'd all miss the place, and Summer would be unemployed.

Then there was Clive and how he'd feel about it. She was

reluctant to admit it, but his opinion mattered to her. At the thought of him her stomach swished, and she bit her lip as she fondled Viva's ears.

'What a mess, eh?' she whispered to the little dog. 'How on earth did this happen? I didn't know I could still feel this way.'

Or *ever* feel this way come to that. How had someone like Clive proved to be such an attraction? He was nothing like Ted. Or Glenn. Maybe, she thought ruefully, that was the point. They'd been wealthy, middle-class men, with refined tastes and posh accents. Clive was so different to them. He was a working man, with a beautiful soft Scottish accent and down to earth tastes. She couldn't imagine him being an opera buff like Ted, or a connoisseur of fine wines like Glenn.

She thought about him soothing that poor little foal and her heart melted all over again. He'd been so good with him. She'd seen the compassion in his eyes, heard the kindness in his tone of voice, and it had moved her more than she cared to admit.

Was she getting confused about her feelings? Was it just because he was nothing like the two previous so-called loves of her life that she'd developed this attraction to him? Or because he was clearly a caring man and she felt she could trust him?

Was it—and she reluctantly had to admit it was a possibility —because he was a link to Joseph, and all those years with her brother she'd missed out on?

Whatever these feelings were, she didn't know how to handle them. Not that it mattered, because she'd seen him looking at Jennifer, and she was almost sure he had feelings for *her*. The last thing she needed was to fall in love with a man whose heart lay elsewhere. She should have learned that lesson by now, surely?

'I really need to pull myself together,' she told Viva, who eyed her sympathetically and licked her hand in a show of solidarity.

Bethany laughed. 'Thank you for that. I think I need to talk to someone who can actually talk back. No offence, Viva.'

She took out her mobile phone and called Helena, who answered within a couple of rings.

'Bethany! How are you, darling? Still up there knee deep in horse manure?'

Bethany felt a pang of guilt at the thought that she should be, really. Well, not knee deep, but helping in the stables. She'd done a bit of mucking out and some of the messier jobs, but she hadn't had much to do with the horses themselves. She wasn't sure why. Maybe it was because she'd been away from them so long she no longer felt sure of her competence. Or perhaps it was because she'd tried so hard to avoid getting emotionally attached to them. Having been around the foal she knew how easy it would be to do so, and where would that leave her? She had to be practical. She was selling Whispering Willows, and the horses would need a new home, so she couldn't form any sort of bond with them. She'd had to leave one pony behind who she'd loved dearly. She couldn't go through that again.

'More up to my eyes in bacon fat and cups of tea,' she said lightly. 'I'm here for six every morning so I can make the workers their breakfast.'

'Six o'clock!' Helena sounded appalled. 'Rather you than me. Can't they make their own breakfasts?'

'They could,' Bethany admitted. 'But I have to say, I quite enjoy it. It's my favourite time of the day actually. We all sit round the table and have breakfast together and chat.'

'Who's all?' Helena enquired.

'Me, Clive, Lennox and Maya—you know, the two teenagers I told you about.'

'Oh, how very cosy. Like a proper family,' Helena said. 'Do I take it you're getting quite attached to this new way of life then?'

'I never said that,' Bethany said quickly.

'Well, you did really. Just not in so many words.' Helena laughed. 'You sound in much better spirits anyway. Did you get Joseph's accounts sorted out at last?'

Bethany rolled her eyes. 'I'd hardly call them accounts. Scraps of paper just shoved in a drawer in no sort of date order at all. Honestly, I can't imagine how he managed. But yes, I've got them in order at last.' She paused. 'He really was in trouble, Hels. Financially, I mean. He'd gone through almost every penny he had. Mum's inheritance, his pension, the lot. I don't think Whispering Willows could have continued much longer anyway.'

'I'm guessing you're paying for the horses' keep now then.'

'Obviously. I can't touch Joseph's bank accounts yet, and I doubt there'll be much in them. Judging by the final demands I found he didn't have the funds to cover his debts. I've just paid the feed bill and the farrier. Aw, the farrier was lovely about it. He even said he'd be happy to waive what was outstanding, but of course I wouldn't hear of it. He's getting married soon and has two young children to support.'

'Ooh, sounds like you've had a good long chat with him.'

'He lives locally,' Bethany explained. 'He's marrying a woman I knew when she was a little girl. I vaguely remember him, too, although mostly because I remember his mother who was a complete dragon. Thankfully he's nothing like her.'

'Sounds like you're really settling in there,' Helena said, clearly surprised. 'Do I take it you're softening towards Tuppenny Bridge?'

'Not at all!' Bethany was quick to deny it. 'Nothing's changed. I'd just forgotten that some of the locals are nice people, that's all.'

'So when are you coming, er, home?'

Bethany sensed the hesitation on Helena's part when she referred to her house as 'home'. She wondered if Helena was deliberately drawing attention to the fact that it wasn't

Bethany's home after all, and maybe she should be thinking of moving out permanently. Or was she just being over-sensitive because the thought had been preying on her own mind for so long?

'I've got a lot to sort out here,' she admitted. 'Things are so complicated, what with the financial situation and the state of the place. Then there are the horses...'

'Have you still not found new owners for them?' Helena asked. 'Surely you've managed to rehome at least some of them by now?'

Ashamed, Bethany had to admit she hadn't even tried. 'I'm thinking of doing some repairs to the stables,' she said.

'You're *what*? What on earth for?'

'You should see the state of them. One's bulging so much it looks like it's been filled to the brim with something and is about to burst. Anyway, it will add value to the property, won't it?'

'I wouldn't have thought so,' Helena advised. 'To be honest, in this day and age people are more likely to pull stables down or convert them into something else. You'd probably be wasting your money.'

'That's what Clive said,' Bethany said, trying not to feel put out.

'Sounds wise. Actually, I'm surprised he didn't encourage you to go ahead, given how he's hoping you'll keep the sanctuary open. What ulterior motive has he got for telling you not to invest, do you think?'

'He's not like that,' Bethany insisted, with perhaps a little more haste than she should have. 'He was just being honest with me. I said I might spend some cash on doing up the house and he pointed out that it might be pulled down and replaced with a holiday park or something.'

'Sounds to me like he's just trying to frighten you into not selling,' Helena said. 'You're not falling for that trick, are you?'

'He's not trying to trick me,' Bethany said patiently.

'Besides, he's got a point when I think about it. It's such a beautiful area round here. The Dales are so popular, and it wouldn't be unreasonable to assume that Whispering Willows could end up in the hands of a leisure company. It could, best case scenario, become a small hotel or guest house. There's no guarantee it wouldn't be demolished though, and then anything could happen. Log cabins, caravans, tents—'

'Yurts. Shepherd's huts. Tree houses. I've seen it all. Glamping. They could make a fortune. Hey, there's an idea!' Helena sounded enthusiastic. 'Scrap that. Cut out the middle man and do it yourself. Pull the house down and turn Whispering Willows into a glamping and holiday site. You could make a fortune.'

'The people of this town would never forgive me,' Bethany said darkly.

'What do you care? You won't be there!' Helena laughed. 'Don't you even want to consider it?'

Bethany nibbled her thumbnail, thinking of Clive's face if she suggested such a thing.

'I've still got to find homes for the horses and ponies and donkeys, whether I do up the house or not,' she mused, ignoring Helena's suggestion.

'Have you rung round any local sanctuaries? There must be some in the area who'd be willing to take them?'

'Clive says it's a real problem at the moment. The cost-of-living crisis is having a massive effect and there are so many abandoned horses. Oh, Hels, you should have seen what I saw.'

She proceeded to tell her friend all about Shirley Bassey and Dylan Thomas.

'Honestly, it would have broken your heart. Clive can't guarantee the little one will make it, but I've told them all if he does he's welcome to recover here, along with his mum of course.'

'Are you insane? You're supposed to be getting rid of all those animals, not adding to them!'

'I know, I know. But he just looked so sweet, and so vulnerable. He's had such a rotten start in life, and I wanted to be able to help him.'

'And what happens when you sell the stables around his sweet little ears? Where does he go then? You've not thought this through,' Helena reproved her.

'At least it will buy him some time until we can find him another home.'

'You can't even find homes for the thirteen you already have! What on earth's wrong with you? Can't this vet keep them, or at least find homes for them when they're discharged from his care?'

'I told you, it's not that easy. I'm sure if Clive had equine facilities he'd have kept them however long it took, but this other vet... Well, who knows how long he'll be willing to care for them? He might discharge them early to make room for new patients. Did I tell you that Joseph was considering turning part of Whispering Willows into an equine hospital for Clive? Stepping Stones is only a little way along the road from here and it would have been an ideal solution. It's a shame it never happened.'

'But if it had you'd then have had the problem of what to do with that when you sell the place,' Helena pointed out. She sounded puzzled. 'And then you'd have had more guilt.'

'I suppose you're right. It just seems a shame. Clive's so good with horses and I'm sure his equine unit would be much better than this Walter chap's.'

She narrowed her eyes as she heard muffled laughter down the phone. 'Are you laughing at me?'

'Sorry, but have you any idea how many times you've mentioned Clive? Is there something you're not telling me, Beth?'

Bethany's face burned with embarrassment. 'Don't be ridiculous! Like what?'

'Oh, I don't know. But it sounds to me like this Clive fellow has made quite an impression on you.'

'He's just a decent man,' Bethany protested. 'Not many of those about.'

'If he's that decent he'll find homes for those horses and you can leave it in his capable hands,' Helena said firmly. 'Come home, Bethany. Let other people deal with this headache. You've got other things to do, like finding your own place for a start.'

Bethany pushed away the scintillating thought that had popped into her head when Helena mentioned Clive's 'capable hands'.

'They're my responsibility,' she said stubbornly. 'Joseph might not have given much thought to their future, but I must. I won't let them down.'

Not after she'd let Pepper down so badly. She couldn't have any more animal suffering on her conscience.

'So I guess you'll be stuck in Tuppenny Bridge for quite some time then,' Helena said with a sigh. 'Maybe you should think about making some improvements to the house after all. You can't stay with Miss Lavender forever.'

'You're right,' Bethany agreed. 'I can't. Maybe I *will* invest a bit of money in the place. If I can increase its value it might put off leisure companies looking for a quick buck. In fact,' she considered, feeling a sudden twist of excitement in her stomach, 'I should turn it back into a proper family home. That would encourage buyers who actually want to live in it.'

'Are you sure about this?' Helena sounded doubtful.

'Absolutely sure,' Bethany told her, feeling happier than she'd felt for a long time. 'I'm going to transform Whispering Willows and make sure it becomes a lovely family home again.

The way it used to be when Grandma and Grandad owned it before *he* destroyed it.'

'And then what?'

Bethany swallowed. 'And then I'll sell it and get out of Tuppenny Bridge as fast as I can. What else?'

'Hmm.' Helena didn't sound convinced, and Bethany didn't blame her.

For the first time ever she'd had a sudden thought that perhaps she'd quite like to stay around here. Not in Whispering Willows, but in Tuppenny Bridge. Just for a while at least.

She couldn't think where that idea had come from and dismissed it immediately. It was never going to happen.

EIGHTEEN

Bethany had decided to shake things up a little and make a continental breakfast instead of a traditional English one. She'd filled the table with plates of bagels and cream cheese, Danish pastries, croissants, pancakes, syrup, fruit, yoghurts, and dishes of jam and butter.

She wasn't sure how Clive, Maya and Lennox would react to the change of menu, but Miss Lavender had certainly been surprised earlier that morning.

'My goodness. You certainly know how to feed them,' she'd said, blinking bleary eyes at Bethany and stifling a yawn.

Bethany, who'd been packing the food into a bag, gave her a guilty look. It was only half past five and Miss Lavender should have been tucked up in bed, fast asleep.

'Did I wake you?' she asked worriedly.

Miss Lavender shrugged and forced a smile. 'Don't worry about it. It's not your fault. I'm a very light sleeper. Not like Boycott and Trueman. Those two are still fast asleep in my room. Wonderful guard dogs they make, I must say.'

'I'm so sorry. I really did try to be quiet.' Bethany sighed. 'Maybe these early mornings aren't working.'

'Well,' Miss Lavender said hesitantly. 'I didn't like to say anything, but I do think you're putting yourself out for nothing. I'm sure the workforce can sort their own breakfast out. I don't think Joseph or Summer ever provided food, and why should they? Can you think of any other job where the staff has breakfast cooked for them by their employer?'

'I'm not their employer, though,' Bethany pointed out. 'They're all volunteers, coming in every morning to help me out. I owe them. The least I can do is provide them with a good meal to start the day.'

'So that's what this is about?' Miss Lavender waved a hand in the direction of the kitchen worktop which was covered in supplies. 'Guilt?'

'Gratitude,' Bethany said firmly. 'It's my way of saying thank you for all their hard work.'

'But you've just said yourself the early mornings aren't working,' Miss Lavender pointed out.

'I meant they're not working for us. You and me. It's not fair on you that, as quiet as I try to be, I'm disturbing your sleep every day. I think it's time I moved out of here.'

Miss Lavender's eyes widened. 'Move out? But where would you go?'

Bethany took a deep breath. 'Back to Whispering Willows. I've made a decision, Miss Lavender. I'm going to restore the place to the sort of family home it was in my grandparents' day.'

'Restore it? In what way?'

Bethany smiled. She'd been thinking about it all night and had lots of ideas. 'The first thing I'll do is hire a team of cleaners to get it super clean. It's too big for me to do it by myself. Then I'll hire decorators to get rid of all the old wallpaper and freshen the rooms up one by one. New flooring and carpets. New doors. New window furnishings. New furniture. I'll have to get someone in to check the roof's okay, naturally, and also the wiring. I'm not sure about the boiler and central heating system.

It all seems fine to me, but I don't know how old it is. I'll ask Clive. I'm sure he'll know.'

Miss Lavender shook her head, looking dazed. 'That's a huge undertaking, Bethany. Are you sure you've thought this through? It will be an expensive job, you know.'

'I know that. But the thing is, as it stands now, the chances are that Whispering Willows could be bought by investors who'll either turn the land into a holiday park or maybe develop it for housing. Either way, there's a chance the house itself could be demolished. I really don't want that to happen. I want it to be a family home again, and the best way to ensure that happens is to make it attractive to families.'

'I suppose you have a point,' Miss Lavender mused. 'It would be a shame to see the house pulled down, and of course, we wouldn't want a holiday park or anything like that in its place. But even so, it's a lot of work and a lot of money. Are you certain?'

'I'll get my money back on it,' Bethany assured her. 'After all, the house cost me nothing to buy, so anything I sell it for is pure profit. Even if I spend every penny I'm likely to make from the sale it hasn't left me out of pocket, has it?'

'No.' Miss Lavender eyed her thoughtfully. 'And you intend to live there while all this is going on?'

Bethany smiled. 'For one thing, I think I've outstayed my welcome here. No—' she held up her hand as the old lady began to protest. 'I know you'll say I haven't but look at us now. I've made you lose sleep and it's not the first time, I'm sure. Besides, it will be something for me to do. I'm quite looking forward to it.'

Standing in the kitchen of Whispering Willows, she realised that was true. She glanced down at the table which was groaning under the weight of all that delicious looking food and felt something akin to satisfaction. She *was* looking forward to it. It was something to keep her occupied, and much more fulfilling than simply turning up every morning with breakfast. It would fill her empty days and make her feel useful. Now that she'd made the decision she was determined to give it everything she had. Finally, after what felt like forever, Bethany had a purpose.

'This,' she said aloud, 'is the start of a new phase of my life.'

In fact, maybe this was what she was destined to do. Maybe that was why she'd never been able to settle anywhere. Maybe her future lay in buying up old houses, doing them up and selling them on. She could live in them while she did them up, she wouldn't mind that. Perhaps her fate was never to really have a permanent home, but a series of temporary ones that she could improve ready for their forever owners.

She wasn't a forever kind of person, and maybe it was time she accepted that.

Unexpectedly, her heart sank at the thought, but before she could question why, the door opened and Clive walked in.

Her poor confused heart, which had only just settled in the pit of her stomach, seemed to leap up into her throat, and she realised her frown had changed into a wide smile at the sight of him.

It didn't take her long to see, though, that he wasn't smiling in return. In fact, he looked quite stricken as he stared at her, seeming not to notice the table of food despite her best efforts to make it look as attractive as possible.

'Bethany...'

His eyes were sad. Bethany swallowed.

'What is it? What's happened?'

He moved slowly towards her, and as he neared he put his hands on her arms and held her as he looked steadily into her eyes. At any other time she'd have been thrilled at his actions, but now she was afraid. This wasn't like Clive.

'It's the wee man,' he told her softly. 'I called Walter this morning. I'm so sorry. He didn't make it.'

Tears sprang into her eyes. 'No! He can't have... It's not possible. You said Walter was a good vet. You said he had excellent equine facilities.'

'Aye, and so he does. But I also told you that Dylan had been through an ordeal, and he wasn't in good shape. We always knew this might happen, didn't we? He just wasn't strong enough to recover.'

Bethany pulled away from him and sank into one of the chairs. It felt as if a dam was breaking within her. She covered her face with her hands as she began to cry—softly at first, but with increasing emotion and intensity.

'I know, I know,' he soothed.

He sat down in the chair next to hers and put his arm around her shoulders, and after a moment's hesitation she leaned against him and continued to cry. She wasn't sure any longer what she was crying for. The thought of that poor little foal and the terrible state he'd been in when they'd found him broke her heart. She could only imagine how distressed Shirley must be, grieving for her lost child.

At the thought of that she cried even harder. Images of Joseph, the brother she'd loved and lost, swirled through her mind. Pepper, the pony she'd adored who'd been so brutally shot by her father. Her mother, unable to face another day on the same planet as her husband, even though it meant abandoning her two children.

It all seemed too much to bear.

Dimly she became aware that Clive had moved his chair closer to hers, and that both his arms were wrapped around her now. As she sobbed into his chest she heard him murmuring something to her but couldn't make out what he was saying. He was stroking her hair. She couldn't remember the last time someone had done that. Perhaps it had been her mother all those years ago, comforting her after she'd fallen, or after her father had said something nasty to her.

She didn't think Ted had ever stroked her hair, but then, she'd never needed soothing when she'd been with him. She hadn't felt anything deeply enough. Life had been very much on an even keel with Ted. No real lows, but no great highs either.

She hadn't even cried much when Ted and Helena told her they were in love. Yet here she was, breaking her heart over some little foal she'd only seen once.

Clive must think she was pathetic.

She pulled away from him slightly, feeling foolish, but the feeling dissipated when she saw the grief in his own eyes. He understood. He wasn't judging her at all.

'I'm so sorry, Bethany,' he said gently. He pushed a strand of hair away from her eyes then his gaze returned to her.

She stared tearfully back at him and saw him swallow hard.

Something stirred within her. Something so unexpectedly powerful it momentarily pushed all thoughts of Dylan away.

For a moment it was as if they were both frozen, and yet she could feel a magnetic pull towards him that she fought hard to resist. It crossed her mind that, just possibly, he was feeling it too.

Then the back door opened, and Lennox said, 'Aye, aye. What's going on here then?'

'Shut up, Len!' Maya sounded cross and Bethany realised Clive had jerked away from her and was on his feet.

She wiped her eyes and turned to face the two teenagers, who were watching them with obvious curiosity and—in Lennox's case at least—wry amusement.

'We've had some bad news,' Clive told them gently. 'That foal we told you about? I'm sad to say he didn't make it.'

Their faces changed instantly.

'Aw, no! I'm so sorry,' Maya said. 'Poor little Dylan Thomas.'

'That's crap,' Lennox admitted. 'I hope they find the person who owned him. They want locking up. I'd throw away the key an' all.'

Maya hurried over to Bethany and put an arm around her shoulders.

'Are you all right?' she asked, the concern in her voice almost making Bethany cry again.

She forced a smile. 'I will be. It's one of those things we have to get used to, isn't it? We can't save them all, as much as we want to.'

But oh, she wished she could! Was that, she wondered with a start, how Joseph had felt? Had seeing what happened to Pepper made him feel as wretched as she now felt? Maybe, for the first time, she could understand why he devoted all his time to saving horses and ponies in need.

What would happen to the residents of Whispering Willows when the sanctuary closed? She was absolutely determined that, however long it took, she would find each and every one of them good homes.

'I've made you a continental breakfast,' she announced, keen to restore some sense of normality to the morning. 'I hope you like it.'

'What's a continental breakfast when it's at home?' Lennox demanded.

Maya nodded at the table. 'That,' she said bluntly.

He wrinkled his nose. 'Are them cakes or summat?' he asked, eyeing the Danish pastries and croissants suspiciously. 'For *breakfast*?'

Maya sighed. 'You're such a peasant, Lennox Turner. It will do you good to try something a bit different. I'm up for it anyway. Thanks, Bethany.'

She squeezed Bethany's shoulder.

'I'll put the kettle on, shall I?'

As she moved away to make tea, Lennox settled himself at the table and, after a slight hesitation, reached for a Danish.

Clive gave Bethany a weak smile and she returned it.

'Sit down,' she told him. 'Eat.'

She doubted that he was hungry, though. She certainly seemed to have lost her appetite and, judging by the way he seemed in no hurry to sample any of the food on offer, she thought he was feeling the same.

Was it only down to the loss of the foal?

She had to admit that, for her at least, it was also about the shocking intensity of her feelings when Clive had been sitting with her moments earlier. She'd known she liked him. She liked him a lot. But now...

As he sat opposite her, staring quietly at his plate and picking listlessly at a bagel, she couldn't help wondering if he'd shared the experience with her, or if she was imagining the whole thing.

It wouldn't be the first time she'd been wrong about such things after all.

NINETEEN

When Miss Lavender invited you somewhere you went, whether you really wanted to or not. Bethany's mother had told her that years ago, and she remembered her words when the old lady telephoned her a couple of days later at Whispering Willows.

'Lunch at The Crafty Cook Café,' she said without preamble. 'Shall we say twelve thirty?'

Bethany blinked, confused. She was, after all, still living at Lavender House, and they'd be seeing each other that evening and having their evening meal together. Why would they need to meet for lunch?

'I'm a bit busy,' she mumbled uncertainly.

'Really? Doing what?'

Bethany glanced down at the laptop that was sitting on the table. She'd been going through a list of local tradespeople, checking out their websites, and reading the reviews. She needed an electrician to examine the wiring, and a roofer to check the roofing on both the house and the stable block, and decorators and carpet fitters and...

She sighed inwardly at the thought of all the upheaval that

lay ahead, before reminding herself that it would be worth it in the end. At least she didn't have to worry about the boiler and central heating system. Clive had assured her that Joseph had dealt with all that about three years ago when the old boiler packed in. She'd thought guiltily that, really, that should have been her responsibility. Whispering Willows was her house even then, and Joseph had never asked her to do anything to it. She supposed he'd had to deal with quite a few running costs and repairs that she'd never considered before.

'Finding people to do the work on this place,' she admitted.

'Nothing that can't be put off for a couple of hours,' Miss Lavender said. 'Besides, there might be someone who can recommend various tradespeople to you.'

Bethany's suspicions increased immediately. 'What do you mean, *someone*? Who else is coming to this lunch?'

'Don't sound so worried,' Miss Lavender said brightly. 'The Pennyfeather girls have been giving crochet lessons in the café this morning, as they do every week, and we always meet for lunch afterwards. Katherine usually joins us, and er, there might be a couple of others.'

At first, Bethany was too busy coming to terms with the Pennyfeathers being addressed as 'girls' to notice Miss Lavender's evasive tone, and it was only after she agreed to be at the café for twelve thirty and had ended the call that she realised the old lady had been decidedly shifty.

She had a funny feeling she was about to face a mass interrogation.

Reaching the top of the stairs in The Crafty Cook Café, Bethany quickly realised the place was busy. Miss Lavender, who had met her outside, assured her it was always like this.

'Puts the Market Café in the shade,' she said cheerfully. 'And no wonder really. Such a marvellous idea to have a craft café, and of course, the food is excellent here. I can recommend the coffee and walnut if you're undecided which cake to choose.'

'We'll see.'

Bethany gazed around the café, which was above the craft shop that had previously been Pennyfeather's Wool Shop. Apparently this had once been a two-bedroomed flat, though you'd never know that now. It was surprisingly light and spacious, with areas set aside for crafting groups. Two walls were entirely taken up with shelving units housing craft supplies, and there was a friendly, informal vibe to the place that Bethany liked immediately.

Rita and Birdie called out to them before she'd even had the chance to look around for an empty table.

'Eugenie, we're over here.'

Miss Lavender rolled her eyes. 'Well of course you are. You're always there after your crochet lesson. Honestly, those two,' she said, shaking her head. 'Come on, dear. Let's join them.'

'Over there?' Bethany frowned as she saw the Pennyfeathers were still sitting in the craft corner, which was sectioned off from the rest of the café. 'Shouldn't we move into the main eating area?'

'Normally we would, but today's a special day.' Miss Lavender beamed and marched over to the sisters, leaving Bethany no real choice but to follow her.

Rita and Birdie were wearing bright yellow dresses today, along with patchwork crocheted waistcoats and—Bethany was a little taken aback to discover—lime green Crocs. Rita's dyed red hair was pinned up with a variety of purple hairpins, while Birdie was sporting a shocking pink hairband.

'We're so glad you could make it,' Birdie told her, ushering her into the seat next to hers. 'I'm so excited. As if she thought she could get away with it!'

'Who would get away with what?' Bethany asked nervously.

'Ooh, here's Dolly and Clemmie!' Rita stuck her arm in the air and waved wildly. 'Coo-ee! Over here!'

Bethany looked round, half relieved to see Clemmie and half wondering what on earth was going on. Behind Clemmie was the woman Bethany had seen her talking to at the open day at the art academy—presumably her Aunt Dolly. They were both carrying bunches of white helium balloons.

Bethany peered closely at the writing on the balloons.

'Kat's Hen Party,' she read aloud, then turned to the others. 'A hen party in here?'

'Tell me about it.' Dolly flung herself into a seat and shrugged. 'I mean, have you ever heard the like? I'm guessing we're not going to be squirting cream on some hunky naked man this afternoon.'

'Certainly not!' Miss Lavender gave her a stony look. 'This is going to be an elegant affair. Daisy has promised us a proper afternoon tea with sandwiches, cakes, and scones.'

Dolly pulled a face. 'Sounds fab,' she said flatly.

'So is this it then?' Clemmie asked, after greeting Bethany and formally introducing her to Dolly. 'Just us?'

Miss Lavender glanced at her watch. 'Sally promised to keep Kat busy downstairs until twenty to one. We've still got five minutes. The others should be here by then.'

'So Kat doesn't know about this?' Bethany asked, amused.

'Nope. She's going to love it, isn't she?' Dolly said with a grin, her voice dripping with sarcasm.

'It's her own fault,' Birdie said. 'She should have had a hen night like anyone else. Fancy saying no. Jonah had a stag, you know. Oh yes! They all went on a pub crawl to Ravensbridge. Did Clive tell you?'

Bethany felt rather hot. 'Why would he tell me?' she asked.

'Just wondered, that's all.'

'So, Clive went on this stag night, too?'

Rita grinned. 'Of course he did! Someone's got to keep them all on the straight and narrow and it's usually Clive. And that's even though they had a former barrister and a vicar with them.' She cackled with glee. 'Rafferty and Zach had a good time, apparently. Not so sure Sally and Ava were impressed.'

'It does men good to let their hair down once in a while,' Miss Lavender said with a sniff. 'They're strange creatures. They need the company of other men now and then, where they can revert to their primitive behaviours. It must be quite a strain on them, having to be civilised the whole time while in the presence of their female partners.'

The others exchanged amused glances and Rita and Birdie nudged each other mischievously.

'I'd quite like to be a fly on the wall when they revert to their primitive behaviours, wouldn't you, Birdie?' Rita said with a smirk.

'You're not kidding,' Birdie replied with feeling.

'I can assure you it wouldn't be a sight worth seeing,' Miss Lavender said firmly. 'And I'd thank you to remember that you're in decent company right now, so please behave with dignity for once in your lives.'

'That's them told,' Dolly muttered. 'Mind you, never thought the old bird would call me "decent company". I feel quite special now.'

Bethany hid a smile, feeling the anxiety that had knotted her stomach begin to ease. Maybe she wasn't going to be interrogated after all.

'It's such a shame Summer's still away,' Clemmie said with a sigh. 'And she'll miss the wedding, too.'

'I should think she's having far too good a time in Australia to care about that,' Dolly told her. 'I don't suppose there's any chance of a glass of wine in here?'

'Daisy doesn't have a licence,' Birdie said glumly. 'It's tea or lemonade this afternoon.'

'Whose bright idea was it to have this do here?' Dolly queried.

All eyes turned to Miss Lavender who glared at them.

'If Katherine had wanted a raucous, alcohol-fuelled party, she'd have gone on a pub crawl like her intended. Clearly, she has more refined tastes. An afternoon tea will please her enormously, I have no doubt.'

'Well, we're about to find out,' Dolly said, nodding towards the staircase, where Sally and Kat were hovering, with Ava and Bluebell just behind them.

Daisy hurried over and led them to the table where the others were waiting.

Everyone yelled, 'Surprise!' and Dolly thrust the balloons into Kat's hand.

She shook her head. 'Well I never. Who'd have thought it?'

Miss Lavender beamed at her. 'Welcome to your hen party, Katherine. We've got an absolutely splendid afternoon tea booked for us. Daisy has promised us a feast, haven't you, Daisy?'

Daisy grinned. 'Just as you requested, Miss Lavender. Would you like me to start serving? Is everyone here?'

'I think so,' Miss Lavender mused, looking round. 'Oh no, Jennifer and Isobel haven't arrived yet, although Isobel wasn't certain she could make it. But Jennifer did say she'd be here, so we should maybe give it another five minutes, and in the meantime I'll just, er, powder my nose.'

She hurried off and Daisy, after giving them all knowing smiles, headed back to the counter.

Dolly nudged Kat. 'So go on then, admit it. You knew, didn't you?'

Kat looked shamefaced. 'Sorry, but yes I did. Don't tell Eugenie, though. I'd hate to spoil it for her.'

'Who told you?' Rita demanded mournfully.

Bluebell shrugged. 'How was I to know Kat was still downstairs in the shop? We were a bit late, so we thought she'd be safely upstairs out of the way.'

'Even so,' Ava said, 'you didn't have to burst into the shop shouting that there'd better be champagne at this bloody hen party, did you?'

'There isn't,' Birdie said bluntly. 'Champagne, I mean. Daisy hasn't got a licence. It's tea or lemonade.'

'Bloody hell,' Bluebell said. She glanced at her watch. 'I'll give it half an hour.'

'Charming,' Kat said, laughing. 'Anyway, I'd already guessed, so it's not your fault. It was pretty obvious that Sally was trying to distract me, and besides, did you really think I wouldn't notice all of you going upstairs to the café? Never take up spying. You'd have a very short and rather disastrous career.'

'Sorry it's just an afternoon tea,' Sally said, her eyes crinkling with sympathy. 'Once Miss Lavender had made up her mind there was no shifting her.'

'What do you mean, *just* an afternoon tea?' Kat said cheerfully. 'Have you seen Daisy's afternoon teas? I've been dying to try one for ages, but I couldn't justify the calories. I'm looking forward to this.'

'Well, my stomach thinks my throat's been cut, so I hope they get on a move on and bring us some grub,' Dolly grumbled. 'Never mind waiting for Isobel and Jennifer. With any luck, Isobel won't bother, and we all know Jennifer won't turn up. She never does.'

'Sorry to have kept you waiting.'

They all turned to see Jennifer hovering by the craft table, looking a bit awkward. Bethany wondered if the others felt as embarrassed as she did. There was no way Jennifer hadn't heard Dolly's words.

Dolly clearly knew that, too. She went a bit pink and said, 'Sorry, love. I wasn't—'

Jennifer slid into a seat between Bethany and Sally. 'It's okay. I know my track record in these things isn't very good, but I'm trying to change that. Thank you all for inviting me. I'm looking forward to one of Daisy's teas, and I wouldn't miss this for the world.' She turned to Kat. 'I'm so happy for you. You know that, don't you? And I just know Leon would be happy for you, too.'

Kat's smile looked forced, even to Bethany. Clearly, mention of her dearly departed boyfriend still hurt, all these years later. Miss Lavender had told her all about Kat's relationship with Jennifer's eldest son, and how devastated poor Kat had been when he was killed in a car accident. Apparently, he'd been Jonah's best friend, too. It was, she thought, quite lovely that the two of them had finally got together.

It occurred to her suddenly that it was a similar situation to Clive and Jennifer. After all, Jennifer had lost Julian, and Clive had been his best friend. Was that why Clive had feelings for her? Were those feelings reciprocated? Hard to compete with a couple who had so much history between them, yet she wasn't certain. Maybe she'd imagined the looks Clive had been giving Jennifer at Monk's Folly. They'd had enough time to get together if they wanted to, after all. She just wasn't sure what to think.

'I'm really glad you came, Jennifer,' Kat said, reaching across Sally for Jennifer's hand. 'It wouldn't be the same without you. And you'll definitely be at the wedding?'

'Try and stop me,' Jennifer said with a smile.

'Oh cripes,' Kat said, looking at Bethany suddenly. 'I'm so sorry! I meant to drop you an invitation off just after the open day at Monk's Folly, and I completely forgot. Bethany, would you like to come to the wedding? You'd be very welcome.'

Bethany looked around, surprised. Everyone was smiling and clearly waiting for her answer.

'Me? Are you sure?'

Kat laughed. 'Of course I'm sure. Me and Jonah would love to have you there.'

Bethany wondered where those tears that were suddenly pricking her eyes had come from. 'Well, thank you very much. I'd love to be there.'

'Great. Uh-oh, we have another guest,' Kat murmured, and Bethany looked round to see Miss Lavender returning arm in arm with a woman of around Kat's age.

Judging by the mumblings and uncomfortable shuffling around the table, Bethany guessed that whoever this person was she wasn't exactly popular.

'Bethany,' Miss Lavender said, 'let me introduce you to my great niece-in-law, Isobel. She's Noah's wife.'

Isobel, an attractive woman with blonde hair and blue eyes, gave her a brief nod and squeezed into a spare seat between Miss Lavender and a dismayed looking Rita.

'Pleased to meet you,' Bethany said, aware of the awkward silence that had suddenly fallen. 'I've heard a lot about you.' As Isobel raised an eyebrow, she added quickly, 'From Miss Lavender. You run Petalicious, don't you?'

'That's right.' Isobel gave her a cool smile. 'And you're Bethany, Joseph's sister. I've heard a lot about you too.'

Somehow, the way she said it made it sound less than complimentary, and Bethany couldn't help but wonder what, exactly, she'd heard.

Daisy hurried over. 'Time for tea?' she enquired. 'Only, I've got a bit of a lull on at the moment so now would be a good time to bring it all over, if that's okay with you.'

Everyone agreed that they were ready for some food, so Daisy took their orders for preferred sandwich fillings and cake. Kat offered to help but Daisy refused, and the others were adamant that Kat was the star of the show, and waiting on tables was definitely out of the question.

Sally and Dolly went with Daisy instead, while Bluebell rummaged in a bag and drew out a sash, which proclaimed, 'Bride-to-Be' and draped it over a blushing Kat.

Ava placed a tiara on her head and said, 'There you are. Now you look the part.'

When afternoon tea was served there were delighted murmurings of appreciation. Bethany had to admit it really did look amazing. Everyone had three types of elegant finger sandwiches, a slice each of a rather yummy cheese and tomato quiche, salad, coleslaw, crisps, a scone with jam and cream, and their choice of cake. Bethany had taken Miss Lavender's advice and gone for the coffee and walnut, but others had chosen Victoria sandwich, lemon sponge, or a rather gorgeous looking caramel and white chocolate cake which made her regret not looking more closely at the options.

Everyone tucked in and soon there was a contented silence, broken only by the occasional crunching of crisps and delighted murmurings of appreciation for how tasty the food was.

'So how was Zach after the stag do?' Dolly asked Ava, even though her cheeks were bulging with food. 'Had a good time, so I heard.'

Ava rolled her eyes but waited until she'd swallowed the quiche she'd been eating before replying. 'He probably did, but he can't remember much about it,' she confessed.

'Same as Rafferty,' Sally said, amusement in her eyes. 'Never seen him in such a state. I had to call in reinforcements cos there was no way he could do his shift in the pub the next day.'

'I must say,' Miss Lavender said, dabbing the corner of her mouth with a napkin, 'I'm rather disappointed in our vicar. It's just not done for a man of the cloth to behave so badly in public.'

'He's still a human being, Eugenie,' Ava reminded her. 'He's a vicar, not a saint, and he's entitled to a bit of fun now and then. It's not as if he makes a habit of it.'

'Even so...'

'Oh, Eugenie, don't be such a killjoy,' Birdie said. 'Let him have his bit of fun. You said yourself, men need to let the primitive side of themselves out now and then. Even those with a direct line to the Almighty are entitled to a few beers on a stag night.'

'Hmm.' Miss Lavender pursed her lips but said nothing more.

Bluebell's eyes twinkled with mischief. 'Did your Noah go on this stag night then, Isobel?'

Miss Lavender looked smug as Isobel said primly, 'Certainly not. I'm afraid he had far too much work on to spare the time. Besides, it's not his sort of thing.'

Bluebell and Ava exchanged glances.

'More a tea and cake sort of chap, is he?'

'Hardly.' Isobel, who so far had refrained from eating anything but her salad, gave her a superior look. 'He doesn't eat cake. We're both very health conscious.'

'Really?' Bluebell shrugged. 'Funny, cos it looks like he's enjoying a big slab of that caramel and white chocolate cake to me.'

Isobel's eyes widened and they all turned to follow Bluebell's gaze. Bethany hadn't seen Noah before, so she had no idea what to expect. Vaguely, she'd imagined he would look like his half-brother, Ross, but the man she saw sitting at the corner table, tucking into the cake with a blissful look on his face, was nothing like him. Slender and a bit pale, he had tawny coloured hair and was clean-shaven. As she watched, Daisy approached him and placed a pot of tea in front of him, along with a cup and saucer.

She said something to him, and he rewarded her with a

wide smile, which she returned before heading back to the counter.

'I don't believe this,' Isobel said. 'What's he doing here?'

'Well, it's his lunch hour,' Miss Lavender reminded her.

'So why isn't he at the school? He usually has his lunch there.'

Dolly frowned. 'Does it matter? So he fancied a bit of cake for a change. So what?'

Isobel was already pushing back her chair.

'Oh, Isobel, leave him alone,' Kat said, as everyone murmured their agreement.

'It's supposed to be Kat's hen party,' Clemmie reminded her, rather timidly. 'Let's not worry about what Noah's doing.'

'I'm not worried,' Isobel said tightly. 'Just curious, that's all. He's always telling me I've got to watch my weight, and there he is tucking into cake.' She looked round at them all, clearly aware that she'd surprised them. She nodded. 'Oh yes, he's a stickler for it. I was just worried when I saw him, because if he saw this,' she gestured to the three-tier cake stand in front of her, 'he'd assume I intended to eat it all and he wouldn't be pleased.'

'I'm sure that's not the case,' Miss Lavender said uncertainly. 'He wouldn't mind you eating cake, especially on a special occasion like this one.'

'Wouldn't he?' Isobel said darkly.

They all exchanged glances and Bethany could see that the others were as uncomfortable as she was. What sort of control freak was this Noah? If he was bullying Isobel about the food she consumed that set off alarm bells in her mind. Not to mention the hypocrisy of him happily tucking into that rich cake with no hesitation.

'Well, he hasn't noticed us since we're hidden away over here in the craft area,' Ava said gently, 'and if he does notice and come over we'll make it quite clear that you've eaten nothing but salad. Although,' she added sympathetically, 'I do wish you'd just eat whatever you wanted. A little of what you fancy does you good.'

'So they say,' Birdie said with glee.

'Chance would be a fine thing,' Rita added.

For once, Miss Lavender didn't reprimand them. She nibbled thoughtfully on her scone, looking quite subdued.

There was a distinct change in atmosphere around the table, as everyone ate and drank quietly. It was as if they were all suddenly afraid of drawing attention to the table, Bethany realised. The atmosphere only picked up again when Noah got up, waved a thank you to Daisy, and headed back downstairs.

It was as if they all heaved a collective sigh of relief, and it was only then that Bethany noticed that Isobel had cleared her plate. Evidently, she'd decided what was good for the goose was good for the gander, and about time too.

'I dunno. Marriage, who needs it?' Dolly said with a sigh. 'Are you sure you want to go ahead with this, Kat?'

'Dolly!' Clemmie said, horrified. 'Of course she does. She loves Jonah, don't you, Kat?'

'He's my world,' Kat confirmed dreamily. 'Jonah and the kids. They're all I need in my life, and everything I ever wanted.' She blinked suddenly and gave Jennifer an apologetic look. 'I'm sorry, Jennifer. I didn't mean—'

Jennifer smiled. 'Kat, darling, you don't have to apologise. I'm just so pleased that you and Jonah found each other after all these years. And I'm so pleased for Hattie and Tommy, too. It's wonderful that you're a little family. There's nothing more important.'

Isobel gave Bethany a smile that she thought was probably meant to convey sympathy, but actually made her nervous. For some reason the knot in her stomach returned.

'Such a shame that you have no family left,' Isobel said. 'And how sad that you didn't get to see Joseph before he passed away. I suppose you didn't get the message in time?'

Bethany swallowed. 'I didn't, no. Helena tried to get in touch with me, but I'd turned my phone off, so...'

'Helena.' Isobel sipped her tea, watching her thoughtfully. 'Is it true that she was married to your ex-husband? That she stole him from you, in fact?'

Bethany wondered how that nugget of information had got round. Fleetingly she wondered if Clive had mentioned it to anyone but dismissed the idea immediately. The only other person who knew was Miss Lavender, but surely she wouldn't gossip about her?

Isobel sat up straight. 'I'm so sorry. Was it supposed to be a secret?'

'Not really,' Bethany said flatly. 'I just didn't realise it was public knowledge.'

'Birdie, Rita, you really should have warned me,' Isobel said, giving the Pennyfeather sisters a disapproving look.

Rita and Birdie looked shamefaced as Miss Lavender glared at them. Bethany guessed that she'd confided in the Pennyfeathers, and they hadn't exactly been discreet.

As Miss Lavender turned to her, clearly embarrassed, Bethany said, 'It's all right. Like I said, it's no secret.'

'But you're still friends with the woman?' Bluebell had evidently decided that, if it was no secret, the floodgates had opened, and she was free to gather more information. 'How come?'

Bethany pushed away her half-eaten scone. 'Helena and I have been best friends since we were at St Egbert's together,' she explained. 'I wasn't about to lose her friendship because she'd fallen in love with my husband. Not when our marriage was already over in all but name when they began seeing each other.'

'He sounds like a proper ratbag,' Dolly said. 'And she doesn't sound much better.'

'They're good people,' Bethany said hotly. 'I mean, Ted was

a good man. They felt terrible that they developed feelings for each other, but it was all okay. They were far better suited to each other than Ted and I ever were.'

'So you forgave her, just like that?'

Bethany shrugged. 'More or less. It took a bit of getting used to,' she admitted, 'but I cared about them both and didn't want to lose them, any more than they wanted to lose me. Ted and I stayed friends until the end, and Helena... I don't know what I'd have done without her when I left Tuppenny Bridge. She was the one I moved in with, you see. When I walked out of Whispering Willows I went to her. She put a roof over my head until my inheritance came through. I owed her so much, and when Ted died I felt I could be there for her and maybe give something back.'

'I think she'd taken quite enough from you,' Birdie said indignantly. 'You're more forgiving than I'd ever be.'

'I think maybe Bethany understands the frailties of human nature very well,' Ava said kindly. 'I'm quite sure it wasn't as black and white as it appears.'

'I think you've been married to a vicar too long,' Dolly said. 'I'd have walloped the pair of them.'

'I'd have thought that, after going through all that, you'd have wanted to come home,' Isobel said. 'To Joseph, and to Whispering Willows.'

'Well,' Miss Lavender said briskly, 'she didn't. Would anyone like more tea?'

'But why not?' Isobel persisted. 'You were away an awfully long time. What happened between the two of you?'

Bethany's face burned. This was the inquisition she'd feared was coming. She should have known better than to give them an opening. They'd never let her get away now.

'I'd rather not talk about it,' she said, wondering how she could make her escape.

'Is it true that Whispering Willows is actually yours?' Isobel asked. 'How come you let Joseph live there if the two of you weren't speaking?'

'Isobel,' Jennifer said firmly, 'it's really none of our business.'

She smiled at Bethany, who gave her a grateful look in return.

'I'm just taking an interest in my neighbour,' Isobel said. She gazed around the table and laughed. 'Let's face it, I'm not the only one who's dying to ask. She stayed away from her own brother for well over thirty years and didn't even come back for his funeral, so clearly something massive happened between them. Don't tell me I'm the only one who's curious because I know for a fact you've all been speculating.' She nudged Rita. 'It wouldn't surprise me if you weren't taking bets on it.'

'Bets?' Bethany croaked.

'Oh yes, didn't you know? The Pennyfeathers are renowned for taking bets on events in this town. Sally and Rafferty's relationship, Ben and Summer's relationship...' She smirked at Clemmie. 'Ross's relationship with the lovely interior designer he was working with earlier this year.'

Clemmie went pink.

'The father of Kat's baby,' Isobel continued. 'Not,' she added, 'that anyone's been paid on that one. Still a mystery to us all, isn't it, Kat?'

Kat gave her a cool look. 'Not to me,' she said. 'And not to Jonah either. That's all that matters.'

'Quite right,' Rita said. 'Nobody's business but your own.'

'Yet you still took bets on it,' Isobel pointed out. 'How lovely to do that to your own great-niece.'

Rita and Birdie looked indignant, and Sally said, 'They don't mean any harm. We all know that.' She smiled at the sisters. 'Hearts of gold, the pair of them.'

'Anyway, it's Eugenie who's in charge,' Birdie said, clearly having no compunction about dropping her friend in it. 'And we give all the profits to the Tuppenny Bridge Fund, don't we, Eugenie?'

Miss Lavender looked as if she'd like to throttle Birdie.

'If no one wants more tea I think perhaps we should get the bill,' she said, looking round for Daisy with some desperation.

'So,' Isobel said, as if she hadn't heard Miss Lavender's suggestion, 'what was it? What did Joseph do that was so bad you left him to rot in that place all those years? Or was it,' she added, a gleam in her eyes, 'that it was *you* who did something unforgivable? Come on, Bethany. We're all friends here. No judgement, right, ladies?'

Bethany felt trapped. Her face was burning, and she had no idea what to say. She'd been dreading this moment. They were all going to start demanding answers now, she could feel it. Why had she agreed to come here? The minute she'd realised it was a gathering she should have had the sense to leave.

'Right.' Bluebell threw her napkin on the table. 'I've had enough of this. It's supposed to be a pleasant little afternoon tea to celebrate Kat's marriage to Jonah, not the bloody Inquisition.'

'It's nobody's business but Bethany's,' Ava added firmly. 'I suggest we change the subject.'

Everyone nodded in agreement and Clemmie leaned across the table and squeezed Bethany's hand. 'Whatever went on, we're all really glad you're back in Tuppenny Bridge now, aren't we?'

There was a resounding agreement to her question and Bethany felt a lump in her throat. She'd thought they would all interrogate her and had believed it inevitable that once Isobel started asking questions the others wouldn't let her go until they'd got some answers. It seemed she'd been very wrong about them.

Perhaps she didn't have to hide away from them.

'Now that's sorted,' Miss Lavender said, 'I think I *will* have another pot of tea. And while we finish our lovely food, perhaps some of you will be able to offer Bethany some recommendations for tradespeople. She's renovating Whispering Willows and needs reliable electricians, roofing people, and decorators. Any suggestions?'

Everyone immediately began discussing work they'd had done on their own homes and scribbling names and website addresses for Bethany.

She could barely keep up with the fast-flowing and light-hearted conversation after that.

Maybe, she thought, spreading jam on the second half of her scone, Tuppenny Bridge really wasn't so bad after all.

TWENTY

Kat and Jonah's wedding took place on Saturday May 11th at All Hallows Church, Market Square, Tuppenny Bridge. They were married by a beaming Zach Barrington. Jonah's best man was his seven-year-old son, Tommy, who proudly handed his father the wedding rings when called upon to do so. Fifteen-month-old Hattie made a beautiful flower girl, aided and abetted by a clearly delighted Sally, who was Kat's best friend and matron-of-honour.

The Pennyfeather sisters sat in the front row on Kat's side of the church, sniffling into their handkerchiefs and adding a distinct splash of zing to the mostly pastel palette of colours on display.

Not for them the pale blues, pinks, creams, and lemons of their fellow female guests. Rita and Birdie were visions in matching scarlet dresses, with large orange hats, and sunshine yellow shoes.

'At least they're dressed the same so they're not clashing with each other for a change,' Miss Lavender was heard to say with some despair. 'It's the best we could hope for really.'

Kat was a vision in ivory lace, and Jonah looked extremely

handsome in a dark suit with a white shirt and a dusky pink tie that matched Tommy's own tie, the sash around Hattie's waist, and the flowers that made up the bridal bouquet and buttonholes, as well as adorning the church.

Afterwards, the wedding party headed to The White Hart Inn, where an informal buffet had been laid on. The stunning wedding cake had been lovingly baked by the proprietor of Bridge Bakery, and everyone posed for photographs, their smiles genuinely happy. All were delighted for the couple, who'd been through so much and deserved their happy-ever-after.

Bethany hadn't had much time to decide what to wear, but luckily she'd got into the habit of packing for all eventualities and had brought with her a pale lemon shift dress and a white bolero jacket which she decided would be perfect for the occasion.

'I'm so glad you came,' Kat told her as Bethany dropped a kiss on her cheek and congratulated the bride and groom. 'Help yourself to food. It's all very informal here.'

Actually, it was possibly the most informal wedding Bethany had ever been to, but she rather liked it that way. Kat and Jonah had put some money behind the bar for a certain number of drinks for their guests, but Rafferty had apparently doubled that, so everyone was in good spirits. The food was tasty and there was no waiting around for it to be served, which people clearly appreciated. There were no formal speeches either since there was no father of the bride present, and the best man was only seven.

Jonah, however, did get to his feet and, amid much cheering, thanked Kat for agreeing to marry him, and for making him the happiest man in Tuppenny Bridge.

As everyone clapped and toasted the bride, Jonah called for quiet. Kat reached for his hand and Jonah squeezed it before turning to face the guests.

'And there's one more thing we'd both like to say,' he said, 'apart from thanking you for all being here, naturally. Thing is, me and Kat, we've got some more good news. We're expecting a baby. Our little family is expanding, and the new arrival will be with us some time in November.'

Bethany joined with the others in clapping loudly at this news and Jonah and Kat gave them all delighted smiles, while Tommy loudly and proudly announced that he'd managed to keep the secret for a whole two days since his mum and dad had already told him and Hattie.

They were such a lovely family. Bethany thought wistfully that, just maybe, happy endings were possible for some people. She couldn't be anything but pleased for them, even though her own story seemed destined to end in a very different way.

Turning away from the bridal table her eyes fell on Clive. He was sitting with Ben and the rest of the Callaghans, and there was a wistful expression on his own face. Was he wondering about his own happy ending, she wondered. As she watched she saw Jennifer say something to him. The wistful expression vanished to be replaced by a smile and he nodded at her. What had Jennifer said to put the smile on his face?

Bethany blinked, aware suddenly that she was staring at them, and that people would notice. Then again, perhaps not. No one seemed aware that she was even here. She wondered if she ought to go home. The pub was full of people chatting in couples and groups and she felt detached from them all. Maybe this hadn't been such a good idea after all.

As the afternoon wore on several people said their goodbyes and left. Kat and Jonah announced they would be leaving soon as they had to put the kids to bed and get changed, but promised they'd be back in the evening if anyone would like to join them, and there'd be another buffet and a disco, too.

Bethany decided she was ready to go home, and she didn't think she'd be back after tea either. She'd enjoyed the wedding and was glad to see Kat and Jonah married, but she knew no one would miss her if she stayed home, and besides, she was all peopled out. She wasn't used to all this socialising, and it was taking it out of her.

'Mind if I sit with you?'

She looked up, surprised to see Daisy standing by her chair. 'Not at all.'

Daisy was a pretty woman, probably around her mid-thirties. She had dark hair in a shoulder-length bob, large, brown eyes, and a round face that dimpled when she smiled, which she was doing right now as she slipped into the seat beside Bethany.

'I'm feeling a bit out of all this,' she admitted. 'I haven't lived here that long and although everyone's been absolutely lovely to me I still feel like an outsider.'

Bethany relaxed. 'Me, too,' she said with feeling. 'To be honest, I was just thinking about going home. Kat and Jonah are lovely, and I really appreciate them inviting me, but I don't really know anyone that well and I'm not the sort of person who'd just go up to someone and make conversation.'

'Me neither,' Daisy said with feeling.

Bethany laughed. 'You just did!' she pointed out and Daisy laughed, too.

'Okay, but that was different. You looked as lost as I felt. Everyone else is chatting away, whereas you looked like a kindred spirit. I would have thought it would be okay for you, though. You're not a newcomer, are you? I mean, you used to live here years ago.'

'*Many* years ago.' Bethany pulled a face. 'I don't really know anyone here now. Not to talk to with ease anyway.'

'How long were you away?' Daisy enquired, turning over a clean glass and pouring herself a drink from a jug of water.

Bethany considered. 'I was nineteen when I left home, so thirty-five years or thereabouts. Good grief, thirty-five years! It's a whole lifetime ago.'

'My whole lifetime,' Daisy admitted. 'Sorry,' she added with amusement as Bethany winced. 'You know, I did the same thing. Well, sort of. I left the place I'd grown up in about eight years ago now. I doubt very much I'd ever return though.'

'I'm sorry to hear it,' Bethany said. 'Where did you go?'

'To Leeds.' Daisy sighed. 'My brother was there, and we had to put Dad in a nursing home so Tom suggested he might as well go in one close to him and that I could stay with him in his house. I'm from Upper Skimmerdale originally. Dad had a sheep farm, but it wasn't the happiest of childhoods. Tom left home as soon as he could and left me to cope with the old man.'

'Is that why you left? Bad memories, I mean.' Bethany's sympathies were aroused. She understood all too well what a terrible experience childhood could be if you were left with an uncaring father. It seemed Daisy's brother wasn't up to much either if he'd left her alone with him. It seemed they had a lot in common.

'Partly.' Daisy fidgeted a little, as if trying to decide whether to confide in Bethany or not. 'I—that is, there was a man. Someone I thought the world of. I thought him and me...' She shrugged. 'Anyway, he met someone else and that was that.'

'I'm so sorry,' Bethany said. She hesitated. 'I was engaged once,' she said finally. 'Before I married Ted, I mean. It didn't work out.'

'Oh, I'm sorry,' Daisy's eyes softened with sympathy.

'Yeah, well, he met someone else too.' Bethany tutted. 'Mind you, I'm glad he did now. Being married to him wouldn't have been a particularly pleasant experience. I can't imagine what I was thinking.'

As she said the words it occurred to her that she'd had a lucky escape. Glenn had seemed like the answer to all her problems, but in fact he'd turned out to be just another disappointment. Something else for her to deal with.

'I really loved Eliot,' Daisy said. 'He was a widower with three kids. He was a sheep farmer, like Dad, and I helped him on the farm and with his children. I suppose I kidded myself that we were a family. Then he met this new woman, and it was like I didn't exist.'

'How awful for you. It hurts to be cheated on.'

Daisy blushed a little. 'I thought I'd been cheated on, but these last few months I've realised I wasn't. Not really. The thing is it was all in my head. I honestly believed he loved me and that we had a future together, but the truth is he never promised me anything. He never even told me he had feelings for me. I think I was just so desperate to believe it that I interpreted everything he said and did to suit myself. I blamed him for a long time. I blamed her, too. It's not fair really, and it wouldn't have worked because how can you live with someone as man and wife when you know, deep down, that it isn't love?'

Bethany thought of the years she'd spent married to Ted. She'd known, from the beginning, that she didn't really love him. Not in the way she was supposed to love him. How had he felt? Had he really loved her? Or had he just wanted someone to share his life with, the way she had? Someone to take away the loneliness? She thought—no, she *knew*—that he'd only really found true love when he'd married Helena.

Her gaze fell on Clive again. He was sitting quietly, sipping his beer. Jennifer wasn't at the table any more, and Ben was chatting to Jamie.

He lifted his gaze and his eyes met hers. He smiled uncertainly and she smiled back, her heart skipping a little, even as she tried her best to suppress the sudden excitement that had gripped her.

'Anyway,' Daisy said, and she turned back to her, trying to put all thoughts of Clive on hold, 'the thing is, we're here now. Whatever we've both been through it's all in the past, right? I never thought I'd get a chance to make a new life for myself but here I am, with my own business, and a nice little flat above the hair salon. Okay, the flat's rented from Bluebell, but even so, it's my home and I'm happy there. To be honest, life's good. How about you?'

'Life's...' Bethany paused then smiled slowly. 'Getting better,' she said at last.

'Let's drink to that then.' Daisy raised her glass of water and clinked it against what was left of Bethany's wine.

Dolly came over and stood behind their chairs, her hand on Daisy's shoulder.

'Having a good time? Daisy Jackson, can I just say that, as good as this wedding cake is—and it's bloody fabulous, let's face it—I can't get that caramel and white chocolate sponge out of my mind. Did you really make that yourself?'

Daisy's face went pink with pleasure. 'I did. I make all the cakes myself.'

'Well!' Dolly sat down next to her. 'You're a genius. I'm terrible at making cakes. Me and Clemmie, we have cake every dinnertime when we're at the shop. I know, awful isn't it? I keep saying I'll go on a diet, but I'm buggered if I can stick to it. Anyway, we usually nip to Bridge Bakery, but from now on I'll be popping into your café and collecting a couple of slices of that cake, so make sure you have some on standby for us, won't you?'

Daisy looked thrilled and Bethany smiled. It seemed Daisy was fitting in around here more than she'd realised.

'Would you like to dance?'

Bethany's head shot up and her cheeks scorched when she saw Clive smiling down at her.

Dolly gave an audible gasp. 'Dance? Clive Browning, since when did you ever dance?'

'You'd be surprised,' he told her. 'I'm a man of many talents.'

'You've hidden them well then,' Dolly retorted. She gave Bethany a wink. 'Well, there you go, love. Who could refuse an offer like that? If you don't want to dance with him I'll have a go.'

'Please,' Clive joked, 'save me from such a terrible fate, Bethany.'

Bethany laughed. 'I can hardly say no now, can I?'

'Bloody charming,' Dolly grumbled, but there was a twinkle in her eye, and Bethany didn't miss the nudge she gave Daisy as she took Clive's hand and followed him onto the dance floor.

Several couples were dancing so she shouldn't have felt awkward, but even so she knew she was blushing as Clive slipped an arm round her waist and they began to move to a romantic song that Kat and Jonah had requested as their final dance before they left.

'Well,' she said to break the silence, 'I wasn't expecting this today.'

'I scrub up well, don't I?' he said amiably. 'I don't think you've ever seen me in anything but jeans and wellies.'

He'd clearly forgotten she'd seen him dressed smart but casual for the opening of the art academy. He might not have remembered, but she did. She could describe every last detail of what he'd been wearing that day.

'You look very... nice,' she said. She'd been about to say handsome but that would never do. But he did. He looked extremely handsome. Her stomach seemed to be full of butter-flies and she hoped her face didn't reveal how she was feeling. That would be so embarrassing.

She looked around for Jennifer but couldn't see her. She wondered how she'd react if she saw the two of them dancing together. Would she mind?

'What made you ask me to dance?' she blurted out before she could censor herself.

He looked surprised. 'Why not? We're friends, aren't we? It's a wedding. Besides, I wanted you to see there's more to me than worming powders and penicillin shots.'

'I know that already,' she assured him.

'Do you?' His voice was low and there was a slight huskiness to it suddenly.

The wings of Bethany's butterflies flapped furiously.

'Of course. I realised you had hidden depths some time ago,' she said, her voice shaky. What on earth was she doing? He would think she was flirting with him at this rate, and that was the last thing she wanted. Wasn't it?

'I'm glad to hear it,' he told her. 'And I'm very glad you came to this wedding.'

Bethany swallowed. 'Actually,' she said, 'I was just about to go home. I think I've had enough for today. I expect you're coming back this evening?'

He shook his head slightly. 'No, not me. I've had my fill of people for one day. I'm really glad I plucked up the courage to ask you to dance before you left. What a wasted opportunity that would have been.'

'Would it?' What was he saying?

'Of course. I mean, that is, we've been working together for a while now and I'd like to think we're friends. I know we had a bit of a shaky start, but I think we understand each other now, right?'

Her heart sank. 'Yes, of course. Friends.'

'Aye.' Clive pulled her a little closer and said, in a slightly offhand manner, 'I'll walk you home after this, if you like.'

'You don't have to,' she assured him, but he insisted.

'Lavender House isn't that far from Stepping Stones. Besides, the walk will do me good.'

'Well... If you're sure.'

'Aye, I'm sure.'

When the song ended they pulled apart.

'I'll get my jacket,' Bethany said, nodding to where her bolero was draped over the back of her chair.

'I'll just say goodbye to a few people,' Clive said. 'I'll be with you in a minute.'

Bethany said goodbye to a beaming Daisy and Dolly then collected her jacket and shrugged it on, looking around to see where Clive was. She found him by the bar. He was saying goodbye to the Callaghans who were clearly waiting for drinks. Jennifer was with them, and she smiled widely at Clive and planted a kiss on his cheek.

Hurriedly, Bethany turned away. What was going on with those two? And if Clive was so besotted with her, why was he offering to walk Bethany home?

She had no idea what to think but she was sure of one thing.

No matter what the truth of the matter, she was glad he *had* offered. She was glad they'd danced together. She could no longer deny that she was a bit besotted herself.

Shivering, she recalled Daisy's words.

'The thing is, it was all in my head... I think I was just so desperate to believe it that I interpreted everything he said and did to suit myself.'

Was that what she was doing? Maybe the dance meant nothing, the offer to walk her home even less. Yet as she saw him walking towards her, a warm smile on his face, she knew it was worth the risk. She'd been frozen for so long and this man was bringing her alive again. Even if it *was* all in her head, even if it was going to end in heartbreak, she wanted to experience these feelings that had come out of nowhere. It had to be worth the price.

TWENTY-ONE

Clive took Bethany's arm as they left the pub and they walked back to Lavender House at a leisurely pace, chatting easily about the wedding and what a smashing couple Kat and Jonah made.

He thought it best not to mention that he'd seen the Lavender Ladies staring at them as they danced, their eyes gleaming with delight. He had an awful feeling that, by tomorrow morning, there'd be a book running on his and Bethany's future.

Well, good luck to them. If they knew which way this was going he'd be delighted if they'd share their views with him. Frankly, he had no idea.

Jennifer, he thought ruefully, had seemed delighted that he'd danced with Bethany. As he'd gone to the bar to say goodbye to the Callaghans she'd beamed at him, thrilled that he'd taken her advice.

'I told you,' she whispered. 'She's absolutely smitten. Did you see the way she looked when you were dancing?'

He'd flushed, embarrassed. He hadn't noticed how Bethany had looked, but then he'd not been facing her. His gaze had been directed over her shoulder, which was why he'd noticed the Lavender Ladies nudging each other, no doubt trying to calculate the odds on various outcomes of this so-called relationship.

He wished he could calculate them himself, but he had no idea what was going on between himself and Bethany.

That afternoon, he'd been jolted by how attractive she looked. Well, she always looked good, he admitted, but today... She was quite beautiful, and so effortlessly stylish.

But she was Joseph's sister, and it was complicated. Why did he always seem to fall for women with such close ties to his friends? First Jennifer, then Bethany. Not that he'd fallen for Bethany. Well, he didn't think he had.

And there was Jennifer. She'd made it very clear there was no future for him with her, but it didn't mean he could just forget about her. He felt an obligation towards her. He always had. He wasn't sure he could turn off his feelings for her as easily as that, and how would that be fair to Bethany?

That's if Jennifer was correct. He still wasn't a hundred per cent certain that she was. She might have been having him on— wishful thinking so she could palm him off on someone else. Make him their problem rather than hers. Or she might just have been mistaken. Maybe Bethany only saw him as a friend.

How would he feel if she did?

How will you feel if she doesn't?

'You don't have to walk me all the way to Lavender House, you know,' she said, breaking into his thoughts. 'I'm perfectly capable of making my own way. It's not as if it's dark.'

'I wouldn't hear of it,' he told her. He offered her a smile and she smiled back, her eyes shining, and his heart thudded. Right there and then he saw it. What Jennifer had been talking about. It was just for a moment but even he couldn't mistake it. Bethany had feelings for him. Now what?

This changed everything. As they headed onto Lavender

Lane and began the walk towards the house, passing Whispering Willows on the way, his mind raced.

He realised he hadn't really taken Jennifer seriously, but there was no denying it to himself any longer. But what could he do? He had a responsibility to Bethany not to hurt her or lead her on. He couldn't give her false hopes. What if he'd done that already, dancing with her? Even walking her home now could be taken the wrong way.

But *was* he leading her on? He'd danced with her because, watching her chatting to Daisy, he'd felt something within him. A strange and unexpected urge to be close to her. And he'd offered to walk her home on impulse because he'd realised that, when she'd admitted she was about to leave, he hadn't wanted to say goodbye to her.

But why? Did he have feelings for her, too? Or was this some sort of rebound response because Jennifer didn't want him, and he'd waited so long for her that he couldn't bear the thought of a future alone?

He had no idea, and it frightened the life out of him. The last thing he wanted to do was hurt Bethany. He should make it clear, as gently and as tactfully as possible, that this wasn't going anywhere. It was just an offer to walk her home, nothing more.

Because that's all it was, right?

As they finally walked through the gates of Lavender House his mind went into overdrive. What would he do when they reached the door? Was Bethany expecting him to kiss her goodbye? Should he? Did he want to?

He risked a sideways glance at her and there it was again— that weird churning in his stomach. He had a sudden compulsion to stop and pull her towards him and kiss her. Kiss her properly. Passionately. What the hell was going on with him?

He couldn't do that. It wouldn't be fair. His emotions were all over the place and he wasn't sure what he felt for her, so how could he give her the wrong message like that?

Berating himself for his confusion he hardly noticed as they neared Lavender House itself, until Bethany drew him to a halt and he realised they were standing at the side gate, and she was holding a bunch of keys in her hand.

'Well, thanks for bringing me home,' she said, and he realised she sounded almost shy. What was she expecting? He felt a surge of panic. What was he supposed to do? Should he kiss her after all? He realised he wanted to. Oh! He glanced down at her lips and gulped. He *really* wanted to. Bloody hell!

But what would that say to her about them? He should leave. Just tell her she was welcome and bid her a good evening.

Turn around and walk away, you moron.

Instead he stood there frozen, no doubt looking completely gormless, while she waited.

After what felt like forever she said, 'Would you like to come in for a coffee before you head home?'

Well, it was a solution, wasn't it? Clive thought about it. If he had a coffee with her, he could then leave without there being any awkwardness about a goodbye kiss. It was different standing at someone's front door. It was like there was a certain expectation. But indoors...

But 'come in for coffee' had connotations, didn't it? Everyone knew what that meant. What *did* it mean? Did she really expect him to drink coffee, or was she asking him for something else?

'Coffee would be good,' he heard himself saying.

She beamed at him. 'Come on then. We'll let ourselves in at the side door.'

She unlocked the gate, and they headed through into Miss Lavender's private garden. Bethany carefully latched the gate behind her, though she left it unlocked, and led him to one of the two sets of French doors set in the wall at the side of the house. He could hear Trueman and Boycott yelping from inside.

They let themselves into Miss Lavender's chintzy living room, whereupon the two Yorkshire terriers hurled themselves at them, yapping in excitement.

Bethany ushered them outside since they'd been cooped up all afternoon, then, closing the French doors firmly behind them she told Clive to take a seat. She went through into the kitchen while he sank onto the sofa, his mind racing.

He was so out of practice, that was the trouble. He hadn't even looked at another woman since he'd met Jennifer, and how many years was that? Even if he'd wanted to, he wasn't sure he remembered how to kiss, and if Bethany harboured hopes of anything else... Lord, he might have to look it up on the internet. He was pretty sure he'd forgotten what he was supposed to do.

He tutted impatiently. He was getting carried away, letting his mind go off in directions they had no business going in. It was just coffee, and he should be ashamed of himself for thinking anything else. She was a respectable woman and deserved better.

Maybe Bethany had no intention of taking things further and simply wanted to offer him a coffee as a thank you for walking her home. If that was the case, what did it say about him? All these assumptions and fantasies... Where had they even come from? He couldn't remember the last time he'd even thought of Jennifer in that way.

Startled, he sat up straighter as the thought repeated itself. It was true. He honestly hadn't thought of Jennifer in that way for years. Yet here he was, his fevered imagination conjuring up all sorts of scenarios with Bethany. Why?

'Here you go,' she said, entering the room carrying two mugs of coffee. 'I'm so glad to be back. The wedding was lovely, and I really enjoyed it, but I'd forgotten how draining it can be to be around people.'

Reluctantly, he made himself offer. 'I can go if you'd rather be alone,' he said.

She put the mugs down on the coffee table and laughed. 'Don't be daft! I didn't mean you. You're not people.'

'As a qualified vet, I can assure you I am,' he joked nervously, inwardly rolling his eyes at his own feeble humour.

Bethany kicked off her shoes and removed her bolero jacket then sat beside him on the sofa. 'That's better. I rarely wear heels these days and they were killing me.'

'You should have said,' he told her. 'I'd have called us a taxi.'

'Oh, it's okay. We're here now.' She handed him the mug of coffee. 'Would you like a biscuit?'

'No thanks. I'm still full from all the food at the wedding,' he admitted. 'Sally and Rafferty lay on a good spread, don't they?'

'It *was* rather yummy,' she agreed. 'The whole wedding was yummy. Didn't Kat look beautiful? And Jonah made a very handsome groom.'

'Aye, they looked fine,' Clive said.

'And I think it's lovely that they were married by a friend,' she continued. 'Zach, I mean. It made it all even more personal and informal somehow. It's a beautiful church, All Hallows. I'd forgotten. I think I only went in there once or twice as a child.'

'Where—where did you get married?' Clive asked. 'Was it a church wedding?'

'No. Ted was an atheist.' Bethany picked up her mug of coffee and cradled it thoughtfully. 'We got married in a hotel. It belonged to one of his friends, so we got a good deal.'

'Right.' Clive thought how soulless it sounded. Whose bright idea had that been?

'It was a very small wedding,' she said flatly. 'A few members of Ted's family and Helena. That was about it really.'

He thought about Joseph and how much he'd have loved to be at his sister's wedding. It was such a shame it had never happened.

'Isn't it amazing news about the baby?' Bethany took a sip of coffee and sank back in the sofa. 'Three children, though. They're going to have a lot to cope with.'

'They'll manage fine,' Clive said confidently. 'They're great parents. Everyone knows that. A proper blended family, and this wee one will seal the unit good and proper. A happy ending all round.'

'Yes, I suppose so.'

He thought she sounded wistful and took a sip of his drink before asking tentatively, 'Did you never want children, Bethany?'

As soon as he'd asked the question he regretted it. It was way too personal. What had he been thinking?

'I'm sorry,' he said hastily. 'None of my business. Forget I asked.'

'No, it's okay.' She gave a slight shrug. 'I did want children actually, but it turned out Ted couldn't father them.'

'Oh.' He wasn't sure what to say to that. After a long and uncomfortable pause he ventured, 'You never wanted to adopt?'

She was quiet for a few moments, and he thought he'd blundered again and cursed himself. Then she turned to him and said, 'Ted didn't think it would be a good idea.'

The sadness in her voice filled him with a sudden anger on her behalf.

'And what about you?' he asked. 'Did *you* think it would be a good idea?'

She sighed and put her mug back on the coffee table. 'It's not as simple as that. When we got married, everyone just assumed we'd have children, and I suppose I just assumed it, too. Ted wasn't as eager as I was to start a family, but he went along with it. Then, when we found out we couldn't have children naturally, I discovered that, as it turned out, he wasn't too bothered. In fact, I'd go so far as to say he was quite relieved. I mentioned adoption once or twice, but it was obvious he wasn't keen on that either. Eventually we had a proper, frank discussion, and I discovered he'd never wanted children at all. I could hardly force him into adopting a baby, could I? How would that be fair to the poor little mite? So we never discussed it again.'

'I'm so sorry,' he said, meaning it. 'You'd have made a great mother, I'm sure.'

He regretted saying it as tears welled in her eyes. He put his mug of coffee next to hers and turned to her, taking her hands in his without even thinking about it.

'Ach, I'm an idiot,' he cursed. 'I didn't mean to upset you. I never think before I open my mouth, that's the trouble.'

'It's okay,' she said, smiling through her tears. 'It was a kind thing to say. Thank you. We'll never know now, will we? I'm way past all that and I've had to accept that children just aren't going to be part of my life. The irony is,' she added, 'that when Ted got together with Helena, she came with two children and two grandsons in tow, so he became a stepfather and a step grandfather. And you know what? He loved it. I think he'd have been a good dad. He was kind and fun and generous towards those boys, and they adored him. It's such a waste.'

'Life,' he said, as much to himself as to her, 'can be very cruel.'

'Oh well...' She wiped her eyes. 'How about you? Did you never want a family?'

'Me? I'd be a terrible father,' he said, trying to sound light-hearted.

Her eyes narrowed as she surveyed him. 'I don't think that's true,' she told him. 'From what I've heard, you've been a father figure to Ben, and a very good one at that.'

'Ben?' He considered the matter. 'I suppose I did take him under my wing, aye,' he conceded. 'But he was already in his late teens by then. No idea how I'd have coped with little ones the way Julian did. Now he was a natural. And,' he added firmly, 'he was Ben's real father. I'm just a friend. A mentor, maybe.'

She nodded, saying nothing, and he allowed his thoughts to range across subjects he'd closed off from years ago.

'I would have liked a family, aye,' he said softly. 'In answer to your question,' he explained as she glanced up at him. 'But it wasn't to be. I just never met the right woman.'

'You didn't?'

He wondered why she sounded so uncertain. Wasn't that obvious? He was alone, wasn't he? A bachelor at the age of fifty-six.

'Way too late for me to have a family now,' he said. 'But it would have been nice. I think about it sometimes, what might have been. Still, that's the way the cards fell, and there's no sense fretting over what can't be changed. I'm very lucky. I have a nice flat, a profitable business, and I live in a community I love, doing a job that means the world to me. I can't complain.'

'I suppose so,' she said thoughtfully. 'You've a lot more going for you than I have anyway.'

'I'm sure that's not true,' he said. 'You're very wealthy and you have a good friend in that Helena woman, right? And you've travelled. Seen something of the world. Not like me. I left Edinburgh and moved here, and I've been nowhere else since.'

'Did you want to travel?'

He grinned. 'Not particularly.'

'Well there you go then.'

'But you clearly did,' he said.

'Not particularly,' she replied, echoing his own response.

He leaned back, raising an eyebrow. 'Did you not?'

'What I wanted,' she said, 'was a home. Roots. A family. Somehow I lost them all. If I ever had them, which to be honest, I don't think I did.'

It was on the tip of his tongue to remind her that she'd had a home and a brother if she'd just bothered to come back to Tuppenny Bridge, but he stopped himself in time. There was such sadness in her eyes that he knew that, whatever he thought, her reasons for walking away were valid to her. She genuinely believed she'd never had a home at Whispering Willows, and worse, she genuinely believed she'd had no brother in Joseph. He wished things could have been different.

She smiled suddenly. 'We're a right pair, aren't we? We should be counting our blessings. Like you said, we both have them. No point dwelling on all the things we haven't got.'

He could see she was trying to be valiant about it, but the sense of loss and grief emanating from her was palpable.

'We both wanted a home and a family,' he said bleakly, suddenly very aware of how true that was. 'I don't think it's too much to ask really.'

'Other people seem to manage it so easily,' she agreed, her cheerful façade slipping instantly. 'Why couldn't we?'

They sat in silence for a few moments, then Clive drained his mug.

'I'd better get off,' he said. 'Miss Lavender will be home any moment now and can you imagine what she'll say if she sees me here?'

'I think that ship's sailed,' Bethany said ruefully. 'The moment we danced together we sealed our fate. From what I've heard of the Lavender Ladies they'll be taking bets on us getting married even as we speak.'

Clive felt a jolt of shock as she spoke the words, and it seemed she realised what she'd said, too, because her face reddened in a most charming manner. He kindly didn't comment on her words but got to his feet.

'Anyway, I need to pop to the stables, collect Viva and check Maya and Lennox have left everything as it should be. Thanks for the coffee,' he told her. He nodded at the French doors and grinned upon seeing Trueman and Boycott with their noses pressed against the glass. 'We'd better let them in.'

'Oh crikey, I forgot all about them,' she admitted, leaping up and rushing over to allow the Yorkshire terriers back into the living room. They immediately dashed over to Clive, investigating him thoroughly.

'They're wondering what I'm doing here,' he said, laughing. 'It's usually Ben who deals with them these days. I kind of palmed them off on him.'

'I'm surprised they're not registered with the Harley Street equivalent of a veterinary practice,' Bethany said. 'Miss Lavender idolises them. *Is* there a Harley Street equivalent of a veterinary practice, by the way?'

'Probably,' he said, 'but I doubt even they'd be prepared to put up with Eugenie's total disregard for all advice on diet and exercise for these two. Poor Ben. She doesn't listen to a word he says.'

'She's a law unto herself,' Bethany agreed.

They smiled at each other, then Clive cleared his throat, suddenly awkward again.

'Right, I'll be away then. Thanks again for the coffee and... and for the talk. It was nice. I'll see you back at Whispering Willows.'

'You will.'

She followed him to the French doors, and he turned to her as a thought occurred to him.

'Have you decided when you're moving back there?'

Bethany nodded. 'I thought probably next week. I've got an electrician coming round on Monday to check the wiring and the supply, and if that's okay I'll move in on Saturday. I'm looking for a roofer and a builder next. I want them to check over the house but also the stables. They're not in good shape, are they? That bulging building is worrying me, and the roof on the other block will need repairing at the very least.'

'Are you sure?' Clive looked at her doubtfully. 'It's a big investment.'

'I'm sure,' she said firmly. 'Even if the new owners decide to convert the stables into accommodation a good roof will only add to the value. Saves them one job at any rate.'

He experienced a flash of disappointment but pushed it firmly away. 'I suppose so. Well, I'll be away then.'

He turned to leave but froze as she caught hold of his hand.

'Thank you, Clive,' she said, her big, blue eyes fixed on his.

'It wasn't far,' he said, embarrassed. 'Honestly, it was nothing.'

'Not just for walking me home. For everything. For all you've done ever since I got here, and before that. I know you helped Joseph so much, and now you're helping me. I want you to know how much I appreciate it. You're—you're quite an amazing man.'

He glanced at the carpet, not sure what to say to that. 'I help because I want to,' he said at last. 'It's my pleasure.'

She reached up and kissed him lightly on the cheek, then stepped back, her eyes never leaving his.

Without giving it any thought, he bent down and kissed her gently on the lips. It was just a brief kiss, but it sparked something within him that scared the life out of him. The urge to continue kissing her was a powerful one, but he forced himself to step away. He saw the look in her eyes that told him whatever had ignited within himself had also ignited within her.

Time to go. This wasn't fair on either of them.

'Bye, Bethany.'

'Goodbye, Clive.'

He heard the longing in her voice and closed his eyes briefly, wondering if he was completely mad. But he couldn't do it. He couldn't take this any further when he wasn't sure what it was he wanted, and she was so vulnerable. What sort of man would that make him?

Without looking back he hurried out into the garden and made his way to the gate. He knew she'd probably follow him to lock the gate after him, but he didn't turn round. Instead, he strode purposefully towards the drive, heading back to Whispering Willows, his mind whirling with confusion and doubt.

What the hell had he just started?

TWENTY-TWO

Summer returned from Australia on the Monday morning, but it was Wednesday before she came back to Whispering Willows. Bethany wasn't sure whether she was glad Summer had booked the extra day off to recover from jet lag or if it would have been better to get this over with once and for all.

She'd kept her promise to Clive, but now Summer was home, and it was time to be honest with her about her plans to rehome the horses and sell Whispering Willows. She couldn't say she was looking forward to it.

Sure enough, her only employee arrived at the stables bright and early that Wednesday morning and was clearly stunned to find Bethany in the process of cooking breakfast for her.

'Careful,' she said, trying to sound jokey, 'or I'll be expecting this every day.'

'We *get* this every day,' Maya told her cheerfully, as she cut into a succulent sausage. 'Bethany comes here every morning to make us breakfast. Sometimes we get one of them continental breakfasts, but mostly it's the full English.'

Summer looked stunned. She glanced at Clive who was sipping from a large mug of tea.

'Wow, things have changed around here,' she said lightly. 'Who'd have thought it?'

'Aye, it makes a cracking start to the day,' he said, smiling. 'It's good to see you, Summer. You're looking very refreshed. How was Australia?'

'Different.' Summer grinned. 'I loved it.'

'Did you get attacked by giant spiders?' Maya asked with a shudder.

'Or see any snakes?' Lennox queried hopefully.

Summer laughed. 'Can't say I did, no. Sorry to disappoint you. Wrong time of year for spiders—or right time, depending on your point of view. They mostly come out in spring and summer and it's autumn over there at the moment. They were probably around somewhere but I didn't see any. Mind you, they don't really worry me anyway, but I think you'd be on permanent alert, Maya.'

'I know. I'll never visit Australia, that's for sure,' Maya said firmly.

'Never mind the spiders,' Clive said, 'how was your holiday?'

'It was great. I loved seeing Billie and Arlo again, and it was smashing to spend so much time with Dad.' She smiled her thanks as Bethany placed her breakfast in front of her. 'I'd forgotten how much I missed him. Wow, this looks great.'

'Enjoy.' Bethany sat down and picked up her knife and fork. 'How long is it since you last saw your dad then?'

'I spent a couple of days with him at the New Year,' Summer told him. 'I wish I could see him more regularly but there never seems to be enough time.'

'Doesn't he live nearby?'

'No.' Summer shovelled some bacon into her mouth and chewed blissfully while they all waited. 'He lives in Bemborough in East Yorkshire, so it's a bit of a hike. I mean, Ben could drive me there and back in a day to be fair, but we're both always busy so... Mind you, I've decided I'm going to make more of an effort. He's great company and I do love him so much.' She gave a wistful smile. 'It's funny how you forget—the good times, I mean. I'd been so focused on remembering the bad stuff I'd forgotten that he can be lovely. Besides, he's changed a lot since he and Mum split up. Even Billie said so and she's always on the lookout for him to revert to type.'

'What type's that?' Bethany asked curiously then blushed. 'Sorry, didn't mean to pry.'

'Oh, it's okay. It's hardly a secret.' Summer shrugged. 'Dad was a womaniser and a liar. Gave my mum an awful time of it until she'd finally had enough.'

'I'm so sorry.' Bethany remembered the times her own father had flaunted his affairs. She clearly remembered Joseph raging at his father about his other women, demanding to know how he could treat his wife so badly, and she'd been aware that Father had 'female friends' even at such a tender age.

Funnily enough, she didn't remember her mother ever saying a word about it. Maybe that was what the tears had been about all those times when they'd sat together in All Hallows' churchyard, but somehow Bethany didn't think so. She thought those tears were about something far more complicated than her father's affairs. 'Your poor mum.'

Summer looked surprised by her response and her fork hovered midway between her plate and mouth for a moment as she stared at Bethany. Then she blinked and said, 'Yeah, it wasn't good.'

'But it's all fine now,' Clive said quickly. 'A happy ending for your mum at least.'

'Absolutely.' Summer popped a mushroom into her mouth and said, 'She got together with Rafferty, and honestly she couldn't be happier.'

'And your dad's okay?' Bethany asked tentatively.

Summer ate the mushroom before she replied. 'He is now.

He was heartbroken when they split up. Sounds mad, doesn't it? But he really loved her, even though he did all those awful things. He's pulled himself together now, though, and seems to be much more contented.' She grinned suddenly. 'Actually, he met someone in Melbourne. She's not Australian. She's from Derbyshire, but she was on holiday with her sister and brother-in-law, visiting her nephew. The two of them really hit it off. They exchanged phone numbers and promised to meet up soon so who knows?'

'Well, let's hope he gets his own happy ending then,' Clive said. His gaze flickered over to Bethany, and she tried not to read too much into his comments.

They'd hardly spent any time together over the last couple of days as he'd been busy with the horses, and she'd been dealing with the electrician and contacting various decorators.

She'd been relieved to discover that the wiring at Whispering Willows was in good condition but had booked the electrician to install some new sockets in various rooms where there weren't enough, and to replace some of the older sockets and light fittings.

Bethany had told Clive the good news over breakfast yesterday, but he hadn't said much. In fact, he'd hardly spoken to her at all since the day of the wedding and she couldn't help wondering if she'd scared him off. She had, after all, kissed him, if only on the cheek. But then, he'd kissed her back and if he hadn't wanted to no one had forced him.

She'd seen the look in his eyes and was quite sure he'd felt the same way she had the moment their lips touched. But then he'd just walked away without looking back and since then he hadn't mentioned their kiss at all, so she wasn't sure what to think. After all, it had only been a couple of light goodbye kisses. Nothing too serious. She was probably overthinking this.

But perhaps his talk of Summer's dad's happy ending meant something, the way his glance had fallen on her as he said it.

Was that his way of telling her he hoped they'd get their own happy ending at last?

Breakfast continued with Maya and Lennox pumping Summer for information about her holiday before they decided it was time to start work.

'Tell Summer about Shirley Bassey and Dylan Thomas,' Lennox said to Bethany. 'Proper drama we've had while you were away, Summer.'

Summer laughed. 'Who?'

'Len! She doesn't want to hear all that on her first day back,' Maya chided him. 'Come on, let's get out there or we'll be late for school.'

Clive drained his cup of tea and got to his feet, giving Bethany a sympathetic look.

'I'd better make a start, too. I'll see to Barney this morning. Summer, take your time with breakfast, there's no rush. Ease your way back into work, okay?'

'When are Maya and Lennox finishing here?' Summer asked. 'I mean, the morning work and the couple of evenings they've been doing?'

'They'll be back to Saturday mornings and Sunday after-noons this weekend,' he told her. 'And I'm back to the day job on Monday, so you'll be pretty busy. Are you sure you can cope?'

'I've managed so far,' Summer said. She hesitated. 'Maybe we can think about taking on someone to help permanently?' She gave Bethany a hopeful look. 'Even if it's just part time.'

Clive looked at Bethany, whose heart sank. There was no more putting this off. She'd have to be honest with Summer.

'Do you need me to...' Clive's voice trailed off and he shrugged slightly.

'It's fine,' Bethany said. This was, after all, her decision. Having made it she should at least have the courage and decency to break it to Summer herself. 'I'll see you later.'

He nodded and left, but not before giving Summer a compassionate look which she missed, as she was dipping the last of her bread in her tomato gravy.

'So, who are Shirley Bassey and Dylan Thomas?' she asked at last, after eating the last mouthful of her breakfast and pushing the plate away. 'I mean, I know who the real ones are of course, but I'm guessing we're talking about someone other than a singer and a poet, right?'

Bethany's expression softened. 'Shirley's a beautiful little Welsh Mountain pony, and Dylan is—*was*—her foal.'

'Was?' Summer gave her a stricken look. 'What happened?'

Bethany falteringly explained about the call-out she and Clive had gone on, and how they'd found the ponies in such a terrible state.

'I thought they'd be treated at the equine unit and then come to us,' she admitted sadly, tears welling up as she remembered Dylan's little face. 'Sadly, the foal didn't make it. It's just awful. I hope whoever abandoned them there is caught and punished.'

She looked over at Summer and swallowed down her own tears as she saw the girl was quietly crying.

'That's so awful,' Summer managed. 'Poor little thing. He barely had any life at all and what he did have was just...' She shook her head. 'This is why it's so important,' she said passionately. 'Whispering Willows, I mean. Joseph was determined to help as many ill-treated horses, ponies, and donkeys as he could, and he gave so many of them happy lives after rotten starts just like Dylan's. You see how much it matters?'

Bethany stared at her, feeling sick. 'I—I know, but—'

'What about the mare?' Summer asked suddenly. 'What's happening with Shirley?'

Bethany admitted, with some shame, that she had no idea.

'You didn't find out?' Summer said incredulously. 'So is she still at Walter Harding's or has she been rehomed or what?'

'I really don't know. Clive never mentioned her, so I just assumed she was okay.'

Summer got to her feet. 'But we have to find out! Maybe she's still at the unit. She can come here, can't she?'

'I really don't think...' Bethany began, but Summer wasn't listening.

'I'll ask Clive for the number. I'll call him. We can bring her home to Whispering Willows. She'll be grieving for her foal. She needs us!'

She headed towards the door and Bethany knew the time she'd dreaded was finally here. No more putting it off.

'Summer, wait!'

Summer turned, clearly puzzled. 'What? We need to act fast, or this vet might place her somewhere else.'

'She—' Bethany swallowed hard. 'She might be better off somewhere else. It will be less unsettling for her.'

Summer frowned. 'What do you mean, less unsettling?'

She walked slowly back to the table and sat down, eyeing Bethany suspiciously.

'What's wrong? You look as white as a sheet.'

Bethany closed her eyes and silently prayed for courage. When she opened them again Summer was looking at her with something approaching horror.

'Don't tell me,' she whispered. 'You're not...' She shook her head, denying the possibility. 'No, you wouldn't. Would you?'

'I'm sorry,' Bethany said, feeling ashamed. 'The fact is, Whispering Willows is going up for sale soon, and I'll be looking for homes for the horses we already have here. I can't take on any more. Not even Shirley Bassey.'

'But—but you said you wanted her here! Her and Dylan! You said—'

'I know what I said, but I was thinking with my heart instead of my head. The fact is, taking them in would have been a mistake, because they'd barely have settled, before being moved on again. It's better for Shirley if she gets a new, permanent home. You must see that?'

Summer stared at her in disbelief. 'You're serious? You're really getting rid of all our residents? You're selling Whispering Willows?'

Bethany nodded. 'I'm sorry,' she said again. 'I understand how hard this must be for you to hear. I know it's your job and I promise, I'll give you excellent references, and of course there'll be redundancy pay and—'

'You think I care about that?' Summer leapt to her feet and glared at her. 'References? Redundancy pay? What about the horses? What about Barney and Diamond and Sapphire and Chester? What about Midge, Titch, Smokey, and Fudge? What about—'

Bethany held up her hand. 'I know all their names,' she said wearily. 'You don't have to list them for me.'

'Do you? So you've learned what they're called,' Summer said. 'Have you learned their histories? Do you know what they've been through? Why they ended up here? Did you bother to learn all that, Bethany, or didn't you care?'

'Of course I care,' Bethany cried. 'How can you say I don't?'

'If you really cared you wouldn't dream of selling this place!' Summer was openly sobbing now, her voice thick with a mixture of sadness, anger, and frustration. 'You said you were thinking with your heart instead of your head when you considered taking in Dylan and Shirley, but I find that hard to believe. You don't have a heart. If you did you wouldn't be doing this. Where do you think you're going to find new homes for all these animals? Have you any idea how hard it's going to be? And if you can't find homes before you sell this place, then what? Will they end up in cans of dog food? Is that what you want?'

Bethany blanched. 'Of course I don't want that. It won't happen. I'm going to make enquiries at other sanctuaries. See if they can take them.'

She should have done that already, she realised. Before Summer got back. If she'd secured good homes for the animals to go to Summer wouldn't have been so angry or upset. Or afraid. And right now, she *was* afraid, Bethany could see that.

'I won't let anything bad happen to them, Summer,' she said gently. 'I promise.'

'You *promise*?' Summer's lip curled. 'Forgive me if I don't trust your promises. You don't strike me as someone who cares much about anything or anyone. You couldn't even be bothered to see Joseph, who was the kindest, most decent man that ever lived. You didn't even turn up for his funeral. So don't make promises to me, Bethany, because you're wasting your time. I don't believe a word you say!'

She gave a strangled sob and ran out of the house, no doubt to find the others. She could picture them all now, standing together in the stables having a good rant about her terrible, selfish behaviour.

Could she blame them?

The awful thing was, she couldn't really. She wished things could be different but couldn't see a way out of this mess.

She gazed tearfully around the kitchen. There were times she wished she'd sold Whispering Willows the moment she'd inherited it, even if it did mean making Joseph homeless. Now was most definitely one of those times.

TWENTY-THREE

Bethany almost changed her mind about moving into Whispering Willows. Summer was so hostile around her that she didn't feel welcome there at all and had to keep reminding herself that it was her house, and she was entitled to be there.

Summer had boycotted future breakfasts with them, saying she'd eat at home and start work while the others ate in the kitchen.

Maya and Lennox had quickly discovered what was behind her odd behaviour and couldn't hide their own resentment. Maya especially had been hurt and bewildered by Bethany's decision.

'I thought you loved the horses,' she said accusingly. 'Yet here you are about to chuck them onto the streets like they don't matter at all.'

'I'm not going to make them homeless,' Bethany told her. 'I'll find them good homes first, I promise.'

'They've already got a good home,' Maya said sulkily. 'The best. At least, it was when Joseph was here.'

With that she'd flounced out of the kitchen and, after a

longing look at his half-eaten breakfast, Lennox had followed her.

It seemed she was *persona non grata* at Whispering Willows. The hardest part was that she didn't blame them. They had every right to be angry with her.

At least Clive was on her side. Well, maybe not on her side —after all, he wanted the horse sanctuary to stay open as much as anyone—but he understood and seemed to have accepted her wish to sell, even if he didn't agree with it.

When she'd tearfully admitted to him that she felt terrible about Summer and hurt by Maya and Lennox, even though she didn't blame them in the slightest, he'd put an arm around her shoulders and told her she had to do what was best for her.

'But you wish the sanctuary could stay open, don't you?' she said, gazing up at him.

Clive gave a heavy sigh. 'I'd be lying if I said I was happy about its future,' he admitted. 'It meant so much to Joseph, and working here you can't help but be invested in these animals and worried about what happens to them. But you've promised they'll get good homes, and you won't close the place until they're all rehomed, and I can't ask any more of you than that.'

'I just feel so guilty,' she confessed. 'I can barely look the young ones in the eye.'

'But you can't stay here out of guilt,' he said. 'In the end, you have to do what makes you happy. What feels right for you. It's a terrible shame that the two things don't align, but there it is. All you can do is make sure you do the right thing by our residents.'

'You're taking it so much better than the kids have,' Bethany said with a miserable sniff.

'Aye, well, I've had longer to get my head around it. You were straight with me from the beginning,' he reminded her. 'You never gave me any real reason to believe you'd changed your mind. This is a shock to Summer and the others, but they'll come to terms with it in the end. Give them time.'

'But they'll never really forgive me,' she said wistfully. 'I thought we were getting close, becoming a unit. They've— they've told me they won't be coming for breakfast any longer.'

'Well, their hours will be changing in a couple of days anyway,' he said reasonably. 'They'll only be doing Saturday mornings and Sunday afternoons. Probably don't think it's worth it.'

'That's not the reason and you know it. They could still come here for breakfast on Saturday mornings. And Summer's here every day but she's said no. I guess it will just be you and me from now on.'

Clive had shuffled awkwardly and removed his arm from around her shoulders.

'About that... Really, there's no point. I can sort myself out for the rest of the week and I'm back at Stepping Stones from Monday. Honestly, you might as well have a lie-in. And you're moving in here on Saturday, so you'll not have time to cook anyway.'

'I see,' she said sadly.

'It was a lovely thing to do,' he assured her, 'but that time's past now. Things are changing here, and we've got to accept that. All of us,' he added heavily.

He was right, but it hurt. And she had to admit, it hurt even more that Clive seemed to have accepted she was leaving and made no more attempts to talk her out of it.

She knew she was being unreasonable and unfair but even so...

Briefly, she considered staying at Lavender House after all. Did she really want to be around Summer and the others when they seemed so hostile towards her? Only the fact that she'd already told Miss Lavender she would be leaving, and that she wanted to be around to oversee the work at Whispering Willows made her go through with her plans.

Saturday was an emotional day. Bethany arrived at around nine o'clock feeling quite wrung out after a fond farewell from Miss Lavender.

Her generous host had made her a hearty breakfast and given her a 'welcome to your new home' card, which Bethany thought couldn't have been more inappropriate if it tried. She'd also presented her with a bouquet of extravagant looking blooms, 'to cheer the place up'. Bethany thought it would take more than some expensive flowers to brighten Whispering Willows, but she was grateful to Miss Lavender for trying.

She'd then been hugged and assured by the old lady that she was welcome at Lavender House at any time, and if there was ever anything else she needed she only had to say the word.

Bethany had been moved to tears by her generosity and had promised to keep in touch. This time she meant it.

It hadn't taken much effort to pack up her few belongings and remove all traces of herself from Lavender House. As she drove into the yard at Whispering Willows she kept a wary eye out for Summer but there was no sign of her, or anyone else for that matter. She guessed Maya and Lennox had already gone home. As for Clive—maybe he was with Summer somewhere out in the fields.

She carried her small suitcase and the bouquet of flowers into the house and closed the door behind her, taking a deep breath. So here she was, back again. Had she done the right thing?

'It's just a house,' she murmured, filling the sink, and placing the flowers in the water for now. 'No one can hurt you ever again.'

The trouble was, she knew that wasn't true. Her parents and Joseph were gone, and if she could just learn to let go of the past their actions could no longer make her miserable. Deep down she knew that.

But Clive was a different matter altogether. He had a powerful effect on her and was in her thoughts constantly. She didn't want to examine the reason for that too closely because she had a feeling that, if she did, she'd have to open herself up to the possibility of her heart being broken yet again.

So it wasn't exactly true that no one could ever hurt her again. Clive could. The only thing that offered her comfort was knowing he was a good, honest man and not likely to play games with her feelings. If only she could figure out what those feelings were.

After making herself a cup of tea and gathering her strength it was time to do the thing she'd dreaded.

She picked up her case and carried it upstairs, pausing on the landing as she considered her options. She'd avoided going in these rooms all this time. Now she knew there was no more putting it off. She'd already decided which room would be hers so she could have chosen not to investigate the others, but somehow, having decided to move back in here, she knew it was time to face her demons.

Taking a steadying breath she opened the door to her old room. It was almost exactly as she'd left it all those years ago, except for one puzzling thing. There was a rocking horse in one corner. It was well crafted, and looked like something from a storybook, with a dapple-grey coat, a black mane and tail, and large, dark eyes. It wasn't very big. Clearly it was meant for a young child. There was something familiar about it, but she couldn't think what it was. Anyway, what was it doing in her room? In fact, what was it doing in Whispering Willows at all?

There hadn't been young children in this house since she

was little. Had there? She thought she'd ask Clive about that. It was a complete mystery to her.

Putting that aside she already knew she didn't want to stay in this room. It was quite small and overlooked the side of the house, and, besides, she wasn't sure it was somewhere she wanted to be any longer. Not with all the memories it held for her.

Joseph's room overlooked the stableyard and was larger, but there was no way she was ever going to sleep there. As for her parents' room...

She opened the door and peered in, her heart thudding as if she expected to find them both sitting up in bed. Not that they'd be together. Her father had spent a lot of nights sleeping out, and she didn't have to guess where he'd been. Even when he was at home he'd taken to sleeping in the box room. Bethany wondered if that had ever upset her mother, or if it had come as a relief to her. Even after she'd passed away he'd continued to sleep in that small room he'd made his own. She'd liked to think he felt too guilty to return to the marital bedroom but doubted it.

Nothing had been changed in here. It was like a shrine, and she wondered if that had been deliberate on Joseph's part, or if he simply hadn't had the heart to do anything about it. She shivered, seeing the dressing table with her mother's hairbrush laid out as if it were waiting for her to sit down and start using it. Her eyes strayed to the mirror, and she fancied, for a moment, that she could see her mother sitting there, brushing her hair, that familiar vacant expression on her face.

Terence Wilkinson had destroyed her, but how, Bethany suddenly asked herself, had he done that? Did it mean Coral had truly loved him once? Because surely, no man could break your heart the way he'd broken hers if you didn't love him? Or was it the lack of love that had broken her? Had she realised she'd never experienced true love and never would, and that was why she'd given up on her hopes and dreams, her marriage —her life?

She felt too sad to linger any longer in this room and closed the door gently behind her. For the first time in many years she felt more compassion than anger towards the woman who'd been so lacking in hope that she'd found nothing left to live for. Bethany had experienced sadness and betrayal, and she'd had times when she wondered what the point of anything was, but she'd never come close to feeling as wretched as her mother must have felt. She was, she realised now, very lucky. She wished her mother had been as fortunate.

There were two more bedrooms up here. The box room, naturally, which she had no intention of going in, and the one next to it which had been laughingly referred to as the guest room, even though they'd never had guests to stay as far as Bethany could remember.

She pushed open the door and stepped inside. It was here that Clive had stayed while Joseph had been ill, and she could understand why he'd chosen it. The carpet was frayed, and the wallpaper was faded, but it had a large window which overlooked the paddocks with views to the river and hills beyond, and it was easily big enough for a double bed, a large wardrobe, and a dressing table. Other than her parents' bedroom it was the biggest room on this floor, and she'd already decided it would be the perfect place for her to stay while the work was being done on the house.

After unpacking her case and hanging her clothes in the old wardrobe, Bethany set to work making the bed. She'd bought new bedding during the week, having made a trip to Kirkby Skimmer. She could have ordered it online, but she'd needed an escape, and it had to be said her day out had done her the world of good.

Kirkby Skimmer, the largest town in Skimmerdale, was a pretty place with lots of independent shops. She'd revelled in the May sunshine, and for the first time in ages she'd felt normal as she walked among residents, holidaymakers, and day-trippers, completely anonymous and feeling relaxed for once.

The shops were quite expensive, but she hadn't cared. She'd chosen two lots of good quality bedding, new pillows and a duvet, and some new towels, plus a few little bits and pieces that would make whichever bedroom she chose a bit more bearable.

She'd purchased a new three-piece suite as well because she couldn't stand that awful old sofa any longer. It would take a few weeks to arrive but at least it was on its way. She reasoned that it wasn't a waste of money as she could take it with her when she left, even if that meant putting it in storage until she found a house of her own. She could also take the double bed she'd impulsively ordered, which would be delivered in a week's time.

Straightening the duvet she stepped back and admired the new bedding. She'd chosen well. It was pretty and brightened the room up. She decided she'd put Miss Lavender's flowers on the bedside table, as they would cheer the bedroom even more.

Heading downstairs she hunted in the kitchen for a vase. She should have thought about that. The bouquet might have to stay where it was for the foreseeable if she couldn't find one. In the end she found two, shoved under the sink. One was a large, rose-patterned jug that looked vaguely familiar, the other a smaller ceramic container which looked more like a miniature milk churn. It was too small for the bouquet, so she left it in its place and set to work arranging the flowers in the jug.

It was a gorgeous bouquet of gold and purple blooms, including roses and lisianthus. Bethany wasn't familiar with the names of most flowers, but she could appreciate a beautiful display when she saw one. These must have cost a fortune, and it was very kind of Miss Lavender to think of her. She would take the jug upstairs later but for now it could stay on the mantelpiece in the living room. At least it would add a bit of cheer to the dingy room.

She thought wistfully that it would be nice to have Viva back here. She could do with some company and the little bichon frise was such a sweet, friendly dog. Was she missing her old home? Maybe she'd like to come back here. She dismissed the idea almost immediately, realising it wouldn't be the kindest thing to do. She couldn't let Viva settle back here then uproot her again, sending her back to Clive when Whispering Willows was sold. That's if Clive would even part with her. He was clearly attached to her, and Bethany had no right even to ask.

She glanced out of the kitchen window, just in time to see Summer coming out of a loosebox pushing a wheelbarrow. She didn't even glance over at the house, though she must have seen Bethany's car and knew she was moving in today. No chance of a thaw there any time soon.

Rummaging in the cupboard under the sink she found some dusters and polish and set to work polishing and dusting the living room. She'd hired a team of cleaners to come in last week and they'd done an amazing job of washing and scrubbing the house. The place had been thoroughly deep cleaned, and even the old bathroom looked halfway decent, but dust had a habit of accumulating so she might as well keep on top of it.

She put Joseph's old radio on as she worked, singing along to some hits of the eighties as she valiantly tried to keep her spirits up. She needed to feel at home here, at least for a short while. She couldn't let Whispering Willows drag her down again. Vaguely she thought she heard the back door open and wondered if Summer had come in to use the toilet or get herself a drink. Since there was no point in trying to talk to her she continued working, so when she heard Clive's voice behind her she almost leapt into the air in fright.

'Working well there, Bethany.'

She spun round, duster in her hand, her face burning as she switched off the radio. 'I didn't realise you were here!'

'No, well, I've been a bit busy.'

He stepped forward and handed her a small bunch of flowers.

'Housewarming gift,' he said awkwardly, then nodded ruefully at the jug on the mantelpiece. 'Mind, I can see someone's beaten me to it, and they look a lot better than these.'

'Oh no, I love them!'

Bethany's enthusiasm was as great as her surprise. Clive had chosen a pretty, informal bouquet of colourful mixed spring flowers, cobalt blue sea holly, and—she inhaled the scent and smiled—eucalyptus leaves.

'They're gorgeous!' she enthused. 'And I love the sea holly. They remind me of Scotland and thistles.'

'Aye, me too,' he said, smiling with clear relief. 'You like them then?'

'I love them! These,' she added firmly, 'can go in my bedroom to cheer me up every morning when I wake up. I've got just the vase for them, too.'

She hurried back into the kitchen and set to work arranging the flowers in the milk churn container.

'There, don't they look gorgeous?'

'They do,' he agreed. 'I'm glad you like them. I admit, my heart sank when I saw that gorgeous bouquet in the living room. Who bought you those?'

'Miss Lavender,' she told him. 'Wasn't it kind of her? She got me a card, too.' She pulled one of the drawers open and took it from where she'd stashed it, not keen on putting it up on display.

He glanced at it and raised an eyebrow. 'New home? It's hardly that.'

'Exactly, but she was being thoughtful, bless her. Would you like a cup of tea?'

'I'd love one if you're not too busy. If you want to get on with cleaning I'll make us both one,' he offered.

'I've finished for now,' she said hastily, putting the duster and polish back under the sink. 'I'm ready for a cuppa myself.'

She filled the kettle and took out two mugs as Clive sat at the table.

'Did you get the flowers from Petalicious?' she enquired, as a way of breaking the sudden silence that had fallen.

'No. I got them from a florist's down in Upper Wharfedale,' he told her. 'On my way back.'

'Your way back?' She dropped teabags into both mugs and spooned sugar into his. 'Where have you been? I thought I hadn't seen you around,' she added, hoping she sounded casual and not as if she'd been fretting about his whereabouts ever since she'd got here.

'I was over there making some enquiries on your behalf.'

The kettle clicked and, rather shakily, Bethany poured boiling water into the mugs. 'What sort of enquiries?'

'I hope you don't mind,' he said, sounding a bit worried. 'I just wanted to help take some of the burden from you, so I got in touch with a donkey sanctuary down there to see if there was any chance of them taking our wee girls. They said they could, so I drove over today to have a look around the place.'

Bethany placed the mugs of tea on the table and sat next to him.

'And?'

He shrugged. 'Can't fault it. It's well run, clean, efficient. They have lots of very contented donkeys there and they obviously care. I think the girls would be happy and well looked after.'

Bethany swallowed, thinking of elderly Diamond and Sapphire, cheeky Oona, and gentle Mayflower. It suddenly all seemed very real.

'Have they said they'll take them then?' she asked hesitantly, surprised to find she was half hoping he'd say no.

'They can, but not for a few weeks. They've just bought some more land and they're donkey-proofing it, plus they're having new shelters built. They reckon it should be ready for them some time in June. Not too long for you to wait, right?'

Not long at all.

'Summer's going to be devastated,' she murmured, cradling her mug of tea.

'She's going to be devastated whatever we do,' he said gently. 'At least this way she knows they'll be looked after. We were lucky they'd just expanded the premises or there'd have been no room for them.' He eyed her with some concern. 'Are you okay?'

'Yes, yes of course.'

'And you didn't mind me acting on your behalf?'

'Not at all. It was very kind of you.'

'They gave me a number of an animal sanctuary that might be able to take some of the other residents,' he said. 'It's a bit further away, on the North York Moors in a village called Bramblewick, but she said they're very good. She doesn't know if they can take all the horses and ponies but thought they might have room for some of them. What do you think?'

She should have been thrilled, so why did she have a sinking feeling in the pit of her stomach? Summer, she thought dully. That was the problem. She knew Summer would never forgive her and that she was about to break the girl's heart. That was why she wasn't feeling more relieved.

'I could ring them for you?' he suggested tentatively. 'If you like?'

'Thank you,' she said gratefully, acknowledging that it wasn't his responsibility, and she didn't deserve his thoughtfulness. 'You're very kind.'

'I promised Joseph I'd make sure his animals were taken care of,' he said roughly. 'I intend to keep that promise.'

She gulped down some tea. So it wasn't really about her at all then. This was all about his obligation to her brother. She should have known. 'I'll keep looking, too,' she promised. 'To find decent homes for the rest of them, I mean.' It was, after all, the least she could do.

He glanced around the kitchen. 'How does it feel to be back properly? Have you been upstairs yet?'

'I have,' she said lightly, keen to hide her disappointment from him. 'I've put my things in the room you stayed in. My old room's too small and, besides, it has bad memories. As for the other rooms...'

'I can imagine,' he said sympathetically. 'Must be very hard for you, especially given the circumstances.'

'At least my mother didn't die here,' she said. 'In this house, I mean. That's something.'

No, she'd taken herself away to the banks of the Skimmer at the boundary of her property. There she'd taken the mixture of drugs she'd somehow hidden from her husband and doctor, lay down beneath the long, drooping branches of one of the willow trees, closed her eyes and allowed her life to ebb away from her.

'You won't recognise it by the time it's finished,' he said encouragingly. 'When do the decorators arrive?'

'Not for another fortnight. The electrician's coming next week to put the new sockets and light fittings in, and Ava's put me on to a good builder so I'm going to contact him next about the stables. I need him to look over that block which is bulging. He might be able to recommend a roofer, too. I wouldn't be surprised if the stables need a completely new roof. Oh, and the doors will need replacing, too. Probably the windows as well.' She managed a weak smile. 'Summer should approve of that anyway.'

He didn't look convinced, and she thought he was probably right. Why would Summer care if the stables were repaired at last when it was too late for the horses and ponies she loved? If any horses reaped the benefit of the renovations they wouldn't be Whispering Willows' horses. And, if Bethany was being really honest with herself, the chances were the stables would be converted into a holiday let, so there'd be no equines in there at all once Chester and Barney stopped using them.

She sighed inwardly and sipped her tea, not really tasting it. Then she remembered something and frowned.

'Clive, did Joseph ever mention a rocking horse to you?'

He gave her a puzzled look. 'Rocking horse? No, why?'

'There's one in my room,' she told him. 'My old room, I mean. It definitely wasn't mine and I assume I'm the last child who ever lived here, so what's it doing here? Who does it belong to?'

'I have no idea,' he confessed. 'As far as I know there were no children here. Certainly not while I've been living in Tuppenny Bridge. I can't imagine what it's doing here.'

'Strange. It's really pretty and just the sort of rocking horse I'd have loved when I was little, but...' She shrugged. 'Oh well. Just another question Joseph will never be able to answer.'

Clive watched her curiously. 'What were the other questions?' He shook his head. 'Sorry, didn't mean to pry.'

Bethany hesitated. 'Did he ever tell you what happened with Glenn?' she asked, almost reluctantly.

He looked surprised. 'Glenn?'

'My ex-fiancé,' she said flatly. 'The man I thought was going to rescue me from this terrible place. You know, the handsome prince saving Rapunzel from the tower?'

Clive gave her a gentle smile. 'No, sorry. He never mentioned him.'

'No,' she said bitterly. 'I don't suppose he would.'

'But *you* could tell me,' he said. 'If you want to. No pressure,' he added as she shifted in her chair. 'Just, I'm always ready to listen if you ever want to talk.'

Her heart raced as she looked into his kindly grey eyes. She knew he *would* listen, and he would probably be sympathetic. But how far would that sympathy go, given his history?

Even so, if she wanted a chance with this man she knew it was time to be honest.

'I thought I loved him,' she admitted. 'Well, obviously or I wouldn't have got engaged to him, would I? Looking back at it now I can see it wasn't love, or anything close. I just wanted an escape route. I was nineteen. I wasn't going to inherit anything from Mother until my twenty-first birthday and I was desperate to get away. Glenn seemed like the perfect solution. He was kind and funny and made me feel like the most important girl in the world.'

'How did you meet him?' Clive asked curiously. 'Was he from this town?'

'No. His father owned a chain of pubs, and he was considering buying The Lady Dorothy at the time. Glenn had been sent here to look it over and decide if it was worth pursuing. He was invited to a tour of the Lusty Tup Brewery while he was here, and Joseph was in charge of showing him around. He invited Glenn back to Whispering Willows as a courtesy, since Glenn was staying in a hotel and didn't know anyone in the area, and they'd already struck up a friendship. As soon as I saw him I convinced myself he was the man for me, and I'm not lying when I say he gave me every impression that he was pretty keen on me, too.' She ran a hand through her hair, her face burning with humiliation as she remembered how naïve she'd been.

'So, what happened?' he asked. 'How soon were you engaged?'

'Very soon,' she admitted. 'Too soon, I should have thought it was odd. He was almost desperate to get that ring on my finger, and his father was over the moon, while mine was furious. I must admit, that was part of the attraction. Knowing my father didn't want me to get married and that he was powerless to stop me felt good.

'But although I was glad Glenn's dad was happy for us, he seemed almost *too* eager. He started planning the wedding before I'd even had chance to absorb the fact that I was going to be married. Joseph *did* try to warn me. He said it was happening way too fast and I should think about what I was doing. He said he didn't think Glenn was the right man for me. Naturally I didn't listen. I loved Joseph, but I thought he just didn't understand love. He'd never had a girlfriend and I figured he never would. He was way too introverted. He didn't really go anywhere to meet anyone, except work. Even so, despite his own lack of experience, he seemed adamant that Glenn was wrong for me, and I should slow down.'

She noticed Clive was looking pensive.

'Are you sure you don't know about this?' she asked suspiciously.

He took her hand, and she felt her insides melt as he squeezed her fingers.

'I promise I don't,' he said softly, 'but I've an awful feeling I can guess.'

'You knew about Joseph then?' she asked.

'Aye. He never hid that side of himself from me and why should he?'

'I wish he'd hidden it from Glenn,' she said bitterly. 'As you've no doubt realised, the two of them were having an affair behind my back. And his father knew, of course. Oh, not about Joseph, but about Glenn's sexual preferences. That was why he'd practically steamrollered us into getting married. Couldn't believe his luck.'

'How did you find out?' Clive's thumb stroked the palm of

her hand, making her shivery. It was almost enough to soothe the pain of those awful memories. Almost.

'In the worst possible way. I walked in on them in the stables. It was the day before my wedding, can you believe it? I was supposed to be picking up the orders of service from the printer in Limmer-on-Skimmer but I only got as far as Chestnut Lane when the car broke down.' She gave a tight smile. 'It had never played up before. Was it fate, do you think? I've often wondered what would have happened if I hadn't walked back to Whispering Willows to see if I could borrow Joseph's car. Would I ever have found out? Would Joseph have stood back and let me marry Glenn, all the while knowing they were in a relationship? Would they have carried on their tawdry affair behind my back?'

'He wouldn't do that,' Clive said, then bit his lip. 'Then again, I wouldn't have said he'd ever sleep with your fiancé. I'm sorry, Bethany. It must have been awful for you.'

'That doesn't begin to cover it,' she said. 'I was devastated. He, on the other hand, seemed more concerned that I'd tell Father. He was terrified in fact. I broke it off with Glenn and I never saw him again. As far as I was concerned both he and Joseph were dead to me.'

She inhaled sharply and Clive squeezed her hand again. 'Did you tell your father?' he asked.

'No I didn't.' She couldn't take credit for that though. She wasn't so noble as he might suppose. 'Not for Joseph's sake. I didn't care if he was shamed. No, it was for Magnus. I told you what Father was like. How he punished our animals instead of us. I couldn't even bear to imagine what he might do to Magnus if he found out Joseph had slept with Glenn. Not that he'd be bothered by my broken engagement, but he was never the most liberal minded of men. He'd have been disgusted if he knew Joseph was gay and Magnus could well have been punished for what Father perceived to be Joseph's sin. I couldn't do that. I couldn't be responsible for his suffering.'

She wiped away a tear. 'Anyway, after enduring a couple of months with Father gloating at my broken engagement and Joseph skulking around in silence, avoiding me at all costs, I accepted Helena's offer to move in with her in her flat in York. I'd been talking to her on the phone for weeks, pouring out my feelings, and she was furious on my behalf. She kept telling me that Joseph didn't deserve to be forgiven when he quite clearly wasn't going to apologise, and that I should leave home and start again. Finally, I agreed. I left in the early hours the next day. I did a secretarial course in York and got jobs temping for an agency, which was how I met Ted. You know the rest.'

'So that's why you left Tuppenny Bridge,' he said sadly. 'Such a shame for you both. And you've stayed angry with Joseph all these years, even though he didn't stay with Glenn? Even though you realised you never really loved Glenn?'

'Are you judging me?' she asked, feeling a surge of resentment.

'Not at all,' he said. 'It's just, well, it seems an awful long time to nurse a grudge. I know, I know!' He held up his hands. 'He broke your heart. He betrayed you. He let you down. I get all that. But thirty odd years, Bethany? Even after you'd married Ted and moved on?'

'You don't understand,' she said bitterly.

'Then explain it to me. I'd like to understand.'

She wasn't sure she wanted to. Would he judge her all over again? Dismiss her feelings as if they didn't matter at all? She didn't think she could bear that.

'If you must know,' she said reluctantly, 'I would probably have forgiven him years ago. I missed him. Yes, I know that sounds weird, but I really did. Until what happened with Glenn, Joseph was all I had. He was my brother and I—I *loved* him.'

To her horror she began to sob. Where on earth had that come from?

Clive put his arm around her and held her.

'It's okay. If you want to stop you can.'

'I don't want to stop,' she wept. 'I need to tell you.'

He nodded, saying nothing but continuing to hold her.

'He never got in touch with me,' she said brokenly. 'That's what I could never forgive him for. If he'd written to me or telephoned me or turned up in person I'd have been ready to listen. I was ready to listen the day I left home. I needed him. I needed him to prove to me that he was still the brother who'd taken care of me and loved me all those years. That I hadn't been wrong about him. About us. All I wanted was an apology, but it never came. He never bothered, Clive. I never heard a word from him and now I never will.'

It felt as if a dam had broken inside and a torrent of emotion poured from her. So much grief, anger, and pain that it overwhelmed her.

Clive held her tightly and stroked her hair, kissing the top of her head now and then and making soothing noises while she sobbed desperately as she finally accepted that Joseph was gone, and she'd never get to make it up with him. How she wished she'd got the message in time. How she wished she could have been with him before it was all too late. Now she'd never get that chance and it broke her heart.

'It was easier to hate him,' she managed at last, mumbling into the handkerchief that Clive had pressed into her hand. 'Far better to channel my emotions into despising the brother who'd let me down than accept how much I missed and needed him.'

'I think he missed and needed you, too,' Clive said. 'I know you don't believe that, but—'

She shook her head in denial. 'He can't have done. He knew where I lived. He must have known! Miss Lavender told me that my marriage to Ted was in the local papers—all that *local girl marries multi-millionaire* stuff they love so much—and I know Joseph read those. Ted was a well-known businessman, easy to trace. He could have found me if he'd tried. Look how quickly Miss Lavender tracked me down and that was after I'd been divorced and Ted had passed away! He just didn't care enough about me and that's what really hurts, Clive. That's what I can't forgive or understand. And he'll never be able to tell me, will he? He'll never be able to answer the one question I really need the answer to.'

'What question's that?' he asked, his own eyes shimmering with tears.

'What did I ever do to him to make him stop loving me?'

Clive closed his eyes and pulled her closer. 'You didn't do anything wrong, and I don't believe Joseph ever stopped loving you. Maybe it was just guilt and shame that kept him from trying to find you. Maybe he thought you wouldn't be interested.'

'But he could have tried,' she sobbed. 'Couldn't he? Wouldn't you? If you loved someone and you'd done something to hurt them, wouldn't you risk rejection to try to put it right with them?'

Clive sighed. 'Who knows what we'd do in those circumstances? We're all different, aren't we? I can't say why Joseph didn't find you but, please believe me, I'm sure he loved you to the end. I wish you could have had some time with him before it was too late. I wish you could have got the answer to your question, Bethany, I really do.'

Bethany wiped her eyes and sat up. 'Thank you,' she said at last.

'For what?'

'For letting me cry and not making me feel an idiot.' She realised she must look bloody awful and felt embarrassed. 'Your tea's gone cold,' she said, trying to smile.

'Ach, that hardly matters. I'll make you a fresh one if you like?' he offered.

'I don't want one,' she said. 'I just...'

She couldn't think what she wanted right now, except to sit here with him. His presence was a reassuring comfort to her. She didn't want him to leave.

'I like you being here,' she said, wondering as she did why on earth she'd blurted that out.

'I like being here,' he told her. 'I like being with you.'

'And I with you.'

Their gaze held and she felt something stir within her. By the look in his eyes she was certain he was feeling the same thing.

Slowly, with a hint of uncertainty, he leaned towards her and kissed her softly on the lips.

Bethany cupped the back of his neck and kissed him back, probably with far more passion than he was expecting, but to her relief and delight he responded and put his arms around her, holding her tightly as he kissed her.

'Aw, Beth,' he said, moving away almost regretfully.

No one but Joseph had ever called her Beth, but she rather liked hearing it from Clive's lips.

'I'm sorry. I should never have done that.'

'Why not?' she asked. 'I wanted you to. Didn't you enjoy it?'

He gave her a rueful smile. 'I enjoyed it a bit too much, but now's not the time. You're emotional and vulnerable, and I took advantage of that. I should have thought. It's not right.'

'You didn't take advantage of me,' she protested. 'If anyone instigated this it was me.'

'But you were in a state with yourself,' he said. 'I should have taken control. I'm so sorry.'

'But, Clive—'

'You know what?' he said, giving her a warm smile, 'I need to get out there and do some work. Summer will be wondering where I am, given I've been missing in action most of the day.'

'Right,' she said, confused.

'It's all right,' he said, kissing the top of her head as he got to his feet. 'Don't worry. I just think, well, now's not the time. Not when you're feeling like this.'

She tried to hang on to his words of comfort. Was he telling her that the time would be right when she wasn't so emotional about Joseph? Did that mean he was genuinely interested in her? Or was he just being kind?

'I won't mention the donkey sanctuary to Summer yet,' he said. 'She's still reeling from the last lot of news, so I'll wait a few days. And I'll call the other sanctuary later today, find out if there's any possibility of them taking some of ours, okay?'

She nodded. Back to business then. Like the kiss had never happened.

Clive frowned and sat back down. 'You're even more upset now, aren't you? I'm sorry. I should never have kissed you and—'

'It's not the kiss that upset me,' she said hastily. 'It's...'

'It's what?'

'Well, you just seem to want to pretend it didn't happen. It's like you can't get away from me fast enough.'

He ran a hand across his forehead. 'I'm an idiot. I never meant to make you feel that way, but I seem to be getting it all wrong lately.' He gazed steadily into her eyes. 'I'm not trying to pretend it didn't happen. And I'm not going to pretend I didn't want to do it either, because I did. I've wanted to kiss you for some time now.'

'You have? So what's the problem?'

'It's just...' He shook his head. 'Nothing. Like I said it wasn't right that I took advantage of you when you were so vulnerable. I'd just be a complication you don't need right now. Can we revisit this another time when we're both thinking a bit more clearly? My head is so busy right now.'

She supposed she could understand his concerns. He was an honourable man. Too bloody honourable. In the end she couldn't deny he was trying to do right by her.

'Fair enough,' she said, looking down but managing a smile.

'You're okay, Bethany?' he asked her, concern in his eyes. 'I've not hurt you?'

'Of course not,' she said lightly. 'Go on back to work. I'll get on with the cleaning.'

He smiled, clearly relieved, and headed outside. Bethany stared into her cold cup of tea.

Had he hurt her? Well, a bit.

The trouble was, she had a feeling that, if he chose, he could do more than hurt her. Clive Browning could rip her heart, and her entire world, apart.

TWENTY-FOUR

'Penguin?'

'Oh, Ben, you really know the way to a man's heart.' Clive laughed and accepted the chocolate biscuit with thanks.

'*Your* heart anyway. You're obsessed.' Ben grinned. 'One day I'll frighten you to death and offer you a plain digestive. That'll be the day.'

'I'd never speak to you again.' Clive unwrapped the Penguin and leaned back against the counter with a contented sigh. 'Had a good morning?'

'Not too bad. Hamster with an abscess and a cat with an eye infection are two of the highlights. It's good to have you back again, though. Don't get me wrong, Piotr was a good vet and very easy to get along with, but I've missed you, grouchy as you are.'

'Grouchy?' Clive said indignantly. 'Me?'

'Well, when the supplies of Penguins are running low...'

'Ah. Fair point.' Clive crunched his biscuit thoughtfully. 'Have you spoken to Summer lately?'

'Every day,' Ben said, amused. 'I take it you're fishing for information about something?'

'Not fishing exactly.' Clive sighed. 'Has she told you about her falling out with Bethany?'

Ben nodded. 'She's not a happy bunny, but can you blame her? Have to say, I felt so guilty when she kept banging on about Bethany selling up and how duped she felt. I wanted to tell her I already knew about it, but I was worried she'd feel there was no one on her side if I did. I suppose I'll have to tell her sooner or later.'

'I don't think you should. Look, you wanted to tell her, and it was me who made you keep the secret. We both know she'd never have gone to Australia if we'd let the cat out of the bag, and look how much she enjoyed herself! She'd have missed all that. It wouldn't have benefitted anyone if she'd been told from the beginning and it won't benefit anyone if she finds out you already knew, so stay quiet, Ben. The last thing Summer needs right now is more stress.'

'I suppose you're right,' Ben said thoughtfully. 'Although I don't feel good keeping secrets from her.'

'That's because you're a decent man,' Clive told him fondly. 'Always have been.'

Ben's face coloured. 'Not always,' he reminded him ruefully.

'Ach, away with you! That was the boy. All right, you were a wee scamp back in the day, but as an adult you've always been exceptional. I'm proud of you. Have I ever told you that?'

Clive watched, amused, as the flush on Ben's face deepened. 'You're way too modest, you know.'

'Don't be daft!' Ben clearly decided the best way to deal with this unexpected compliment was to offer a distraction. 'Have you heard the Lavender Ladies are taking bets again?'

Clive groaned. 'Don't tell me. They're running a book on our wedding date. Mine and Bethany's I mean.'

Ben laughed. 'Not exactly. Actually,' he said, suddenly serious, 'speaking of you and Bethany... *Is* there something between you? I mean, we all saw you at Kat and Jonah's wedding and you looked very intimate, and you walked her home, didn't you? And Summer says she's been cooking you breakfast every morning. Is that true?'

'She's been cooking breakfast for Maya and Lennox, too,' Clive pointed out. 'And she'd have cooked breakfast for Summer, but Summer dug her heels in and decided she didn't want anything from Bethany.'

'I see.' Ben hesitated. 'So you're not *involved* with her then?'

'Involved?' Clive wasn't sure what to say but in the interests of honesty he couldn't outright deny there was something going on between them, even if he hadn't a clue what that was. 'It's complicated,' he said finally.

Ben stared at him. 'Seriously? So you and she—'

'I don't know what we are, Ben, okay?'

'But you like her?'

'I like her fine,' Clive admitted. 'But like I say, it's complicated.'

'You mean because she's leaving soon?' Ben sounded sympathetic. 'That's what the bet's about. The Lavender Ladies' latest book is on whether she'll move away from Tuppenny Bridge or stay here. With you. *Because* of you actually.'

Clive swallowed. 'And what are the odds?'

'Evens,' Ben admitted. 'I don't think anyone's quite sure of the outcome.'

'Join the club,' Clive said glumly.

'Oh heck,' Ben said. 'You really do like her. I'm sorry. I thought it was just rumour and gossip. It must be awful not knowing what she's going to do.'

'Oh, I know what she's going to do.' Clive threw his empty Penguin wrapper in the bin. 'She's selling Whispering Willows. Her mind's made up on that, and I can't really blame her. It has awful memories for her.'

'Maybe,' Ben said hopefully, 'she'll sell Whispering Willows but stay in Tuppenny Bridge. Maybe she'll move into the flat above here with you. What?' he demanded as Clive gave him a scornful look. 'Why wouldn't she?'

'Because Stepping Stones is still in this town, and it's not just Whispering Willows that holds bad memories for her. This whole place, it reminds her of sadness and betrayal. She can't wait to get away. I doubt very much I'd be enough to keep her here and I wouldn't want to be the reason she stayed anyway.'

'You wouldn't?'

Clive shook his head. 'It would never work. It would be trapping her, just the way she was trapped here when she was younger. I couldn't do that to her, and anyway, she'd end up running away again at some point. If she does stay here it has to be because she's come to terms with her past and wants to be here, not because she has to stay because it's where I am. And somehow I doubt that will ever happen.'

Ben looked worried. 'I don't suppose you're planning to move away with her?'

Clive gave a mirthless laugh. 'You're joking, right?'

'I mean, I wouldn't want you to,' Ben said slowly, 'but if it's what you want. If it will make you happy.'

'But it wouldn't,' Clive said heavily. 'My life's here. I love this town and the people in it. I love my job and Stepping Stones and...'

He'd been about to say, 'And you', but couldn't make himself do it.

'And everything,' he finished lamely. 'Bethany's always on the move. She doesn't settle anywhere, so how could I work? How could I feel at home? And that's what I need, Ben. Home. It's where I'm happiest. I suppose the truth is we're a bad match. At least, for now. Rotten timing, I guess. She says she wants a home of her own, but she's had years to find one, hasn't she? I think maybe the truth is she'll never settle, and I can't live like that.'

Which was one of the reasons he hadn't followed up on their kiss. Thinking about it now he felt a mixture of emotions. He'd been taken aback by how much he'd enjoyed it, and by how powerful the urge to take things further with her had been. But he'd quickly realised that it would only make things more complicated. He had other obligations, and she would be leaving soon, so what was the point of trying to start a relationship with someone when they wouldn't be around much longer? Plus Bethany had been emotional and vulnerable. She probably wasn't thinking straight. He'd known she had feelings for him, and he couldn't help worrying he'd taken advantage of her when she was at a low point.

Then there was Jennifer. There was always Jennifer. He was, he realised wearily, so confused.

'I'm really sorry, mate,' Ben said. 'I hope things work out for you; I really do.' He tilted his head, a gentle smile on his lips. 'It's funny, I never thought I'd see the day when Clive Browning fell in love. I can't believe it's finally happened.'

'I never said I'd fallen in love,' Clive reminded him.

'You didn't have to,' Ben told him. 'It's written all over your face. Anyway, I'd better get off. I've got another call-out to Hillside Farm.' He clapped Clive on the shoulder. 'It will work out, one way or the other.'

'Aye, no doubt,' Clive said airily. 'And right now we've more important things to worry about, like Mike Gray's sick heifer. Get yourself away to Hillside.'

Ben nodded and left the consulting room. Clive ran a hand over his tired eyes before sinking into the chair.

What a mess! How had he ever got himself into this situation? It had taken him years to pluck up the courage to confess his feelings to one woman and now here he was, just weeks later, falling for another one.

But I'm not in love with Bethany, he thought anxiously. Am I?

And if he was, where did that leave Jennifer?

What, he wondered, would Julian make of all this?

At the memory of his old friend he felt the familiar flood of shame. Julian had been such a wonderful, decent man. Generous, kind, and so bloody noble and brave it had taken Clive's breath away.

He remembered that afternoon when he'd gone to Monk's Folly to visit his friend. Julian had been through gruelling treatment and was weak but optimistic. Jennifer had shown him into the living room where Julian lay on the sofa covered with a blanket despite the warm day.

He'd been so overcome at seeing how ill his friend looked he hadn't been able to say a word. He'd almost fallen into the armchair and Jennifer had sat in the other one. She'd given Clive a sympathetic look but there was also a warning in her eyes, as if she was telling Clive not to show Julian how worried he was.

Evidently he'd failed. Julian had never been daft.

'Don't look like that. There's still hope,' he'd told Clive, who'd blinked away tears and tried to pull himself together. If Julian wasn't crying he certainly couldn't justify giving way to his emotions. 'I'm not written off just yet so don't look so glum.'

Jennifer had passed Julian a glass of water and poured Clive a whisky, then she dropped a kiss on her husband's forehead and left them to it.

As she closed the door behind her, Julian said softly, 'I love that woman so much.'

'I know you do.' The words had almost stuck in Clive's throat as guilt tried to force them back down.

'She's so good to me,' Julian continued. 'And all I want is for her to be happy. To have a good life.'

'You'll give her a good life,' Clive had managed. 'As soon as you're well again think of all the things you can do together. The places you can go.'

Julian smiled at him. 'You think?'

'Of course I think! You've just said yourself there's still hope. You can't change your mind now!' He gave his friend a weak smile. 'I won't allow it. No talk of defeat here.'

'But that's just it, Clive,' Julian said. 'I need to be honest. I'm putting on a brave face for Jennifer's sake, but with you I want to be truthful. With myself as well as you.'

Clive had gulped down some whisky, not wanting to hear it but knowing Julian needed him to listen, and that it was the least he could do for him.

'I might get through this,' Julian told him, 'but there's a good chance I won't. It's okay,' he said quickly as Clive opened his mouth to speak, 'I don't need platitudes or reassurance. This is me being brutally honest with you, okay? While Jennifer's not here. While it's just you and me.'

Clive nodded dumbly.

'I can accept that,' Julian continued. 'It's bloody rotten but life *can* be rotten, can't it? When I first got the diagnosis, all I could think was, *why me*? But the truth is, why not me? What's so special about me that I shouldn't be affected? Thing is, it can happen to anyone. It does happen, in one form or another other, to about half the population. Just got to get on with it, haven't we?'

Clive drained his whisky and stared down at the carpet. He wasn't sure he could be half as stoic as Julian if it ever happened to him.

'It's not me I'm worried about,' Julian admitted. 'It's Jennifer. And Leon, and Ben, and little Jamie.' He swallowed down a sob at that. 'Jamie's just a baby,' he said. 'Bad enough that I'll leave my boys behind, but Jamie won't even remember me.'

'You don't know that!' Clive protested. 'You're looking at the worst-case scenario.'

'I know. I know I am. But that's because it's just you and me and I can do that with you. With everyone else it's all very positive and *look on the bright side*, and sometimes I actually mean it. I know things might work out well, but while you're here I must tell you something. Just in case.'

Clive frowned. 'What is it?'

'If the worst does happen, I can't bear the thought of Jennifer having to cope with it all on her own. This house takes some looking after. Jamie, as I said, is just a baby. Ben's all over the place. I don't know what's going on with him lately but he's getting into all sorts of bother at school. It's the last thing his mum needs. Leon's a good lad and I know he'd step up for her and his brothers, but I don't want his life to be all about sacrifice and responsibility. He's way too young for all that. So, I must ask you, Clive. Would you be there for them? Would you take care of my family for me?'

Clive stared at him. He genuinely had no answer to that. It was so unexpected he could only sit in guilty silence.

Julian shook his head. 'Don't look like that. I know what you're thinking but it's okay. I know how you feel about Jennifer. I've always known.'

Clive's heart thudded. 'What—what do you mean?'

'We haven't got time to play games, mate,' Julian said, glancing at the door. 'She could come back any second. It's time for straight talking. I've seen the way you look at her and I realised way back that you were in love with her. I think you fell in love with her the moment I introduced you to her, didn't you?'

The truth was, Clive had briefly met Jennifer in Market Square before he ever knew she was Julian's wife, and he'd fallen in love with her instantly. He'd been devastated to find out she was married to his new friend and had done all he could, over the years, to push his feelings for her away. He honestly thought he'd hidden them well. Clearly, he'd failed.

'I'm so sorry,' he mumbled miserably. 'I tried so hard—'

'It doesn't matter. I know you haven't acted on those feelings, and I know Jennifer would never betray me. I trust you both. I love you both. And that's the thing, Clive. I can't think of anyone better to look after her for me if I do die. I can't bear the thought of her being alone, struggling with all this responsibility. You're a good man and I know you'd take care of her and my boys. I know you'd do everything you could to make them happy and give them a decent life. Will you please consider it? For me?'

Of all the things Clive had expected to hear this was the very last of them.

'Julian, I couldn't—'

'But you could! Don't you see? It would be perfect. You already love her. She's not the sort of woman who should be alone. I'm terrified that, if the worst happens, she'll spend years cooped up here alone with the boys, struggling to get by. She deserves to be loved. She deserves to be loved by someone like you who'll make sure she'll continue to live without me and, more than that, that she'll be happy. Please.'

Clive couldn't hold back the tears. Being with Jennifer was everything he'd ever wanted, but not like this. Never like this. He'd gladly sacrifice every moment with her if his friend could survive. She belonged with Julian, not him.

'Jennifer's totally in love with you,' he said, his voice thick with grief. 'She wouldn't want me even if I tried to help.'

'I think she might surprise you,' Julian said. 'She's an emotional, passionate woman. She needs a man in her life. Be that man, Clive. I can't think of anyone else I'd want to be her husband, or a father to my children. Promise me.'

It was an overwhelming statement to hear, and Clive had felt humbled and unworthy. He didn't deserve such generosity.

Even so, he knew Julian was desperate for reassurance. He needed peace of mind, and maybe if he had that guarantee he could gather his strength and focus on the fight that lay ahead of him. If he was no longer worrying about his family's future he might have a better chance of beating this thing. Of surviving. Of living his life with his wife and children. Then all this would be forgotten, and Clive would happily step back and leave them to it.

'I promise,' he said quietly.

The smile on Julian's face had almost broken his heart.

'Thank you,' he'd said, then closed his eyes as if this discussion had drained him of all energy.

Clive had left him to sleep and, after bidding a brief and embarrassed farewell to Jennifer, he'd left Monk's Folly, his mind whirling, praying he'd never have to keep that promise.

In the end, of course, he hadn't. Not really. Things had changed so drastically since then, with events that neither he nor Julian could ever have predicted. Who, for example, could have imagined, that afternoon in Monk's Folly, that Julian would outlive his eldest son? Clive had seen the effect Leon's death had on both Jennifer and Julian, and in a way he'd known from that moment his friend wasn't going to make it.

After Julian's remains were buried close to Leon's in the Garden of Ashes in All Hallows churchyard, he'd thought about approaching Jennifer, just to see if she needed any help, but she'd hurried away from him, shepherding Ben with almost frantic haste.

He'd tried to speak to her several times after that, but she'd been cold and unyielding, and had made it clear she wanted nothing from him and that she was managing perfectly well without his help.

Maybe, he'd thought then, he should give it some time. His promise to Julian kept nagging away at him but now, more than ever, he felt it had been a mistake to make that promise. Yet make it he had. He owed his friend. He needed to make sure Jennifer was okay somehow. He just didn't know how.

Then one day she'd turned up at the surgery with one of the family's dogs, who was ill. Ben had been with her, and she'd told him the young lad was currently devouring every James Herriot book and was obsessed with becoming a vet.

He knew Ben had been through an ordeal. Losing his brother and father had changed him. He'd grown up way too fast. No longer a rebellious, badly-behaved boy, this fifteen-year-old had the weight of the world on his shoulders, and it showed.

Jennifer said proudly that he'd really turned things around at school and was working hard at last. He wanted to go to university and qualify. Be a vet just like James Herriot. Just like Clive.

And that was the moment he saw a way of keeping his promise to Julian. Not in full, but partially. He could mentor Ben, pay for his textbooks and equipment, supplement his student loan, and give him work experience. If Ben passed his exams he would offer him a job and make sure he was well-paid and well-treated. It would be a weight off Jennifer's mind. One less thing for her to worry about. And it would help the family financially, too.

He hadn't really given much thought to what might go wrong. Many years later he'd realised that Ben could have been a disaster. He might well have changed his mind about his future career. He might have failed his exams. He might have been the worst vet ever.

In the event he'd turned out to be a real blessing to Clive. He was hard-working, honest, reliable, compassionate, and skilled. He looked like his mother, but he had his father's nature. It wasn't long before Clive saw him the way Julian had wanted him to—as the son he'd never had. By supporting Ben he'd helped both Jennifer and Jamie financially, and he'd tried his best to counsel Ben and be there for him through the darkest times. He felt he'd done right by the boy.

But Jennifer was a different matter.

Despite his promise to Julian he'd never tried to get close to her until recently. He'd never broached the subject of their relationship. He'd never told her of her husband's wishes, or how he'd made a promise, or how he'd happily marry her and take care of her.

He'd failed Julian in that respect. But when he'd finally confessed how he felt to Jennifer he'd been soundly rejected. She didn't need him. Julian had thought she would crumble without a man, but Jennifer was happy at last. It had been hard for her, but she'd made a new life for herself. She loved her new home and her new job.

How ironic that it was Julian himself who had made things so difficult for her. If he hadn't drummed it into her how much he loved Monk's Folly, she might have let it go years ago, and life for the Callaghans would have been so much easier. He hadn't really been able to do anything about that apart from gently and repeatedly telling Ben that he should sell the place.

The worst part of it was that he knew Julian had only changed his will after Leon died, leaving the house to Ben, because he'd been so sure Jennifer would be taken care of by Clive and wouldn't need it. He'd inadvertently shackled his grieving son with the heaviest burden of all, and it had taken Summer's arrival in Tuppenny Bridge for Ben to finally see the light and get rid of the place. Nothing to do with Clive at all.

Jennifer didn't want him in her life. Not as a romantic partner anyway. He should feel free to pursue Bethany and be happy at last. But he didn't. Not really. Because he'd broken his promise to Julian, and he'd let Jennifer down badly. He'd let himself down, too, and he'd paid the price ever since for his weakness. How could he move on knowing that?

He couldn't give Bethany what she needed from him while

he still felt obliged to the Callaghans. And Bethany might be moving away anyway, so what was the point?

'Evens,' Ben had said about the bets being placed on Bethany's future. The whole town was unable to decide whether Bethany would stay or go. If the Lavender Ladies couldn't figure it out how was he supposed to?

But if she did leave Tuppenny Bridge...

His heart sank like a stone at the thought of it. He might never see her again and how did he really feel about that? It scared him as he realised it made him depressed beyond words. What he'd said to Ben was true. He didn't want Bethany to stay for him. He knew that wouldn't work, that she'd never be happy. What if she stayed but never came to terms with her past? She'd walk away at some point. She'd have no choice, and he wouldn't want her to remain there just because she felt obliged to stay with him. The last thing he wanted to do was trap her again.

But maybe, if he could give her the love she desperately needed, he could help her come to terms with everything that had happened before? Just maybe there was a chance they could both put their pasts behind them and move on together into a brighter future. A future that included Tuppenny Bridge, despite all the sad memories it held for them.

It had to be worth a shot, surely? They deserved happiness. They deserved a chance. Julian would forgive him. Wouldn't he?

And Joseph—how would he feel?

He felt a smile tugging at his lips as he imagined his friend's wry response to that question.

Don't be mithering about me. Life's too short. Do what makes you happy and bugger everyone else.

His smile faded as he remembered that Joseph had done what *he* wanted, and he'd broken his sister's heart in the process. Sometimes, following your own heart's desire came with too high a price.

'You can't hurt the dead,' he murmured to himself. No one alive right now would object to him and Bethany being together. It was only the memory of his two departed friends that was making him hesitate. He couldn't live the rest of his life for them. He'd put his life on hold for far too long already.

He wanted Bethany and she wanted him. It was time for them to find their own happiness.

TWENTY-FIVE

'Dinner at yours?' Bethany clutched her phone tighter as Clive's words sank in.

'Aye.' He sounded a bit awkward she thought, imagining him shuffling as he plucked up the courage to ask her out. Ask her out! Was this it? Was he finally arranging a date?

'I thought we'd be better at my place rather than being gawped at by everyone, and it's time you saw where I lived so you can see how house trained I am.'

Bethany's heart leapt. It *was* a date!

'I'd love to,' she said breathlessly. 'What time?'

'Come by about seven?' He paused. 'Look, I have to confess something first.'

She waited, half expecting him to say something she wouldn't want to hear, like, *Don't get any daft ideas. We're just friends, okay?*

'I'm a terrible cook.' He sighed. 'There, I've said it.'

She almost laughed with relief. 'That doesn't matter. I'm a good cook. I'll make us something if you—'

'Certainly not!' His obvious indignation made her smile. 'I've got loads of takeaway menus, so I thought I'd order us something. I know it's not the same but, trust me, your stomach will thank me for it.'

Now she did laugh. 'Okay. Seven it is. Thank you.'

'Great,' he said warmly. 'See you later.'

She ended the call and gazed unseeingly around the living room. Clive had asked her out! Finally, things were happening.

Bethany spent over an hour getting ready for her date with Clive that evening. She hadn't even taken that long to get ready for Kat and Jonah's wedding, and this was supposed to be a casual thing. She was, after all, only popping across the road to Stepping Stones for a takeaway. Put like that it seemed ridiculous to worry but she couldn't help it.

Bethany was starting to wonder what on earth had happened to her lately. She was acting like a schoolkid with a crush, and she was far too old for this sort of thing. Nevertheless, she tried on at least half a dozen outfits and took so much care with her make-up that she ended up, ironically, making a complete hash of it and having to do it all again.

By five to seven she was knocking on the front door of Stepping Stones, dressed in jeans and a simple cream top with three quarter length sleeves and a hanky hem.

'Smart casual,' she muttered to herself as doubt attacked her. Was she *too* casual? Would he be offended that she was wearing jeans? But if she'd worn something smart would he think she was crazy, given they were just...

Whatever the heck they were. Perhaps she'd read too much into this. He might see her as a pal. He might just want to check if she'd made any progress finding homes for Joseph's precious equines. But he could have asked her that on the phone, couldn't he? Oh, she was overthinking this. She was simply going to have a takeaway with a friend.

Don't expect anything else, Bethany. I'm warning you. That way you won't be disappointed.

She heard Viva yapping and forced a smile as the door

opened. The smile, however, became genuine almost instantly as he greeted her and invited her in.

Oh, lord! He looked *gorgeous*. She was relieved to see he was wearing jeans, too, but smart jeans, not like the ones he wore around the stables, thank goodness. And he had on a navy-blue, checked, brushed flannel shirt which, judging by the creases on the back, he'd taken fresh out of a packet.

She couldn't help but feel amused. Clearly his ironing skills were as good as his cooking skills since he'd decided to attempt neither.

He scooped up Viva, who was keen to say hello to their guest, and said, 'She's pleased to see you again. You, er, look lovely by the way. Shall we go up?'

It was years since she'd been inside Stepping Stones and she'd never been upstairs. She was amazed that she'd forgotten the spacious hallway with its tiled floor and the sweeping staircase that led to Clive's living quarters. This was a Victorian house that had clearly been built for people with money, and she followed him up the stairs thinking jeans didn't seem so appropriate any longer. She felt as if she should be dressed like someone from a George Eliot novel.

That feeling disappeared when she reached the landing, though. It was clear immediately that Clive's flat was thoroughly contemporary. Few of the original features remained intact up here, unlike downstairs, and she was ushered into a living room that was bright, airy, and modern in style.

It was also sparkling clean and spotlessly tidy. Clive might not be brilliant at ironing or cooking, but she couldn't fault his cleaning skills.

'Make yourself at home,' he said, putting Viva down. She noticed the slight tremor in his voice and realised he was as nervous as she was, which gave her hope that this was, indeed, more than just a meeting of two friends. 'Would you like a drink? I've got wine. Red and white. And there's whisky? Or maybe you'd prefer a soft drink,' he finished worriedly. 'I never thought. I might have some squash in the fridge...'

Bethany laughed. 'White wine sounds good to me,' she said. 'Thank you.'

His face brightened. 'Great. I'll be right back.'

He shot into what she presumed was the kitchen and she glanced around, eyeing his living room curiously while Viva settled herself in a squashy leather armchair, looking as if she'd already made herself quite at home here.

So this was where Clive lived. It was certainly nothing like Whispering Willows, but she had to admit it was more to her taste than her childhood home. There was good quality wooden flooring here, rather than the shabby carpet that graced, or rather *dis*graced, her own living room. The walls were painted in a slate grey which contrasted well with the white ceiling, skirting boards, architraves, doors, and coving. White shutter blinds added a contemporary twist to the large bay window, which dominated one wall.

There was no fireplace in here. Evidently it had, at some point, been blocked off. Instead there was a modern electric wall fire—the sort that could be operated by a remote control. Above that was a large, flat-screen television. In either recess stood oak wall units which housed a few books and assorted items, including, she noted with interest, several framed photographs of various adults, babies, and children.

In front of the chimney breast was a shaggy rug, which added texture and warmth to the wooden floor, while an oak coffee table stood in the centre of the room, bearing a vase of flowers not dissimilar to the ones he'd bought for her.

Bethany gazed around her, thinking she felt quite at home here. It was, perhaps, a little too perfect if anything. Too tidy. Too neat. But then, he'd probably smartened it up for her benefit. She was sure that, usually, there'd be mugs on that coffee table, the television on, perhaps books or newspapers lying around. She tried to visualise Clive actually living in here and smiled. He must have cared about Joseph an awful lot to give up this place to stay at Whispering Willows!

'Right, here you are.' Clive entered the room carrying two glasses of white wine and a stack of takeaway menus. 'I wasn't sure what sort of food you fancied so I've brought every leaflet I've had shoved through the letter box for the last two years or so. As you can see, there's plenty of choice.'

He grinned at her, and her insides fizzed with delight. She took the glass from his outstretched hand and said, 'I really don't mind. Whatever you want is fine by me.'

'No, no.' He shook his head in denial. 'It's your choice. I invited you and it's only right you decide what we have.'

'Well...' Bethany felt ridiculously pressured to choose the right thing suddenly. What if she selected something he hated? He might decide they were incompatible.

For goodness' sake, Bethany, you're not twelve! She honestly couldn't imagine what had happened to her lately.

Tentatively she suggested a curry from the Indian restaurant that had apparently opened in the town just before Christmas. They also delivered, and Clive immediately checked the online reviews on his phone and approved.

'Do you always check reviews?' she asked, amused.

'I do. And hygiene ratings from the council,' he admitted. 'Sorry. It's just my thing. What do you fancy?'

You, she thought dreamily, but said firmly, 'A chicken tikka masala for me.'

She waited for him to point out that chicken tikka masala had been invented in England and wasn't an authentic Indian dish at all, the way Ted had often done, but he didn't.

'Do you want rice and naan bread?' was all he asked.

She smiled, relieved that he hadn't disappointed her. 'I love naan bread, but I never eat it all, so it seems a waste.'

'We could share one?' he suggested. 'They're huge after all.'

'That sounds perfect.'

Clive ordered the food, including a lamb rogan josh for himself and was told the food would be with them within the hour.

'I should have asked you what you wanted and ordered it earlier,' he said ruefully. 'Never thought. Sorry. Are you really hungry? I can make us a snack if you are.'

'If I eat anything now I'll never manage the meal,' she said. 'It's okay. I'm not exactly starving.'

'That's good,' Clive said. He leaned back in the sofa and sighed. 'I'm not very good at this, Bethany. It's been a long time since I invited anyone round for dinner, as you can probably tell.'

She wondered who that had been and couldn't help but think it might have been Jennifer. She hadn't forgotten the way he'd looked at her that day in Monk's Folly. But surely if he wanted Jennifer he'd have asked her out by now? And why would he bother with Bethany if that was the case?

'Please don't stress,' she told him kindly. 'Honestly, it's just a treat to be away from Whispering Willows. Besides, I've been dying to see where you live.'

'You have?' He looked surprised. 'Would you like a guided tour? Not that there's much to see, I'll warn you.'

'I'd love one,' she admitted. 'If that's okay with you.'

He looked relieved to have something to do, and leapt up with enthusiasm, placing his wine glass on the coffee table. 'Come on then and I'll show you round.'

Viva immediately jumped off the armchair and trotted behind them, accompanying them on their grand tour.

It was a large flat, which she supposed wasn't surprising given the size of the house. Even so, she was taken aback at how big the kitchen diner was. Like the living room, it was thoroughly contemporary and utterly spotless.

'It's gleaming! You could operate in here,' she said, impressed.

'I have done on occasions,' he told her, then burst out laughing when she wrinkled her nose. 'I'm joking! Of course it's gleaming, I never cook.' He patted the ceramic hob and sighed. 'I don't think I've even switched this on apart from to heat up the odd tin of beans and fry eggs for butties. Mind, my microwave gets a good workout with all those ready meals.'

'You ought to teach yourself to cook,' she said sternly. 'It's not good for you to eat ready meals and takeaways.'

'And Penguins,' he said, a twinkle in his eye. 'Have I ever mentioned I'm partial to a Penguin?'

'Oh well, as long as you have variety in your diet,' she teased. 'I'll buy a few packets and keep them especially for you at Whispering Willows.'

Except, he wouldn't be visiting Whispering Willows any more, would he? He was back at his usual job now, and the only time she'd see him was if one of the animals got sick, God forbid. And even then it might be Ben who turned up.

'That would be grand,' he told her warmly, and she smiled. Maybe he meant to visit anyway, even if it wasn't to work. The thought cheered her immensely.

Apart from the living room and kitchen diner, the flat consisted of a small study, a bathroom, two good-sized bedrooms, and finally the largest bedroom, which turned out to be Clive's room, complete with an en suite.

For the first time he looked embarrassed, as if he'd somehow overstepped the mark by bringing her into his room. She determined to put him at his ease.

'Wow, it's so tidy! Don't you ever make a mess?' She gazed round at the beautifully neat and clean master bedroom and shook her head. 'I thought men couldn't do housework.'

'I can't abide mess,' he confessed. 'I think I had it drummed

into me by my mother. She's very house-proud and had me
helping with the cleaning from being a wee boy.'

'Your mum lives in Scotland?' she asked as she followed him
back into the living room.

'Oh, aye. Both my parents do. And my brothers. Well most
of them.' He waved a hand at the wall units. 'Got all their
photos on display. They keep sending me them in case I forget
what they look like,' he added jokily.

'I didn't realise you had brothers.'

'I've got four of them.'

'Four!' She gasped. 'Your poor mother! How on earth did
she cope with five boys?'

'We were all angels,' he assured her, a glint of amusement in
his eyes.

'So you're still in touch with some of them?' she asked,
settling herself back on the sofa, glass of wine in hand.

Clive collected his glass and joined her, both positioned so
they were facing each other with Viva lying in between them,
her head on her paws.

'I'm in touch with them all,' he said, sounding surprised at
the question. 'I go back up to Edinburgh once or twice a year
and we talk on the phone all the time. Dad's health's not so good
these days but he doesn't grumble. It's Ma who does that. Says
he gets under her feet.' He grinned. 'She loves him to bits, but
she'd never admit it.'

'And your brothers? Are they still in Edinburgh?'

'Two of them are. One's up in Aberdeen but the other one
moved to London.' He shook his head, clearly finding that
amusing. 'My parents have never got over the shame.'

She laughed. 'And are any of them married or...'

'Or miserable old bachelors like me?' He took a sip of wine.
'All married. All fathers. I've got eight nephews and three
nieces. Christmas is a damn expensive time; I'll tell you that
much.'

Bethany gazed into her wine glass wondering how hard that must have been for Clive. He'd already admitted he'd wanted a family of his own. Knowing he had four brothers who were married with children she thought each new arrival must have cut deeply. She remembered how she'd felt when Helena had her two sons. She'd been happy for her friend, of course, but it had hurt, although she'd rather have died than admit it to Helena—or Ted for that matter.

'Are any of your brothers vets?' she asked, wanting to turn Clive's thoughts away from the children in case it was as painful a subject for him as it had always been for her.

'No. The eldest works on the oil rigs. Two of them are farmers, like Dad. They manage the family farm. The one in London works in IT. We can't think what went wrong with him.' He laughed and Bethany's insides fizzed again. She loved to hear him laugh.

'So you were brought up on a farm?'

'I was indeed. It was a mixed arable and livestock farm, but my brothers have diversified somewhat. They specialise in Highland cows now—good for the meat. Very popular because it's low cholesterol.' He rolled his eyes. 'They're also a real draw for tourists who love them, so my brothers converted some of the outbuildings into holiday lets and had a restaurant built on site. People come for miles to eat there. It's set in beautiful countryside, but less than half an hour from the centre of Edinburgh.'

His eyes shone as he spoke of his old home and Bethany couldn't help but ask if he missed living up there.

'I do sometimes,' he confessed. 'It's always a pleasure to go back there. As I said, I usually manage it twice a year, but with Joseph... Well, anyway, I didn't make it back for Christmas or Easter, but I've promised I'll go up at the end of summer.'

'It sounds amazing,' she said. 'And do your brothers live on the farm with your parents?'

He laughed. 'Hell, no! They'd destroy each other. One

brother, Marti, he lives there with his wife and kids. Fraser lives in town because his wife's a GP there. Ma and Dad moved out of the farm a few years ago. They've got a nice bungalow just outside the city and it's much easier for them to manage, even though Dad misses the farm. I don't think Ma does. She's taken to urban living like a duck to water.'

'It must be lovely, having such a big family,' she said wistfully.

'I suppose it is,' he said thoughtfully. 'I don't see that much of them, but I can't imagine life without them.' He gave her a sympathetic look. 'There was a big age gap between you and Joseph. I suppose you didn't really get the chance to bond that well.'

She shrugged. 'He was nearly twelve years older than me so yes, quite a gap. He always looked out for me and took the best care of me he could, but I didn't really have anyone to play with or talk to. Not until I met Helena anyway. We were at St Egbert's together—you know, the public school?'

'Aye, I know it,' he said. 'Ben's younger brother goes there.'

'Well, Helena was a godsend. We were like sisters, even though I didn't see her in the school holidays because we lived quite far apart. She was a boarder, whereas I was a day pupil,' she explained. 'We bonded from the first day of term, so I guess she sort of made up for not having any siblings around my own age.'

'Did...' Clive sighed and shook his head. 'Sorry, forget it.'

'No, go on.' Bethany fondled a sleepy Viva's ears. 'What were you going to ask me?'

'Well, it's none of my business really, but I was just wondering how soon you realised Helena and Ted were involved with each other?'

Bethany drained her glass and Clive immediately offered to top it up. She assured him she could wait until their takeaway had been delivered and settled back on the sofa, her gaze fixed on the little dog rather than on him.

'I'd been living with Helena in her flat in York. She insisted. She was so good to me, putting a roof over my head when I needed one. I was working part time in a shop and going to college to learn secretarial skills. When I finished there, I enrolled with an employment agency and, as luck would have it, my very first job was working for Ted. He was already successful even though he was only thirty.'

'How old were you?' Clive asked, curious.

'Twenty by then. I suppose I felt comfortable with him because of Joseph. Anyway, he might have been my boss, but he never intimidated me. I liked him and it was soon pretty obvious that he liked me, too. He came from a wealthy family, but he never flaunted that. And the best thing about him was that he didn't ask too many questions. He knew a bit about my background but didn't press me to fill in the details, which I appreciated more than I can say. Within eighteen months we were married. Helena was my maid of honour.'

She sighed. 'I think there was a spark between them even before we got married if I'm honest. I've never really gone over it with her. There didn't seem much point. I'm certain that nothing happened between them at that time, even though there was clearly an attraction. About a year after we got married Helena announced her engagement and had her own wedding six months after that. I assumed she was happy. Well, they went on to have two sons and she seemed to be in her element being a mother.'

Viva lifted her head and gave her a sympathetic look, as if she'd picked up on the sadness that Bethany was trying to hide.

'But Helena's marriage obviously didn't last,' Clive said.

'No. They broke up when the boys were still quite young. I found out later that Helena was already in love with Ted and her husband was a poor substitute. I felt terribly sorry for him. I still do. He's a nice man and a good father to the boys, despite everything.'

'Sounds like Helena and Ted were both pretty selfish,' Clive observed.

'They weren't. Not really. You can't help who you fall in love with.' She thought about Joseph and Glenn and felt a sudden shame. Joseph's life had been so lacking in love and happiness, could she really blame him for acting the way he had? After all, she'd forgiven Helena so easily. Why hadn't she forgiven her own brother?

Because Helena apologised. Helena was truly sorry. Helena stayed in your life.

She mentally shook her head. She couldn't go into all that again. Not now. 'They really did try not to get involved but things weren't good between Ted and me by then. I mean, we didn't argue or anything. Maybe,' she admitted, 'it would have been better for us if we had. As it was, we barely spoke. No anger or nastiness. Just... Nothing. We were living separate lives. Helena was my shoulder to cry on. What I didn't realise was that she was also Ted's, and that things were developing behind my back. Anyway, in the end they realised they couldn't carry on deceiving me, so they came clean and begged for forgiveness.'

'And you forgave them.'

'It hurt. I cried a bit. I raged a lot. I felt humiliated.' She shrugged. 'After I'd got that out of my system, I realised I was actually okay about it all. Ted and Helena were good people and they cared about me. I didn't want to lose either of them as friends, and it wasn't as if they left me destitute. Ted wanted to keep the house we'd lived in, which was fine by me. It was too big for me anyway and, besides, it had been his long before he even met me. I moved out and Ted gave me an incredibly generous divorce settlement, even though I told him I didn't need it or want it. I suppose it was his way of making amends.

But really, the way he made amends was to stay friends with me. I needed them both. I needed their friendship. I've been very lucky.'

She looked up and saw the way Clive was watching her. His expressive grey eyes clearly told her that he didn't think she'd been lucky at all, and he didn't think much of either her late ex-husband or his second wife.

'Honestly,' she said, 'it's not as bad as it sounds. Don't judge them too harshly.'

He bit his lip, and she had an awful feeling he was longing to point out that she'd judged Joseph harshly.

'Maybe I will have that glass of wine,' she said.

The doorbell rang and Clive got to his feet, looking relieved. Not half as relieved as Bethany felt.

'That'll be the food,' he said cheerfully. 'About time, too. I'm famished.'

Viva leapt off the sofa, suddenly wide awake, and followed Clive onto the landing. Bethany closed her eyes and wondered if she'd just soured things between them. Had she come across as way too understanding of Ted and Helena and far too unkind to her brother? She'd never thought of it before, but she could see why Clive might think that. Perhaps she'd ruined things between them already.

'This smells so good,' Clive told her on his return, his eyes gleaming. 'Come on, let's get the plates. Shall we eat in the kitchen at the table, or would you prefer a tray on your lap?'

Smiling she followed him into the kitchen, glad to see that he'd evidently forgotten all about their conversation and was far more interested in dishing out the food.

Viva was persuaded into her basket and Clive and Bethany washed their hands before dishing out the curries. They split the naan bread, and both agreed it had been a good decision to share one as it was enormous.

'This is yummy,' Bethany said approvingly, as they sat at the table tucking in with relish. 'Ross mentioned it was a decent restaurant when he popped into Lavender House one evening. Apparently he's taken Clemmie there a few times.'

'Aye, I've heard good things about it. Maybe we should eat there one night, rather than get a takeaway?'

He sounded hesitant but Bethany beamed at him. 'I think that's a great idea.'

He smiled back and for a moment they forgot all about the food, until Viva whined at them, evidently still reproachful that they weren't willing to share the curry.

They took their time over the food, chatting and drinking wine in between mouthfuls of tasty lamb rogan josh and chicken tikka masala.

'I meant to mention,' Clive said, 'I might have found somewhere for some of the ponies.'

Bethany tried to dismiss the sadness she felt at the news. 'Really? That sanctuary in Bramblewick?'

'That's right. Folly Farm.' He paused, holding his half of the naan bread between his fingers and staring into the middle distance as if he was thinking about something.

'Are you all right?'

'Eh?' He blinked and laughed. 'Sorry, I was miles away. It's just, it's a bit of a quandary really. They can take two of the Shetlands but no more. They're absolutely overwhelmed with animals at the moment and Folly Farm is only small. We had quite a chat. It's as I suspected; the sanctuaries are really struggling right now. The owner, Xander, asked me if we had any suitable to send out on loan as riding or companion ponies. You know, to individuals rather than another sanctuary. He thought that might be our best chance of rehoming them.'

Bethany frowned. 'On loan?'

'Yes, they'd still belong to you, but they'd live with other people, who'd take care of them. It would have to be a legal agreement, obviously. I was just trying to think if any of them would make good riding ponies or horses. I suppose Pan and Tink might be an option. What do you think?'

Bethany was ashamed to admit she wasn't sure which of the animals Pan and Tink were.

'The two Welsh cobs who are friends with Chester. They used to work at a trekking centre until someone reported the neglect that was happening there. Turns out the owners were complete amateurs, and the ponies and horses were suffering. Joseph offered to take three of them in but only two of those survived treatment, sadly. Peter Pan and Tinkerbelle. They've been at Whispering Willows for four years now, though, and they're in good condition. He's only fourteen and she's thirteen, so they might be okay, although obviously they've not been ridden for all this time and whoever took them would need to take it very slowly. That would have to be made clear.'

'They'd probably need their fitness building up,' Bethany said. 'Maybe some lunging first, see how they go. It could be that they're fine, but it might also be that they'll need to start all over again and then it would be a case of treating them as if they were just breaking them for the first time.' She frowned. 'We'd really have to trust the people who took them. What if they were as bad as the previous owners?'

'It would entail careful checks and vetting their homes, obviously.'

'Homes plural? We couldn't keep them together?'

'Well...' Clive sounded doubtful. 'I mean, it's possible, but not likely.'

Bethany's heart sank. Pan and Tink spent all their time together. How would they cope apart? And then there was Chester. He relied on them. What would it do to him if they were taken from him? He was already grieving for his late owner.

She blinked, realising Clive was still talking.

'And references. And we'd have to make clear there'd be regular visits from us to make sure he's okay.'

Bethany couldn't bring herself to point out that she wouldn't be in the area to make any visits. How was she supposed to keep an eye on the horses and ponies if she couldn't be around for them?

As if he'd read her mind Clive said slowly, 'You could always sign them over to me if you wanted. They'd be my responsibility then and I'd do the checks. I mean, with you not knowing where you're going to go from here.'

The silence hung heavy between them, and Bethany prodded at a piece of chicken, feeling suddenly miserable.

'Anyway,' Clive said, trying to cheer things up, 'it's something to think about. How do you feel about the Shetlands going to the sanctuary I mentioned?'

Bethany straightened, realising she hadn't fully taken in what Clive had said about that.

'I don't think it's a good idea. The Shetlands arrived together. Summer told me all about them when I first got here, and she showed me how bonded they are. They're a little family. It would be awful to split them up. If the sanctuary can't take all four we'll have to wait and look for somewhere else.'

'It could be a long wait,' he advised. 'We'll be hard pushed to find anywhere willing to take all four.'

'It's okay. I'm not in any great rush. I've got the house to see to anyway, remember, and that's going to take some time.'

Clive smiled. 'So you have. You're going through with it then?'

'I am. I want Whispering Willows to appeal to families and I'm sure I can make that happen. I've been looking at magazines and websites for ideas. I'm quite excited about it. I never got the chance to do anything with my old home—Ted's home. It had been in his family for ages when I met him, and it was all done to his taste. I never liked to suggest changing anything.

Whenever things needed updating he just hired people and they took care of it between themselves without any input from me.'

'How very considerate of Ted,' Clive said drily.

They finished their meal and cleared the plates. Clive stacked everything in the dishwasher then poured them both another glass of wine before leading her back into the living room.

'I'm glad you're not going to separate the Shetlands,' he told her softly as he clinked his glass against hers. 'They'd have pined for each other I'm sure.'

'We can't have that, can we?' she said, gazing into his eyes. 'They belong together. They shouldn't be separated.'

'I'll drink to that,' he said, and they both took a sip of wine, their eyes locked on each other as Bethany's heart thudded.

'What are you thinking?' she asked when he didn't speak.

He looked a bit embarrassed. 'Honestly? I'm thinking maybe having a curry wasn't such a good idea when I really want to kiss you right now.'

She couldn't wipe the smile from her face. 'But we've both had curry. I think they cancel each other out, a bit like garlic.'

'Are you willing to risk it?' he asked, his eyes twinkling.

'I am if you are,' she said.

'Oh, I'm willing,' he assured her, putting his glass of wine on the floor. He took her glass from her hand and put it next to his own then leaned over and kissed her.

Bethany forgot all about the curry and judging by Clive's reaction he had too. And if he noticed that Viva had followed them into the room and had leapt up into his lap, he gave no indication. He seemed completely focused on kissing Bethany, and that was just fine by her.

Was it ever! She never wanted this kiss to end, except, that wasn't quite true. She wanted to take it further. She needed more from him than this, however good it was.

She almost groaned with frustration when, once again, he pulled away from her.

'Go on,' she said. 'What's the excuse this time?'

He blinked. 'I'm sorry?'

'You're going to tell me that was a mistake, aren't you? That I'm vulnerable and you took advantage of me because—oh, I don't know—because I've had a couple of glasses of wine or something.'

'Really? That's what you think?'

'Well,' she reminded him, 'it's what you said last time.'

'Aye, I did,' he said heavily. 'I've a feeling I hurt you a lot more than you let on, too. I'm sorry.'

'So why did you say it?'

'Lots of reasons. You had just been crying your eyes out over Joseph, remember. Whatever you say I shouldn't have kissed you at that moment. But the truth is, I really did want to kiss you for ages before that, and I just couldn't help myself. But then I thought, you're not sure where you're going to end up. Is there any point in starting something when you're not going to be around for long? Could I really deal with that?'

He'd been worried he'd be hurt? She hadn't even thought about that possibility, and it made her want him even more. 'Do you still feel that way?'

'A bit,' he admitted. 'But the thing is, I've been giving a lot of thought to my two friends, Joseph and Julian. Life's short, Beth, and the truth is, all we ever have is now. We get so hung up on worrying about the future but what if the future never happens? I don't mean that to sound gloomy but it's a fact. So what we should be doing is living in every single moment as it comes and making the most of each one. And that's what I want to do.'

'I don't know where I'll end up,' she told him softly, 'but I do know that, right now, all I want is to be with you.'

She put her arms around him, and they kissed again, this

time with less gentleness and more urgency, barely noticing when Viva gave an indignant yelp and tumbled off Clive's lap onto the floor. When they finally released each other, she saw the desire in her heart reflected in Clive's eyes.

'Beth,' he said awkwardly, 'it's been a while... Years.'

His words were heavy with anxiety and her heart melted.

'It's been a while for me, too.'

'Maybe,' he mumbled. 'But what if I let you down?' He tried to smile. 'I might have forgotten what to do.'

She cradled his face in her hands.

'Then we'll figure it out together.'

Tenderly, he stroked her cheek. 'Are you sure about this? You don't think it's too soon?'

'We're consenting adults who are old enough to know our own minds,' she pointed out.

'And it's what you want?'

'Definitely.' A sudden doubt attacked her. 'Unless—I mean —if it's what you want, too?'

She'd thought she'd read his signals correctly but maybe she'd got carried away. Maybe she'd made too many assumptions.

His smile this time was genuine. 'Do you really have to ask?'

'Well then,' she said, relieved, 'what are we waiting for?'

He took her hand and, heart racing with anticipation, she followed him to his bedroom, leaving a rather cross Viva behind.

TWENTY-SIX

June had arrived and the weather had warmed up beautifully. The mornings were brighter and the evenings longer and lighter. Tuppenny Bridge was a wonderful place to be.

Clive had visited Whispering Willows three times in the last ten days or so and Bethany had been to his flat in Stepping Stones twice. They'd watched films together, eaten snacks, gone for long walks in the surrounding countryside, talked, laughed, and spent quite a lot of time in bed.

Everyone knew about them. Well, that's how it felt to Clive, who'd got quite used to the knowing grins and nods from not only his clients but his staff, too.

Jane, his receptionist, and Hannah, the veterinary nurse, were beside themselves with excitement. They'd been thrilled about Ben and Summer he thought ruefully, but this was on another level.

'You can't blame them,' Ben told him, laughing. 'Jane especially. She's been with you for years and she's never seen you like this before.'

'Like what?' he'd asked, perplexed.

'Loved up,' Ben said, laughing even harder as Clive's face burned. Was he blushing? He never blushed!

'Get away,' was all he could manage in response.

There was no denying it, though. His feelings for Bethany had surged since that evening in Stepping Stones. He felt like a new man.

'Well,' she'd said as they lay in bed that first time, 'if that's you out of practice I don't think I could have coped with you at your peak.'

He'd amazed himself, quite frankly. He'd honestly thought he'd be a dismal failure, but being with Bethany it was as if he'd been given a new lease of life.

'Maybe you never really forget,' he said thoughtfully. 'Like riding a bike.'

'Charming!'

He'd given her a stricken look. 'I didn't mean—' Then he'd seen her face and started to laugh.

'You're so easy,' she said. 'I'm going to have fun winding you up, I can see that.'

'Wind me up all you like,' he told her, delighted to see the smile on her face. 'If it makes you happy I'm willing to make that sacrifice.'

She'd given him a suggestive look. 'I tell you what would make me happy...'

'Bloody hell,' he said in mock horror. 'I can see I'm going to have to start taking multivitamins.'

If he hadn't been so uncertain about where he stood with her he might have moved things on, but he still feared she'd leave town and how would he feel then? He hated even imagining the day she left so he tried not to dwell on it at all.

Two things gave him cause for optimism. The first was her obvious excitement about doing up Whispering Willows. She'd been looking at new kitchens and a suite for the tired old bathroom.

Apparently she had a sofa and two armchairs on order, and a brand-new double bed had been delivered earlier that week. He'd helped her put it together in her room which had been... interesting.

'You know,' she'd said thoughtfully as she wandered out of his en suite one night, 'I quite like the idea of an en suite myself. That box room at my place...' She shuddered at the thought of it. Clearly, in her mind it was still her father's room. 'It would make a good-sized bathroom. I could knock through, make it the en suite to the room I'm using. It's not going to be much of a loss, space wise, as a bedroom and it might add value. What do you think?'

What Clive was actually thinking was that she'd called Whispering Willows 'my place' without any hesitation. It might have been a throwaway remark, but he hoped it revealed more about her state of mind than she realised.

The second thing was her determination not to separate the four Shetland ponies. Clive had been touched that she was seriously putting their welfare before any other consideration. He'd suggested contacting the sanctuary again to ask if they'd take Barney instead, as he was quite small. He knew the sanctuary was tiny and already overstretched, and that he couldn't ask more from them, but thought the little Exmoor might be okay there. To his surprise Bethany had vetoed the idea, citing Barney's skin problems as a reason to hang on to him.

Clive had pointed out that the staff would know what they were doing and that many horses and ponies suffered from a severe reaction to midge bites, so they'd be able to continue his routine of barrier cream and hooded rugs from April to October with no real problems. Even so, she'd been reluctant to even consider it.

'He's been through enough, and Summer's so good with him.'

'But he'll have to go at some time, Beth.'

Her eyes had glistened with tears. 'You think I don't know

that? But not yet. He should be the last to go really. I mean, for Summer's sake. It's hard enough having her scowling at me all the time, but if I let Barney go first she's going to be impossible. No, we'll leave Barney until last because I can't deal with any more of Summer's attitude, I really can't.'

Clive strongly suspected that her reaction had nothing to do with Summer. She obviously cared about the ponies very much and was worried about their futures, which was a huge improvement on her initial stance. Surely that could only mean she was reconsidering her decision? Maybe, if things continued the way they were, she'd choose to stay. He hoped so, anyway. The alternative was too painful to consider.

Summer was clearly unimpressed that their relationship had developed. She didn't trust Bethany, and now that Clive was involved with her she didn't trust him either.

'I thought you, of all people, would be on my side in this,' she told him resentfully one morning when she'd called in at Stepping Stones to see Ben on his break.

'Summer don't drag Clive into all this,' Ben had begged her. 'Whatever's going on with Whispering Willows it's got nothing to do with him.'

'He's sleeping with the enemy!' Summer's eyes were wide with indignation. 'She's selling the house and letting all our lovely residents go who knows where!' She fixed an accusing stare on Clive. 'Don't you care what happens to them?'

'Of course I care,' he said heavily. 'Believe it or not, so does Bethany. You have no idea—'

'She's got a funny way of showing it,' Summer said. 'I'd be careful if I were you. If that's her way of caring, you could be in trouble. When you're no use to her she'll get rid of you just as easily, you wait and see.'

'Summer!' Ben shook his head. 'Stop it. I know you're upset—'

'Upset? If you think I'm upset how do you think Joseph

would feel?' She jabbed a finger at Clive. 'You were supposed to be his best friend. You promised him you'd look after Whispering Willows. Instead you're too busy mooning over his heartless sister who couldn't even be bothered to turn up for his funeral, and you're just standing back and letting her destroy all his hard work. I hope you can live with yourself.'

She'd given both Clive and Ben furious looks before storming out of the surgery.

'Well,' Ben said with a sigh, 'that went well.'

'I'm sorry,' Clive told him. 'I don't want you two falling out over this.'

'She'll come round. Thing about Summer is, when she feels strongly about something she flares up, but she calms down again pretty quickly. I mean, she won't change her mind about Bethany, but she'll not take it out on me. Anyway, it's not your fault. I know you're in love with Bethany and it must be awful for you, torn between your feelings for her and your feelings for Joseph.' He hesitated. 'Is there no chance you could change her mind? Talk her round.'

Clive shook his head. 'I can't do that, Ben. Especially not now. This has to be her decision and I'm the last person who should be pressuring her.'

'But you must want her to stay?'

Clive gave a broken laugh. 'Of course I want her to stay! But only if *she* wants to. I've explained all this. I'm not going to make her change her plans for me. It would never work. She'd be like a caged bird at Whispering Willows, and I won't be responsible for that. No,' he shook his head firmly, 'this is all up to Bethany. It always has been. I admit I put pressure on her when we first met, but as I got to know her and understood her reasons for wanting to leave I stopped doing that because it wasn't fair. Now I'm—' he hesitated before shrugging, slightly awkwardly, '—*involved* with her it's even more important that I don't try to influence her. Do you understand?'

Ben sighed. 'I guess so.'

'Has Summer started looking for another job?' Clive asked sympathetically.

'She's been searching for a job connected with horses but it's not easy in this area. There was a job advertised over at the stables at East Midham but they needed someone who could ride.'

Clive raised an eyebrow. 'Summer can't ride?'

'No. Didn't you know? Her mum and dad couldn't afford lessons for her, and I don't think Bemborough was a particularly horsy area, so she never got the opportunity. It was only when she left school and volunteered at an animal sanctuary that she got to spend any time with horses at all.'

'Well I never,' Clive mused. 'I'd imagined her spending all her childhood weekends at stables, like Maya I suppose. Thought she'd have been a pony club girl. Just shows you.'

'Sally and Rafferty have said she can her old job back at The White Hart Inn,' Ben continued, 'but Summer knows they already covered her when she increased her shifts at Whispering Willows. They might need extra help in the summer months but after that they'd be paying her for work they don't really need doing, just because she's family. She doesn't want that.' He rubbed his forehead. 'I honestly don't know how this is going to end.'

He wasn't the only one. It was all very well Clive saying Bethany's future had to be up to her, but it wasn't just her future in the balance. Summer's life would change forever if Bethany went through with her plans. All the equine residents of Whispering Willows would be sent away, which would be a big upheaval for them—especially the ones who'd been there for years. Even Maya and Lennox would face big changes.

As for him, he didn't want to imagine what life would be like if Bethany moved back to Somerset. He'd be devastated to see Whispering Willows sold. To have to say goodbye to

Joseph's legacy, knowing how heartbroken his friend would be at the way things turned out.

And his own heart? Well, he thought it might just shatter for good if he had to watch Bethany drive away from him. He could only pray that she would change her mind and decide she wanted to stick around after all. Not for him, but because Tuppenny Bridge was the place she felt most at home. It was a long shot, but it was all he had to cling to.

TWENTY-SEVEN

'One caramel latte, and one slice of lemon drizzle cake.' Daisy put the tray on the table and beamed at Bethany. 'Ooh, are those house brochures? Anything interesting?'

'A few,' Bethany admitted. She glanced around the café, noting it wasn't particularly busy for once. 'Have you got a few minutes? You could join me if you like.'

Daisy looked over at the counter. A young couple had just come up the stairs and were now loitering there, waiting for service.

'I'll just see to these two and then I'll see what I can do,' she promised, rushing off to greet her customers with a smile.

Ten minutes later she returned with a cup of tea and a slice of ginger cake. 'Might as well make the most of the lull,' she said, sitting down opposite Bethany. 'So, are you house hunting then?'

'I've been browsing.' Bethany shuffled the papers she'd been perusing and settled back in her chair, latte in hand. 'But I thought I'd also find out what sort of places were selling in Skimmerdale, what prices they reach, what buyers are looking for, that sort of thing.'

'Sounds like a plan,' Daisy said, biting into her ginger cake. She chewed thoughtfully for a moment then asked, 'You don't look too happy about it. I take it you're disappointed with what you've found out?'

'I had a chat with a couple of estate agents,' Bethany said. 'Basically, they were both of the opinion that, with a house the size of Whispering Willows, and with all that land in a prime location, it has the potential to make a decent price, but they did agree that more leisure companies and building firms might be interested in the land, given the poor state the house is in now. One told me it would probably be in my best interests to do no work to the place at all, just sell it as it is. They admitted the house might well be demolished. If the new owners could get planning permission for a new house or even a few houses the land could sell for a whole lot more. In fact, they suggested I might want to apply for planning permission myself. If it was already in place I'd be in a much stronger position.'

Daisy wrinkled her nose. 'I can't see that going down well with the people round here,' she said. 'Mind you, I take the agent's point. Dad's farm didn't sell for as much as we'd hoped for. Granted, we'd already sold off some of the land, but even so. It was run-down, you see. Like Whispering Willows. We were lucky because we sold it to a family looking for a project.'

'I don't want Whispering Willows to be demolished though,' Bethany said wistfully. 'And I certainly don't want it to become a housing estate.' She sighed. 'The other agent said there's some demand for high-end equestrian properties in this area, if I wanted to market it that way.'

Daisy looked doubtful. 'Is Whispering Willows high-end?'

Bethany broke off a piece of her lemon drizzle cake. 'You've never been there, have you? Believe me, high-end is not how I'd describe it. It would take a huge amount of money to make it the sort of equestrian dream prospective buyers would be interested in.'

Daisy sipped her tea thoughtfully. 'And are you prepared to spend that much?'

Bethany broke off a piece of her lemon drizzle cake and considered the matter. 'I was, at first. For ages I've been talking about making improvements to the house and putting a new roof on the stables, but now...' She gestured to the leaflets stacked up beside her plate. 'These places are amazing, and the prices they're going for are impressive. But their stables look nothing like the broken-down ones at my place. All of these have state of the art stabling and a manège and all sorts! I mean, listen to this.'

She picked up one of the leaflets and read, 'Enclosed stable-yard with twelve looseboxes, each with rubber matting and automatic drinkers. Separate block with tack room, feed room, and washroom with toilet, sink, and hot water.'

She shook her head. 'Believe me, that does *not* describe the facilities at Whispering Willows. They even have sensor lights in the stableyard!' She shook her head. 'Oh, I don't know!'

Daisy surveyed her thoughtfully. 'Can't say I blame you. That sounds like a really expensive project to me.' She chewed another bit of ginger cake. 'It would take time, too,' she said at last. 'And you want to leave here as soon as possible, don't you?'

Bethany folded her arms defensively. 'Yes. No. I mean—it's complicated.'

'Because of Clive?'

Bethany sighed. 'I suppose that's all round Tuppenny Bridge?'

'Of course it is! What did you expect?' Daisy laughed. 'I've only been here five minutes, but I've already figured out there are no secrets in this place. Kat's aunties are running a book on you both, did you know? Everyone's waiting with bated breath to see what happens next. So things have hotted up with the sexy vet, eh?'

Bethany couldn't hide the smile that spread across her face at the thought. 'They have a bit,' she admitted.

'Only a bit?'

Bethany laughed. 'Okay, they've hotted up a lot.'

'That sounds more promising.' Daisy wiped her fingers on a napkin. 'So maybe you're thinking of staying then? In which case, why are you looking at these brochures? Just do the house and stables as you want them, never mind what might suit the market best.'

'It's not that simple.' Bethany massaged her temples, feeling the pressure. How had it come to this? When she'd arrived in Tuppenny Bridge she'd had one clear goal in mind. Empty the house and put Whispering Willows on the market. She'd had no idea that she'd have to take into consideration three horses, four donkeys, and six ponies, a bichon frise, a justifiably furious employee, and a vet she couldn't help but fall in love with.

Now it was no longer just about what she wanted. She had to think of the futures of all those animals and people, too. The worst of it was, she couldn't even make up her mind what it was *she* wanted these days. And it had just got even more complicated.

'I had a visit yesterday,' she said reluctantly. 'A builder and a roofer came to look at the place. Thankfully, the house isn't a problem. Structurally it's sound. Just needs a few tiles replacing on the roof which I'm very grateful for, and some of the plaster needs replacing in the kitchen and hallway, which I'd already guessed. When I tapped the walls I could feel it had come away. It's not a huge job, though. The stables, however, are a different matter.'

'Oh. How bad?'

'Let's put it this way, they were of the opinion that it would be much cheaper to demolish the whole lot and build again from scratch.'

'You're joking?'

'I wish I was.' Bethany felt cold at the memory of the two men shaking their heads at her in sympathy.

'Fact is,' one of them had told her, 'the spread on the roof over time has bowed the walls so far out—around eighteen inches in fact—that it's likely the foundations have gone. They'd need re-doing and that's far from cheap.'

'What do you mean by "spread on the roof"?' she'd asked, puzzled.

'The rafters on the roof are inadequately supported,' the other one explained. 'So the ridge tiles on the top of the building push down, forcing the tops of the walls to bulge out. The door frames have come away from the walls, too, see?'

'I see,' she'd said anxiously. 'And it's an expensive thing to repair?'

'To be honest, it would make more sense to knock it all down and start again. Apart from anything else it would be quicker, never mind cheaper. Of course, it's up to you, but you asked for our advice, and that's what we're giving you.'

'Right. Well, I appreciate that. Thank you. I'll be in touch when I've given it some thought,' she'd promised them, her heart sinking.

'I guess it makes more sense to just leave things as they are then,' Daisy said. 'If I was putting my sensible hat on and pushing aside all emotions I'd say cut your losses and get Whispering Willows on the market.'

'I know you're right,' Bethany admitted. 'And there wouldn't be any losses. I mean, it might not go for much in its present condition but then, it didn't cost me a penny anyway. It's all pure profit.'

'So forget about doing it up or demolishing the stables. Just focus on buying a place for you to live in.' Daisy watched her curiously. 'And figuring out whereabouts it is you want to settle.'

'But if a building company does buy Whispering Willows,' Bethany said anxiously, 'how would everyone react to that?

Even if it becomes a holiday park or something, they're not going to be happy. And anyway, I can't just put it on the market. I have responsibilities to the animals in my care.'

'Yes, of course you do.' Daisy sighed. 'Sounds like you've got a lot of thinking to do.'

'Tell me about it.'

'Hey, why don't you come over to my flat on Saturday night?' Daisy asked eagerly. 'I haven't had anyone round before and you could be my first guest. We could get fish and chips from Millican's and put the world to rights. Might even figure out a plan of action for you.'

Bethany hesitated and Daisy slumped. 'Sorry. Of course, you've probably got plans with Clive on Saturday night.'

'Nothing definite,' Bethany assured her. She smiled suddenly. 'I'd love to. Fish and chips from Millican's. Sounds like it could be just what I need. I'll bring a bottle of wine, shall I?'

'Perfect!' Daisy beamed at her. 'Oh, I'd better get back to work. Looks like I've got some new customers,' she said, glancing over at the counter where no fewer than four people now hovered.

She got to her feet and Bethany hastily gathered her leaflets. 'And I'll get back to Whispering Willows. I've got an awful lot to think about now. See you on Saturday, Daisy.'

'About six?' Daisy called as she headed back behind the counter. 'Looking forward to it. And don't worry. We'll figure something out between us.'

Bethany headed down the stairs thinking ruefully that it would take more than a portion of fish and chips and a chat with Daisy to sort this mess out. She honestly had no idea what to do for the best.

TWENTY-EIGHT

As Clive approached Daisyfield Cottage he thought he couldn't be feeling more different than he had the last time he'd visited the Callaghans' home. He remembered his anxiety on walking up the path to the front door and felt a sudden embarrassment. He'd been so sure he was in love with Jennifer. So convinced that his future lay with her. Yet, how easily she'd changed his mind. It had taken only minutes for her to set him on a completely different path and, given how set he'd been on his previous course for so many years, that was quite an achievement.

He should thank her. If she hadn't pointed out the way Bethany had been looking at him at Monk's Folly he might never have recognised his own feelings for her. Thank God he'd finally plucked up the courage to talk to Jennifer. He fleetingly thought it was a shame he hadn't done so many years ago but dismissed that immediately. It hadn't been the right time, and he hadn't been ready to hear it. Maybe if Joseph hadn't died, if Bethany hadn't arrived in Tuppenny Bridge, he still wouldn't be ready. He just hoped she'd forgotten how pathetic he'd been the last time she saw him.

To be honest, he was surprised he'd been invited over. It was all a bit of a mystery, and he still didn't know what this get-together was about. The telephone call had come out of the blue and there'd been little in the way of an explanation, as he'd told Bethany yesterday morning.

They'd been having breakfast in bed at Stepping Stones. Bethany had spent the night there, not for the first time, and he'd impressed her by making them both bacon sandwiches and mugs of tea before she'd even woken up.

'You shouldn't have bothered,' she'd protested, struggling to sit up in bed as he walked into the room, tray in his hands, already showered and dressed. 'I know you've got work this morning. I could have eaten some cereal when I got home.'

'It's no bother,' he'd assured her, carefully settling himself on the bed beside her and handing her a plate and mug, which she put on the bedside cabinet. He put his own breakfast on the cabinet at his side of the bed and reached down to place the empty tray on the floor. 'I've fed Viva and let her out, too. She's happy enough.'

'Shall I take her back with me?' Bethany offered. 'I can take her for a walk later while you're working.'

'Are you sure you don't mind?'

'Of course not. I like being around her. She's adorable. I can see why Joseph loved her so much.'

He'd smiled inwardly, aware that she'd mentioned her brother a few times lately, with no prompting, no hesitation, and no signs of sadness or anger. That, he thought optimistically, had to be a good sign that she was coming to terms with the past. He hoped so, anyway.

'You never told me what the builder and the roofer said,' he reminded her, reaching for his bacon sandwich. 'You said you'd fill me in later, but you never got round to it.'

'Oh.' Bethany shook her head. 'Nothing much. Mostly what

I'd expected. Some plastering needs doing in the house, and a few roof tiles need replacing. Nothing too drastic.'

He chewed some bacon, nodding in relief. 'That's good,' he said at last. 'And what about the stables?'

She swallowed some tea and he waited for her to continue. 'Pretty much as we thought. Needs a new roof.'

'Ach, that's a shame. Are you going for it then?' he asked.

Bethany shrugged. 'I said I'd think about it,' she said lightly. 'Might be best to get a few different quotes, don't you think?'

'Definitely. Good business sense.'

'That's what I thought.' She smiled at him. 'I've got another builder coming in a couple of days so he can give me his opinion and I'll go from there.'

He eyed her thoughtfully. 'You seem different.'

'Do I?' She tilted her head. 'In what way?'

'I don't know.' He really didn't either. There was just something about her. 'You look lighter. Happier. Like a weight's lifted.'

'Why wouldn't I be happy? The man in my life has just made me a bacon sandwich and I didn't even have to ask. What more could any woman want?'

He laughed. 'Put like that. Oh, you hadn't got anything in mind for tomorrow night, had you?'

'As a matter of fact, I had. I'm going to Daisy's for a fish and chip supper. We're going to put the world to rights.'

'Are you indeed? Look out, world! Well, that's all right then.'

She broke off a piece of her bacon sandwich. 'Why? Do you have plans of your own?'

'I do actually. Jennifer's invited me round for dinner. You know, Ben's mum?'

Bethany stilled. 'I know who Jennifer is,' she told him. 'That's, er, nice for you. I didn't know you two were on such intimate terms.'

'Intimate terms?' He'd frowned at the expression, surprised to see she was no longer smiling. 'Hardly that. We're old friends, and it's just a bit of dinner, that's all.'

'You never mentioned,' she said.

'She only called me last night, just before you came round. I was going to tell you but...' He grinned. 'I got a bit distracted with other matters.'

Hadn't he just! They hadn't even remembered to eat their evening meal until almost nine o'clock.

'Oh, okay.'

He was puzzled. 'You don't mind, do you?'

She gave him a bright smile. 'Why on earth would I mind? As you said, you're old friends. If you want to have dinner together, so what? I'm having a meal with Daisy after all.'

She was saying all the right words, but he couldn't help feeling something was bothering her.

'It's a bit weird really,' he admitted.

'What is?'

'Well, it's all very last minute, and Jennifer asked me not to mention it to Ben or Summer, so don't say anything to her today, will you?'

'I'm hardly likely to,' she said drily. 'We barely exchange two words these days, do we? So, Ben and Summer don't know you're going round there?'

'No.' He shook his head. 'I'm wondering if she needs some advice about something. I hope everything's okay.' He took another bite of his bacon sandwich and chewed, mulling over the situation. He had, after all, told Jennifer she could always call on him if she needed anything. Maybe something had arisen that had made her take him up on his offer.

'I'm sure everything's fine,' she said, putting her plate back on the bedside cabinet.

He lifted an eyebrow. 'Are you not going to finish that?'

'I ought to be getting ready,' she said, climbing out of bed and reaching for her robe. 'Do you mind if I get a shower before I head home?'

'Of course not. There's no hurry, though. You don't have to rush off just because I've got work.'

'No point in hanging around here,' she said over her shoulder as she headed towards the en suite. 'You get yourself off to work and I'll let myself out.'

As he eyed her with some concern her face changed. She broke into a smile and walked back to the bed.

'Stop looking so worried,' she said, dropping a kiss on his lips and ruffling his hair.

'So we're okay?' he asked.

'Of course we are! Now eat that sandwich and get off to work or I'll drag you into the shower with me, and we both know where that will lead.'

He grinned, relieved. 'Well, it beats work.'

'Go on with you!' She'd laughed and headed into the bathroom, closing the door behind her, and he'd settled back on the bed to finish his sandwich, thoroughly reassured.

Now, as he approached the front door of Daisyfield Cottage, his thoughts returned to the purpose of his visit. Was Jennifer in need of help? He hoped it wasn't anything to worry about.

It was Sally who opened the door and Clive stared at her in surprise.

'What are you—?'

The question was cut off as she grabbed his arm and pulled him inside.

'You're late!' she said as she closed the door behind them. 'They could be here any minute.'

'Who could?' he asked, bewildered.

'Ben and Summer!' she said, exasperated. 'Who else?'

'Oh, Clive, you made it. I'm so glad.' Jennifer hurried into the hallway, a smile on her face. 'They're not here yet, thank goodness. Let's go into the living room before they arrive.'

'What's going on?' he asked, feeling everyone had gone mad. He was more or less pushed into the living room where he found Jamie, Eloise, and Rafferty waiting, along with Sally's mother, Mona, of all people.

'Didn't you tell him?' Sally asked Jennifer who admitted, rather shamefaced, that she hadn't.

'I meant to, but then I heard Ben coming down the stairs, so I ended the call. I was going to ring him back, but I forgot all about it. Sorry, Clive,' she said. 'You must be wondering what on earth's going on.'

'You could say that,' he agreed. 'So what *is* going on?'

Mona rolled her eyes. 'Is he blind or tuppence short of a ha'penny?' she asked, with her usual charm.

Clive gazed around and realised there were banners strung around the edges of the room, along with bunches of white balloons.

'Congratulations on your engagement,' he read, and his eyes widened. 'They're engaged? Ben and Summer?'

'Give the fella a coconut,' Mona said.

'Oh shut up, Mam.' Sally shook her head, clearly despairing of her mother's sarcasm. She turned to Clive. 'They are! And do you know they actually thought they'd get away with not having a celebration of any kind. I mean, is it likely?'

'Well,' Mona said, 'if this is all there is they pretty much *have* got away with it, haven't they? I'm not sure I'd have come all the way from Bemborough if I'd known this was it.'

'Don't worry, Mona,' Rafferty said, 'there's plenty of food and drink in the kitchen, and a smashing cake from Daisy at the café.'

'When did this happen?' Clive asked, amazed. He couldn't deny he felt a bit hurt that Ben hadn't confided in him. He'd thought he told him everything.

'They only told us the day before yesterday,' Jennifer said softly, as if she understood how he was feeling. 'And even then they only told me, Sally and Rafferty, and Summer's dad. Even Jamie isn't supposed to know yet.'

'I know,' Jamie said indignantly. 'I think that's well harsh.'

'You know what they're like,' Sally said kindly. 'They don't want any fuss. Just want to quietly get engaged and people can find out organically. No big announcement.'

'Yet here we are,' her mother pointed out. 'You couldn't wait to ring me up and drag me here for this so-called party. Our Summer's going to love you. Not.'

'It wouldn't have been the same without you, Mona,' Rafferty said.

'Aye well, that's true enough,' she agreed, nodding. 'And at least there's cake.'

They all stood stock-still and stared at each other in horror as the front door opened.

'They're here,' Eloise whispered.

'Isn't that what we want?' Mona asked drily. 'Wouldn't be much point to this if they weren't. Are we allowed to smoke in here?'

The living room door was pushed open, and everyone yelled, 'Surprise!'

Well, everyone except Clive, who hadn't known he was supposed to, and Mona who was too busy fumbling in her bag for her cigarettes and lighter.

Ben and Summer looked aghast.

'Wh—what's going on?' Ben asked.

'It's your engagement party,' Jennifer told him, rushing over to hug the happy couple. 'Now,' she added, stepping back, 'I know you said you didn't want any fuss—'

'Yeah,' Ben remarked, 'that's exactly what we said.'

'But we couldn't let the occasion pass without throwing you a little party,' she finished. 'It's not every day my son gets engaged, and I'm so excited. And so are your parents, Summer.'

Summer raised an eyebrow. 'Both of them? Gran! What on earth are you doing here?'

'Charming,' Mona said. 'You could at least pretend to be pleased to see me.'

'I am, honestly!' Summer hurried forward and hugged her gran. 'Where's Dad? Is he coming?'

'He wanted to, love, but it was a bit short notice for him, what with work and everything,' Sally said. 'He's dead chuffed for you both, though, and he said he'd love you to go over to his place one day when you can spare the time and he'll treat you both to a meal out.'

'Aw, that's lovely of him,' Summer said.

'Er, I'm right here,' Mona informed her. 'I made the effort, even if he didn't. And,' she added, 'I've got you a card and a present, despite the fact I was only given a few hours' warning. What do you think you're playing at getting engaged and not telling anyone? Anyone would think you were ashamed or something.'

'I'm not ashamed,' Summer assured her. She linked arms with Ben. 'We're very happy, aren't we?'

'We are,' he said, smiling. 'In fact, show them where we've been today.'

Summer held out her left hand and they all crowded round to admire the ruby and diamond engagement ring on her finger.

'Isn't it gorgeous?' she asked proudly.

Everyone agreed it was and Mona asked if it would be okay for her to smoke, to which Jennifer promptly directed her into the back garden before telling everyone else to help themselves to the buffet.

Summer put her arms around Clive, who was rather taken aback at her unexpected display of affection.

'I'm glad you're here,' she told him. 'I'm sorry things have been a bit off between us. It's not your fault, and I know I've been a moody mare.'

'You're worried,' he said. 'I understand that.'

'I still shouldn't have taken it out on you. You're not to blame. I'm sorry, Clive.'

'It's okay, don't worry about it,' he reassured her.

She nodded and smiled, then followed her family into the kitchen.

'I can't believe you're engaged,' Clive admitted, clapping Ben on the back.

'I'm sorry you had to find out this way,' Ben told him. 'Honestly, I wanted to tell you myself and I was going to do that on Monday. We wanted to get the ring before we announced it to anyone other than our parents. I can't believe Mum's done this. You must think I'm horrible.'

Clive laughed. 'Don't be daft. I'm happy for you, truly. So when's the wedding?'

'Oh, probably not until next year,' Ben said. 'So that will give you plenty of time.'

'Plenty of time for what?' Clive asked, puzzled.

'To prepare a best man's speech,' Ben said quietly. 'That's if you'll agree to being my best man of course. Will you?'

'Ben.' Clive was speechless for a moment. 'Are you sure?'

'You've been there for me for most of my life,' Ben told him warmly. 'I don't know where I'd be without you, I really don't. I can't think of anyone I'd rather have at my side when I get married.'

Clive beamed at him. 'You've just made my day, you know that? I'd be honoured, Ben. I truly would.'

He hugged the young man who'd become like a son to him, his eyes blurry with tears, and reflected that, on balance, he couldn't remember a time in his life when he'd been happier.

He'd been through a lot, and it had been a particularly painful few months, but now everything seemed to be working out for him at last. He was, indeed, a lucky man.

TWENTY-NINE

'Well,' Bethany said, scrunching up the fish and chip paper, 'that has to be the best meal I've had in ages.'

Daisy nodded in agreement. 'It's a really good chippy, isn't it? And they always taste better in paper than on a plate. Weird that. It's a bit too handy for me, though. I could get addicted.'

She stood up and took the paper from Bethany's grasp. 'Do you want to wash your hands? They're very good fish and chips but you can't avoid the grease.'

'Please.'

Daisy led her into the kitchen and dropped the papers in a bin while Bethany washed her hands. As Daisy followed suit, Bethany gazed out of the window.

'You're in a great location here, Daisy. Look at that! The craft café's just across the square from here, and you've got the chippy, and the sweet shop, and the pubs on your doorstep. And Maister's supermarket not a ten-minute walk away.'

'And Bluebell's salon downstairs,' Daisy remarked, grinning. 'No chance of hiding from the landlord if I can't pay the rent.'

Bethany turned to her, alarmed. 'Are you struggling?'

'It was a joke,' Daisy said, drying her hands on the towel. 'I'm really happy here, and the café's doing well. Much better than I expected. And I'm even getting orders for cakes for special occasions now. I don't think the people at Bridge Bakery will be impressed with me as I'm stealing some of their business.'

'Good for you,' Bethany said, impressed. 'Considering you've not been here long that's such good going.'

'Thanks.' Daisy smiled shyly. 'I never thought I'd get the chance to run my own business. To be honest,' she admitted as they headed back into the living room, 'I never thought I'd be able to leave my brother's house. Yet here I am.'

'You sound so contented.' Bethany settled herself on the sofa and smiled at her.

'I am. I spent years thinking I had to be with a man to be happy, but I've finally realised that's not true. I can be happy on my own with friends and a job I love. And,' she added, gazing round the little flat in delight, 'my very own place. I know it's cheap and cheerful but it's home, and I couldn't be happier.'

'You've figured out where you belong,' Bethany said. 'Once you realise that everything else makes sense.'

'And how about you, Bethany?' Daisy poured them both a glass of wine. 'Have you figured out where you belong yet?'

Bethany took the glass she was offered. 'Perhaps,' she said, a teasing note to her tone. 'Let's just say I did a lot of thinking recently and some things fell into place at last.'

'That's great. Whatever you've decided it's obviously made you happy. You've got a different look about you somehow.'

'That's just what Clive said,' Bethany remembered. She shook her head slightly, not wanting to think about their last conversation right now. That worry could wait for another time. 'So, you've decided to stay single, or are you still looking?'

'Oh, I'm definitely happy being single for now,' Daisy said.

She sipped her wine and shrugged. 'I mean, I'd like to meet someone eventually but I'm starting to accept that the future I had mapped out for myself might not happen. I'm thirty-five. I might never have the family I always assumed I'd have.'

Bethany understood that pain all too well, and she wasn't sure she'd ever accepted it really, even though she'd thought for a long time that she had.

'You never know,' she told Daisy. 'I believe Kat was in her mid-thirties when she had Hattie and look at her now. A baby, a stepson, and another child on the way! And happily married to Jonah who, I have to say, is quite a hunk.'

Daisy's eyes twinkled with amusement. 'He is a bit of all right, isn't he? Kat's lovely. She's been so good to me. If it wasn't for her I'd never have been able to get the café up and running. She deserves this.'

'I wonder what she really thought to that hen do,' Bethany said, giggling. 'It wasn't exactly a typical one was it?'

'Nope. I felt awful when Miss Lavender told me what she'd booked the table for and then asked me to provide those afternoon teas. But then again, Kat had insisted she didn't want a hen night, and of course she knew she was pregnant so she wouldn't have been able to drink alcohol. I guess it was better than nothing.'

'And kind of Miss Lavender to organise it,' Bethany admitted. 'I thought I was going to be interrogated you know. I was horrified when I got there and realised so many people were going to be there, but everyone was lovely. I mean, there was a dodgy moment or two but generally everyone accepted that I didn't want to answer questions and left me alone.' She pulled a face. 'Except for Isobel Lavender. What *is* her problem, by the way? No one seems to like her very much.'

Daisy sighed. 'I have no idea. She's got everything going for her from what I can see. Her own business, a husband who's got a good job, a lovely home. She's very pretty, too. I don't know. Some people are never satisfied.'

Bethany remembered suddenly what Isobel had told them and her smile faded. 'Do you think she's being bullied by Noah?'

Daisy spluttered into her wine glass. 'Noah? No way! Why would you ask that?'

'When she found out he was in the café she got a bit worried. Said he wouldn't like her eating cake, and that he kept an eye on her weight and diet.'

Daisy put her glass on the table and turned incredulous eyes on Bethany. 'Noah? He's not like that!'

'How well do you know him?' Bethany asked curiously.

Daisy shrugged. 'Well, not that well,' she confessed. 'He comes into the café once or twice a week, just to escape the school for half an hour I think. He's very partial to my caramel and white chocolate cake, I'll tell you that much. Does that sound like a man who worries about calories and weight?'

'No,' Bethany said slowly, 'but maybe it's not *his* diet and weight he's bothered about. Only hers. Some men are like that, aren't they? Control freaks. He's a headmaster, isn't he? Maybe he's used to being in charge, giving orders.'

'I really can't see it.' Daisy looked extremely doubtful. 'He's a sweetie. We've chatted a few times. He's very polite, very gentle. He just doesn't seem the type to bully anyone. And have you met Isobel? Does she strike you as someone who'd be bullied?'

'No,' Bethany admitted. 'But that doesn't prove anything. What goes on between a man and woman in their own home can be very different to the way they behave in public, can't it? I'd hate to think she was being abused in any way. And really, when you think about it, it could explain why she's so edgy and unhappy all the time.'

'I suppose.' Daisy looked suddenly depressed. 'I don't want to think it possible of him, but as you said, who knows what goes on behind closed doors? I guess we can't rule it out. I'd be gutted if it's true, though, as I like him, and he seems so decent. And I'd hate to think she was suffering. Maybe we ought to keep an eye on her. I hope she's got someone she can confide in, but I can't think of anyone she's particularly close to offhand.'

'Hopefully we've got it all wrong.' Bethany sighed and swilled the wine round in her glass. 'Can you ever really trust any man one hundred per cent though?'

Daisy's eyes widened. 'Uh-oh. That sounds ominous. Don't tell me you're having doubts about the magnificent Clive already.'

'Of course not!' Bethany was quick to deny it but there it was again, that nagging feeling that she couldn't quite dismiss. 'It's just...'

'Just what?' Daisy leaned forward, her tone encouraging. 'It's okay, Bethany, you can tell me anything. I promise it will go no further.'

'I'm being stupid,' Bethany said, shaking her head. She took a sip of wine. 'It's just, he's round at Jennifer's tonight. You know, Jennifer Callaghan?'

'And?'

'I know it sounds silly, but I think there might be something between them. Maybe not now, but in the past perhaps. Or maybe he wanted there to be. Oh, I don't know.' She took another large gulp of wine. 'Like I said, I'm being stupid.'

'Why do you think that?' Daisy asked sympathetically. 'Has he given you any reason to doubt him?'

'No. Not really. It's just that I saw him at the opening of the art academy. Honestly, he couldn't take his eyes off her. And he's quite close to her son, which sort of includes him in their family. And tonight... I mean, why did she invite him round?

She didn't give him a reason. And,' she added triumphantly, as if this was conclusive prove, 'she told him not to tell Ben and Summer he was coming round.'

'Ah.' Daisy settled back in the sofa looking less worried. 'I don't know about anything else, and I can't give you any details, but I can tell you there's a reason for the invitation and it's nothing sinister, I promise you that.'

'Really?' Bethany eyed her uncertainly. 'Are you sure?'

'Positive.' Daisy smiled. 'But are you sure he was looking at her in that way at the art academy? Is it possible he was simply relieved to see her doing so well for herself in her new job, given her past? I've heard all about it from Kat and the poor woman's had a hard time of it. He must be pleased she's getting out into the world again. Maybe it was just that.'

Bethany considered it. 'Maybe,' she said slowly. 'But I can't shake this feeling that there's something he's not telling me about her. Oh, you're right. I'm probably reading way too much into things.'

'Jealousy,' said Daisy carefully, 'is a terrible thing. I was awful to Eliot. I accused him of some terrible things and caused him a lot of pain. If I'd stopped to think about it I'd have realised that he would never cheat on me if he thought we were together. He just wasn't like that. He was a decent, honourable man, and if we'd truly had an understanding he wouldn't have looked twice at Eden. But it was, as I've explained, in my head. Our relationship, I mean, not theirs.'

She gave Bethany a sympathetic look. 'I know it's hard to be objective about these things, but you know Clive. Do you think he's the sort of man who'd cheat on you? Really?'

Bethany hesitated then shook her head, ashamed. 'No,' she said quietly. 'Like your Eliot, he's a decent, honourable man.'

'Eliot wasn't mine,' Daisy reminded her. 'That was the trouble. But Clive *is* yours, and I think that's how he likes it, so I don't believe you have anything to worry about. You know the kind of man he is, so hang on to that. Believe in him. I hope, one day, I'll be lucky enough to meet someone like Clive and Eliot again, and this time I hope he cares about me as much as I care about him.'

She was right, Bethany realised. Clive was all she'd ever hoped for and more. She was, indeed, a lucky woman.

THIRTY

Clive and Summer were in the stables the next morning with Barney. Clive had popped round to Whispering Willows expecting to find Bethany having a lazy Sunday breakfast, but she'd already gone out. According to Summer she'd said vaguely that she was heading out for a day of shopping.

He'd been going to suggest they went out for the day themselves. Not shopping, but maybe a wander along the river at Kirkby Skimmer, and a tour of the abbey there. Perhaps a pub lunch or a cream tea.

Plans scuppered, a disappointed Clive had offered to help Summer bath Barney. Now they were putting a clean rug and hood on him and applying the barrier cream he needed to keep the midges at bay.

'Did Rafferty speak to you last night?' Summer asked as she worked the cream into Barney's legs.

'About what?' Clive asked her, amused. 'I take it you don't mean to tell me how good he thought the cake was.'

'No. Not that.' She peered up at him. 'About the horse sanctuary in Norfolk.'

Clive frowned. 'No, he didn't. What sanctuary's this?'

'He remembered there was one near where he used to live in Hoxbridge. It's nothing like this one. It's massive. They've got over a thousand horses apparently. It's a registered charity and they've got a great reputation. He suggested we contact them about our residents. He thinks they might even be able to take all of them. I mean,' she added dully, 'there are only nine to rehome aren't there? Now *she's* found somewhere for the donkeys.'

'It's quite a long way from here,' he said dubiously.

'I know. But at least they'd all be together, and we'd know they were safe.'

Clive was surprised and a bit sad that Summer had finally accepted the animals needed to find somewhere to go. He knew he should be glad, but somehow it made it all so much more real now that Summer was facing up to the situation.

'I'll tell Bethany,' he said quietly. 'She can ring them later.'

If she still wants to. If this is still what she's planning, even now.

Was she? She hadn't said anything specific, but her attitude towards the horses had definitely changed, and would she really think about turning the box room into an en suite if she still planned to leave? He knew he might be grasping at straws, but he just couldn't imagine it. Was he seeing what he wanted to see, or had Whispering Willows finally started to feel like home to Bethany?

Maybe, he mused, it was time they had a proper talk. He needed to see how she was feeling about everything now. She'd seemed so much happier on Friday night that he was certain she'd changed her mind.

'Looks like we've got a visitor,' Summer said, straightening up. She nodded towards the stableyard where a van had just pulled up.

'I'll see what they want.' Clive headed out of the loosebox, carefully shutting the lower door behind him, and strode into the stableyard, where a man was climbing out of the van, which had V.B.B. Building Services written on the side. Must be here about the plastering in the kitchen he thought, greeting the man with a smile.

'Hi, can I help you?'

The man beamed at him. 'Now then. Sorry to disturb on a Sunday morning but I was in the area on my way to another job and I thought I'd pop in to see you, rather than have another conversation on the phone. So, about the demolition job. I've had a look in my books and I'm a bit pressed for the next six weeks, but after that—'

'Wait, demolition job?' Clive stared at him. 'What are you talking about? I thought you were doing some plastering inside the house not pulling it down.'

The man laughed. 'Oh, we're doing the plastering next week, never fear. It's not the house that's coming down any road. It's the stables.' He frowned suddenly. 'You didn't know? I spoke to your lady wife about it, and she assured me that was what you wanted.'

'If you mean Bethany, she's not my wife,' Clive said dully.

'Oh. You're not Mr Marshall then?' The builder rubbed the back of his head. 'Is she around?'

'She's out for the day,' Clive told him. 'Perhaps you could tell me why the stables are being demolished and when this was decided.'

'Well, not sure I can actually.' The builder backed away towards his van. 'If you're not Mr Marshall I'd be best speaking to Mrs Marshall about this. No offence, mate, but I don't know you from Adam.'

'I just want to know—'

The man climbed into the van and started the engine. 'Ask

the owner if you want to know anything, mate. Tell her I'll give her a ring tomorrow.'

With that he drove out of the stableyard leaving Clive staring after him in dismay.

He was so lost in thought he didn't even hear Summer walk up behind him.

'So that's that then,' she said flatly. 'She's demolishing the stables. We'd better contact that sanctuary because it seems we only have six weeks to rehome the horses.'

'She wouldn't do that. Not without telling me.' Clive spun round to face her, feeling sick with misery.

Summer evidently saw he was in shock and her expression softened.

'But she has, Clive. You heard the man. She's had this all planned behind our backs. Obviously she didn't tell you what she intended to do.'

'She said they were just going to do some repairs on the roof and do a bit of plastering,' he murmured. 'She told me the stables needed a new roof but no mention of any demolition. Why would she keep that from me?'

'Makes you wonder what else she's keeping from us, doesn't it?' She sighed. 'I'm sorry. I know it's not what you were hoping for. Look, can you do me a favour? Can you take Barney up to Harston Hill? I need the loo.'

He nodded dumbly and while Summer headed into the house he collected Barney who, bless him, looked like Batman in his hood and rugs, and led him to his favourite grazing area, where the midges were less likely to bother him due to its exposed location.

Returning to the house he went into the kitchen to make a cup of tea for himself and Summer, stooping to fuss Viva who'd been left in there while he saw to Barney. At the distinct sound of a drawer being closed in the living room he straightened and spun round, noticing the living room door was slightly ajar.

Tentatively pushing it open, he peered round, his mouth falling open as he saw Summer busily rifling through the cupboards in Joseph's old dresser.

'What on earth are you doing?'

Summer jumped guiltily. 'Sorry, but I had to look.'

'Look for what? What are you up to?'

Summer gave him a defiant stare. 'She's lied to you about the building work, and she's kept the plans to demolish the stables to herself. Aren't you curious about what else she's hiding?'

'Summer, you can't just go spying on her like this. It's not right!'

'Do you think keeping us in the dark is? We have a bloody right to know, Clive, and if she won't tell us we'll have to find out for ourselves.'

'What's that?' he asked, nodding at the folder tucked under her left arm.

'I don't know yet. I haven't had the chance to look. I'll do that now.'

'No you won't.' He took it from her and returned it to the cupboard, closing the door firmly. 'You've no right to do this, Summer. Besides, you won't find anything.'

'That's where you're wrong. Look.'

She beckoned him over and, half reluctantly, he moved to stand by her side. 'What are we looking at?'

She jabbed a notepad with her finger. 'See? Exhibit one.'

Clive peered at what was written there in Bethany's neat handwriting.

Russell from Greystones Estate Agency
Viewing Monday 10th June 2pm.

'Right,' he said heavily. 'So she's getting someone to value

Whispering Willows.' She hadn't changed her mind about leaving then.

'Exhibit two,' Summer said.

To his discomfort she pressed play on the telephone answer machine.

'Summer, you can't!'

'Listen,' she hissed, and despite his misgivings he did.

'Message received yesterday at fifteen hundred hours.'

The voice was friendly but professional.

'Hi, Mrs Marshall, this is Rachel at Folly Farm, just returning your call. Sorry to have missed you yet again but if you'd like to give me a call back we can discuss the matter in full. Thank you.'

'She's contacted Folly Farm?' He felt dazed. 'But she was so adamant. She said if they couldn't take all four Shetlands they weren't having any, and when I said they might have room for Barney instead she wouldn't hear of it.'

'Well,' Summer said bitterly, 'seems she's changed her mind, doesn't it? If you ask me she's been in talks with the estate agents round here and they've told her she'll make more money if the stables are gone because of the work they'd need to fix them. She's got pound signs in her eyes.'

'But—I don't understand.' Clive sank into an armchair, barely noticing as Viva jumped into his lap. He really didn't understand at all. He was so sure she'd changed her mind, that she wanted to stay. How had he got her so wrong?

He hadn't wanted her to stay in Tuppenny Bridge just for him, but he had to admit he'd hoped he'd at least be a consideration. It seemed she wasn't swayed by their relationship at all. All the progress he thought they'd made had been in his head. She hadn't budged from her initial decision to get rid of Whispering Willows, and what hurt him the most was that she'd been arranging all this behind his back.

'She could at least have told me,' he murmured.

Summer sat down next to him and ruffled Viva's ears. 'I'm so sorry. You really liked her, didn't you?'

'I did. I mean, I do.' He just couldn't take it in.

He'd been so besotted with Bethany he hadn't seen what she was up to.

Maybe it was true what they said. *No fool like an old fool.* And he suddenly felt very old and very foolish.

THIRTY-ONE

It had been a long and busy day for Bethany, but it had been worth it. She was smiling widely as she pulled into the stable-yard, and her smile grew even wider when she spotted Clive's SUV parked up near the house.

She wondered how long he'd been waiting there. Not too long, she hoped. It would have been lovely to spend the day with him, especially as she hadn't seen him yesterday, but this had been too important to put off and she was sure he'd agree it was good news all round. In fact, she could hardly wait to tell him.

She grabbed her handbag from the passenger seat and locked the car doors before heading happily into the house.

Clive was sitting at the kitchen table, Viva at his feet. He had his head in his hands but as she shut the door behind her he looked up and she saw the bleak expression in his eyes.

'Clive, what it is it? Has something happened?'

Oh, lord! What if Jennifer had given him bad news last night and he'd needed her? She'd been out all day. She should have told him she was going, given him the chance to tell her if he wanted to talk to her.

She pulled out the chair next to his and took hold of his hand. It lay unresponsive in hers and she squeezed it gently, hoping he'd show some sign of affection in return.

When he didn't she frowned. 'What's the matter, Clive? You're worrying me.'

His gaze ranged over her as if he was only just seeing her. 'Why didn't you tell me?' he asked her.

She straightened. 'Tell you what?'

'You had a visitor today,' he said. 'Some builder. He assumed I was *Mr Marshall*. I hear you're planning to demolish the stables.'

She groaned inwardly. It was meant to be a surprise! Stupid Mr Belper telling Clive like that.

'That's true,' she said reluctantly. 'But you see—'

She leaned back, startled, as he placed a piece of paper on the table in front of her.

'Got an estate agent coming to value this place, too.'

She stared at the reminder she'd scribbled on the pad after speaking to the estate agent on the phone.

'What are you doing with that?' she asked, bewildered.

'I found it,' he said. 'And I also found the message on your answer machine from Rachel. So you've changed your mind about sending Barney to Folly Farm? Or have you decided it's no big deal if the Shetlands are separated after all?'

Bethany glared at him. 'Are you seriously telling me you've been snooping? You listened to my answer machine messages? Where the hell do you get off doing that? You had no right.'

He sighed. 'I know,' he said simply. 'I shouldn't have done it. I hold my hands up. But, Bethany, how could you do such a thing, especially behind my back? I thought you were better than this.'

The injustice gnawed away at her. 'Did you indeed? So that justifies you listening to my private messages? And you must have been looking in the dresser, too, because that phone pad was in the cupboard.'

He at least had the decency to look ashamed, but she was so disappointed in him she didn't know where to begin.

'I thought I could trust you,' he murmured.

She glared at him. 'You thought *you* could trust *me*? I think it's me who should have the trust issues around here!'

'Hang on,' he said, 'I may have listened to a message I shouldn't have, but you've been arranging all this stuff without even mentioning it to me. The builder reckons he can start work in six weeks. Six weeks! You've not left much time to rehome all the animals, have you? I suppose that's why you've lowered your standards and have decided Folly Farm is suddenly good enough. Any port in a storm, right?'

'I don't know how you've got the cheek,' she said. 'I'm not the one who can't be trusted around here. And I'm certainly not the only one keeping secrets!'

He stared at her. 'What do you mean by that?'

'You and Jennifer! Don't tell me there's nothing between you because I know there is.'

Actually, she'd almost persuaded herself that she'd been imagining the whole thing. Her talk with Daisy had reassured her that Clive simply wasn't the sort of man to do such a dishonourable thing, but knowing he'd been spying on her had made her think perhaps she'd been naïve. And now, looking at the expression on his face, her heart sank as she realised she might genuinely be onto something.

'What makes you think that?' he said weakly.

It was hardly the outright denial she'd hoped for, and she pulled her hand from his.

'I'm not stupid,' she said coldly. 'I saw the way you were watching her at Monk's Folly that day. You looked pathetic. Like a lost little puppy.'

She was being cruel now and she knew it, but she was hurt

and bewildered. She couldn't believe she'd been planning to surprise him with so much good news and all the time he'd been snooping on her and lying to her.

'There's nothing between me and Jennifer,' he said quietly, staring at the table. 'Nothing.'

'Look at me and say that,' she said tearfully.

With evident reluctance Clive faced her.

'Go on,' she said. 'Say that again.'

He took a deep breath. 'There's nothing between me and Jennifer.'

His voice sounded odd, and she had the strongest feeling he wasn't telling her the whole truth.

'And was there ever?'

There was no mistaking the stricken look in his eyes and the way his cheeks reddened slightly.

'No,' he said slowly, making it so obvious he really didn't want to answer that question that she was incensed.

'Oh my God! You're lying,' she whispered, hardly able to believe it.

'I'm... That is...'

'You know, I'm such a bloody fool,' she said, running her hands through her hair in despair. 'First Glenn, then Ted. Why should you be any different?'

'Bethany,' he said, reaching for her hand, 'it's not like that. I swear to you.'

'Don't bother,' she said, pushing his hand away. 'You know what? I was so excited today. I was going to tell you my big news and I thought you'd be over the moon but instead this is what I get. You're a liar and a cheat. I wish I'd never been stupid enough to fall for you.'

'I'm—I'm sorry.'

'Save your apologies. Shall I tell you something, Clive? I was planning to stay in Tuppenny Bridge. Despite everything that's happened, despite all I've been through in this town, I was going to put that behind me and make a new life here with you. I was such an idiot. The estate agent? Yes I'd been in touch with one because I was looking for somewhere to buy round here. I might not want Whispering Willows, but I wanted to stay in this town for you. That's how much I cared about you.'

Clive swallowed, seeming unable to put into words what he wanted to say. At last he managed, '*Cared* for me? Past tense?'

Bethany blinked away the tears. Of course she still cared for him. Did he really think she could change her mind about that so quickly? But she was too hurt to reassure him, so she simply stared at him, saying nothing.

'Well,' he said at last, 'at least we both know where we stand now.'

'Do we?' she said, amazed that he could believe that. 'Lucky you, because I'm still waiting for an answer. What went on between you and Jennifer? And is it still going on? What was I? A bit of amusement on the side?'

Clive shook his head slightly. 'You know, I never wanted you to stay here just for me, Bethany. I never expected it, and I wouldn't have asked it of you.'

Was he really saying he didn't want her to stay? After everything that had happened between them was she really so unimportant to him?

'You said you wanted me to stay!' she protested.

'But not for me! Don't you see? It would never work. This had to be about you and what you wanted for your future. Finding where you could be happy, not for my sake but for your own.'

'Well,' she said, 'I guess I'm rethinking that right now. Fact is, you're not what I thought you were at all, so why would I stay? Thank goodness I've got somewhere to go.'

'Back to Helena's?' he asked sadly.

She nodded. 'For now.'

He got to his feet. 'I see. Well, I hope things work out for you, Bethany.'

'And that's it, is it?' she demanded. 'You're going to walk out of here without telling me the truth? You'd rather I left here for good then admit what's going on with you and Jennifer?'

'Do you really believe there's anything going on?' he asked her.

'I know you're lying about something,' she told him. 'There's something you're not telling me, that's for sure.'

'Seems we're both good at keeping secrets then, doesn't it?' He sighed heavily and glanced down at Viva. 'I take it you want me to keep her?'

Bethany was struggling to keep her composure. She certainly couldn't risk looking at little Viva.

'That would be appreciated,' she said, hoping her voice didn't betray how utterly broken she was feeling.

Clive scooped Viva into his arms. 'Will you keep in touch with Summer?' he asked. 'Let her know what's happening? You don't have to contact me, but she needs to know. Our first priority has to be the animals in our care.'

'I'm aware of that,' she said stiffly. 'Although really, that's between me and Summer, isn't it?'

She heard him take a sharp breath and closed her eyes briefly, determined to hold back the tears that were threatening to fall at any moment.

The next thing she heard was the back door closing, and then there was only the sound of her heart breaking.

THIRTY-TWO

'Oh, Clive.' Jennifer's eyes crinkled with sympathy. 'I'm so sorry to hear about Bethany leaving, I really am.' She shook her head slightly and stepped aside. 'Come in. You look awful, you poor thing.'

'How did you know?' he asked, following her down the hall and into the living room of Daisyfield Cottage. Then he gave an abrupt laugh. 'Please don't tell me the Lavender Ladies have got hold of all this?'

'No, don't worry,' she said, directing him to the armchair nearest the window. 'Summer confided in me. She's terribly worried about you and she can't help feeling responsible.'

'It's not her fault,' he said. 'This was all me, believe me.'

'She told me she'd been snooping and had discovered some things that threw Bethany's motives into doubt,' Jennifer said cautiously. She sat near him on the sofa and surveyed him with sorrow in her eyes. 'She doesn't seem the sort of person who'd behave like that, but Summer says having been caught out she fled back to her friend's house in Somerset. Surely that's not true? There must have been another reason she left.'

Clive didn't know where to start. He gave a slight shrug, knowing this was going to be a difficult conversation.

'Where are Jamie and Ben?' he asked warily.

'Jamie's gone to the cinema with Eloise,' she said. 'And Ben's round at The White Hart Inn with Summer.'

He nodded, distracted. He'd hoped the boys would both be out with it being a Saturday evening. At least they wouldn't be interrupted but God knows this was going to be hard.

'I needed to talk to you,' he said reluctantly. 'You see, Bethany leaving, it concerns us.'

'Oh, Clive, no!' Jennifer held up her hands in despair. 'I thought we'd sorted this out. I thought you understood—'

'It's not what you think,' he told her. 'Far from it. It's just, Bethany's got it into her head that there's something between us.'

'Which you denied, obviously.'

'Of course I did. But...'

She stared at him, her face pale. 'But what? What did you tell her, Clive?'

'Nothing. That's the trouble. I didn't tell her anything because how could I? And she knew I was lying. Seems she can read me like a book and now she doesn't trust me. Really, why should she? So she's gone. As you can see it's all my fault, not Summer's.'

Summer might have been the one to do the snooping, for which he'd taken the blame, but that wasn't what had driven Bethany away. It was his own failure to be honest with her that had done that. But what choice did he have? It was such a difficult situation, and he knew, when he woke up that morning to the realisation that Bethany had left Tuppenny Bridge and returned to Somerset, that if he didn't do something about it he'd never get her back. Even now, six days after their argument, it might be too late, because when she knew what had happened she might never forgive him. Maybe she'd decide she was right not to trust him because, the truth was, he wasn't the man she thought he was. He never had been.

'Oh, Clive.' Jennifer leaned back in the sofa and sighed, staring out of the window beyond him, her thoughts clearly miles away.

'I know,' he said softly. 'It's a mess.'

'You could say that. Just when I thought everything between us was finally sorted out.' She drummed her fingers on the arm of the sofa, deep in thought. 'You know,' she said at last, 'I really enjoyed the party last Saturday. It was lovely to celebrate with Ben and Summer of course, but I also enjoyed the fact that you were here as a friend, with no barrier between us at last. It's been a long time since I felt that way.'

He hung his head. 'I know.'

'Julian told me,' she said suddenly, making Clive shoot a puzzled glance at her. 'What you and he arranged between you. How you were going to step in and take his place after he died.'

Clive reddened. 'It wasn't how you think,' he said.

'Wasn't it? Well, it sounded like that to me. He was very ill at the time, but he was insistent that I listen to him.' Her eyes filled with tears. 'He told me I wasn't to worry. That even though he couldn't be here to take care of me, he'd made arrangements with you, and you were going to ensure Ben, Jamie and I would want for nothing.'

'Is that why...?' Clive shook his head. 'Is that why you wanted nothing to do with me? Why you made it very clear I wasn't wanted in any capacity.'

'You know, I loved Julian very much,' she said, 'but I was furious. Furious with the pair of you. How dare you arrange my future for me that way? Was I supposed to just sit back and meekly accept that, from then on, you would be taking care of me and my children? Like I was some favourite possession to be handed down in a will! As if I had no mind of my own.'

'He was just trying to protect you,' Clive said. 'That's all.

He was worried you wouldn't manage on your own and he knew he could rely on me...' His voice trailed off and he added miserably, 'At least, he thought he could.'

'I'm not a trinket to be passed from one person to the next,' she told him. 'I didn't say anything to Julian of course. Not that I'm sure he'd have taken it in anyway. He wasn't really in any state to at the time. I thought it would be kinder to let him think I'd go along with his ridiculous plans. But you! I can't believe you agreed to that. What were you thinking?'

'I tried to persuade him it wasn't a good idea,' Clive said wearily. 'He was so insistent and, in the end, I thought it would be better for him to believe that's what would happen. When he extracted that promise we didn't know for certain what the prognosis would be anyway. I hoped he'd pull through and we could both forget we'd ever had the conversation. He was just worried; he didn't want all the responsibility to fall on Leon's shoulders. I'm sorry, Jennifer. I just wanted to take one of the worries off Julian's mind, that's all. I never really thought I'd be keeping that promise. Not in the way he meant anyway. I intended to help you out as much as I could, but I never assumed I could just step in and marry you the way Julian imagined.'

Jennifer was quiet for a moment. 'When Julian told me, I thought...'

Clive gave her a bemused look. 'You thought what?' Then his face cleared. 'Oh no. You didn't? No wonder you put the barriers up. You thought that what happened was because of the promise I'd made to Julian. That I didn't really care. That it meant nothing!'

Jennifer wrapped her arms around herself defensively. 'I was so hurt,' she admitted. 'I felt betrayed by you both.'

'I'm so sorry,' he said. 'It was never like that, I promise you. I would never have done that!'

'I suppose I knew deep down,' she said sadly. 'You're not

that sort of person, are you? But the truth is, I was so terribly unhappy, and in so much pain that it was easier to be angry with you and punish you then face up to the truth. And the fact is it was easily as much my fault as yours. More really. I knew how you felt about me, and I took advantage of that for my own selfish reasons. If anyone owes anyone an apology it's me to you.'

She gazed up at him with tear-filled eyes. 'I really am sorry. The way I've treated you all these years, and after everything you've done for Ben...'

'Don't, Jennifer,' he begged her. 'Don't cry. There's been enough sadness in your life. Please don't let me be the cause of any more. It's done now. Over with.'

'Except it isn't,' she pointed out. 'It's still causing you problems. Bethany's left because you couldn't be honest with her and, knowing you, that was for my benefit, wasn't it?'

'It's not just my secret to tell,' he reminded her gently. 'I couldn't betray you like that.'

She shook her head, looking anguished. 'It was one night, Clive. Just one night! Did I really deserve to be punished so badly for it?'

'Of course not.' He sat beside her and put his arms around her. 'No one deserves what you went through. I've hated myself ever since so I didn't blame you for pushing me away. I thought it was all about that. I had no idea Julian had told you about the promise I'd made him. No wonder you wanted nothing to do with me. But, Jennifer, you must believe me, I did love you. I always loved you from the moment I met you. Otherwise none of that would have happened, I swear to you, promise or no promise.'

She nodded, wiping her eyes with her sleeve. 'Clive, you have to tell Bethany,' she said at last.

He frowned, not sure she was thinking straight. 'That's an awful big leap of faith,' he said. 'Not just for me but for you.

Especially for you. You have far more to lose than I do if she can't keep a secret.'

'If you don't risk it she'll never come back to you,' Jennifer said. 'And you want her back, don't you?' She peered into his eyes, a slight smile on her lips. 'I'm right, aren't I? You do want her?'

He hesitated, not wanting to hurt her any more. 'Aye,' he said at last. 'I'm in love with her, Jennifer.'

'I'm so glad,' Jennifer said, her smile widening. 'You deserve this, Clive. You really do. So you see, we have no choice. You must tell her. There's no other way because she'll see right through you, and anyway, that's no way to begin a relationship.'

'I was going to ask you,' he admitted. 'That's why I came here today, for your permission.'

She shook her head, a look of amazement on her face. 'You see? You didn't just tell her and save your skin. You wanted my permission first. And that, Clive, is why you deserve to be happy. Why you deserve to be loved. You have my permission. Go to Bethany and tell her what happened between us. If you trust her, I trust her. *Do* you trust her?'

He hesitated. 'She's been acting strange. Doing things without telling me.'

'That's not what I asked,' she said. 'Summer told me all that and I agree it looks odd, but that doesn't mean it's an open and shut case. So I'll ask you again. Do you trust her?'

He nodded. 'I do, yes. I was just so hurt when I found out she'd rung the sanctuary and then there was the whole demolition thing, but maybe she's got her reasons. She's a good person, and I know she's grown to care for the animals in her care. I was wrong about the estate agents. She was looking to buy a house round here so she could stay with me. So yes, I was wrong to react the way I did. I trust her.'

'So go to her and sort this out,' Jennifer said. 'Only when

you've both been completely honest with each other will you know if you have a future together.'

'You're right,' he said. 'Thank you.'

'Thank *you*, Clive,' she said, putting her arms around him and hugging him tightly. 'For all you've done for Ben, for what you tried to do for Julian, and for putting up with me after what happened. You have the patience of a saint. We've both been so unhappy for so long, but it's time for us to grab life and start living again, isn't it?'

He smiled. 'It is. And we will.'

He just hoped he hadn't pushed Bethany too far. He needed her to understand and forgive him, but was that asking too much when he'd been unable to understand and forgive himself for so many years?

THIRTY-THREE

Bethany had barely slept that night. She'd tossed and turned in her old bed in Helena's spare room and had finally given up at five in the morning, getting up as quietly as she could and heading downstairs to make coffee for herself.

Helena rose at seven, wandering into the kitchen yawning. She frowned when she saw Bethany sitting at the table and, shaking her head in despair, she tightened the belt on her dressing gown and headed to the coffee machine.

'Would you like a top up?' she asked, nodding at the mug in front of Bethany.

'That would be good, thanks.'

Bethany drained her mug and carried it over to where Helena was taking another one out of the cupboard.

'I take it you didn't exactly have a good night's sleep?' Helena asked sympathetically.

'You could say that. Honestly, I can't believe the way things have turned out. Just as I thought my life was finally beginning to make sense.'

Her eyes filled with tears again and she blinked them away.

She'd never felt so lost and alone and given her past that was saying something.

'Sit down,' Helena said gently. 'I'll bring your coffee over.'

Minutes later they sat opposite each other at the table in thoughtful silence.

'It won't do to brood you know,' Helena said at last. 'I knew it would be a mistake for you to go back to Tuppenny Bridge. After everything that went on there when you were younger how could you ever think you'd be happy there? All those plans you made! I was so worried about you. I really couldn't understand what was keeping you there.' She shook her head. 'I can't believe you fell for that vet! I mean, the man who did nothing but emotionally blackmail you and try to manipulate you into keeping Whispering Willows, just because of his devotion to your brother. It's crazy.'

'He was just thinking of the animals,' Bethany said sadly.

'Yes, and to hell with what was best for you! And the minute he discovered you were going ahead with the sale he just dropped you, as if you'd never mattered at all.' She shook her head. 'You always were too trusting you know.'

Bethany bit her lip as the thought popped into her mind that Helena might be right about that because look how trusting she'd been of her and Ted. She could hardly say that, though. They were her friends and hadn't meant to hurt her, so it wouldn't be fair. Even so, she couldn't agree with Helena's verdict on Clive.

'He didn't emotionally blackmail me or manipulate me,' she said reluctantly. 'He was the one who warned me about spending money on the house and stables, remember? If he'd really wanted me to stay at any cost he'd have been all for it.'

'I think he was just being clever,' Helena said. 'Calling your bluff. That's what I mean about manipulation. By making you think he was only saying that for your sake he actually made you believe it was your decision. Really it was what he intended all along. I know his sort. Thank goodness you saw through him in the end before you'd wasted too much money. I'll bet he got an awful shock when he saw the note about the meeting with the estate agent.'

Bethany hesitated, reluctant to burst Helena's bubble. She could imagine the scorn on her friend's face if she told her the whole truth and decided a partial confession would suffice. 'The meeting wasn't about Whispering Willows,' she said. 'It was to view another house in Tuppenny Bridge.'

Helena's face was a picture. 'You're joking? You seriously considered staying in that town after everything you said?'

Feeling stupid Bethany had to admit she'd done more than consider it. She'd made her mind up.

'Well!' Helena sipped her coffee, her eyes narrowed. 'I guess Clive did you a favour in the end then. Snooping around, prying into your private business. At least now you know what sort of man he is, and you don't have to feel bad about leaving. Good job he showed his true colours before you did something foolish and signed a contract.'

Bethany couldn't reply. She was feeling too emotional to speak.

Helena sighed and squeezed her hand. 'I'm sorry, Bethany. I can see this is hard for you and I really wish I could make it better. I'm just sad you had to go through all this, even though I did warn you that it would be a mistake to go back there. I wish you'd listened to me.'

'So do I,' Bethany managed.

If she hadn't returned to Tuppenny Bridge she'd never have met Clive and would never have experienced what it felt like to fall in love. She was heartbroken that it was over, but was the heartbreak worth it? Would she really have preferred to live her life without ever knowing the joy of loving someone so completely and overwhelmingly? She wasn't entirely sure she would.

She may be feeling devastated right now, but she'd had such good times in Tuppenny Bridge. Not just with Clive, but with Daisy and Clemmie and Kat and Jonah. With kind Miss Lavender and the funny Pennyfeather sisters. At the opening of the art academy and Kat's hen party. Eating breakfast every morning with Maya and Lennox, sitting round the table at Whispering Willows. Making tea strong enough to stand the spoon in for Lennox and weak enough to barely colour the water for Maya. Dancing with Clive at Kat and Jonah's wedding...

She felt an almost unbearable weight of sadness pressing on her chest. The thought that she'd never see all those people again was so painful she couldn't stand it. How was she going to get through the rest of her life now? She'd started to feel like part of the community, and she'd truly thought they liked her. She was sure they had.

But then, she'd thought Clive loved her, and he'd let her go so easily.

I never wanted you to stay here just for me, Bethany. I never expected it, and I wouldn't have asked it of you.

But why not? Why hadn't he expected it? Why wouldn't he ask it of her? Why hadn't he wanted her to stay just for him? Because she hadn't mattered anywhere as much to him as she'd thought?

So it must be about Jennifer, she thought wretchedly. Why else had he lied about her? No matter how much it hurt she simply had to put the last few weeks behind her and start again. Back to house hunting. Back to searching for that elusive forever home.

She glanced around her at Helena's smart, modern kitchen.

'You've done a great job with this place,' she told her. 'What did the kids think to it?'

Helena smiled. 'Oh, they loved it. They were very impressed with the renovations and the boys adored the garden.

They were outside playing for hours each day. They want me to get a tree house put in at the end of the garden. I looked online and can you believe there are companies that actually do that? I thought I might have it done for them before the summer holidays as a surprise.'

'You won't have long,' Bethany observed. 'It's June now.'

'Oh, if I offer them enough money they'll fit me in,' Helena said airily. 'Anything for my grandchildren.'

She gazed round the kitchen, a satisfied smile on her lips. 'It's not bad here,' she admitted. 'And it's far cheaper to run than the old house and in a much more convenient location.'

'Do you miss the old house?' Bethany asked, curious. 'It must have been a wrench leaving it, with all your memories of Ted.'

'Not really.' Helena patted her chest. 'Ted's in here, not in a pile of bricks and mortar. He'd have understood. He might have owned that house for a long time, but he was never emotionally attached to it after all. As he said, it's the people in it that make a house a home. A house on its own is just a shell.'

Bethany nodded. 'I suppose you're right. I never thought about it before, but Ted wasn't particularly fond of it, was he? Maybe it's because it was a family home and he never got to choose it for himself.'

Although, she thought suddenly, if that was the case why hadn't Ted sold it and bought himself somewhere else? When he married Bethany it would have been the perfect time to do so. They could have chosen somewhere together. Or if not then when he'd married Helena.

Helena laughed. 'Why would he bother? As far as Ted was concerned it was just a place to stay. As long as he had all his comforts around him he didn't care where it was. Why do you think he got interior designers to sort out the décor for him? He really had far more important things to think about than a house.'

'And that didn't upset you?'

Helena looked astounded. 'Why on earth would it? It saved me a job. After you left he offered to have the whole place redecorated so I could make it my own but, as I said to him, nothing in there was to your taste anyway so what did it matter? It was stylish and comfortable, so why put ourselves through all that upheaval?' Her mouth twitched in amusement. 'It's not as if it was ever as dire as Whispering Willows. Now that sounds truly awful. I don't know how you stood it there as long as you did.'

Bethany thought about the old house in the Dales where she'd grown up. It was in an awful state now, but it hadn't been bad when she was little. She'd been shocked and saddened to see how much it had been neglected. But she knew from photographs how lovely it had looked in her grandparents' day, and before that it had been a grand house. It was only after the First World War that a whole wing of the house had been demolished to make it cheaper and more manageable. Before that it had been much larger, and she could imagine how proud the Parkinsons must have been when they first purchased such an amazing property.

She felt a sudden anger towards her father who had brought nothing but sadness and despair to Whispering Willows. The house hadn't deserved that. Neither had the people within it.

'I'll need to talk to my solicitor,' she said listlessly. 'I must sort things out once and for all. And I need to call Summer.'

'Summer?'

'The manager of the sanctuary. She needs to be put in the picture.'

At least she thought, she could put the girl's mind at rest at last. And she had some good news that might even put a smile on Clive's face, even though she wouldn't be there to see it.

Helena gave her a suspicious look. 'What are you up to?'

Bethany shrugged. 'Nothing much. Just, I've decided not to sell Whispering Willows.'

'What? But I don't understand! That was the whole point of you returning—to get it ready for sale. Surely you're not going back there? Please tell me this isn't about that vet.'

'No,' Bethany said. 'It's about the house and the horses. The fact is, I don't want the house pulling down or turning into some glorified guest house or a holiday park. And as for the animals...' She shook her head, more certain than ever that she was doing the right thing. 'I can't let them go. Whispering Willows is their home. I wanted to tell Clive that day but never got the chance. I'm going to keep it running. Put Summer in charge and pay her a proper wage.'

'Are you insane? Have you any idea how expensive that will be?'

'Yes. Which is why I want to see my solicitor. I need to look into setting up a registered charity. I'm sure Summer will be all for it and of course I'll hire more people to help her.'

'And the house?'

'I'll get it renovated and rent it out. I'm sure I'll find tenants for it easily enough, but even if I don't I'll be able to let it as a holiday home. That will pay for its maintenance going forward.'

Helena stared at her. 'You've really thought this through.'

'Of course I have. The truth is,' she said, taking her courage in both hands, 'I realised something while I was living in Tuppenny Bridge.'

Even as she said the words it finally struck her how true it was. She'd never articulated the thought to herself before but now it was there, fully formed in her mind, and it was a revelation.

'I thought I was incapable of love. Of any deep feeling at all. I'd been so withdrawn and closed off for so long that I forgot what true emotion felt like. But being back there changed me. The truth is, I enjoyed being part of the community. I realised that I liked the company of my neighbours and that, given time, they could become friends. I fell in love with Clive—something I never could have imagined in my wildest dreams. And no, it didn't work out, but I'm still glad I got to experience it because I never thought I would. And as for Whispering Willows...' She paused, shaking her head in amazement. 'Maybe that's been the biggest revelation of them all. What happened to me there, living in the shadow of my father's behaviour and my mother's suicide, it coloured my whole perception of the place. I detested that house and all I wanted to do was get rid of it.'

'But now you don't,' Helena said flatly.

'No, I don't. I can't. Because the thing is, Hels, what Joseph created there mattered. Those horses, ponies, and donkeys, they'd suffered. No one wanted them. They'd been hurt and abused or cast out because they were too old. But Joseph took them in and cared for them. He gave them new hope and a future they might never have had otherwise. Whispering Willows is a place of love and compassion, and I'm not about to shut that down. Ted was right, you know.'

Helena gave her a puzzled look. 'About what?'

'It's the people that make a house a home. A house on its own is just a shell. And Joseph—despite everything he'd suffered from our father—made Whispering Willows a home. For the animals he loved, who loved him back. It isn't a place of misery and despair at all, and that's what took me so long to see. Joseph transformed it into a welcoming and loving home, not for himself but for them. That's why he spent all his money on the sanctuary and let the house decay. He was thinking with his heart and I, for one, am very grateful that he did.'

Helena pushed her coffee cup away. 'Are you saying... Bethany, are you saying you forgive Joseph?'

Bethany swallowed. 'I don't know what happened to him, Hels. I don't know why he betrayed me, or why he never apologised or tried to make it up with me. I don't know what went wrong and the fact is, I never will now. Can I forgive him for that? Maybe not. Not fully. But at least I can step back and see the bigger picture. Who he was. What he tried to do. Maybe after Father's behaviour he was too damaged to love another human being, but he had the capacity to show love for other living creatures, which proves to me that he wasn't a bad person.'

She wrapped her arms around herself, wishing she'd seen that earlier. 'I forgot that for so many years. I forgot about how he used to look after me and protect me, how he used to coax Mother outside and try to cheer her up. I got lost in the bitterness and where did it get me? I ended up as closed off as he was in the end. Worse maybe, because I couldn't even express my love to the horses I used to love so much. I was afraid they'd get through my armour, make me vulnerable. But loving Clive has made me see that, sometimes, the pain is worth it. I wouldn't have missed these past few weeks for anything. I've never been happier. So maybe I haven't totally forgiven Joseph, but I don't hate him any more. I can look back and remember him with love. And you know what, that makes me happier than I've felt in decades, despite everything that's happened.'

She looked up and gave a wry smile, seeing the stunned look on Helena's face.

'You think I'm mad, don't you?'

To her amazement, a tear rolled down her friend's cheek.

'No, Bethany. I don't think you're mad. But I think you're going to be shocked by what I have to tell you now.' She slipped off the chair and held out her hand. 'You'd better come with me.'

THIRTY-FOUR

Bethany couldn't help but feel a little anxious as Helena led her upstairs into the box room at the end of the landing.

'What's this about?' she asked.

Helena didn't look at her. 'You'll see,' was her only reply.

She led Bethany inside the room and headed over to one of the many bags and boxes which were piled up inside. Clearly, the box room was only used for storage, and looking round Bethany realised most of the stuff in here had once belonged to Ted.

Helena opened one of the boxes and rummaged around inside.

'You might want to sit down,' she said, indicating an old ottoman chest at the end of the room.

Frowning, Bethany settled herself on it, her eyes never leaving her friend. Just what was going on?

Eventually, Helena straightened and walked slowly towards her, carrying a large canvas bag.

'What's in there?' Something was warning Bethany that whatever Helena was about to show her it was important.

'What you have to understand,' Helena said, 'is that he did it for your own good, as did I. Promise me you won't overreact.'

'Overreact to what?'

'Promise me.'

Bethany shook her head. 'How can I promise if I don't know what you're talking about?'

Helena hesitated then shrugged. 'Very well.'

She placed the bag in Bethany's lap. Bethany frowned, not understanding what any of this was about, but opened the bag and peered inside.

'What are these?' she asked, but even as the words left her mouth she knew. She gasped and reached into the bag, dragging out a handful of envelopes, all sealed.

'These letters! They're from Joseph!'

She'd recognise his handwriting anywhere, even all these years later. Frantically she rummaged in the bag, realising there were dozens and dozens of them.

'He wrote to me? When? When did these start arriving?'

Helena sank onto the ottoman beside her. 'Honestly? Not long after you and Ted got married. I guess he saw your marriage announcement in the newspapers and tracked Ted down.' She folded her arms. 'Ted told me he wrote once a week, every week for five years.'

'Five—five *years*?'

Helena nodded. 'There are birthday cards and Christmas cards in there, too, I think.' She looked embarrassed suddenly. 'There were more, but I...'

Bethany stared at her. 'You what? What did you do?'

'You must understand, you were my friend, and you were upset! Joseph had broken your heart, that's what you said. You told me you wanted nothing to do with him. So when he turned up at my flat looking for you I told him just that and sent him away.' She turned her face away as if she was suddenly too ashamed to look Bethany in the eye. 'He came back but you were at college, and I told him you'd left and that I didn't know where you were. I don't think he believed me. I think he thought you were hiding in the flat. That's when he started writing. Every week for the entire two years you lived with me.'

'What? But how didn't I know about that?'

'He was regular as clockwork.' Helena shrugged. 'I quickly learned when to make sure I reached the door first when the postman came. Besides, mostly you were at college. It was only holidays I had to be careful, but with my shifts I found it pretty easy to get there before you did. So I—I took them to work and shredded them in the office.'

She turned to look at Bethany and her expression changed. 'Don't look at me like that! I acted in your best interests, as did Ted.'

'So Joseph was writing to me from the first?' Bethany could barely get the words out, she was so choked. 'All this time I thought he didn't care. That he wasn't sorry. And you kept these from me. Kept him away from me. How could you do that?'

'You said he was dead to you,' Helena reminded her. 'And when I told Ted about them, he said I did the right thing.'

'You told Ted? When?'

'Just before your wedding,' she admitted. 'I wasn't sure what to do but he said there was no point in upsetting you. That you had him now. Us. We'd look after you. Then, not long after your wedding, the letters stopped coming to my flat and started going to your house. Ted took care of them, and when Joseph turned up at the door—'

'Wait, what?' Bethany felt sick. 'Joseph went to the house?'

'Yes, but only once or twice. Ted made it very clear you weren't interested and after that he didn't visit again, but the letters kept coming. Then, after five years, they just stopped. We guessed he'd finally given up.'

Bethany gazed down at the letters in her hand and then at all the dozens of others nestled in the bag. All that time Joseph had tried to contact her. He'd tried to talk to her. He'd even visited her at the flat in York and the house in Somerset! And she'd thought he wasn't bothered that she left. That he hadn't cared. But he must have cared, mustn't he?'

Feverishly she tore open one of the envelopes, a gasp escaping her lips as she saw his beautifully written letter.

Dear Beth,

That man you've married says you want nothing to do with me and it breaks my heart. How long will you keep punishing me? How many times can I say I'm sorry? I've tried and tried to explain it all to you and I know I hurt you, believe me. I hate myself for it. But I can't lose you, Beth. You're my sister and I love you. I'll never stop loving you.

Your husband says you'll only put this letter in the fire like you have all the others, but I'll keep trying until you agree to see me. Please let me explain in person. Maybe if we can meet face to face you'll understand.

Your loving brother,

Joseph xx

She turned anguished eyes on Helena. 'Ted told him I put his letters on the fire!'

'Bethany,' Helena said gently, 'Ted was just trying to do the right thing by you, that's all.'

'By keeping my own brother from me? By letting me believe, all these years, that he didn't care about me?'

'Joseph had hurt you and Ted couldn't bear that. Neither could I. We wanted to protect you from being hurt again.'

Bethany could hardly contain the torrent of emotion that was building up inside her.

'And that's why you had an affair, is it? To protect me from being hurt again?'

'Bethany!' Helena sounded shocked that she could bring such a thing into the conversation. 'I thought we'd been through all that. I thought you understood.'

'I thought I understood, too,' Bethany managed through her tears, 'but maybe I'm only now beginning to understand.'

Helena got to her feet. 'I'll pretend I didn't hear that,' she said calmly. 'I know this has come as a shock to you, so I'll leave you to it. When you've had the chance to take everything in I'm sure you'll realise we were acting in your best interests. I'll be downstairs when you're ready to talk rationally.'

She walked with dignity out of the room, leaving Bethany staring down in despair at the bag on her lap. Swallowing, she gathered up all the letters and carried them into her own room, where she tipped the bag up on her bed and spread out every single envelope.

She sorted them into chronological order which took ages. It took even longer for her to read them all. She ignored Helena calling up to her to ask if she wanted any lunch. She didn't respond when her so-called friend rang her on her phone, then texted her to see if she wanted a cup of tea bringing up.

She read through all the letters and cards feverishly, tears streaming down her cheeks as she absorbed Joseph's heartfelt apologies and his repeated pleas for forgiveness.

I don't know why I did it. I can't explain. It wasn't an affair. It was just that once, I swear to you. He was so kind to me, so gentle, and he was the first man who'd ever behaved that way towards me. I shouldn't have done it, but I couldn't help myself. Maybe I just wanted to feel the way you did. I wanted to feel love. But it wasn't love, Beth. I realised that straight away and I was so ashamed.

I wanted to tell you so many times how sorry I was. I'd have done anything to take it back. But it was too late. And the shame and the guilt just got worse and worse, until I couldn't even look at you any more. I couldn't make myself apologise because I knew you wouldn't forgive me, and I couldn't bear to see the hatred in your face.

Glenn meant nothing. You mean everything. You always did. I just want you to come home, or if you can't stand to come back, at least meet me somewhere. Let's talk. Let me try to make it up to you somehow. You're my little sister and I've always looked out for you. I hate that I'm the one who's hurt you by taking away the man you loved.

Please, Beth, just write back to me, or pick up the phone. We can sort this out, can't we? Please tell me it's not too late.

But it *was* too late. Far too late. Because of Ted and Helena she'd never get the chance to sort things out with her brother.

Dear Beth,

I'm sorry to have to tell you this in a letter but I think you have the right to know. Our father passed away in the early hours of this morning. As I told you, he'd had several minor strokes over the last couple of years. Well, this time it seems he had a massive stroke and died in his sleep.

I'm not sure how I feel about it all. I suppose I should be relieved and maybe, soon, I will be. Right now, I just feel numb. There's so much to think about. So much to organise.

I'm getting a visit from the vicar soon. No doubt he'll be expecting that Father will be buried in the family plot next to Mother. Well, he'll soon find out that's not going to happen. I can't do it, Beth. She's not getting stuck with him again. I'm not sure what to do with him, to be honest. If you have any thoughts, you could always call me.

I don't know if this will change anything between us. Now he's gone maybe you'd think about coming back here—just to talk? We could start again. What do you think?

There's no pressure but if you want to pick up the phone, or if you feel you'd like to be at the funeral, please know you are always welcome. It's still the same number we always had. I'm not one for mobile phones.

Take care of yourself and know that I'm forever

Your loving brother,
Joseph xx

So Joseph *had* written to tell her of her father's passing. He hadn't just left her to find out from an obituary in the newspaper. Something else she'd resented him for that he hadn't even done. With shaking hands Bethany opened the last letter.

Bethany, it's clear to me now that you're never going to forgive me. It breaks my heart, but I've finally realised I've got to accept it. I suppose I thought that, once our father had passed, it would somehow change things between us. Obviously that's not the case. You might want to know I had him cremated in the end, or perhaps you don't care one way or the other.

It's okay, Beth. I know the chances are we'll never meet again. I just want you to know that I love you so much and I always will.

But I get the message now. I'll stop writing and leave you in peace. I hope you have the happiest of lives, my darling sister, with all the love and kindness you deserve.

Your loving brother,
Joseph xx

Bethany's hand flew to her mouth. He'd given up because he truly believed she wasn't bothered about him. That she hadn't even taken the trouble to reply to him when their father died. He must have thought her so cruel, so unforgiving, yet he'd still signed himself as her loving brother.

As tears rolled down her cheeks, she spotted, out of the corner of her eye, an envelope sticking out of the canvas bag. She put the letter down and reached for it, realising it wasn't another letter but a card. A Christmas card perhaps? Or a birthday card.

She gasped as she checked the postmark. This card had only been sent last November! After such a long gap why had Joseph suddenly decided to write to her again?

As an awful thought struck her, she tore open the envelope and pulled out the card. It had a picture of two donkeys on the front, which was typical Joseph. Inside there was no printed verse, only Joseph's handwriting—not as neat as it usually was as he poured out his final message to her.

My darling Beth,

Oh, this is a hard letter to write. Even harder than all those letters I used to send you all them years ago. Even so, I have to do this. I have to contact you one last time.

I haven't been very well, Beth. Well, the plain fact is I'm very poorly. I've had all the tests and there's nothing more they can do. I'm not sure how long I've got but judging by the expressions on people's faces I'd say not that long. So I've had to put pen to paper once more before I get too frail to walk to the post box on my own and while I can still think clearly.

I've missed you, Beth. I saw a wedding announcement for that fella you married and Helena, and you could have knocked me over with a feather. I never expected that. I really hope it's not as bad as it sounds and them two didn't do the dirty on you. I'd hoped that you'd found your happy ever after, but it seems he wasn't the man for you after all.

Maybe you've already found someone else. I hope so. You deserve to be loved. You were always such a sweetheart. The light of my life.

I'll never forgive myself for how I drove you away but if it's any consolation I've paid the price. All these years without you have been hard to bear at times. Not your fault and there's no blame attached to you. Everything I got I asked for and I know it. I'm not writing this to make you feel guilty. I just needed you to know a couple of things.

Firstly, about Pepper. When he passed away I had him cremated. I didn't want to get rid of his ashes because I thought you might want them some day. Then I read about some young lass who'd had her pony's ashes put into a rocking horse, and I thought, bingo!

I had a rocking horse made especially for the job and I got them to make it so it looks just like that one you wanted when you were a little girl. Do you remember that, Beth? That day in

Kirkby Skimmer at the toy shop? Aw, you loved that horse and I wish I'd been able to get it for you. You broke my heart that day. Maybe this is the only way I can even try to make it up to you. I've had the ashes placed inside the horse's belly and it's in your old room waiting for you. I hope that's okay with you.

The other thing I have to tell you is a bit trickier. I've been running a horse sanctuary at Whispering Willows. Not a big one by any means. Just taking in a few waifs and strays as and when I could. But now, the way things are, they're going to pass into your care when I'm gone.

I'm not so daft that I don't know you'll likely sell Whispering Willows the minute I'm gone, and I don't blame you for that. But will you please promise me that you'll find good homes for my animals? You won't have to do it alone. Clive and Summer will help you I'm sure.

Clive's a vet but he's also my best friend and the finest, most decent man you could ever hope to meet. And Summer's the little lass who works for me. She's been a godsend to me, she really has. She's so kind and hardworking and compassionate. She reminds me of you when you were her age. Except, I never saw you at her age, did I? I haven't seen you since you were nineteen years old and by heck, that gave me a shock when I realised it.

I don't know who you are these days, but I do know that you'll still be the loving person I knew back then, and that's why I trust you to do the right thing by my residents, and by Viva. She's my little dog and if you can give her a home, I'd be so grateful, but Clive has promised me he'll take her if your circumstances don't allow it.

Well, that's all I have to say now, Beth. I guess this is it. I won't expect a reply and I can only hope that you're still at this address, despite the divorce, and that you will read this letter and not just throw it on the fire unopened.

I would have loved for us to make it up before it's too late, but I know now that won't happen and I've made my peace with it.

Do you remember when you were a little girl, and I used to tell you that it would all be right? Well, this time it's going to be a bit difficult.

Maybe one day you and I will be reunited, and all this pain and sadness will be forgotten. I hope so, Beth. Until then be happy and know that I love you now and always have.

Your brother
Joseph xx

Bethany covered her face with her hands and sobbed. Oh, Joseph! She should have been with him. If she'd just read this letter back in November, she could have gone to him and been with him for his final months. They could have put all that stuff with Glenn firmly behind them because she knew now it hadn't mattered. None of it had mattered. Glenn had been a small blot on her past while Joseph had been her everything. She'd loved him so much.

How, she wondered, had she forgotten about the rocking horse? She remembered it now so clearly. That day in Kirkby Skimmer...

She'd been about six years old and it had been about a week before Christmas.

Mother had been holed up in her room for days and Father had been 'entertaining' a lady friend in the living room which had made Joseph angrier than Bethany had ever seen him. That seemed to amuse Father no end, and eventually Joseph had told Bethany to put her coat and shoes on because he was taking her out for the afternoon.

They'd driven all the way up to Kirkby Skimmer in Upper Skimmerdale. Joseph hadn't said much on the way there and at first his face had been dark and angry as he stared fixedly at the road ahead. Gradually though, he'd started to relax and by the time they reached the large market town, he was all smiles again.

'Let's have something to eat,' he'd suggested, aware that neither of them had stopped to eat any dinner before they left Whispering Willows.

He'd taken her into a cute little café which she'd been thrilled about. They'd had a tasty meal followed by syrup pudding and custard because Joseph knew that was her favourite.

'Right,' he said after paying the bill. 'Let's go and find a really good Christmas present for Mother.'

It hadn't been as easy as she'd expected. They'd realised fairly quickly that their mother seemed to have no interest in anything and had expressed no desire for any gifts. They'd found an antique shop and Joseph had bought her a silver locket from the two of them. Bethany was sure she'd love it as it was so pretty.

Holding Joseph's hand, she'd skipped along the street, gazing around in delight at all the shop windows which were decorated for the festive season.

'Well, look at this, Beth,' Joseph had said, stopping outside the toy shop. He'd scooped her into his arms so she could see the window display more clearly, and they'd both gazed through the glass at the assortment of wonderful items: the latest doll that everyone in Bethany's class seemed to want; a little pink type-writer; packs of plasticine; boxes of Lego; a nurse's outfit complete with hat and cape; and a toy sweet shop with a set of scales and a till.

'Do you think Father Christmas will bring me something nice?' she'd asked him wistfully. Somewhere at the back of her mind she'd known, even then, that with her mother not being so well and her father having no interest in her whatsoever, there was a very good chance that Christmas wouldn't be so good this year.

Joseph had looked at her, sadness in his eyes. 'I'm sure he will,' he'd promised. 'Hey, why don't we go inside and look around? I might even treat you to some of those stickers you like.'

She'd been thrilled at the prospect and had happily followed him into the shop, holding his hand tightly as she stared at the amazing displays of dolls, board games, jigsaws, and brightly coloured children's books on the shelves.

Over in one corner she'd spotted some doll's prams and some bikes with stabilisers and a large and very expensive looking doll's house.

'Some lovely dolls in here, Beth,' Joseph had murmured. 'If Father Christmas were to bring you one of them, which one do you hope it would be?'

But Bethany had barely registered what he was asking her. Her eyes had fallen on a beautiful rocking horse at the far end of the shop. Without thinking, she managed to free her hand from Joseph's grasp and ran over to inspect it more closely.

It was so pretty. A gorgeous dapple grey with a black mane and tail, wearing a leather saddle and bridle. It had large, brown eyes which were so irresistible that Bethany threw her arms around its neck and hugged it.

'Wow, this is a beauty,' Joseph said, reaching her side.

'Do you think Father Christmas would get him for me?' she'd asked hopefully.

He'd turned over a label attached to the browband of the rocking horse's bridle and frowned before looking down at her.

'Er, maybe not for Christmas, Beth.' He'd paused, his gaze far away as he seemed to be thinking about something, or working something out. 'But maybe in June for your birthday? What do you say?'

'Father Christmas doesn't work in June,' she'd reminded him, making him smile.

'I know, but big brothers do. I could ask the shopkeeper to order another one especially for you. Would you like that?'

'Oh, Joseph!'

She'd stared up at him in delight then turned to hug the rocking horse again. But as she breathed in the scent of the artificial hair, wrinkling her nose as it tickled her, a sudden feeling of sadness had overwhelmed her and she'd stepped away.

'It's all right,' she said. 'I don't want him.'

Joseph had stared down at her, clearly perplexed. 'You don't want him? But why not?'

Bethany shrugged. 'Just don't.'

'Okay, Beth, what's the matter? You loved him to bits a minute ago so why...?'

'I don't want Father to hurt him,' she mumbled.

Joseph had inhaled sharply before crouching down in front of her. 'You don't want...'

'If I do something wrong, he'll hurt him,' she'd burst out. 'Like he hurt Magnus last week when he was mad with you. And I know I'll do something to make him mad with me because, even though I try really hard to be good, I keep getting things wrong and he gets so cross. Magnus is so big compared to this horse and Father would only break him.' She'd shaken her head sadly. 'I don't want him to come home to Whispering Willows, Joseph. He's better off here.'

Joseph had straightened and closed his eyes for a moment.

Swallowing hard he'd said, 'Right, well... Shall we go and see what else is going on in town today? The market's on after all.'

Taking her hand, he'd led her outside and straight to the market where he'd bought her a little plastic bracelet and a bag of sweets before they headed back towards the car park. Nearing the church, they'd seen a crowd gathered round the steps where the Salvation Army band were playing Christmas carols.

Joseph and Bethany had stood, hand in hand, listening to Silent Night. Bethany had no idea why, but the music had a strange effect on her. She thought about her mother locked away in her bedroom. She thought about Joseph getting cross about their father's friend being at the house, and how Father had laughed at him. She thought about Magnus and the beautiful rocking horse in the shop. Suddenly it all seemed too much.

Joseph bent down and wiped away the tears she hadn't even noticed. 'What's wrong, Beth?'

'I don't know,' she admitted. 'I'm just sad.'

He'd immediately picked her up and held her tightly to him. 'It won't always be like this,' he'd told her fiercely. 'I swear to you, things will get better. And you'll always have me to look out for you. Remember that. It's going to be right, Beth. It's all going to be right. Promise.'

Bethany could hardly see for the tears blurring her eyes. She'd forgotten all about that day, but Joseph hadn't. She'd never got the rocking horse, but she had unwrapped one of the lovely dolls she'd admired in the toy shop window—no doubt a gift from her brother. And all those years later he'd had a rocking horse just like that one made especially for her so the ashes of her real pony would be kept safe for her.

Oh, Joseph! I'm so, so sorry. You deserved so much more than you got. You were always looking out for me and because of one mistake I let you go. And now it's all too late.

If only Ted and Helena had told her about the letters it would never have got this far. All she'd wanted was to know Joseph was sorry and that he still loved her. She'd needed to believe that her brother truly cared about her, but all those years she'd heard nothing and believed he didn't love her. Now Joseph was gone and there was nothing she could do to put things right. She'd never be able to tell him how much she loved him or how sorry she was for the way she'd behaved. It was all far too late.

Suddenly her grief turned to anger. Ted! How dare he keep these letters from her? What right had he had to turn Joseph away and not even tell her? To let her think her brother had abandoned her just like her mother had.

And Helena! Helena had been her best friend since schooldays. How could she have acted so cruelly? She and Ted had colluded to keep her away from her own brother.

For her *protection*. Because it was *best for her*.

What gave them the right to decide what was best for her?

And just like that Bethany began to see things as they truly were. Helena had encouraged Bethany to leave Whispering Willows and come to York to stay with her, rather than try to work things out with Joseph. When she'd met Ted he'd taken charge in their relationship from the first; even their wedding had been arranged by him with no input from her. He'd insisted they move into the home he already owned, even though she'd suggested they look for somewhere that would belong to both of them. He'd refused to let her decorate it to her taste, instead instructing professionals to make the few alterations he wanted.

She shook her head, her face in her hands. She'd wanted children. All right, so it wasn't Ted's fault he couldn't have them, but they could have adopted. He'd made it obvious that wasn't on the agenda, despite knowing how desperate she was for a child of her own to love. She wasn't even allowed to have a bloody dog!

And his affair with Helena... All this time she'd told herself they'd been kind to her about it. Unselfish even. Done all they could to make it up to her because they were sorry. How sorry had they actually been?

Not sorry enough to stop themselves from starting the affair in the first place. Not sorry enough to end it when it became serious. Not sorry enough not to break it to her that they were in love.

Ted had wanted a divorce. He'd wanted his house. She'd moved out to make things easy for them and he'd paid her off with a hefty divorce settlement and she told herself it was because he was kind and wanted to stay friends with her.

But money meant nothing to Ted. It never had. He'd had far too much of it to mind giving her a bumper payout to shut her up. So long as it didn't disrupt his life he would have paid her twice that amount if she'd asked.

She'd been so pathetically grateful that they'd stayed in her life because she'd needed them. She'd needed to belong somewhere to someone.

And all the while she'd kept quiet and plastered on a smile, watching from the sidelines as Ted played father to Helena's children, loving grandad to her grandsons.

Helena hadn't invited her to move in with her after Ted died out of the kindness of her heart. She'd asked her to move in because she was lonely and sad. But when her children came to stay, she'd been quick to ask Bethany if she'd mind going away for a while to give her little family time to be together as a unit.

A unit, she thought with startling clarity, that didn't include her. *When it suited.*

And all that time, all those years, these letters had been hidden away from her. Why had Ted kept them? Why hadn't he burned them? Was it some sort of power trip? Some perverse pleasure knowing he had the means to change her life forever but was choosing not to?

And Helena... Even knowing Joseph's fate, she still hadn't admitted that he'd written to her recently. Instead she'd shoved that final card in the bag with all the others, robbing Bethany and Joseph of their last chance to be reunited. How could she call herself a friend?

They'd controlled her for years; she could see that now. Both of them. She'd been a puppet and they'd pulled her strings, with her too blinded by her need for them to realise it.

She thought about Clive.

I never wanted you to stay here just for me, Bethany. I never expected it, and I wouldn't have asked it of you.

And he hadn't, even though she was sure he'd wanted to. The difference was, Clive treated her like an adult. He respected her and wanted her to do what was right for her whatever the cost to himself.

He hadn't told her everything about Jennifer. She was sure of that. But even so, sitting here surrounded by all the evidence of Ted's and Helena's betrayal, she knew for certain that he wasn't like them.

Whatever Clive hadn't been able to tell her it wasn't what she'd assumed. He just wasn't that man and deep down she knew it. But she'd jumped to conclusions because that's what she'd come to expect, and her self-esteem had been so low, so damaged that she'd thought it was inevitable. And she'd done what she'd always done, ever since she was a teenager.

She'd run back to Helena. Her friend.

Her *friend*!

Bethany stared at the letters on the bed and gave a strangled sob.

'Oh, Joseph! I'm sorry. I'm so, so sorry.'

Frantically she shoved them back in the bag then pulled her suitcase from under the bed. No more of this. She was taking back control of her own life and to hell with Helena.

She was going back to Tuppenny Bridge.
She was going home.

THIRTY-FIVE

It almost felt wrong that the sun was shining on Bethany as she made her way along the footpath at the side of the church and headed towards the Wilkinson family grave.

Somehow she'd have felt more comfortable if it had been pouring with rain, the way it had been when she'd first arrived here on the day of Joseph's funeral.

The skies were blue and unbroken by clouds, and the scent of flowers hung in the air. It was mid-June and the days held warmth and beauty and the promise of better times. She could only hope it would keep that promise.

Her steps slowed as she neared the plot, her heart thudding with anxiety and grief. She'd avoided this place the whole time she'd been here but there was no more avoiding it. She'd come back to Tuppenny Bridge to put things right and she'd already made a promising start.

Summer had clearly been stunned to see her pull up in the stableyard at Whispering Willows, and Bethany had expected a tirade of abuse from her. She couldn't have been more amazed when Summer dropped the wheelbarrow she'd been pushing and ran over to her.

'Bethany, you're back! Oh, I'm so glad to see you.'

'You are?' Bethany frowned, not at all sure she understood what she'd done to merit such a greeting.

'I wanted to see you, to tell you. About Clive. You've got it all wrong.'

She was babbling, clearly distressed, and despite her own nerves Bethany had taken her into the house and made them both a cup of tea so that Summer could calm down and explain.

'This is all my fault. I'm sorry I was such a cow to you. I was so upset about the sanctuary and Joseph and the horses I just couldn't see how painful this must all be for you. Clive sat me down and made me look at it from your point of view. I still don't like it,' she added honestly. 'And I'm still worried sick about the residents, but I get it, honestly I do. You have to do what's right for you, and I had no right to treat you the way I did.'

Bethany smiled. 'That's very noble of you, Summer, but—'

'But I have to tell you the truth about Clive,' Summer added hurriedly. 'It wasn't him! I mean, it wasn't his fault. It was all me. If you want to blame anyone blame me, even though I know he let you put it all on his shoulders even though he tried to stop me and wasn't pleased with me at all.'

'Summer,' Bethany said, confused, 'what exactly are you talking about?'

Summer took a deep breath. 'It wasn't Clive who was snooping on you that day. It was me. I sent him up to Harston Hill with Barney and while he was up there I came in here and started looking around to see what you were up to. It was after that builder had been. I heard him telling Clive you were having the stables demolished you see.'

'Right,' Bethany said slowly. 'So you put two and two together and decided to find out what else I'd been keeping from you.'

'Yes! Not Clive. He just wouldn't do that sort of thing. I

found the phone pad in the dresser cupboard with the message on it about the estate agent, and then I thought, maybe they'd left a voice message on the answer phone which would confirm you were selling this place, so I played it. Clive was furious with me when he walked in on me.' She blushed. 'I saw a folder with leaflets in it and I wanted to have a look, but he pulled me away and wouldn't let me, even though he must have been dying to know what was in there.'

'I see,' Bethany said.

'You know Clive,' Summer pleaded. 'You *should* do by now. I'm so miserable that, because of me, you two broke up and you left him. Please don't punish him for what I did.'

Bethany gave her a reassuring smile. 'Summer, I believe you. Don't worry about it. I should have known. As you say, he's just not like that.'

'So you'll call him, or maybe go to Stepping Stones?' Summer asked hopefully. She glanced at her watch. 'He'll be there now. Surgery—'

Bethany shook her head. 'Right now I need to talk to you.'

'Me? About what?'

Bethany smiled. 'The future, Summer. The future of Whispering Willows, and what I've got planned for us all.'

Now, approaching the grave, she knew that one piece of the jigsaw had fallen into place. She just wasn't sure if she'd be able to complete the picture.

Taking a deep breath to steady her nerves she gazed down on the headstone.

Joseph's name had been added, which came as no surprise to her. Clive had explained to her, very carefully and with as much tact and gentleness as he could muster, that Joseph had transferred ownership of the grave to him when it became clear Joseph wasn't going to get well. Clive had, therefore, taken it upon himself to contact a stonemason to add to the inscription as Joseph had requested.

She read the words on the headstone through blurry eyes.

Coral Fiona Wilkinson, nee Parkinson.
Beloved daughter and darling mother.
"My peace I give unto you".
John 14:27

Joseph Alistair Wilkinson
Beloved son and brother.
"Come unto me all ye who labour and are heavy laden, and I will
give you rest".
Matthew 11:28

There was no mention of her father. Joseph had kept his promise not to bury him with their mother. She should have known he would. She should have trusted him. She'd let him down in so many ways.

'Joseph,' she said, taking a piece of paper out of her pocket and unfolding it, 'I didn't know. All those letters you sent—no one told me about them. I've only just found out. I'm so sorry.'

Her voice cracked with emotion and she cleared her throat. 'I've written you a reply at last,' she told him. 'I know it's far too late but I wanted you to finally get an answer to your letters.'

She took a steadying breath and began to read:

'My darling Joseph. How do I even begin? All these years I thought you didn't care about me and I kept wondering what I'd done to make you abandon me the way our mother abandoned us.

'I was wrong. You hadn't abandoned me and neither had she. I understand that now. She was ill and couldn't stay. I hope she's found peace at last, and I hope you're together again.

'If I'd known, Joseph, if I'd got the letters, I swear to you I would have come back to see you. I think, all those years, I was just waiting. I was just waiting for you to tell me you still loved me and that you were sorry for what happened with Glenn. I would have been with you at the end. I would have held your hand. I would have told you none of that mattered anymore and that it hadn't mattered for years. Decades.

'The truth is, I never loved Glenn. Looking back on it all it's so clear now. I never loved Ted, either. You were the love of my life, Joseph. You saved me. You were there for me all those years when our parents failed us. You were my light in all that darkness as I was in yours.

'We might say fate pulled us apart, but that would be too kind. The truth is, bad people pulled us apart. People who believed they knew what was best for me. People who pretended to care about me when really they only cared about themselves, and wanted to control me. And we allowed it to happen because, deep down, we didn't believe in each other. Our upbringing had ensured that we felt unlovable so it was far easier for us to think the worst of ourselves. You thought I couldn't forgive you. I thought you didn't care about me. We were both wrong, and I see that now. I can see everything clearly now. I see that Ted and Helena took advantage of my low self-esteem and they manipulated me and lied to me, and to you. I see that you really did love me, and Joseph, I always loved you.

'Now I've found Clive and you were so right about him. You said he was the kindest, most decent man, and he is. I've messed things up with him, too, but I've learned my lesson this time. I won't let things drift along until it's too late the way I did with you. This time I'm going to fight for what I want, for the person I love.

'I know you'd be happy for us, Joseph, because you loved both of us. Well, I want you to know that we both love you, too, and we'll never forget you.

'I know you're sorry for what you did, but I need you to know that I'm so sorry, too. I should never have left you alone with Father like that. I should have sorted things out with you instead of running away. I've run away all my adult life, but now it's time to stop running. It's time to take control of my own life, and because of you, because of the strength your letters have given me, now I know I can. Thank you, Joseph. Your loving sister, Beth.'

She folded the letter back up and put it in her pocket, staring down at the headstone and praying that, somehow, her brother had heard her. She so needed to believe that.

'Bethany, are you all right?'

She looked up, embarrassed to find Zach Barrington standing there watching her.

He gave her a warm smile. 'I'm sorry to disturb you. You look so sad that I thought you might want to talk, but if you want me to go I will.'

Bethany wiped her tear-streaked cheeks. 'Just finally saying my goodbyes,' she admitted. 'I've been avoiding coming here because of him. My father, I mean. I was so worried he'd be buried here but I found out recently that Joseph had him cremated.'

'I'm sorry, I assumed you knew. I wasn't here at the time,' Zach explained, 'but Joseph told me all about it. You know, when we were discussing...' His voice trailed off and Bethany waited.

'Well, I understand this was meant to be a family plot for all four members of your family, but Joseph admitted that, when your father passed, he couldn't bring himself to put Terence in there with Coral.' He cleared his throat. 'I understand things weren't so good between them in life and he said he had no intention of saddling her with him in death.'

Bethany swung round to gaze over at the Garden of Ashes. 'So he's in there?' she asked.

'Er, no. I'm sorry. As far as I'm aware Joseph scattered your father's ashes out at sea. I'm afraid there's no exact record of where he did that but maybe Clive—'

Bethany burst out laughing.

Zach stared at her in obvious bemusement. 'Did I say something funny?'

She beamed at him in delight. 'Father wouldn't even go on a rowing boat. He got seasick.'

Zach lifted his eyebrows. 'I, er, see. I think.'

'So do I,' she told him, unable to wipe the smile from her face. 'I thought he was here, you see. All this time. I thought Joseph had put him next to our mother and had then chosen to spend eternity in the same grave as him. But instead, he gave the old goat the send-off he truly deserved. Scattering his ashes out at sea!' She giggled again. 'Oh, Joseph, that's priceless. You absolute star.'

'Well...' Zach sounded a bit doubtful about that, but nothing could dim Bethany's relief. She crouched down and blew a kiss to the headstone.

'I love both of you so much.' She got to her feet and said softly, 'Rest in peace, my two angels.'

'Are you okay, Bethany?' Zach asked gently.

'You know what?' Bethany said, feeling a new hope surge through her. 'For the first time in decades, I actually think I am.'

THIRTY-SIX

Clive folded a pair of jeans and stuffed them as neatly as he could into the holdall.

'Okay, will that be enough?' he wondered aloud, frowning. It was hard to say because he had no idea how long he'd be in Somerset. The truth was, Bethany might take one look at him and send him straight back to Yorkshire. On the other hand, if she'd listen to him and believe him, if she'd forgive him, he might be able to stay a couple of days. She might even come back with him.

His stomach churned at the thought. What if she wouldn't listen, though? Or what if she heard everything he had to say and believed him but then said what he'd done was unforgivable and she could never love a man like him.

Could he blame her? Not really. She'd already been through so much, what with Joseph letting her down with Glenn, and then Ted and Helena.

His jaw tightened whenever he thought about Bethany's ex-husband and her so-called best friend. He knew she thought the world of them and had forgiven them everything, but from what he'd heard he couldn't imagine why. She seemed completely oblivious to the way they'd treated her. He supposed she loved them, and love could make you blind to another's faults. Sometimes.

'Toothbrush and toothpaste,' he said and headed into the bathroom to collect them. Once he'd packed a bag of toiletries he thought that should do it. He zipped up the holdall and carried it through to the living room.

'Car keys, wallet...'

There was a knock on the door and Ben called, 'Clive, are you there?'

Clive rolled his eyes. Where else would he be? He'd promised Ben he'd pop his head round the surgery door to let him know when he was heading off. He hoped there wasn't a sudden emergency downstairs because it was going to be evening before he reached Chimneys as it was, and if this Helena woman wouldn't let him in he'd have to search for a bed for the night. Either that or sleep in the car.

'Aye, right here. Come in.'

He continued hunting for his keys and wallet, expecting Ben to walk in. Vaguely he heard voices outside the door and paused, puzzled. What was going on out there? Then there was the distinct sound of Ben's footsteps on the stairs. He was going back to the surgery. What was that all about?

Sighing he realised he'd have to check Ben was all right and hurried to the door. As he pulled it open to shout down, his mouth dropped open. Bethany was standing there, her hand raised as if she was about to knock on the door. She hurriedly dropped it and stared up at him.

'Hello, Clive.'

'Beth! What are you doing here?'

'Don't sound too pleased to see me,' she joked, clearly nervous.

He gulped. 'Sorry. Come in, please.'

Feeling dazed he led her into the living room. She stared pointedly at the holdall.

'Are you going somewhere?'

Bloody hell! How stupid did he feel now? Oh well, she already thought the worst of him. Might as well be a source of amusement to her, too.

'Aye,' he said heavily. 'I was. I was going down to Somerset to see you.'

Her eyes widened. 'You were?'

'I wanted you to listen,' he told her, tilting his chin determinedly. 'You might not like what you hear but you deserve to hear it anyway. What you do next will be your choice.'

He couldn't have been more amazed when she rushed towards him and threw her arms around his waist.

'Oh, Clive! That's what I love about you. You have no idea how much.'

What I love about you? Present tense? Clive hadn't a clue what this was all about, but he closed his eyes and offered a silent prayer of gratitude as he held her tightly.

'What are you doing here?' he asked her eventually, unable to believe his luck.

'Don't you know?' She raised her face, gazing up at him with tear-filled eyes. 'I missed you. I was so stupid, Clive, and I'm so very sorry.'

'Aw, Beth...' He didn't know what to say. He wanted to tell her he'd missed her, too, and how much he loved her, but he had to be honest with her first. She had to know the truth about him and what he'd done before she said anything else she'd probably regret later. 'Sit down. We've a lot to talk about.'

She pulled him onto the sofa beside her and took hold of his hand as if she'd never let it go.

'Can I go first?' she asked. 'There's so much swilling around in my head and I need to tell you before I go pop.'

This wasn't what he'd expected at all. He'd had a whole

speech rehearsed and this wasn't going the way he'd imagined, but as she gave him a beseeching look with those beautiful dark blue eyes he could only nod.

Immediately Bethany began to tell him what she'd discovered at Chimneys. How Helena and Ted had colluded to keep Joseph away from her, and how they'd hidden his letters all these years. Clive's jaw tightened with anger as he thought of how his friend had been treated. He imagined Joseph's growing despair as each letter went unanswered and his heart broke for him, and for Bethany, who'd believed all that time that her brother didn't love her.

She told him what she'd finally realised about her relationship with Ted and Helena, and Clive could only be thankful that, at last, she'd opened her eyes to what had really been going on.

Finally she revealed she'd visited the family grave at All Hallows and told him about her chat with Zach.

'I think I shocked him when I burst out laughing,' she confessed, 'but really, it was such a relief! All this time I've assumed Joseph had been buried with both my parents, but knowing he'd refused to put Father with Mother, and best of all, that he'd scattered his ashes at sea, well it made my day!'

She gave a peal of laughter, and despite his anxieties, Clive couldn't help but laugh with her.

'He did. Took him to Whitby and got a boat out to sea. We both went. Made a day of it actually. We got back on land after the deed had been done and I saw a weight had lifted from Joseph, so I said, why don't we stay here for a few hours and have some fun? So we did. Went in the amusement arcade, ate fish and chips and an ice cream, had a wander around the abbey. It was a great day.'

'Oh, I wish I could have been there,' she said sadly.

Clive squeezed her hand. 'So do I,' he said. 'And I'm sure Joseph would have loved that.'

'I'm so glad you were with him, though. Joseph would have had no one if not for you. Everybody's told me that. You must have been such a comfort to him when I couldn't be.'

Tears rolled down her cheeks at the thought and Clive pulled her to him. 'It's okay. It wasn't your fault. You both suffered, each believing the other didn't care, and all the time... Ach it makes me so angry, Beth! What right did those two have to keep him from you?'

'I don't know. And I don't understand why I didn't see what they were doing from the start. I suppose,' she admitted sadly, 'I just let my need for them blind me. They were all I had. They'd made sure of that.'

'But why? They had each other, why keep you tied to them like that?'

'I honestly don't have a clue. I like to think none of this was deliberate, or even specifically aimed at me. I think maybe that's just the way they are. Perhaps that's why they got on so well. I'll never really know but I do know I don't want to give them any more headspace. They're my past now, whereas my future is in Whispering Willows.'

'Whispering Willows?' Hope flared within him. 'You're not selling?'

'I'm not.'

'When did you decide this?' he asked.

She gave him a smug look. 'Well, for your information I'd already decided it before we had that argument. That's what I was trying to tell you.'

'But the estate agent's appointment! It said you were viewing another property.'

'And I was. The thing is, I'd realised that I didn't want to leave Tuppenny Bridge because I couldn't bear to leave you. I was also worried about the horses. So I decided that I'd keep the house going and I'd look for another house for me to live in. You see, my plan was to keep the sanctuary going and rent the house out. I had it all worked out that day and I couldn't wait to tell you, but Summer had played detective and ruined the whole thing.'

'Ah,' he said sheepishly.

'Yes, it's okay. Summer told me it was she who listened to the phone message and hunted through my belongings for information, not you.'

'You've seen Summer?' he asked, surprised.

'My first stop when I arrived back in Tuppenny Bridge was Whispering Willows. I had a lot to tell her. She and I had quite the chat and let's just say I think we're pretty much best friends now.' She laughed. 'In fact, I think she might love me more than she loves Ben.'

Clive grinned. 'You're really intriguing me now. What are you up to?'

'What I was always up to, except for one big change. You see, it's true that I'd arranged with the builder to demolish the stables. Realistically, the section that was bulging was beyond saving anyway, and he'd advised it would be cheaper to knock it all down and start again. And then I got to thinking about the stables as a whole and how old and ugly they are, and how badly designed the whole area is. And I thought it would be the perfect time to design it all from scratch and build it to contemporary standards. The horses deserve nothing less, right? And that way if we get any unexpected arrivals there'll be room for them.

'So that was the first idea. And I realised that meant I could apply for charitable status for Whispering Willows, so I'd started looking into that. And I thought I'd take Summer on as my permanent full-time manager, and I'd hire some more people to help her with the animals while I'd work in the admin side, so I'd have something to do as well.'

'Wow,' Clive murmured. 'You'd really figured it all out.'

'I called the sanctuary about the donkeys and told them

they were staying here after all. Honestly, Summer nearly burst with excitement when I told her that,' she said, laughing.

'But wait, what about the message from Folly Farm?' he asked, suddenly remembering. 'If you'd decided to keep the horses why had you rung this Rachel?'

'Well, before I rang her I rang Walter Harding. I desperately wanted to know what had become of Shirley Bassey. He told me she'd been discharged and had been sent to Folly Farm on a temporary basis until they could find another home for her. So I rang Xander and Rachel who run it and left a message asking them to contact me about that. Unfortunately I'd rung them from the house phone, so naturally Rachel returned the call on the same phone, which was why she'd left a message since I was out. I'd completely forgotten that and had been waiting for a call on my mobile all day. Anyway, the upshot is, I spoke to her the other day, and she confirmed Shirley Bassey is there and they're trying to find a new, permanent home for her, and I said she must come to Whispering Willows. So she is. They're bringing her over next week.'

'Oh, Beth,' he said, awed at what she'd been getting up to all this time. 'That's amazing!'

'I know.' She shrugged. 'I wanted it all to be a surprise for you, but it went a bit wrong.'

'That was my fault,' he said guiltily. 'I jumped to conclusions. I'm so sorry.'

'You're not the only one,' she told him, suddenly looking pensive. 'I jumped to conclusions, too, didn't I? About you and Jennifer.'

He frowned. 'What do you mean?'

Bethany stared up at him with guilt written all over her face. He recognised it all too well because he'd struggled with it himself for so long.

'I don't know what's going on with you and Jennifer,' she said at last, 'but I do know you. I know you wouldn't start a relationship with me if you were involved with her. I trust you, Clive, so if you want to tell me the truth about the two of you, well, I'll listen. If you'd rather not I'll deal with that, too.'

He could hardly believe it. 'You're serious? You're willing to put that much faith in me?'

She took his other hand and squeezed them both, her expression deadly serious. 'Yes, I am. These past few days have taught me a lot about human nature and about my own refusal to see what's right in front of my nose. All the signs were there with Helena and Ted, but I didn't acknowledge them. All the signs were there with Glenn, too, but I refused to see those. Yet I knew Joseph, and I know you. Two good, honest men who genuinely care about me, and I was willing to believe the worst of both of you.

'What's that saying? *If someone shows you who they are believe them.* Ted, Helena, you, Joseph, you'd all shown me clearly who you were. I think it says more about me and the feelings I had for myself than it does about either of you that I got things so badly wrong. I'm so sorry. I can never make it up to Joseph, but I can make it up to you. If you'll let me.'

He'd never felt more humbled, or more undeserving.

'I have to be honest with you,' he said reluctantly. 'We can't have our fresh start if I don't, and you deserve the truth. You might decide I'm not the man you thought I was after all, and if you choose to walk away I'll understand. I just hope it won't affect your plans for Whispering Willows.'

'It won't,' she said confidently. 'I'm going nowhere.'

He was glad about that and could only hope she meant it.

'Jennifer and I—we're not having an affair, Beth, I promise you that. But there was something between us once. You see, I met her when I first moved to Tuppenny Bridge. We were in Market Square. The market was on, and she was buying some fruit.'

In his mind he was right back there that day. The sun was

shining, and the crowds were jostling. He'd been passing the fruit stall when it happened. Jennifer's thin carrier bag had given up under the strain of all the fruit and vegetables she'd bought, and the food had spilled out onto the ground.

Clive had helped her pick it all up and put it back in two new carrier bags, and she'd smiled a thank you at him. He'd gazed into her bright blue eyes and had fallen head over heels right there and then. He was twenty-eight years old, living permanently away from his family for the first time, a stranger in a new town, and he'd been smitten.

All he knew about her was the name she gave him. Jennifer. He was too afraid to ask around, and besides, how many Jennifers might there be in Tuppenny Bridge? He'd returned to the market every Wednesday and Saturday for weeks hoping he might bump into her again, but he never had.

Then Joseph had introduced him to Julian Callaghan, his colleague at the Lusty Tup Brewery. The three of them had developed quite a friendship. He'd liked Julian immediately. He had an easy manner and a great sense of humour, and when Joseph didn't want to go out to the pub he'd gone with Julian. Eventually, Julian had invited him round to his home, Monk's Folly.

'Come and meet my wife and two boys,' he'd said cheerily. 'In fact, come for tea. We'd love to have you.'

So he'd gone, and the bottom had fallen out of his world when he'd been introduced to the wife Julian had so often mentioned but had never named.

Jennifer.

He wasn't even certain she remembered him, but he'd been unable to hide his shock as she shook his hand, smiling. He thought he'd masked his feelings for her, and convinced himself that they would fade gradually, but as the years passed every moment he spent with her only made him fall more deeply in love with her. Of course, he'd never said a word about that to her or to Julian. He would never embarrass her like that, and he'd certainly never betray his friend.

What he hadn't realised was how perceptive Julian was, or he might have been better prepared when his friend confronted him that day. The day he'd extracted a promise from him that he should never have made.

'I just thought he'd pull through,' he told Bethany quietly. 'I was so sure of it. And I thought we'd simply forget all about it and move on.'

'But then he died,' she said sympathetically. 'Did you tell Jennifer what he'd asked of you?'

'No. It turned out he'd already confessed to her, although I only found that out very recently. She wasn't happy about it. Can't blame her, can you? As she said to me quite forcefully, she wasn't a possession that he could pass on to me. She had a mind of her own and she'd make her own decisions, and she'd quite clearly decided that she didn't want me or any other man.'

'Well, good for her,' Bethany said. 'It was a stupid thing to make you promise, Clive, but I can understand why you felt obliged to make it.'

'That's not the worst of it though,' he said, shame washing over him at the memory. 'You see, things went from bad to worse with Julian's health. Ben was playing up at school, getting into all sorts of bother, and they had Jamie to see to. He was no more than a baby. Jennifer was exhausted and sinking into depression. I tried to be there for her—not from any ulterior motive but because I was genuinely worried about her, and I knew Julian was too. I tried talking to Ben to make him see reason. I didn't really succeed but I tried. I helped her clean the house. She was fine with the cooking as she said it helped relax her, but Monk's Folly is a big place, and it was getting on top of her. You know I love cleaning, so I was happy to help. We just got closer. She started talking to me, telling me how she felt. All the old feelings I'd had for her started to come back and this time...'

Bethany's eyes widened. 'They were reciprocated?'

He nodded, not wanting to look at her. 'It wasn't real,' he said heavily. 'We were both just tired and sad I think, and Jennifer was so low. We arranged for her to come round here, to this flat. We told ourselves we deserved it. *She* deserved it. She needed just one night away from Monk's Folly. Just one night where she wasn't thinking and worrying and suffocating in all that grief and misery. One night to forget everything and be herself again. That's what we told ourselves. One night only and then we'd never speak of it again.'

He ran a hand over his forehead, dreading how she was reacting to all this. 'You see, we thought it would make everything feel better. We were both so unhappy. We needed a release. It wasn't about sex or love in the end. It was just about escaping reality. We honestly thought it would help us to cope with everything, but the minute it was over we both knew we'd made a terrible mistake. All it did was make us feel worse, adding guilt to the misery.'

'So it was just that one night? It was never an affair?' Bethany asked hesitantly.

He shook his head. 'Oh no. No! It was one night only all right.' He raised his gaze to hers, bracing himself for the look of disgust on her face. 'But, Beth, it was *that* night. The night Leon was killed. Jennifer would have been at home normally, and she'd have been the one to collect Ben from the police station when they rang. But she'd told them she was staying with a schoolfriend in Harrogate and because of that, it was Leon who went to bring Ben home. And there was an accident and Leon never made it.'

Bethany's hands flew to her mouth. 'Oh my God! Poor Jennifer!'

He waited for the condemnation, but none came. 'All these

years... I can't imagine... All that guilt.' Tears spilled from her eyes. 'I know how it feels to be so weighed down with guilt, wishing you'd done things differently, knowing it's far too late and can never be fixed. Oh, Clive, you must have felt terrible. Both of you. I'm so sorry.'

'Don't waste your sympathy on me,' he said roughly. 'I don't deserve it. But Jennifer does. She was in pieces, Beth. She just couldn't forgive herself. It was the only time she'd left Julian's side and look what happened! She thought it was a punishment and after that she just got lower and lower. By the time Julian died she was a different person. She stopped going out, didn't meet up with anyone. She became a recluse in that wretched house. I wanted to help her, but I was the last person she'd have anything to do with. I understood why but what I didn't know was that she was also under the misapprehension that I'd only slept with her because I'd made some sort of bizarre pact with Julian. She was devastated and wouldn't let me help her at all.'

Bethany considered the matter for a few moments. 'But you found a way,' she said slowly. 'By helping Ben. So he only works for you now because you made a promise to Julian?'

He was amazed that she'd figured out where Ben fitted in already but he had to make one thing very clear.

'No! God, no! Ben's more than paid me back, trust me. He's worked so bloody hard and he's a brilliant vet. I love him to bits, I really do, and I'm so proud of him. Ben deserves this job. I'd be lost without him. To be honest, I'm thinking of making him a partner. He's got a great future ahead of him, and he's such an asset to Stepping Stones.

'But back then I had no way of knowing that. He could have been a disaster. Even so, it was the only thing I could do to help the family, and I needed to help them so badly. Not just because I'd promised Julian but because I needed to do something, however small, to try to make amends for the way I'd betrayed him. He was my friend, Beth, and look what I did to him!' He gave her a desperate look. 'So now you know. That's the sort of man I really am.'

Bethany shook her head and smiled. 'I know what sort of man you are, Clive. A very good one.'

He swallowed a sob. 'How can you say that after everything I've just told you?'

'Because good people sometimes do bad things,' she said simply. 'And broken people sometimes do the wrong thing because they think it will fix them.'

He hung his head, not sure he deserved for her to be so understanding.

'You and Jennifer have paid for what you did a thousand times over,' she told him. 'And the truth is, neither of you deserved to suffer this way, any more than Joseph did for the mistake he made. It's time you forgave yourselves and moved on with your lives. Jennifer seems to be making good progress at last, so what about you? Are you ready to move on? With me?'

Clive blinked away tears. 'You're sure that's what you want? Even now?'

'I've never been more certain of anything in my life,' she promised him. 'It's all I want. Is it what you want, too?'

Was it what he wanted? He thought about Julian and how his friend had wanted him to be there for Jennifer and his boys. He hadn't done exactly what he'd been asked, but he'd done his best. And yes, he'd made a big mistake, but it had been born of his and Jennifer's love for Julian and their grief. Neither of them had wanted to hurt him. Surely Julian would understand that? Maybe Beth was right and they'd both suffered long enough.

He needed to forgive himself and take this chance with Beth because if he couldn't, he would lose her forever, and he knew, more than ever, that he couldn't face that. He loved her. He needed her. He wanted to be the man she believed him to be.

'Aye,' he said softly. 'It's what I want more than anything in the world.'

She gave him one of her brilliant smiles that lit her face from within, and his heart skipped with joy as she said, 'I'm very relieved to hear it. And I'm glad you were singing Ben's praises, too, because I've had a thought about the future of Stepping Stones myself.'

'You have?'

'What I was also thinking when I was planning my great surprise, is that while I was having the stableyard redesigned and all the stables rebuilt, why not incorporate an equine veterinary unit there? There's certainly enough room, and you said yourself you'd love to work more with horses if you only had the facilities. So why not put those facilities at Whispering Willows? It would mean you and Ben get to expand your practice, and we'd always have a vet on hand if one of our horses got sick, so they wouldn't have to travel to Walter Harding's or even further afield. It's a win-win as far as I can see. What do you say?'

Clive was speechless. After everything he'd just told her she was still considering sticking around? Not only that, but she was offering him the kind of facilities he'd been dreaming of for years.

'Are you serious?'

'Of course I am. Naturally, you'd have to work with an architect to design the unit. I mean, I wouldn't have a clue. And you'd be responsible for equipping it, but if you're up for that I certainly am.'

'Bethany,' he said, not sure she'd understood what he'd told her, 'about Jennifer... Can you really forgive me?'

'Forgive you?' she asked, smiling tenderly at him. 'There's nothing to forgive. I have so much respect for you because I know it can't have been easy telling me all this. Thank you for trusting me. You're still the man I thought you were, believe me. If anything, I might just love you more.'

He rested his forehead against hers, overwhelmed with relief and gratitude.

'I hope Jennifer has finally accepted it wasn't her fault,' she murmured. 'The accident I mean.'

'Ben blamed himself for years,' Clive told her. 'He thought, if he hadn't got in trouble with the police Leon would never have driven out that night to collect him. I think, when he finally admitted how much he was struggling with guilt, Jennifer realised that she'd been doing the same. She was able to tell Ben, honestly, that it wasn't his fault, and by doing that she finally accepted that it wasn't hers either. Fate.' He shook his head. 'Life can be so cruel at times.'

'And don't we both know it,' she said. 'So it seems to me we've got to grab every moment of happiness we can. You and Jennifer, how do you feel about each other now?'

At least he could smile about that. 'We're friends,' he said firmly. 'That's all we'll ever be and all either of us want.'

'And you don't have any lingering romantic feelings for her?'

'Of course not! Aw, Beth, for so long I wasn't sure. It was all mixed up with feelings of obligation and shame and duty and guilt. I thought that was love but it wasn't. It was only when I fell in love with you that I realised it never had been. Not really. I've never felt for anyone what I feel for you. You've changed everything.'

'So let's make a promise,' she said. 'Let's not waste any more time with the past. Let's you and I enjoy every moment as it comes and live each day to the fullest.'

She kissed him gently and he saw the love shining in her eyes.

'I can do that,' he said uncertainly, as he cupped her face in his hands. 'So you and me...?'

'I think,' she said firmly, 'you mean *us*.'

THIRTY-SEVEN

'You know,' Lennox said thoughtfully as he pushed his plate away, 'I think maybe next time we have a continental breakfast I'd like some pains au chocolat. What are the chances, Bethany?'

'What do you know about pains au chocolat?' Maya asked incredulously. 'You'd never even heard of a croissant until the other week.'

'Dad took us for an all-you-can-eat breakfast at that pub over in Lingham-on-Skimmer last Sunday. I mean, we didn't have the continental breakfast naturally, not when there was sausages and bacon on offer, but I did see them in a basket, and I thought they looked all right. Chocolate for breakfast. You can't knock it till you've tried it after all.'

Bethany and Clive exchanged amused glances. 'I'll see what I can do but remember these breakfasts will be on hold from Monday,' she reminded him. 'The kitchen's getting ripped out then and it's going to be chaos in here while the new one's being installed.'

'It's going to look fabulous when it's done,' Maya said. 'And fancy you getting an en suite put in! My mam would love an en suite, but Dad says they're only for posh people and she should be glad we've got a bathroom at all, cos all he used to get was a weekly soak in a tin bath in front of the fire in his dad's mucky water.'

'Good grief,' Summer said. 'Honestly?'

'That's what he *says*,' Maya said knowingly. 'Mind you, he also told me he was a bookie's runner at the age of nine and that Grandma sang in a bar for gin. Mam told me he's having me on, and she reckons he's watched too much *Peaky Blinders*. She said he was brought up in a semi-detached in Leeds and they had an avocado bathroom suite. He's just too tight to fork out for an en suite.'

Bethany and Clive smothered their laughter.

'All right,' Clive said, 'that's enough of the idle chit-chat. Hurry up and eat your breakfasts because we've got work to do. Shirley Bassey arrives today, remember?'

'I can't wait to meet her,' Summer said. 'Poor little thing has been through so much. She's going to need a lot of love while she's grieving.'

'Maybe Chester can help her with that,' Lennox suggested, his cheek bulging with Danish pastry. 'He's been missing his owner after all. Perhaps they can give each other therapy? They say it's good to talk.'

'Sometimes, Lennox, you astound me.' Clive shook his head in amazement. 'And who knows but you might be right. Worth a shot anyway.'

'I just wish Dylan Thomas was coming with her,' Summer said sadly.

'It's horrible that he didn't make it,' Maya agreed. 'But not all of them can, and he never stood much of a chance, did he? At least in the end he was with people who cared about him and wanted to help him. I hope he understood that not all humans are cruel and selfish.'

'Maybe we could name one of the new stable blocks after him,' Bethany suggested. 'It would be a nice way of remembering him. In fact, maybe we could name all the new buildings after some of the horses and ponies we've lost. Like Pepper,' she added, earning a look of sympathy from Clive.

'And Shadow,' Summer begged. 'He was such a lovely old horse, but Ben had to put him to sleep last year because he was in so much pain. Joseph really loved him. What do you think?'

'I think that's a good idea,' Bethany said. 'What about the veterinary unit, Clive? Any ideas what you're going to call that?'

'Oh, I think Ben and I have already decided on a name,' he said. 'It will be the Joseph Wilkinson Equine Unit. What else?'

They all stared at him, overcome with emotion.

'Oh, Clive,' Summer said at last. 'That's perfect!'

'Thank you,' Bethany said softly. 'I'm sure that would mean the world to him.'

She shook her head, dismissing the sadness that had suddenly threatened to overwhelm her. Life was for living and she intended to make the most of every day.

She looked around the table at them all: Summer, Maya, Lennox, and her soulmate, Clive. They were all chatting away to each other, and laughter rang out as they teased and joked with each other.

Really, she thought suddenly, she had a sort of family now after all. Her Whispering Willows family. She never wanted to lose them again.

She gazed around the kitchen, imagining it when it was completed. It was going to look so different, but she thought Joseph would approve, and she was certain her mother would have.

Whispering Willows was already becoming a centre of love and laughter she thought, her eyes crinkling with mirth as she heard Maya telling Clive more stories of her dad's so-called deprived childhood. She was such a character and had so much love for the horses. She was an asset to the sanctuary, without a doubt.

As for Lennox... He might have started working here because he had a crush on Maya, but she was confident he'd grown to love it as much as she did. His heart was most definitely in the right place, and he was a good worker, even if he did grumble about the copious amounts of manure the residents managed to produce.

As for Summer... Bethany watched her now, nibbling on a croissant. She was half listening to Maya, but her thoughts were clearly also somewhere else. She was probably imagining Shirley Bassey's arrival, working out how best to make the little Welsh Mountain pony feel at home. Summer lived and breathed the horses, ponies, and donkeys in her care. They were in safe hands with her and, hopefully, in time she'd learn to think with her head as well as her heart.

Clive had already told her that Joseph had warned him about Summer's determination to save every animal she could, whatever the cost. Bethany knew there would be times when she'd have to be firm with her manager, but she had confidence that Summer would eventually become more practical without losing her passion.

She hoped so anyway. She wouldn't want her to be *too* practical after all. It was lovely to see someone who cared so much and wanted so badly to make a difference. She felt she was lucky to have Summer.

And then there was Clive.

He sat at the end of the table opposite her, already seeming like the head of this Whispering Willows family. It suited him. It was a shame he'd never had the chance to be a father, though she realised he was a real father figure to Ben. Summer had confided as much. Ben adored him and she could understand that. She adored him herself.

He was everything Ted hadn't been. Honest, reliable, gentlemanly, respectful. He treated her as an equal and cared about her opinions. She'd never had that in her marriage. There had been so many things missing in her relationship with Ted, but she knew they weren't missing from this one. She didn't know what she'd done to be so fortunate to find Clive and had no idea why he'd fallen in love with her, but she gave thanks every day that he had.

Sometimes, in her more wistful moments, she liked to imagine that Joseph had sent her to him. She hoped he was happy for them. She thought he would be. They were, after all, the two people he'd loved most in the world.

And now here she was back home at Whispering Willows, determined to make it the beautiful family home it deserved to be. A hub for her sanctuary family. She wasn't going to rent it out after all. Instead she was going to live here, creating a home for the people she loved, and for herself. One day, maybe it would be Clive's home, too.

At last she knew where she belonged. She'd been running for so long, searching for that elusive place where she could put down roots. All those house viewings. All that travelling. All that searching and hoping and disappointment.

And all the time home had been waiting right here for her in the very last place she'd thought to look.

Home was Tuppenny Bridge with its friendly and welcoming community. It was Whispering Willows with its horses, ponies, and donkeys, its dedicated and compassionate staff, and the memories of her mother and Joseph oozing from every stone, wrapping themselves around her with warmth and love.

Home was Clive, the man who'd unfrozen her heart, helped her to forgive herself and her family, and had taught her what true love really felt like.

They were never going to be lonely again.

Thank you, Joseph, she thought. Thank you for everything.

And it was as if she could hear his voice inside her mind.

It's going to be right, Beth. Haven't I always told you that? It's all going to be right.

A LETTER FROM THE AUTHOR

Dear reader,

Thank you so much for reading *Coming Home to Tuppenny Bridge*. I hope you enjoyed being part of Bethany and Clive's emotional journey. If you want to join other readers in hearing all about my new Storm releases and bonus content, you can sign up here:

www.stormpublishing.co/sharon-booth

I also have my own chatty monthly newsletter where you'll find my latest news, cover reveals, giveaways and more.

www.sharonboothwriter.com/newsletter-sign-up

If you enjoyed this book and could spare a few moments to leave a review that would be hugely appreciated. Even a short review can make all the difference in encouraging a reader to discover my books for the first time. Thank you so much!

I've loved horses, ponies, and donkeys since I was a little girl. My favourite programmes all those years ago were *Black Beauty*, *Flambards*, *White Horses*, and – best of all – *Follyfoot*. This was a programme all about a young woman called Dora who worked for her uncle at Follyfoot Farm, caring for rescued equines. I've been fascinated by horse sanctuaries ever since.

I invented an animal sanctuary in my Bramblewick series

and called it Folly Farm in tribute to my favourite childhood programme. Sharp-eyed readers might have noticed that Folly Farm and its owners, Rachel and Xander, are mentioned in this book! I knew, when I created Tuppenny Bridge, that a horse sanctuary would be a big part of the town, and that the people who lived and worked there would be very special indeed, with their own stories to tell.

Finally, with this book, I've been able to write my very own version of *Follyfoot*.

Back in the early 1990s I saw a newspaper advert for a horse sanctuary in Norfolk called Redwings. You could adopt a horse, pony, donkey, or mule from them and the money you paid for that privilege went towards the costs of keeping all the rescued animals.

I adopted a beautiful bay pony called Pepper. You might realise where Bethany's childhood pony came from! These days I sponsor Lady, a gorgeous half-Shire horse. Redwings is an incredible place but it's sad to know that sanctuaries like this are still needed. I read the newsletters from the sanctuary and some of the stories have me in tears. Writing about little Dylan Thomas was painful because that scene was inspired by two real-life stories I'd read. Redwings and other sanctuaries do such amazing work, but it costs such a lot of money to give these beautiful creatures a new start and a happy home.

If you'd like to adopt a horse, pony or donkey from Redwings, or make a donation, you can do that here: www. redwings.org.uk

Thanks again for visiting Tuppenny Bridge with me and I hope you'll stay in touch – I have so many more stories and ideas to entertain you with!

Love Sharon xx

KEEP IN TOUCH WITH THE AUTHOR

www.sharonboothwriter.com

facebook.com/sharonbooth.writer

x.com/sharonbwriter

instagram.com/sharonboothwriter

pinterest.com/sharonboothwriter

ACKNOWLEDGEMENTS

As I've said before, it takes more than one person to produce a book. It might be my name on the cover, but I've had a lot of help and support behind the scenes.

First and foremost, I must thank my editor, Naomi Knox. This is the first time I've worked with Naomi, and it's been a pleasure from start to finish. Her encouragement and insights helped me not only finish writing the book but added depth and clarity to the writing, making it a story I could truly be proud of.

Thanks also to Shirley Khan for the copyedits, to Liz Hurst for the proofreading, and to Debbie Clement for another lovely cover.

There are at least five other members of the Storm Publishing team I should acknowledge. Thank you to Kathryn Taussig, Oliver Rhodes, Alex, Anna and Elke. If I've missed anyone out, I sincerely apologise!

On a personal note, I want to express my gratitude to my dearest pal, Jessica Redland, who kindly read the first part of this book when I'd convinced myself it wasn't working and didn't know what to do with it. She read the document I sent her in record time and told me in no uncertain terms that she loved it, I was being daft, and I'd better hurry up and finish it because she needed to know what happened next! Her unfailing support and friendship means the world to me.

I must also thank my brother, Rick, for answering my persistent messages about roofing, bulging buildings, and demolition! Thanks so much, Rick. I knew you'd come in useful one day!

Finally, thank you to The Husband, who does everything he can to make life easy for me by supplying me with endless mugs of coffee, chauffeuring me to my catch-ups with writer pals, and even agreeing to go on holidays to the places I need to research. I don't know how I'd do any of this without him. He truly is a star.

Printed in Great Britain
by Amazon